THE BEGINNINGS PROPHECY

∴∴∴∴∴∴∴∴

KAITLIN OTTEMAN

"Magic is believing"

Kaitlin Otteman

First printing: 2016

ISBN: 978-1-329-78278-5

Chicken Fried Duck Publishing
C/o Tim Otteman
310 Applewood Lane
Mt. Pleasant, MI 48858

For more information about ordering or special bulk discounts, please contact Tim Otteman at the above listed address or via email at tim@imperiument.com

Cover Credits: Tim Otteman, Bettie Ricolo and Bridget Timbrook

ACKNOWLEDGMENTS

I want to thank my mother, Marcie, for always supporting me and being there throughout this whole experience. I want to thank my Nana, Karla Cooper, for taking me to the library for so many years. It has paid off well. I also want to thank my Oma, Suzi Tengen, for the frequent trips to the bookstore and taking such a great interest in my writing.

I give gratitude to my teachers who have always supplied me with plenty of material to motivate me and to my best friend, Juliet, who has told me time and time again that I will be successful.

To the rest of my family and friends, I thank you all for encouraging me during this crazy experience. Your support means the world to me - I hope you all love it.

A very special thank you goes to my dad, Tim, who took the time to edit and format the book, helped me with the cover design and for all the hard work he did to get the book out for the world to see.

And of course, I can't forget to thank, Jacob and Wilhelm Grimm, Jeanne-Marie Leprince de Beaumont, Hans Christian Anderson, James M. Barrie and Lewis Carroll. I could've never made this book without your timeless pieces. They have entertained so many and made countless children smile. Rest in peace.

This is to all who have inspired me
and to those I might have the honor of inspiring.

PROLOGUE

She walked confidently through the square that night but it was only for show, only for those who saw her. Inside her she was shaking, shaking with fear, horror and utter sadness.

Her cloak, coated in rain, clung to her dress and dwarfed her, yet she hurried on. Upon reaching the house she pushed the door open and threw the hood off of her face.

"This cannot be happening," she thought. But thoughts can only cover the pain, they do not diminish it.

She went up the stairs and into her mother's bed chamber. There she lay, still, not lifeless, but still. She halted at the doorway. If she stepped through she was allowing herself to be open to the pain. If she stayed there, it was almost like protecting herself from it.

Her foot crossed the doorway. Unsure of what to say, but what could she say? Her mother was facing the most horrific cause of evil.

Death.

She knelt down beside her and looked at her sleeping face.

The mother was very beautiful, even at the age she was. Her eyes were closed, but she knew the color by heart and memory from seeing them so often. Her black hair, slightly grey with age, was fanned out around her face. Her lips looked thin and were unnatural without their red color.

One hand was tucked into the sheets, but her right lay out, its ring brightened by the candle.

She could feel a tear wiggling its way down her face when her mother's eyes opened. Relief flooded her. A faint smile came to her mouth.

The mother looked toward her daughter. Her face gave away no emotion, happy or sad.

"In fifty years, our world will change, everything will change. The Seven Sins will cloak this land in evil. Four women will go through tremendous things for true love, two girls will fill their craving for adventure, one boy and girl pair will risk anything to save one another and one source of magic must help them. Find this magic, help those wandering souls and prepare," the mother recited in a hoarse breath. She turned her face toward the light and shut her eyes. Still sobbing, the daughter clutched her mother's hand, but knew what had been done was done.

She was gone.

She fled the room and out the door of the house. She ran to the woods, farther and farther away from the house and village she knew. Adrenaline had taken over every one of her fibers and she knew where she had to go. Her mother was now dead, but she had told her of a Prophecy. The last time she had heard about prophecies was when she had heard about a great power that was in this world.

She stopped for a moment. One word was clanging around her brain, ringing in her memory.

Magic.

Her mother had told her of magic. There was only one place she knew she would find answers now.

She ran harder until she reached a clearing surrounded by massive rocks. She stopped and closed her eyes. She thought back to when she was little girl and had wandered into the woods. She had seen a lady that could do an amazing trick.

She could make a house appear!

Her eyes burst open. The trick had come back to her memory. She picked up two flat stones that were behind a pine tree in blackberry bushes. She laid the stones in front of her and then pricked her finger on one of the bushes and let one drop of blood fall right in the center of each stone.

She then clanged the stones together and recited the words.

> *"These words I choose,*
> *Will undo the ruse,*
> *These things I say,*
> *Will open the way."*

She set the stones on the ground again and waited. A moment passed and then a bright beam propelled from the stones and a house formed as the glow vanished.

She was stunned a minute, it had actually worked. Cautiously, she walked in.

The house was small on the outside and looked worn down. On the inside, however, it was much grander. Stone went from the walls to the floor and then wood planks made up the ceiling. A garnet mat lay by the doorway.

As she crept through, a mouse scurried by her feet, frightening her. She fell into a bookcase.

It shifted.

She pushed harder and it gave away, revealing a stairway heading downward. She followed it down a story or so and reached a room. She peaked in the keyhole and saw that same lady bending over a table looking at something. She turned the knob and pushed the door open.

"I've been waiting a long time for you," the lady said without turning around.

"Your mother told you about the Prophecy, didn't she?" asked the lady. "You know why? Because I told her to. The day you first saw me wasn't a coincidence, my dear. She and I have known each other for a quite a while. She believes you have the Gift, my dear. I have seen you, I believe you do, too. I have plans for you."

"You are good, right?" the girl asked the women, her words came out timid.

"Of course I am, darling."

"Then who are you?"

"I am Starletta."

"What are these plans you speak of?"

"I must conduct a spell, a powerful one, and you must help me. By conducting this spell, I will die and you will carry on my doing. This is what your mother always wanted, but she never had that one thing. You do, my darling Marybella. She wanted this for you."

"If it is my mother's dying wish, then I will help you. What must I do?"

"I will teach you magic, you will learn from this book." Starletta pointed to a book, thick and aged. "This book holds all the keys to what your mother had told you. It has everything I will teach you and it will help you help those people."

"I understand. What will happen when you cast that spell?"

"This will be very powerful magic that we will conduct. We only have a small amount of time. Some of your people will stay here, others…they will not."

"What! They're going to die!" Marybella shrieked.

"They will not die. They will be put in a new place, a better place, and they will not remember this world. They will think that has been their only life."

"So, they will not be harmed?"

"No."

"Who will not be affected by this magic?"

"Your friend, Aaron. He must be here, he is significant in one of the woman's future. He is a strong boy and will manage. Several fairies will be here as well. He will be protected."

"And…will you be coming to the new land with me?" Marybella asked.

"Like I said, once I have cast the spell, my time will be up. I will not accompany you, you are strong and you can do this on your own. We are fairies, powerful forces made us who we are. Take pride and confidence in that, you are the magic your mother talked about."

Marybella thought about this a moment and then spoke. "If I am the magic my mother told me of and I can help these people on their journeys, I will do so. How will they know me?"

"You will be more significant in some tales than others, but you will be a part of each none the less. You are a fairy, my darling, one in a very important legacy. Now, we must begin. You have a lot to learn and the clock is ticking."

CHAPTER 1
GRIMM'S FAIRY TALES

"Now, if we were in our two characters' situation, then maybe we would understand better why Elizabeth accepts the second proposal from Mr. Darcy," Ms. Tickens recited. "Does anyone have any comments or questions about this selection?" She scanned the room. No one raised their hand.

Not even me.

I would normally always raise my hand in English.

Not today though. Other than copying notes about *Pride and Prejudice*, which I had mostly liked, I was daydreaming. I didn't normally daydream, but today English was just dull.

"Gwendolyn," Ms. Tickens called into the room. "How about you? Do you have any comments on the book?"

I was startled. I searched my memory for bits of the question I had heard.

"I thought it was interesting, very old minded. People were always thinking of who you married and if you ever did get married," I said in a voice that hopefully masked that I had thought of that on the spot.

Ms. Tickens beamed. "Thank you Gwendolyn, that was a perfect way to look at it. Now, for your next assignment, I would like you all to think of a classic book that would be good for English class. But, to make this more of a challenge, I will assign you each a letter and the book you pick has to have your letter capitalized in the title. You must have it by tomorrow with some facts or a summary written out about the book or the authors. Everyone clear on the assignment?" A number of nods came from the class. "All right, on your way out I will give you your letter." Ms. Tickens walked over to the door.

After English I went to my locker to pick up my things. I thought about the letter I had gotten: *'G.'*

"Hey," said a voice from behind. It was Macy, my most wonderful friend and BFF for the last five years. She was half Italian and half French, but she looked a lot more Italian with her dark hair that had natural curls and mocha skin. Macy was very outgoing and she liked to speak her mind, but she was always there for the people she cared about.

"What letter did you get in English? I got 'C' and I've already thought of a classic book," Macy said.

"What book?" I asked.

"*Charlotte's Web* by…his named rhymed with right," she said.

"E.B. White," I told her.

"Thanks. Anyway, it's a classic, and that was my only homework, so I'm all yours for the sleepover at my place. What time are you going to show up?" she questioned.

"I have to go to the library and find my book before we can do anything. Don't you have math homework?"

"Crap, I do have math homework. Well, how about this…you get your book and I'll finish my homework, which I think is fairly short. Then we meet up to go to that new movie tonight at 5:30 and we can go over to my house after, okay?" I nodded my head.

"Okay, see you then. Ciao," Macy said fluttering her fingers as she walked away.

I headed toward the library which was right by the school, only a few blocks. I called my dad to tell him my plans.

"All homework has to be done first. What is the movie about? What's it rated?" Dad asked when I told him.

"I only have to do this English assignment. The movie is PG-13 and it's that new adventure one you've seen the commercials for."

"Alright, have fun. I'll see you tomorrow afternoon after school. I love you, princess."

"I love you too, Daddy."

I turned off my phone and went inside. The library was one of the biggest spots in town. It had been there for more than one hundred years. Paint was peeling off the bricks and lots could be done to make it look better, but, Mr. Gog, the librarian, wouldn't budge on changing things.

"Excuse me, ma'am, I need some help," I said to the lady behind the information desk. She peered over her thick, black glasses. With her hair pulled into a sleek low ponytail and a dark grey blazer over her white blouse, she looked like she belonged in court. I had seen her before and she sort of intimidated me.

"What can I do for you?" she inquired.

"I need to know where your classic books are located, please," I asked politely.

"Go down those stairs and it will be the shelf closest to the west wall," she instructed and then turned her gaze back to her computer screen.

I followed her instructions and found the wall of classic books. I began sifting through the tightly packed shelf.

"Moby Dick, no, Romeo and Juliet, no, To Kill a Mockingbird, no, " I mumbled as I searched. I knew there were many classics with the letter *'G'* in their title, they just all seemed to disappear at the moment.

I picked up my backpack in surrender. I couldn't find a single book in that shelf with my letter. Maybe I could make up the name of some book they just discovered from ancient times.

As I was picking up my bag, something banged into my head. I rubbed my temple for a moment and then looked on the floor for the object that had hit me. A book had fallen from the shelf. *Grimm's Fairy Tales.* I stared at the book that was clasped in my hands. I knew I had searched that shelf twice, left and right, and had not seen this book once.

I knew two things at this point. One, I knew books shouldn't appear out of nowhere. Two, I had found a book. I looked up some facts on the computer about the book and wrote down them down on a sheet of notebook paper. I checked the book out, slipped it into my backpack and headed downtown to the theater.

The theater was only a few blocks from the library, five at the most. I passed the bank and furniture store that had furnished dad's office. I passed the hospital where my Uncle Thomas worked.

Uncle Thomas had gotten back from being a doctor overseas and was staying with dad and I until his apartment was remodeled. He would sometimes tell me about what it was like to be a doctor for the men who protected our country, but then dad

3

would get mad. He said he was filling my head with horror and that I had gone through enough of that, but I didn't mind. Uncle Thomas was the only person that called me Guinevere. I knew that is what he wanted my name to be. I also knew that's what my mom had wanted it to be too.

When I got to the movies I scanned the room for Macy. She was standing by the candy machine, popping something sweet into her mouth, while talking to a boy. He looked like he could be in our grade. His hair was cut close on the sides, but some hair gel was in the front to spike up his bangs.

I strolled over to them. Once I got close enough, I could see that it was Aiden Morns, Macy's stepbrother. He was a seventh grader and was, in the opinion of several girls, very cute. He played a few sports, but was much more into guitar. And... he was cute. Macy and he looked nothing like each other though. She had darker skin and dark hair and he had light skin and tannish hair.

"Hi," Macy said when she noticed I was there. "I saw that Aiden was here and came over to say hi. I already have our tickets. Aiden was meeting Blaire here to see the new rom-com that's out, but...it looks like she's not here yet," she said, looking around the lobby.

I could see how disappointed Aiden was. He kept looking around and tapping his foot, but who could blame him? Blaire Whitman was his perfect match, in terms of status. She had greyish blue eyes that were highlighted with mascara. She wore clothes that came from designer boutiques. And she rarely had acne, which was the only thing I was ever jealous of. Blaire was beautiful, no doubt, but I had seen what methods she used to get her way. I had seen the people she had tricked. She was one of those girls who did anything to get what she wanted. And she almost always did.

"The movie was supposed to start ten minutes ago and I've gotten nothing from her - no texts, emails, calls," Aiden said, breaking me from my thoughts.

"I'm sorry Aiden. I know that she must have a good reason for not being here," I said in sympathy.

"Maybe," Aiden mumbled under his breath.

Eventually, we had to say goodbye to Aiden to get our seats for the movie. We had missed the previews and the theater was a bit crowded, but we managed to find seats. The movie began, but it was hard for me to concentrate. I kept thinking about that book. Something was off about it. No one had placed the book there, I would've heard or seen them. I was basically zoned out for the first quarter of the movie thinking over every possibility that could've made that book be there and I couldn't see it. I didn't think of anything logical except the book appearing out of thin air. Who said the answer had to be logical?

"I loved that movie, didn't you?" Macy asked as we were leaving.

"Yeah it was really good. I liked the action in it."

"I liked the action *guys* in it," Macy said in her sly voice as she grinned. "Speaking of guys, Aiden is such a sweetheart, You're going to be every girl's envy because he's interested in you."

Macy kept walking, but I stood frozen. *Aiden and I together? Him liking me, when he could date Blaire? It doesn't seem possible.*

"Come on," Macy urged when she noticed that I was lagging behind.

"You know Aiden and I aren't, and will probably never be, an item. Not when he can have Blaire," I said trying to make it sound like I didn't care when I really did.

"Oh, come on!" Macy said, widening her mouth and making her words sound dramatic. "He totally likes you. Why would he have asked me all those questions if he didn't?" Again, I froze. *He had asked questions about me?*

"What kind of questions?" I asked.

"Oh you know. Your interests, hobbies, stuff like that."

"What did you tell him, exactly?"

"I told him that you like vintage things and that you like to read and walk in your woods and that you love action adventure movies. Did I make you a dream girl, with real information I might add, or what?" Macy said holding her hands up and spreading her fingers in a jazz hands motion.

"Okay, I will admit you did make me sound pretty good. But no guy would turn down Blaire for me and I'm totally fine with that. If they're going to diss me, then they're not worth my time," I told her when we started walking home.

"Speaking of Blaire, I wonder where she is. She hasn't texted me all day."

"Sometimes it's strange to remember that you two are friends."

"I know. I know, she can be a bit self-involved, but she can also be sweet."

"To some people," I muttered under my breath.

"Can we please try to find her? She's supposed to come to our sleepover, so at least we can try," Macy said making her please-help-me-and-I-will-owe-you-big-time face.

"Fine, we can look around some of her favorite places. They're pretty close to here anyway right?" I asked. Macy nodded her head. "Alright, come on, let's go before it gets dark."

We turned at the next right corner and headed toward some of the places Blaire went to regularly.

"Well, that got us nowhere," Macy said as we exited Blaire's favorite massage place. "We've checked two of her favorite stores to shop at, her massage spot, where she buys her makeup, where else can we look?" Macy voice quivered as she said this.

I knew she was starting to get upset. "How about we check her hair salon, maybe she's making an appointment." Macy was hesitate at first, but finally agreed that it was worth a look.

We walked a few blocks to the hair salon. There were two in our town. One was where just about everyone went, and then there was *Champagne Styles*, an upper class salon. It was one of the kinds of salons where you were pampered and got deluxe treatments.

Champagne Styles was only open for about twenty more minutes when we walked in. Only two workers were there, both girls. One had her hair in a fishtail braid and the other had her tips dyed blue. The one with the braid was sweeping up hair that had fallen on the floor and the other one was working with Blaire. Macy and I walked over to her chair.

"You know you were a real jerk tonight," Macy said once she got over to her chair. Her voice was steely, yet calm. Blaire didn't turn her head. I noticed she had neon pink earbuds in her ears.

She took them out and noticed that Macy and I were there. "Hi," she said in that sweet voice. "What's up? Sorry I'm taking so long, Georgia here…"

"I don't understand how you could just stand Aiden up like that," Macy said, her tone sounding more hurt than angry.

"Stand him up? What are you talking about?"

"Gwendolyn and I saw him at the movies and he said you were supposed to be there to meet him there. Now, I would like to know what was so important that you had to miss that date with him and not call or anything?"

Blaire tapped her fingers on her knees.

"Well? Spill it Blaire!" Macy said impatiently.

"I was…well you see…"

"What?"

"I was getting my highlights touched up for the school's spring formal that's coming up this weekend. My appointment conflicted with the movie time."

"And you couldn't text, call or email him that you couldn't make it?" Macy snapped.

"Well, I mean, Aiden's sweet and cute, but I really didn't see it going anywhere. This was our second date and I didn't see a third one happening. And, well…Marco Alfano asked me to the dance anyway. I mean, he's gorgeous. I couldn't pass that up, he's the quarterback of the football team, so…"

"You thought of status more than anything," Macy shot at her. Blaire became silent again.

"I can't believe you, you know that?" Macy said to her, shaking her head and laughing a sad laugh.

"You always think of your social rank more than anything. You never consider the actual people you manipulate. You did it to Aiden by standing him up, but making him think you were in to him first. You did it to Tori Fotter, she was the best artist in school and you tricked her into helping," as she did air quotations. "you do your art project in the statewide art competition just to win. You did it to Molly Conners, who was super nice and a fabulous seamstress to make your dress for the seventh grade winter formal and never gave her credit. You said it was designer and that you had bought at this special boutique in Los Angeles just to impress your friends." Macy paused, her face was flushed a furious shade of pink. Her eyes became glossy and her face tensed with fury.

"You even played me, Blaire. You made me think you could be a good person who just sometimes wanted to get her way, which I thought I understood. Now, I see that that was all you wanted. Have fun being at your house alone tonight." Macy grabbed my wrist and pulled me toward the door. Blaire sat shocked and disappointed in her chair.

"Hey, Blaire," I called before I was out the door. Blaire turned her attention to me. "I know this place is high end and all. But if you ever read the labels, you would know that this place uses macaw spit in their hair products. Just thought you should know."

Blaire's mouth dropped and she screamed at the stylist. Then she started rubbing her hands down her hair, attempting to rub it out. I had a small smile on my face as I closed the door.

"Was that true? That they used macaw spit in their hair products?" Macy asked when we were a block away from her house.

"Yeah, I had read it on one of the labels while we were there. Now I know why they put it in super small print."

"You know you didn't have to say it. Even if I really liked seeing her scream, 'There's spit in my hair, get it out, get it out,'" Macy said, making an impression of Blaire.

I laughed. "Yeah, I know I didn't. She just made me so mad right then. I mean you two had been friends for years and then she became such a brat."

"Yeah, she did."

"When did she become so mean?"

"It was the summer before seventh grade. She had invited me to her big before seventh grade summer party. Right when I got there, I went over to her. She basically didn't notice me for like an hour and hadn't even noticed when I had gotten there earlier. I had bought this new dress that I really liked and then I heard her whisper to Laura Com that it made me look 'fuller in my butt.' I talked to her about it later and she said that she had just meant that I looked curvy. She said it was meant to be a compliment. We were never as close after that, but we were still pretty good friends."

I was silent for a moment. "That was a crappy thing to do."

"Yeah, but I don't think I'm going to be dealing with her anymore."

"I know it hurts Mace, but you know it could always turn around. You two can always make up, when the time is right."

Macy nodded her head. "I just got so mad at her, I mean it was my stepbrother for gosh sake. She can toy with any guy's heart she wants, but she picks him."

I didn't know what to say. I knew about pain, family pain specifically. I knew that no matter what people said, it didn't make things better. So, I didn't say anything. I just wrapped my arms tightly around Macy's waist and hugged her. I could feel my sweater getting wet, but I didn't mind one single bit.

We finally got to Macy's house. "How was the movie, girls?" Mrs. Poen asked when we walked in.

"It was good, Mom. We saw Aiden there. He was waiting for Blaire to get there."

"Oh, what were they going to see?"

"It was that new rom-com that came out a few days ago."

"How is Blaire?"

"She's fine." Macy bit her top lip.

Mrs. Poen looked toward her daughter. She saw the expression cast on her face and changed the subject.

"Would you girls like some of the leftover pizza?"

"Yes please," I answered.

Mrs. Poen cut two pieces from the pie and shook them onto two paper plates.

We carried the pizza downstairs to where the Poen's flat screen was. Macy plopped herself into the beanbag chair and I pulled out the folding table for us to put our plates on. Macy turned the TV onto the local news. She was about to flip it when I stopped her. The anchorwoman was saying something about the Grimm Brothers.

"Just a few hours ago, in Germany, was the 214th anniversary celebration of the publication of the *Grimm's Fairy Tales*. The celebration was conducted at the Grimm's burial site allowing the public to come and say prayers and give thanks to these amazing writers. Stories were read later that day and play of the Snow White was put on by the town's children. In other news..."

I clicked the button to another channel. This was crazy! I had the book. I had found it on the 214th anniversary of its publication and I don't even know how I found it.

"Gwendolyn, Gwendolyn, speak to me," Macy said she was shaking my shoulders back and forth.

"I have the book," I said, in a voice lower than a whisper.

"The book?"

"The book they just talked about, the Grimm one. I have it. I got it for the English assignment."

"What does that have to do with anything?"

"I searched the shelf twice and I didn't see that book once. Just as I was about to leave, it hit me on the head. And it's the 214th anniversary of its publication, which to me is weird."

"Maybe it is a little strange. But look, nothing bad happened, you're fine."

I slowed my breathing. I thought about that. Macy was right, nothing happened, it was just a coincidence.

"Come on, let's go in my room and we'll do makeovers, okay?" Macy guided me into her basement bedroom and finally got my mind off of the book, mostly.

"What do you want to look like, an actress, singer or model?" Macy asked.

"A singer, I guess."

"Good choice. I'm going to do your hair too."

"Go ahead, it's a mess anyway." Macy was better at these things than I was and would always fix my makeup and hair before school. I never got to learn how to properly apply makeup or really know how to style hair. I was always watching and listening when Macy tried a new technique.

I could feel the soft bristles of a brush going along my cheekbones and other areas on my face.

Must be bronzer, I thought.

I felt the eye shadow brush sweep on my eyelid and into my crease then the liner tip glide just between the lid and my lashes. I felt the smooth feel of the lipstick and gloss when it came over my lips. I could tell the difference between the two by the texture. I had grown used to being Macy's makeup guinea pig.

Macy then stopped working on my face and moved on to my hair. I felt heat and small strands of my hair being tugged and twisted.

"Can I dress you up?" Macy asked me. She normally didn't, but it was still fun, so I said yes.

She told me to still keep my eyes closed, and then guided me as she had me slip into some silky material. She walked me over and turned me then told me to open my eyes.

I was standing in front of her full length mirror. At first I was in a little shock. I knew it was me, but I looked more mature, different.

"Do you like it?" Macy inquired with a smile. "I know I went a little overboard with the neutrals, but you looked so amazing, I just had to use them."

"Macy, I don't know how you did this, I look like a..."

"Princess?"

"Yes, sort of."

"I'm glad you like it, I thought this was way better than a singer."

"Where did you get the inspiration for this?"

"I actually looked in your fairytale book. It has some great inspiration in there."

"Can I see the picture you used for my makeup?"

"Sure." Macy went over to get the book. "This one, with the girls by the well. I modeled you after the one in the blue."

"She's really pretty. What story is it?"

"I'm not sure, but whoever it is, she's really beautiful. She looks a lot like you."

"Aww, thanks Macy."

"No, I'm serious! She actually looks just like you. Look!"

I stared at the picture. Macy was right, she did look just like me. Same dark brown hair, same jade blue eyes. It was like I was staring at a picture of myself. "You're right, she does look like me."

"I think it's creepy."

"Yeah it is."

"I don't like this," Macy said. She now looked very concerned.

"What do you mean?"

"I'm just getting a bad feel from it, can we just…put it away. I know I'm sounding like a crazy person, but you know my feels and this one isn't good. My feels are rarely wrong, Gwendolyn," she told me sternly. I saw the worry in her face.

"Don't worry, Macy, we can put it away. It was freaking me out too."

"What do you think it means?" Macy asked as I slipped the book back into my backpack.

"I'm not sure. But, whatever it does, so far it doesn't seem good."

"Yeah. Let's get your makeup off and watch a movie, take our minds off it," Macy suggested.

We slipped into our pajamas and watched a movie from Macy's massive collection. When the movie was over, Macy got out her sleeping bags for us and laid them at the foot of her bed.

"You can have the starred one, I know you like that one best."

"Thanks, Mace."

Macy fell asleep right away, but I couldn't get my mind off the book. It had been made over two centuries ago, how could that girl look so much like me? Maybe our eyes were just tricking us, and we only thought she had looked like me. I wanted to get up and check, but I knew I would wake up Macy if I tried. I cursed her owl like hearing.

I finally got the book put out of my mind and drifted off into a slumber.

I could barely open my eyes. They were blurred with tears and my head felt like a brick. Smoke seeped its way into my lungs making me gag. I could hear faint wails of pain and shrieks of terror. I tried to push myself up, but my arms and legs felt numb. I finally got my hand to move, but my wrist landed on a flame and it burned. The sizzle of my skin jolted my heartbeat and I had to grit my teeth to stop the tears, that were already in my eyes, from seeping out.

I jerked awake. I felt my arms. They were warm and my face and eyes were wet. Macy bolted up, too.

"Gwendolyn, please tell me you had a weird dream, too."

"I did."

"I was in this place, I didn't know where, but it was a bedroom. I wasn't in my regular pajamas, I was in a nightgown. I got up from the bed, which was huge and had all these blankets, and I could feel the floor. I walked around the room and felt the walls and curtains. I even went over to the nightstand where there was a candle. I held my finger over it and I could feel heat. I remember what everything felt like Gwendolyn, you don't do that in dreams." Her words became soft as her sentence finished.

"I had a strange dream, too. I didn't know where I was and my body felt numb and my eyes had tears in them. It was like looking at a nightmare, everything was being burned and I could hear people screaming. But they were dreams, they can't hurt us now."

"Gwendolyn, can I see your wrist?" Macy asked, quivering. I held my wrist out for her and I saw what she saw. There was a burn mark just below my wrist.

"If those were just dreams, then explain that!" Macy said crying.

"Is there anything on you?"

"I don't think so. Wait…look!" She pulled a white ribbon off her pajama pants. "There was ribbon on the bottom of the nightgown. It must've come loose."

"We shouldn't talk about this. For one thing people will think we're insane. For another, we need to figure out what this is about," I said in the calmest voice I could muster.

"I can tell you what this is about right now," she pointed to my backpack.

"Okay, yes, this did start happening when I checked out that book, but…"

"There is no other reason, Gwendolyn. We're dealing with a force that is trying to tell us something through our dreams. It's using the book to get into our heads!"

"What are you saying?"

"I'm saying we're dealing with…magic."

CHAPTER 2
STARLETTA FLOWER

When I got to school the next morning, I felt like all the energy had been drained from my body.

Once the bell rang for eighth period, I slunk my way to English class.

I took much longer than normal and wasn't able to snag my regular middle section, front row seat. I instead went to the right section and sat in the middle row, closest to the aisle.

Two more kids sulked in. One was Jenney Meffer, she was shorter than most of the other seventh graders and didn't talk very loudly. She went straight to the back of the middle section and shimmied down into her seat letting her textbooks show only a strip of her head.

Next came in Marco Alfano. He was the football team's quarterback this year and was the 'hottie' of the school according to some people. His hair was always slicked heavily with hair gel and he rarely wore anything other than sportswear. He sat right next to me. I said a silent groan.

"You know, I can't believe you would do something like what you did to Aiden. He's been your friend for what, three years?" I made my tone sound utterly disgusted.

"What do you mean doll?" he asked with a small smirk.

"You had to have known that Blaire was going on a date with Aiden and yet you still asked her to the spring formal. You stole Aiden's chance to ask her."

"You don't sound to upset about it," he stated as he turned toward me.

"I am upset. It was a totally backstab on your part and a real jerk thing to do," I said turning my attention back to the doorway, praying that the next person to walk through would be Macy. And she could show this tool a piece of her mind and get him to shut up.

"Maybe I should've asked you to the formal," he said smooth like.

15

"Look," I said turning my attention back to him. "I know a lot of girls have a crush on you, but sorry to burst your bubble, I'm not one of them. So don't try to win me over, because I think you're such a jerk. Now if you'll excuse me, I'm going to get my assignment out, I actually try to do well in school." Marco stared at me for a moment before he moved to the other aisle, while I pulled out my book and paper.

Macy was able to get to class a minute before the tardy bell rang and she sat down in the empty seat next to me.

"So I looked up some things on our...sleep patterns and found that I was right. This is magic," Macy whispered.

"Did you do more research on this than on your assignment? I muffled a giggle.

"Possibly, but look what I found." She pulled out some typed sheets. "Unusual sleeping can be caused by enchanted garments, objects or animals. It can cause the human or animal to have odd dreams. It can also put the human in a time or place they once lived or be telling them of a mission they must fulfill. It sure sounds like our problem to me," Macy said putting the sheets back in her book bag.

I was quiet for a second. "Do you really, truly think that this could be happening to us?"

"Yes. I know it's crazy, but I think that this is happening. I just don't know why."

"Well, know you have me on your side. I think you're right. I think we are dealing with magic, but who is doing this to us?"

"That's the part I can't figure out."

"Hello, class!" Ms. Tickens sang as she came into the classroom. Her hair looked twice as big today.

"Please pull out your books and papers and set them, neatly, on my desk," she said, emphasizing 'neatly.' She was a stickler about things like that.

"As I read through these, I would like you all to take out your English textbooks and reread pages 203 through 209. You may write down any questions you have. Neatness will count. If I can't read it, I don't count it."

I pulled out my textbook and began to read, occasionally rubbing my eye or resting my head on my hand. It was hard to concentrate on Shakespeare today. Ms. Tickens had us read *A Midsummers Night Dream*, which I thought was beautiful, but today it was hard to follow.

Maybe it was because magic was actually real and my best friend and I were seeing it in our dreams, but that's just a guess.

"Alright, books down. I have read the assignments, and for some of you, I'm very interested in your choices. I would like it if some of you would read your selections to the class. Gwendolyn, would you please come up here?"

I walked to the front and stood in front of the chalkboard. "Would you please tell us a bit about the book you chose?" Ms. Tickens said with a smile.

"The book I chose was *Grimm's Fairy Tales*. It was written by Jacob and Wilhelm Grimm. They were two German brothers and wrote some of the most famous fairy tales that are still around today, such as Snow White and other versions of stories like Cinderella. Some movie makers have even taken the tales and made them into hit movies."

"Thank you Gwendolyn, that was very nice," Ms. Tickens said. I went back to my seat with my book. She had a few others come up and talk about some of their books like *The Adventures of Huckleberry Finn*, *Frankenstein* and *Little Women*.

"I think all of your choices were wonderful. So to make it fair, I'll put everyone's story into this basket," she said as she held up her papers basket. "And draw one out randomly." She wrote down each story and then placed them into her grading basket. Then slightly spinning it around in a circle, she pulled one out.

"And the book is...," she unfolded the paper. "Grimm's Fairy Tales! I'll see if I can order some copies. Tomorrow is Saturday and you know my preference, I don't like to give you homework over the weekend. Since I should be busy finding these copies, there will be no homework, have fun everyone," Ms. Tickens said with a gentle smile on her face.

"Oh Gwendolyn, before you leave, can I have the copy of your book?" Ms. Tickens asked before I left.

"Sure, but I got it from the library."

"I'll make sure it gets turned in. I'm going to go there to look for other copies before I try to order them anyway."

"Well then, here you go." I handed her the book and then caught up with Macy in the hallway.

"She seemed really happy today, don't you think?" Macy asked me as we walked to her locker.

"I suppose, but I think she's always nice."

"Yeah, but she seemed like really happy today. Right around the time you started talking about your book."

"So, now you think the magic is affecting her?" I questioned with a laugh.

"I'm saying it's a possibility," Macy countered back. When we got to Macy's locker I remembered something bad. Macy's locker was two to the left of Blaire's and mine was five to the right of Blaire's. When Macy was mad, it wasn't pretty. When she was this upset, I didn't want to see what was going to happen next. Then, like in some weird twist of fate, Blaire walked out of math class and noticed that we were there. We would have to confront her.

She didn't say anything. She just stood there staring at us. Macy nudged me a little and we went about the business of getting our things. Macy worked on her locker combination and I strolled past Blaire to my own locker.

After we had both gotten our things, we walked outside. Once we were out there, I sensed someone behind us. I could see beams of sunlight catapulting off black metallic fabric and strands of strawberry blond hair swept into the sidelines of my vison. I motioned for Macy to keep walking.

"Yes? Can I help you with something?" I asked without turning around. I felt Blaire's glare burning into my head.

"Who did you tell?" Her voice was low and had a slight growl to it.

"Who did I tell what?" I had turned around. If she got to give dirty looks, I did, too.

"About *Champagne Styles*, who did you tell?"

"No one, but if you're going to be so cranky about it, maybe I should." Now I was shooting fire.

"You wouldn't."

"Oh, maybe I would. I didn't like you when you and Macy started hanging out, but I tolerated you. You know why? Because I was Macy's real friend and I wanted her to be happy unlike you. How many times did you think about your happiness before you made a decision that hurt her?" I shot her my dirtiest look.

"You want to point fingers? You want to call me selfish? You stole her from me! You didn't want me in the picture. That's why you hate me. You wanted me gone and have done everything you could to tear her and I apart," Blaire retaliated.

I was shocked. Blaire felt this way? It was true I didn't like having her around, but did she really think that I would be ruthless enough to try to tear apart her friendship with Macy?

"Don't blame her Blaire, she wasn't the only one who wanted you gone," someone said.

Blaire and I both turned. Before us stood three of Blaire's former friends - Skylar Banks, Jennifer Wang and Tori Fotter.

"Hey Blaire, how have you been?" Skylar asked bittersweet like. "Have you talked to my brother lately? Oh right, you haven't talked to him or me since you dumped him and isolated me from your life." Blaire's face became red.

"Blaire, are you still doing dance? You were really good. You just have to watch someone else's routine for the talent show," Jennifer said sarcastically.

Tori stayed quiet for the moment.

"Blaire, these two wanted to get that out, but I really don't have anything to say. We were hurt by you. Maybe you don't think that we were, but we were. You made us all feel terrible. We thought we were your friends...I thought I was your friend. They wanted to tell you they were hurt, they hadn't had the courage until now. But we've all moved past it." Jennifer and Skylar walked off the grass back onto the sidewalk and left.

She stood there a moment. I heard her sniffle, but she didn't look at me. I knew I had spat at Blaire just as much as those other girls had. I knew Blaire deserved it. I also knew that

19

if I was in that position, I would want comfort more than anything. And maybe that was all she needed.

I went over and I hugged her. I wrapped my arms around her shoulders, squishing the pieces of her metallic black shrug to my face.

"You need someone Blaire. Even with the conflicts we've had in the past, whenever you want to talk, here's my number." I took a scrap of paper from my bag and wrote down my number. I concealed it into the palm of her hand.

I began my walk home again with a few questions harboring in my brain. Why had I hugged Blaire? And given her my number? She certainly hadn't done anything to deserve it at the time. But I did know something for sure - my number one rule. The rule I lived by.

Everyone deserves love, laughter, life and chances. No matter whom they are.

I didn't look for Macy after I talked with Blaire. She had probably already gone home. I saw Tori standing on one of the street corners looking around. I knew that Tori was a popular girl and very beautiful. She had dark, fiery red hair that had naturally curly ringlets. She was a fabulous artist. Her artwork was always in the art shows and she was always generous. I thought she was pretty from the inside out.

"Hey, do you need some help?" I asked her.

"Um, actually yes, can you help me find my way to The Benlock Restaurant? I'm meeting my grandma there for dinner. Our special tradition on Friday night is to go out to eat. She normally picks me up, but she couldn't, so I told her I would meet her there and I got a little turned around."

"Well, I can help you get there, it's actually right by my house. I'll show you on my way."

"Thanks," Tori said. We began talking and laughing as we continued on our way. There was something I wanted to ask her, something I had wanted to ask those other girls. I just couldn't hold it in any longer, I knew it was none of my business, but I just had to ask.

"What did Blaire do that hurt you?"

Tori kept walking, but she was really quiet. She breathed deeply.

"I didn't mean to upset you. I shouldn't have asked, it was stupid."

"A few years ago, Blaire wasn't the queen bee. She didn't care about designer clothes and jewelry. She was quieter and made smarter choices and was nicer. One day she came up to me and we began talking. We went from talking to laughing and from laughing to being great friends. I mean like sister close. I thought she was wonderful. Then, over the summer before this year, she began to be…different. Caring about different things. I didn't do anything about it when she would talk about a girl or act snooty. I didn't want to lose my friend."

"We hadn't really been talking for about a week and then she called me up asking if I could come over. I was thrilled, I thought that this was the night she wanted to talk and tell me that she was sorry she had done the things she had. I told my mom and she gave me a ride over. When Blaire's mom let me in my heart was racing and huge smile was on my face. Until I saw her room."

"Her room?" I said in confusion, then quickly closed my mouth realizing I had interrupted. Tori smiled a little, then continued.

"I knew her room as having light green walls with a loft bed that had a turquoise comforter and stuffed animals up with the pillows. She had a silver painted dresser that held her TV and pictures of her family and friends that was close to the doorway. Across from that, an unpainted bookshelf held all of her books and a desk that always had scrapbooking things on it. A bulletin board held all of her artwork and coupons and other things."

"I didn't walk into that room. It was now painted a royal purple and she didn't have her loft bed. She had a queen size with no stuffed animals and a black comforter that had leopard embellishments on it. Her silver dresser was now not even there, there was this gold one covered in makeup and hair products. Her bookshelf, now painted, wasn't holding books, it was a place for a speaker and music player. No scrapbooking things were on her desk, just a lot of fashion and beauty magazines. Her bulletin

21

board still held coupons, but not for the stores I had known she shopped at. These were for designer things. There was a pageant tiara sitting on that bookshelf."

"I remember her being so happy with it all. Talking about where it all had come from and the pageant she had been in. I asked her why she was into all these things now and she said it was because she now realized who her real self was. I asked her what she meant. Her exact words were 'I'm popular now, I can have anything I want. Because now I'm not being the quiet, average girl, I'm on top. You've shown me that I'm meant for popularity, that's why we're friends.' I was shocked."

"I told her I became friends with her because I thought she was nice and smart and funny and awesome. Not what she was becoming, which was a brat. She yelled at me and told me that I wasn't 'Queen Vicki' anymore, which is what my friends had given me as a nickname. She told me she was the top girl now and that if I couldn't accept that this is who she was, then I should leave. I didn't want to lose the friendship, but I knew it was already lost. I told her I wanted Blaire back, not this, and that I wished we could've made it work. I knew she felt worse, but she still opened the door to let me out. I told her mom that I wasn't feeling good. Then at home, I cried and cried and told my mom all about it."

I gave Tori the nicest hug I could manage and kept my arm on her shoulder until we got to the restaurant.

"Thanks for taking me here. Can you not tell anyone what I just told you. I don't like to bring it up. Skylar and Jennifer don't know."

"Don't worry, I'll keep it between you and me," I said with a smile.

"Here's my number if you ever want to call," she said handing me a sticky note.

"Hey, if you want, Macy and I are getting ready for the formal at my house tomorrow. Would you like to come?"

"That would be great, I would love to."

"Great, we're going to meet at about five o'clock, which should give us an hour to get ready."

"Okay, I'll see you then. Bye." She waved as she walked through the doors.

I walked the half of block I had left to get to my house. When I got home I walked into the living room where I found my Uncle Thomas. His legs were crossed and his thick glasses, or as he liked to call them his 'bifocals,' had slid down his nose a little. A book was in his hand. I swore I had never seen him without a book, whether he was reading it or not.

"What are you reading?" I asked, approaching him.

"*The Secret Garden* by Frances Hodgson Burnett. It's quite fascinating how they portray Mary as very crude and miserable." I loved the way he talked, it was like he was from a different time.

"Really? Why do you think that it is fascinating?" I asked things like this when he was on one of this 'theory runs' as I called them. I loved them.

"Because, I think they have to make her grow like the garden. The garden I believe is a metaphor for Mary. That she just needed care and someone to put work into her to make her grow again, to make her happy."

"I guess you could say the garden was hidden in more ways than one, huh?" I said.

"I guess you could indeed," he said chuckling. "Speaking of hidden places, I have something to show you," he said with a joyful grin displayed across his lips.

He had me close my eyes. By the touch of afternoon air and the tickling of grass, I knew he had taken me outside. The backyard was wide, outstretching to the fields and forests that guarded it like a wall.

"Where are you taking me, Uncle Thomas?" I asked as he guided me forward then slightly turning me.

"I cannot tell you, it would spoil the fun of the surprise," he said.

We walked a while longer. I hunted sightlessly, with my shoes, feeling the grass rub against my ankles and hearing the occasional rustle of an animal in the distance.

"All right, uncover your eyes," Uncle Thomas said with an excitement it seemed he was barely able to contain.

I opened my eyes revealing myself to a world of wonder. I was standing in a semi clearing that was somewhere in my woods. I used to play back in the woods, but I had never been here before or even seen it from a distance.

Towering pines, birch and various other kinds of trees surrounded the area. There was one big tree that held a magnificent treehouse, complete with a self-operating elevator, and access to branches for climbing.

My eyes were attracted to a waterfall. It was fairly large. The rocks that held the rushing water were caged by vines growing a peculiar flower. The water ran between and beneath the rocks reaching a neighboring river that surrounded everything, which made an island with a log bridge as the only way in and out.

I choked on joyful tears. "I…I can't believe this!" I said gesturing my arms about. "It's wonderful! So wonderful I wish I had a better word - marvelous, splendiferous, magnificent. It's all that and more. Thank you, Uncle Thomas!" I ran to him with wide arms then I wound them around his tall body.

"When your mother and I lived here, we used these woods as our escape to unimaginable places. I fixed a few things up and now you can, too. I hope that you find the happiness that we once did."

"Thank you so, so much. I am so happy. I love this place, but I have one question."

"What, love?"

"What is that flower, I've never seen it before." I pointed to the indigo blue flowers poking out from vines on the waterfall.

"Ah, that's a Starletta flower. A wondrous flower that has several colors mixed together to make its unique shade. It grows only near water and blooms whenever it wants."

"Whenever it wants?"

"Yes, some bloom in just fall and some bloom in spring and summer. Some are out all year round, but each flower chooses when it blooms. It's most unusual," he shook his head slightly.

"How come I've never heard of them?" I asked.

"Oh, I've done a study on them and I brought them here just for you. They're quite rare. Well, why don't you stay and have a look around for a bit, while your father and I start on supper."

I explored everywhere. I practiced the elevator, which had a small chamber made of wood without a roof, but bars and a platform to stand on. I would unhook the latch, climb in and then use the rope to pull myself up.

I wandered around, climbing up the jagged sides of the waterfall and splashing my fingertips into its rippled streams of water. I dipped my feet into the river, feeling little pebbles on the arch of my foot.

I examined the Starletta flower. Uncle Thomas was right, it had a mix of indigo and dark blue, light blue, periwinkle with a white star like center. I plucked one from the tangle of plants and studied it closely. I put it in my pocket and planned to put it in a book to press it.

"Guinevere love, it's time for supper!" Uncle Thomas called. I was snapped out of my daydream by the sound of his voice. I lowered myself to the ground and ran to the house.

"I guess I was out there a while, wasn't I?" I asked after I had gotten back.

"Yes, but don't fret about it. Come along, dinner's ready," Uncle Thomas said leading me back into the house.

My nose sucked in the scents of freshly baked rolls settling in the kitchen and steak just reaching the cool air from its hot prison.

I pulled out a chair and sat down. Dad was directly across from me and had already started on his meal.

"How was school today?" Dad asked looking at some paperwork.

"It was fine," I answered finishing one of my rolls. "Ms. Tickens chose my book for our next reading and she thought I did great job telling the class about it." I took some bites of my steak.

"That's my girl," Dad said.

I could see something was troubling my dad. Most likely it was from work, being a lawyer wasn't exactly an easy task.

"David? Is something going on?" Uncle Thomas asked.

"I have a very stressful case I'm working on. Speaking of which, I should probably be getting back to it." He gave me a quick kiss on the forehead before he went downstairs to his office.

I looked down at my plate of half eaten food.

"Now, don't be down honey. You know he gets troubled sometimes," Uncle Thomas said comfortingly, as he rubbed my back.

"He gets troubled *all* the time." I pushed out of my chair and stood up. He nodded in understanding. "I'm sorry Uncle Thomas, but I've lost my appetite. Can I go to my room?" He nodded sympathetically. I took one more swallow of milk before I took my glass and plate to the sink.

I jogged up the stairs to my bedroom. I smiled a bit when I entered. This used to be my mother's room when she was growing up. Most people would want a different room if it had been their missing mother's, but not me. I wanted to be as close as I possibly could be to my mom. This room didn't make me ache or cry, it made me feel secure. This was where my mother was last, it sometimes felt like it was where she was now.

The walls had been painted a creamy white. There were some chips in the paint and there was some age to the light tan carpet, but I liked that. The room was a square. On the west side there was one window with faint, silk pink curtains and a sill outside of it where I could sit or climb down to the flat part of the roof.

Two narrow wooden bookshelves stood on each side of the window and then across from that was a French armoire where I had all my clothes. My bed was a few inches from the left bookshelf with a handmade quilt that had beautiful stitch work. My desk was up against the north side.

Then there was my mother's vanity. She had gotten it for her sixteenth birthday. I hadn't changed anything. It even had the jewelry dish that held my mother's favorite necklace. It had strands of pearls dropping down from a gold chain. I had begged my father to let me keep it in my room and not to put it in the family vault.

I fell backward onto the quilt, stroking my hand along the lines of stitches. I breathed in a few heavy sighs, then looked at my clock. 7:30.

I sat up and pulled my phone from its charger. Three texts from Macy lighted the screen.

Gwendolyn?
R U there?
Call me once you get these ASAP!

I called her and left a voicemail. Almost instantly I got a reply back.

"Gwendolyn, something seriously wacko is going on," Macy said frantically into the phone. "I took a nap earlier and had that freaky dream again, except this time I went outside the bedroom. Into a hallway that was lined with pedestals of all these…fairies or enchantresses or something. They were all holding wands. Then I heard people talking, they were talking about…"

"What Macy? What were they talking about?"

"They said your name - your full name - Gwendolyn Marie Star. I don't know about you, but I think that falls into the super-weird-crazy category."

"They could've been talking about someone else."

"How many other Gwendolyn Marie Stars' do you know?"

"Fair point. What do you think we should do?"

"Well, did you find or get any new things? Something that's strange?" The image of the Starletta flower lit up in my mind.

"Yeah. My Uncle Thomas took me to my mom and his favorite spot as kids. He added some new touches to it for me and one was this rare flower called a Starletta flower. It had all these different colors to make its color and it grows only when it wants to. Like some will only grow in winter or summer or some will only grow in fall and spring, the plant decides."

"Wow, that's cool. Bad, but a lot of cool. But bad. Do you think that brought on the dream?"

"I'm not sure, it's possible. But why would it affect you and not me when it was in my backyard and my uncle brought it here?"

"That is true. But, you haven't slept since you saw it, so maybe once you sleep you'll have a dream."

"Maybe."

"Sorry, but I have to go and get ready for Aiden's guitar concert. You should come, it's going to be fun."

"Are you worried if Blaire will be there?" I asked. I knew Blaire had gone to a couple in the past.

"It may be one of the reasons I'm asking you to come."

"You really don't want to see her do you?"

"Would you just come?"

"Sure, where is it?"

"It's at the Pinetten Theater and it starts at eight. So you have probably enough time if someone drives you."

"Got it, bye." I clicked the 'end' button.

I leaped over to look in the mirror. I looked at the outfit I had worn to school. Dark blue crewneck shirt, light jeans and a three necklace trio.

I knew the Pinetten Theater seats were packed pretty tightly together, so I took off the crewneck and replaced it with a light yellow tank and cream shrug. I kept the necklaces, but pulled my hair into a ponytail.

I swiped my purse off the back of my chair and went down stairs to persuade my uncle to take me to the concert.

"Uncle Thomas, can you drive me somewhere?" I asked at the bottom of the stairs, while trying to tug on my brown ankle boots.

"That depends on where you want to go."

"To a concert. Macy invited me. Her stepbrother, Aiden, is playing. Can you drive me?"

"This Aiden fellow, what's he like?"

"He's smart, kind and cute," I said.

"Sounds like you're smitten with him," said Uncle Thomas with a smirk. My cheeks became deep shade of red.

"Well, I'm not one to keep lovers apart. Hop in the car and I'll take you. Where is this event?"

"It's at the Pinetten Theater. Thank you, Uncle Thomas."

"My pleasure, darling."

When we got there, he gave me a quick kiss on the cheek before he sent me off. I bought a ticket and then got swallowed in along with a group of other late comers.

I found Macy sitting in the middle section and scooted into a seat next to her.

"Hey, you made it!" she exclaimed when I sat down.

"Yeah, though you didn't mention that I had to *buy* a ticket."

"Sorry, my bad."

"Can you help me put on a little mascara? I was trying to do that technique you showed me earlier this week for the formal, but I can't get it."

"Trying to look good for my stepbrother?" she asked with a sly smile.

"Please."

"Sure, I happen to have some."

"Thanks." She handed me a compact mirror when she was done.

"You've done it again," I said admiring my eyes.

"Thank you. Can you give that back to me? The show's about to begin." Macy slipped the things back into her bag and set it on the floor.

We watched as Aiden and his bandmates entered the darkened stage and took their places.

They played for about a half an hour and were great. After the show, Macy pulled me backstage to say hi to Aiden.

"You did great!" Macy said with a big smile as she ran up and hugged him. She was a bit shorter than him. He was 5'3" and she was about 5'1".

"You did really, really well. I loved the performance," I congratulated him.

"Thanks. We'd been practicing a lot, every day after school to be specific. It looks like it paid off for our first performance in front of a paying crowd."

"It was the best $5 ticket I've ever bought," I said with a flirty smile.

"Yeah, it totally was. I have to call my mom to come pick us up, but I'll see you tomorrow evening before the dance," Macy said to me while pulling out her cell.

"Hey, that reminds me. Gwendolyn, would you like to go to the dance with me?" Aiden asked. I could barely speak. He had asked me!

"Well, I was going to go with Macy…"

"She would love to! Don't worry Gwendolyn, I'll make sure he's dressed to impress," Macy said finishing for me with a grin.

"Great! I'll just meet you there if that's all right?"

"That sounds great, we'll see you then," I said rushing through my sentence so Macy couldn't interject anymore opinions. Then I rushed to the door.

I was dialing my uncle to see if I could get a ride home, when there was a tap on my shoulder.

"Is Aiden in there?" Blaire asked.

"Yeah why?"

"I want to ask him to the spring formal," said Blaire.

"He's backstage, but…um…he already asked me to the dance," I said softly.

Blaire bit the inside of her bottom lip.

"Oh, um, well, that's okay because Marco already asked me anyway. I just thought that I should ask Aiden for like a dance at the party you know. I wouldn't want to make him feel bad, but it's good we've both moved on." Her voice sounded surreal, like she knew this could happen, but never believed it would.

"Blaire, it's okay. Maybe Aiden hasn't moved on."

"Thank you for yesterday, I needed it." Blaire said quickly and then she walked off back outside.

When my uncle didn't answer my call or text for a ride home, I began to walk.

I came to a four way intersection and walked north. My feet began aching. The walk never normally took this long, I must have missed a corner or something.

I went back about one block and looked around. Nope, I had gone the right way. The same as I always did when I walked this way.

I looked around, there had to be some explanation. I don't know why, but a signal went to my brain for my feet to move. I began walking forward, not challenging the actions my body was making.

I kept walking north for a long time, maybe three blocks. Then I stopped at the entrance to Lonright Park.

The park looked peaceful at night. The whispered song of the crickets flew brokenly into my ears. Little ripples of water were made by the small breeze and the swaying of trees harmonized a tune.

The park was closed. In fact, it had been closed for only about a minute before I arrived according to my watch and the park schedule. That weird sensation came over my body again. My feet wanted me to move again, but this time my sense of right and wrong took over first. Breaking into the park was definitely on the wrong side.

Then the sensation stopped. I waited a moment and just as I was about to try to go home, the sensation took control. It guided me right of the entrance sign and toward the abandoned golf course that was next door.

A few decades back, the golf course had closed and been abandoned because of bankruptcy. Sometimes teens would go and play on the greens and around the areas of the course since it never got locked up.

The feeling led me beyond one of the greens into the woods. It stopped when I came to a river.

The river was shallow. Sandbars could be seen among discarded tree branches and jagged rocks. They taunted me to come near enough for them to stick their pointed tops into my feet as they had the advantage, hidden among the blanket of oncoming night.

As I stared into that vast night, I saw a glimmer of some sorts on one of those sandbars. It small, but something was there. Now, since I had entered the course, every inch of my body was telling me to go home. Except that one part and it seemed to take over everything. Even my logic.

I slipped off my boots and socks then waded a little ways into the water. It was much colder than I had anticipated and it sent a sharp shiver up my body.

When I came to the small sandbar island, I saw what was glimmering. It was a plant.

It was a glowing plant.

It was *my* glowing plant.

At first I thought I was just imagining it, but it was there. And I was seeing it with my own eyes. That was a Starletta flower on that island and it was glowing, like a tiny light was coming up from its core.

I stood directly over it and looked down. There was a light, a light that was getting brighter. I didn't want to touch it, but I couldn't stop looking at it.

The light went out.

I stood in shock. It was the most beautiful thing, beautiful and strange. Yes, it was strange and strange can mean bad. Another bad thing was being late for curfew.

I ran back out through the woods and the course and went back to the intersection. I was running harder, pumping my legs wildly.

Now I wasn't thinking about which way I had to go, I just ran. Maybe it was instinct, maybe it was memory, but I found my way home in record time and slipped right in. It was one minute before I would've been late, when I shut the door.

I noticed my dad was still in his office. I quietly crept past it.

My uncle was in the living room when I passed.

I froze. *Busted!* But he just nodded like I had been in the house the whole time.

"Did you have fun at the concert?" he asked.

I nodded.

"You should be getting ready for bed, right?"

I nodded again and started up the stairs.

"Oh, Guinevere. Next time you want to go golfing, all you have to do is ask."

I shook my head a little and let a smile take form. I didn't know how he had known I had been at the course, but he hadn't told my dad. And he wasn't mad, that's what really mattered.

Once in my room, I tugged off my boots and changed into a t-shirt and some sweat pants. I crawled into bed and covered my body in warm sheets.

Bzzzzzzzzz. I unlocked the screen to my phone.

Hey! I can't wait to see you and Aiden together at the dance!
Yeah. Thanks for telling me that you were going to ask him to be my date.
I did you a favor, it's not like you were going to ask him.
You don't know that.
I think I do.
Well, I'll see you tomorrow. Bye.
Bye, soon to be not-so-single-lady. Night.

I flicked off my light and let the darkness settle around me. Slowly, the night took its toll and my eyelids became heavy. I watched as the last slip of light faded from my eyes.

My dad would tell me about how dreams would take you from the world of reality to the world of dreams. To a world of magic and adventure and freedom - freedom from the rules of the real world. Freedom from the horrors and scars of the real world. As I learned though, you're still not protected from the monsters of the dreams.

CHAPTER 3
THE CLEARING AND THE CAVE

The earth felt muddy. Rain poured down every inch of me. I found myself lying on the damp ground. I picked myself up and swept off some of the wet dirt from my sweat pants.

This definitely wasn't my bedroom. I wasn't even in a room. I was in the middle of what looked to be a soggy cornfield.

Trudging through the drenched stalks, I came to a farm house. The lights were on and I could see the shadow of a person moving within the house.

That same sensation I felt in the park zipped through my body and made me move toward the house. I went up onto the steps and under the small awning. A girl had just entered the house and was running up the stairs.

The sensation jerked me forward.

The door opened without a sound and I followed the girl upstairs to a bedroom. She was kneeling beside someone. I guessed it was her mother based on the painting of them I noticed on the night table. Her mother's skin was very pale and her eyes were shut. Her dark hair was long and curtained her face.

The girl was weeping at the sight of her mother's condition. Then, her eyes opened and she looked toward her daughter. I moved a little closer into the room. Strangely, I didn't make a sound.

It must be because I'm in a dream, I thought.

The mother began to speak. "In fifty years, our world will change, everything will change. The Seven Sins will cloak this land in evil. Four women will go through tremendous things for true love, two girls will fill their craving for adventure, one boy and girl pair will risk anything to save one another and one source of magic must help them. Find this magic, help those wandering souls and prepare." Her voice was low and scratched. She used great energy to turn her head toward the candle on the nightstand, and then she shut her eyes. I felt tears come to my eyes, but it was nothing compared to the daughter. She began to sob, clutching her mother's limp hand in agony.

She turned away from her mother and dashed out the room. I took one last look into the bedroom. I went over to her mother. As I looked at her I noticed something. The mother sort of looked like...mine.

I knew that it was normal for kids to hallucinate that they were seeing a lost parent. I hadn't been around my mother long enough to actually remember her, but I had dreams where I heard her talking to me.

That's when I noticed the woman's ruby ring.

That was my mother's ring.

It's not possible. It's just me dreaming. It's just me thinking about her, I told myself. But I knew that wasn't true.

My mother's favorite ring had been put in storage for years. It was the only thing they found of hers when she disappeared. Uncle Thomas told me about it once I was older. I knew that that ring was one-of-a-kind, it couldn't be duplicated.

I slipped the ring off of the women's finger and pocketed it.

When I got outside, I followed the muddy trail the girl had left. The path continued for a while, until I came to a forest. The footprints were now harder to see with the pine needles disguising them, but I managed to follow.

I saw the girl standing very still in a clearing. I saw as she jumped a little and then scampered over to a pine tree caged by some berry bushes. She pulled out two flat stones. She pricked her finger on a thorn from the bush. She let a drop of blood drop on each stone and then she smacked them together.

I watched in puzzlement when she started chanting a phrase. I was too far away to catch any more than the last few words. *"Will open the way."*

The girl placed the stones on the ground again and waited.

A marvelous light rocketed from the stones. A rickety house stood when the light had faded.

Upon entering the house, the girl started looking around. I heard her shriek and then I saw a slight movement. I turned to see the girl had moved a bit of the bookcase and was now pushing against it.

It finally budged and revealed a staircase behind it. I walked over to the bookcase and I hurried behind her down the spiral of stone slabs that led to a door. The girl peeked in the keyhole and saw something. I looked in. A woman in a shimmering white robe was standing over a table.

She walked in cautiously. The woman said something to her and she said something back. They exchanged words for the longest time and I heard a few words of the conversation. "*Magic...Prophecy...Spell.*"

"You will be more significant in some tales than others, but you will be a part of each none the less. You are a fairy, my darling, one in a very important legacy. Now, we must begin. You have a lot to learn and the clock is ticking." The woman in the white robe said.

I shot up from my covers, forcing them forward. My breath was hard and rapid.

"It was just a dream, it didn't mean anything." I told myself aloud, but I knew that was a lie. The dream had showed me a woman that looked an awful lot like my mother who was wearing her ring.

I felt something in my pants pocket. I grabbed the object. A beautiful ruby ring displayed itself in my palm.

Fear ran through me.

Was this my subconscious showing me my mother's unproven death?

Who were the lady and girl?

I got out of bed. I couldn't deal with this, at least not now. It was the night of the spring formal. Aiden Morns was my date. I would be getting ready with my friends and I had a gorgeous dress picked out for the occasion.

I pulled together what logic and sanity I still had left and got dressed for the day.

"What's for breakfast?" I asked when I was downstairs.

"I made French toast and bacon. Sit down or it'll be gone soon. Your father is already on his second serving," Uncle Thomas said as he stood over the pan of frying bacon. I took out a glass from the cabinet and let a stream of orange juice fall into it.

"Who is the lucky guy who is taking you to the dance?" Dad inquired as he took a gulp of his coffee.

"How do you know someone asked me?" I asked, my cheeks blushing a smidge.

"Who wouldn't want to take my daughter?"

"It's Macy's stepbrother, Aiden Morns."

"I know his father, Luke. Real nice guy, so is his wife Lily. Now, I haven't seen Aiden in a long time, how is he?"

"He's good. He gets excellent grades and he's a downright gentleman."

"It sounds like he'll be a great date."

We all finished our breakfast. My father went off to work, as did my uncle, and I was left home alone. Once the front door shut I went straight to where I had left my phone.

"Hello? Macy? Are you there?" I asked into the receiver.

"I'm here, doll."

"I had a dream. A really weird one...my mom was in it."

I heard slow breathing on the other end.

"What did you see?" Macy asked.

"I saw a woman lying in a bed. She looked almost identical to my mom and she was wearing my mom's favorite ring. It can't be duplicated. I have never seen it, but Uncle Thomas has shown me pictures of her with it and it's the one. I'm staring at it right now."

"Wait, you're staring at it?"

"That's what I said."

"You saw it in a dream and now you're staring at it."

"Affirmative."

"And you're sure that you didn't just sleepwalk into your basement and get the ring out of one of the boxes?"

"Yes. I don't sleepwalk. I know I don't and how logical is that anyway? I don't even know which box it's in."

"Okay, yes, but if something like this is happening, shouldn't we account for everything?

"Macy, I know I didn't sleepwalk downstairs and grab the ring out of one of the storage bins. I got this from a dream or wherever I went."

"Okay. So, what do we do now?"

"Can you come over a little early? I want to show you that place my uncle showed me."

"I think I can, I mean I only live a couple blocks away. I should be there in twenty."

"Got it." I hung up and readied my backpack. I slipped in a flashlight and the ring.

I was impatiently pacing in the kitchen when Macy rang the doorbell.

"Sorry it took so long, my mom told me to put away laundry. So, where's this place you want to take me?"

"It's in my woods," I said tugging her to the door.

"What's with the backpack?"

"You'll find out when we get there."

"Is it muddy back there?"

"Probably not."

"These are new flats. I can't get them ruined by mud or dirt."

"I understand, just come on."

We ventured into the woods toward the clearing. "Oh my God, Gwendolyn, it's…beautiful. I can't believe it's been back here this whole time and we never knew. I mean, how can you miss something like this!" Macy spread her arms wide.

"I know, I really love it. I think we need answers. For some reason this seems like the place to come."

"How do you propose we find these answers?"

"We do what any person would do. We explore." I climbed to the peak of one of the waterfall's jutted sides and then jumped down to the ground.

"Hold on Gwendolyn. I've got on flats, remember," Macy said, carefully planning her movements down the edges.

"Sorry," I apologized and took Macy's hands to help her down.

We went far back into the woods. I scanned the area, mapping where large rocks and trees were and if we took lefts or rights at passes.

"Hey, come over here!" Macy shouted. I turned my head away from the area I had been observing. Macy was over by a cave coated in moss and twigs. I had never seen it before.

"What?" I asked coming over to the cave.

"Something is in this cave, I can hear it."

"Are you sure it's not an animal? Maybe it's just a bat."

"Whatever made that noise wasn't an animal or at least not a normal one," Macy said.

"Alright, I have a flashlight. We can use that. Let's see what's in here."

We crept into the mouth of the rock and I darted the beam of light around its edges.

"Which way did the noise come from?" I asked when we came to a fork in the path.

"It sounded like it was coming from this direction," Macy said pointing her finger to the opening of the right pathway. Trusting our gut, we headed right. The outside light faded with each step, letting the darkness consume us. We came to a halt if saw any movement or heard any sound.

I put my hand in front of Macy when I saw that a boulder blocked our way. A small depression was carved in the rock. It had a circular shape to it.

I took the ring from my backpack and slid it into the carving. Both of us took a few steps back. The boulder began to move. We ran over and pulled with everything we had to pry it the rest of the way open. After using most of our strength, it was open wide enough for us to go in.

I was about to head in when Macy put a hand on my shoulder.

"Gwendolyn, I know we're looking for answer about these dreams. But...could this really be about your mom? I know it was hard, you don't know where she is, you don't know if she's alive, but...," she took a deep breath.

"But, you've had dreams, too."

"Yes. I don't know how to explain that, but I don't want you to hurt yourself, physically, mentally, emotionally…"

"Macy, you're here with me, I won't get hurt. And you're right, a small part of me wants this to give me answers about my mom, but mostly I want answers on this. This isn't normal, but at the same time, it's sort of…amazing."

"Amazing?"

"Yes, we can see things no one else can. We are living, breathing proof that magic is out there. You even said it yourself. And now, maybe, we're magical in some way," I said it more enthusiastically than I had intended.

"Alright, let's see what's inside." A smile cracked onto each of our mouths as we went inside the rocky tomb.

The walls were smoother inside there. They looked like granite. The room itself seemed to shimmer with a mesmerizing glow.

We heard that weird noise again and watched as a pedestal of crystal rose from the granite. Timidly, we walked toward it. I looked down into the almost clear crystal. I was in a trance as I stared at my reflection in the mineral. As fast as light, I suddenly saw an orb sitting in the center of the pedestal.

I jumped back.

"Holy cow," said Macy, her voice a shocked whisper.

"I made an orb appear. I made an orb appear!"

"How?"

"I…don't know."

"Gwendolyn…maybe we should…"

"Uh-uh. No. We're figuring this out. I just made a flippin' orb appear just by using my mind! That's not an everyday thing for me, so I think I have the right to know why in the world that's possible."

Macy nodded her head in agreement.

I went back over to the orb, which was now semi glowing.

I bowed my head, then placed my hands on the orb and concentrated.

I opened my eyes and I found myself in a village. From what I could tell I was in the center of the town, maybe a square. I looked down. My jeans and tank top had now been replaced by a blue dress with a dusty apron.

People began running into the square. All had frightened looks on their faces.

Black mist swirled into the square, encircling the trees, turning them to ash. Parents took their children into their arms before the mist could reach them and tried to flee.

The mist secured a wall around the crowd, then weeded out all of the fathers, mothers, boys and babies.

Leaving just the girls.

They didn't move. Terror was plastered on their faces, along with stripes of tears on their cheeks.

The mist began stirring up dust and smoke. I placed a hand to my face to block out the bits of grime.

A black, shadowy silhouette came into view. It seemed to be almost floating toward them. A long sleek hood was draped over its head and across its face accompanied by a black floor length cape.

It held a charred vine like stick in its hand. A purple orb was clasped in it. It glowed wickedly.

It swept the hood off its face. Crow colored hair was in a tousled back bun, strands falling over its brows. Its eyelashes were thick and long against dark indigo eyes. They blazed with flecks of the sun.

"Dementia," I heard one of the girls mumble in horror.

She began walking around each girl until her eyes fell on me. She grinned a little.

I heard the soft thump of her boots as she approached me.

Dementia traced her finger along my cheekbone, then dragged it under my chin, pulling it up so I could look at her.

With a velvet voice she said into my ear. "Such a pretty princess."

I opened my eyes. My breathing was calm this time and my heart wasn't going a million miles a minute.

"Are you okay? What did you see?" Macy asked me.

I turned to face Macy and wrapped my arms around her, bringing her into a hug.

"What did you see in there?" she asked again.

I took a gulp of air and licked my lips. "I was in a town square and my clothes had been changed into peasant rags. This black mist began burning the trees and it separated the girls from their families. These girls were like our age, they were all terrified. The mist swirled up all the dust and dirt and then this lady, Dementia, came out from it. She was wearing black, head to toe, and then she pulled off her hood and it showed these eyes. They were purple colored, but with little sparks of orange and gold in them. They looked so menacing. She looked at all the girls and then stopped at me. She put her hand under my chin and then whispered into my ear 'such a pretty princess.' Those exact words."

"Do you think she was the cause of all the smoke and fire in your first dream?" Macy asked.

"I don't know, but that would be a good assumption. Let's get out of here. I want to show you something that's not in a place of orbs and wicked sorceresses."

I led the way back out into the light. I took Macy back to the clearing and took out the Starletta flower I had pressed.

"What is that?"

"It's one of the Starletta flowers, those ones that bloom whenever they want. Uncle Thomas planted them here for me."

"It's really pretty."

"Yeah, I thought that, too. We should be getting back to my house, Tori should be coming soon." I hopped up from the rock I had been crouching on.

"Shouldn't you get your mom's ring?"

"I'll come back for it later." *And learn a little bit more about that cave.*

"Do you think I should go with a small amount of grey or a neutral color?" Macy asked as she sorted through my eye shadow palette. Tori, Macy and I were all picking out our makeup for the night.

"What does your dress look like again?" Tori asked her. Macy held up a royal purple knee length, side strap dress.

"I'd go with the grey, it'll go with the dress," I said.

"Same here," Tori said in agreement.

"That's what I thought. Hey Gwendolyn, you haven't shown us your dress yet," Macy said with an eager grin.

"Yeah, come on, show us!" Tori said happily.

I got off my bed and pulled out the dress from my closet. I was in love with this dress. It was an alluring blue with small gems all down it, making it look like the night sky. It went a little farther than my knees and had sheer blue straps that went over the semi-sweetheart neckline. It came around and connected in the back like a halter.

"Oh my God! Gwendolyn, that's breathtaking," beamed Tori.

"Totally. I can't wait to see Blaire's head pop off when she sees you in this," said Macy.

"I really like it. I found when I was cleaning up the basement. It must've been my mom's. I guess she must have really liked it to make sure it wasn't thrown away."

"Good thing she didn't, you'll look ravishing in it," Tori said.

"Hey, can you two do my hair and makeup?" I asked.

"For sure! I'm great at doing hair," Tori said. The girls went to work on me. Then Tori and I made over Macy and Macy and I made over Tori.

"We're ready!" I said when we came down the stairs.

"You all look lovely," Uncle Thomas said, his coat draped on his shoulder. "Let's get going, I have the car all set."

"I hope you all have a fun night." Uncle Thomas said when he dropped us off at the school.

"We will. Thank you for the ride!" I called back to him.

Inside the gym, which was very large, bodies were moving in every direction imaginable. Some were getting food, some were talking on the sidelines, but most were dancing.

"Great turnout. I love the setup. You did a great job on the decoration committee, Tori," Macy complemented.

She blushed a little. "Thanks, we all worked hard."

"I'm going to try to find Aiden, okay guys?" I said negotiating the bodies to see if any matched his.

"Go get 'em, honey. He's in a white polo and grey dress pants," Macy called to me as I headed into the crowd.

Aiden was standing by the sidelines talking to someone. I stopped. It was Marco Alfano.

"Gwendolyn, it's a pleasure to see you here," Marco said with a snake smile.

"Aiden asked me to be his date." I looked to him with a warm smile that hinted with that I wanted to leave.

"Hey, I want to go get some soda. Care to come, Gwendolyn?" Aiden asked. I walked beside him to the table of chips and drinks.

"I'm sorry I pulled you out of your conversation. I just don't really like Marco," I apologized.

"It's totally fine, I sometimes don't like him either. He likes to show off. Oh by the way, I love your dress. You look really beautiful in it."

I could feel my face burning. "Thank you, I like your shirt. Hey, I was wondering, do you know if Blaire has shown up yet?"

"Did someone say, moi?" Aiden and I turned around to see Blaire standing behind us, arms raised in a dramatic way, which was not unusual. Her hair was pulled into a chignon style bun and she was wearing a dress with jewels fading as they descended the fabric. She had on silver heels that gave her an extra two inches and she was wearing diamond everything - bracelet, earrings, necklace, the whole nine.

"I was just wondering if you had shown up," I said to her sweetly.

"Oh, Gwendolyn, you know I never miss a bash," she laughed a little, eyeing Aiden as much as she could without being obvious. Good thing I was observant.

"I love your dress Blaire, it's really beautiful," I said politely.

"Thank you," she said as she kept eyeing Aiden.

"It does look very nice. Um, Gwendolyn, shouldn't we find…"

"Aiden, could I borrow you for a moment?" Blaire gestured toward an area on the sidelines.

"Well, I was going to ask Gwendolyn to dance with me."

"It's alright Aiden, I'll wait," I said.

I secretly watched as they talked. Blaire stormed off about two minutes into the conversation.

"What did she want to talk about?" I asked as we started dancing on the dance floor.

"She asked me if I wanted to go to a movie with her Sunday. I turned her down. I didn't want to get stood up again."

"I bet she wouldn't do it this time."

"Yeah. She said she had been a bit of a jerk, but personally I don't want to go through that again. You know, waiting in a movie theater lobby for a half an hour and getting no response until finally your mom picks you up is no fun."

I thought this over. "If that's how you truly feel, then okay. But it is Blaire, she is a catch. And she can actually be pretty nice."

"Yeah, I suppose. She can be pretty vain though."

"Yes, but she is a good person." I couldn't comprehend the words that were coming out of my mouth. Why was I was defending Blaire?

Then I thought of the thank you.

It was the only thing I could think of. Blaire had sincerely thanked me for just a simple offering of comfort.

"I think you should go with her to the movie." I took a deep breath. Aiden was the sweetest guy I knew, but maybe this was a second chance for Blaire. One that she needed.

"Why?"

"Because I think you like her and I think she likes you."

Aiden looked down at his feet.

"I want you to go and I think you both would connect if you had a real chance."

"You think so, huh?"

"Yeah."

"All right, I'll tell her. Thanks Gwendolyn, it's really sweet of you." Aiden kissed me on the cheek before he walked off toward where Blaire was chatting with some of her friends. It stung a little to watch him go. I had liked this guy since the sixth grade, but he'd be happy and that's what I wanted for him.

"Where did Tori go?" I asked when I found Macy again.

"She decided to leave. She had this really bad headache. And when I went into the bathroom with her, she actually puked a little and some got on her dress."

"That's crappy. I hope she feels better Monday."

"Same. She looked so pretty. I felt bad that her dress got stained, but onto other things. How was it, did you dance? Did he complement your dress? Ooh...did he ask you on a date?" Macy interrogated.

"Yes, we did dance. Yes, he thought my dress was very pretty. No, he did not ask me out."

"What! How did he not ask you? You said that you danced and he complemented your dress.

"You think that means the guy will ask me out?"

"It implies that the night is turning it in that direction."

"Well, we're not. He did kiss me on the cheek though. I told him to go on a date with Blaire."

She grabbed my elbow pulling me back. "You did what?"

"I told him to go on a date with Blaire."

"Why?"

"I think he likes her more than he realized. And I think she likes him and they need another chance. Truthfully, and you have to listen to me on this, I think that you and her need another chance, too."

"She hurt Aiden. She hurt me, she's hurt others, she's..."

"That doesn't give us the right to subject her to pain. I mean it Macy. I don't think anyone, even someone who has tricked many people, needs to be put through a series of jabs." I stared at her, putting sympathetic firmness into my words.

Macy bit her bottom lip. "How am I going to trust her again?" she said quietly.

"You have to give her some time and some grace. But, first, you have to forgive." I took Macy's hand. "I'll walk you to her."

"Blaire?" Macy was standing a few inches from Blaire who was texting or something on her phone. I stood a few feet away.

"Yeah?"

"I want to talk to you."

"About..."

"I'm sorry about the night in the salon. I was pretty harsh. I was really mad because it seemed like we were drifting farther apart. And then you stood Aiden up and something in me snapped. I remembered the way that you had hurt people and the way you had hurt me. I know I said some things that now I actually regret, but I want to try to have a friendship again."

Blaire was stunned. They just looked at each other.

"I think I'll leave you two alone," I said. I patted Macy on the shoulder and then smiled a small smile to Blaire. I don't know what they said to each other after I left the gym. All I know is, Macy went home with Blaire that night. And when she called me the next day, she sounded happier about the friendship than she had in a long time.

CHAPTER 4
FAMILY HISTORY

"Why didn't Macy come home with you?" Dad asked when I got home.

"She wanted to go home with Blaire."

"I thought you didn't like Blaire?"

"She's okay."

"Well, then how was the dance?"

"It was good. I danced with Aiden and I talked with Macy. Tori had to leave early though because she wasn't feeling well."

"I hope she feels better soon."

"I do, too. I'm going to change out of my dress and start getting ready for bed," I told him.

"Sweet dreams honey, don't stay up too late," Dad called as I climbed the stairs.

I changed into a pair of sweat pants and a t-shirt. I stretched my hands out and placed them behind my head. I fell back onto my bed and stared up at the ceiling.

A thought struck my brain. What was happening? I couldn't believe it had taken me this long, but really *what* was happening? I had begun having weird dreams. They started to happen when I got that library book on fairytales. I had made an orb appear with my mind. I had taken a ring out of a dream.

The ring!

It was still in the cave.

Now I was a good girl. I knew I wasn't supposed to go out in the middle of the night. Especially into the woods, into a magical cave, to find my mother's ring. In a place where I could put myself into a dream world, without someone there to make sure I got out.

But, it was a magical cave where I could put myself into a dream world.

My hoodie cuddled my body against the cool night air. I had brought a flashlight, but wouldn't permit myself to use it until I got into the woods where no one would see its light. I carefully maneuvered through the pines and then, when I was a few feet in, I clicked on the flashlight.

I found my way to the clearing. Even during the night, it was fairly easy to see. I was about to start my climb over the waterfall, when I began to see movement in the trees.

One by one the Starletta flowers began to glow – just like that one had at the old golf course. The glow became brighter and brighter. Dozens of them were shining. Paralyzed by wonderment, I just stared.

Then the flowers did something amazing. Their lights unattached themselves and began floating and flying around me. I swore that I could hear small giggles, like little bells, coming from them.

Suddenly, just like before, the lights went out and the forest became black except for the beam of the flashlight.

I continued on my way, feeling the rocks and ground for similarities from my last journey. I came upon the cave's opening and stepped inside. I saw that my mother's ring was still inside the groove and that the stone door was still open.

I forgot about the ring and walked into the room. It was like no time had passed. The pedestal was still standing and the orb was still there, its glow illuminating the room.

I looked deep into the orb's glassy surface. *Why can't you just tell me what's going on? Don't I deserve to know? Haven't I gone through my share of pain and cluelessness to finally know why things happened the way they did? Why me?*

I brushed away the thoughts and took a few deep breaths. I needed to be calm. After relaxing my heartbeat, I placed my hands lightly on the orb. I thought about my last questions, playing them over and over, letting my head swirl with emotion.

I appeared at a mansion, no…at a palace. Large turrets of white brick reached up to the twilight sky, decorated with emerald vines. Each tower had a small rounded window and a large moat surrounded the fortress.

I looked around trying to find an entrance, when I saw one of the Starletta lights flicker its way over to me. The light guided me to the castle doors. Two guards were standing there. When they saw me, they bowed graciously to the floor. I was thinking this was odd, but the light kept moving, so I followed. Everywhere around the castle, if I ran into someone, they would bow or curtsy.

The light took me down a long hallway to a painting. I had never seen this woman before. She was wearing a golden crown decorated with jewels. She wore a purple dress with several stripes of lace. A plaque under the painting read:

> **Irene Star**
> **The First Queen of Stardon Kingdom**

This woman could have been one of my great grandmothers. I had never heard of Stardon Kingdom, but maybe this was the place I had been coming to in my dreams.

The light went over to the other side of the hallway. There was a portrait of a man. He was in a red, white and gold suit and a large golden crown was on his head. A plaque was under his portrait also:

> **James Star**
> **The First King of Stardon Kingdom**

The light took me down the whole hallway. All of the portraits were of kings and queens of Stardon. I came to the last couple.

> **Scarlett Star**
> **Princess of Stardon Kingdom**
> **Daughter of King Aaron Star and Queen Felicity Star**
> **Went to Modern World**

My mother's name was Scarlett. I had never known about my mother's parents. Dad and Uncle Thomas wouldn't talk about them either. I looked to the other side of the hallway.

> **Thomas Briarwood**
> **Prince of Lakeshore Kingdom**
> **Son of King Daniel Briarwood and Queen Alison Briarwood**
> **Went to Modern World**

This didn't make sense. All of the portraits had been of kings and queens that had been married and ruled the kingdom. If this was my mom then how could she be married to Thomas? My father's name was David. Thomas was my mom's brother.

There was one more portrait left. It was of a baby that Scarlett was holding.

> **Guinevere Star**
> **Princess of Stardon Kingdom**
> **Daughter of Princess Scarlett Star and Prince Thomas Briarwood**
> **Went to Modern World**

Guinevere. The name my mom wanted me to have. This couldn't be real. I was a princess...a princess of a kingdom. My stomach began churning. Like when you're at the top of a roller coaster and your heart races before you start speeding down the first hill.

How could my father be Thomas, but also be David? It didn't make sense. My uncle couldn't be my father. They would never lie to me like that. Would they?

The light pressed itself right on my painting. I just looked at it and shrugged. It came off the painting and pulled my hand to the cloak. I pressed on it and it opened. It revealed a little passage way to a room.

The room was a bit crowded. But with a hidden room in the walls of a castle, I don't know how they could make it comfy. The room had a desk with bookshelves. The bookshelves held many old books and the desk was concealed under piles of papers and documents.

The light guided me over to one of the bookshelves and pulled out a book. The book was old and thick and dusty. The light started to spin in a circle. It spun faster and faster and started to get bigger and bigger. It finally took its form. A lady.

She was wearing a sparkling white robe that went down to her ankles. Her brown hair was pulled into a braided bun that had small threads of grey in it.

"It is such a relief to be out of that dream dust form. It can be quite uncomfortable at times," she said.

"Who are you?" I asked.

"I am Starletta. You may know me as the Fairy Godmother."

"As in *the* Fairy Godmother?"

"The original."

"What are you doing here?"

"I am granting your request."

"My request?" I asked.

"You thought you deserved answers and so did I. That's why I'm here."

"Um…alright. Well, normally I would think I was being crazy, but I am the girl who has been traveling into a dream world. So, I think it is okay to trust you."

"I am a good person to trust. Also, it's not a dream world. It's your home, dear. This is where your family grew up."

"Where *is* this exactly?"

"Well, we have names for all the different kingdoms. But we've been given the name Fairytale World by the modern folk."

"You mean to say I'm in the Fairytale World?"

"Yes. Well, this is only an illusion of it, but it's real," she said as she nodded her head.

"Okay. So, I do have some questions."

"I presumed that you would."

"Was my mother really a princess? Am I really a princess?"

She took a breath. "Your mother was a princess. She was one that this kingdom loved dearly. You're her daughter. That means you are a princess and the heir."

"Why did the Starletta flowers start glowing at night and why did my dreams start happening when I found that book?"

"They were both signs from me. I couldn't communicate with you directly, so I had to get creative."

"When I was in one of these dreams, I heard you say spell and prophecy and magic. What was that about? And who was the woman I saw die? Was it my mom?"

"The woman you saw die wasn't your mother. She simply looked like her. She was actually a merchant who stole magic to make herself beautiful. She stole your mother's ring at one point, but we did retrieve it. She did have a good heart toward her daughters. Her oldest daughter, the girl you saw, her name is Marybella. She...," Starletta stopped for a moment.

"I thought she had magic. I thought she had the magic I needed for a spell. That's how she made the house appear. She copied a trick that I used to hide my house from Dementia, a former student of mine," she said quietly.

"What is that spell, Starletta?"

"The Prophecy you heard from that woman was true. This land was taken by the Seven Sins, seven women with hearts of stone and minds of revenge. Dementia is one of those girls. They are cruel and deceitful. They only think of power and control. I had concocted a spell that would not let those people, the ones you heard about in the Prophecy, be subjected to them. I thought Marybella had the extra magic I needed. I needed her because I didn't have enough. Being over 300 years old, my magic was running out. We trained and trained, practicing everything we could. I should've seen from the beginning that she wasn't perfectly fit, but I was blinded by the lack of time that we all had. What I didn't realize was that the person I needed, wouldn't be born in time. I actually told the people that Marybella was not who they needed, before I cast the spell."

"What was the spell meant to do?"

"It would take everyone from this world into your world. I wanted it to be everyone because I didn't want anyone to ever by hurt by the Seven Sins. I didn't want them to be lost in that new world. The Seven Sins wouldn't be able to reach them because the spell would trap them here. Then, they couldn't enslave people to do their wicked biding. Only a few people would stay back to make sure the land stayed safe."

"Why did you want the land protected?"

"If the land stayed protected, then we could come back. I never had planned to make the memory loss permanent. And with Marybella's limited skills, the spell definitely wouldn't last an eternity. That's why you've been having all those dreams. Technically, they are memories put in a dream form. They were memories your mother and I wanted you to have."

"You knew my mom?" I asked, choking on my words.

"Yes," Starletta said kindly. "Your mother was a wonderful woman. She knew that she was giving birth to a powerful girl, she could feel it. You were the magic I needed at the time for the spell, you just wouldn't make it in time. You would be born in the Modern World. You would not know of this place. I insisted your portrait be put up on the family wall though."

"So, you and my mother gave me all those dreams?"

"Yes. Those were memories that we left you. Like I said, we could come back if the land was protected. Even though the spell would wear off, I always like to have another plan just in case. You were that, my dear."

"How is Macy having these dreams?"

"Macy?"

"My best friend, Macy Poen."

"Poen? Oh, that's right. Macy, well, her name is really Bella. She was like you and started here, but was born in the Modern World. A few memories were lost, so some parents forgot their children's original names, which is why she is named Macy. She's related to Marybella."

"How? I thought Marybella stayed here?"

"I actually don't know where she ended up. I thought she went to your world, but I don't know that for certain. Her younger sister, Ava, I know went to your world. She is Macy's mother, so the Gift could've been passed down to her and that's how she's having the dreams. Macy's magic will be more focused on dreams and their power."

"That's amazing! I did have another question. Why does it say my father's name is Thomas? My dad, or who I think is my dad, is named David. Thomas is my uncle."

"Ah, well, Thomas's memories, like your mother's, were not erased as much as the others. I wanted them to remember a little more. Though I was leaving those clues for you, I wanted someone to explain things to you. It was planned to be your mother, but I haven't seen her in years. Thomas has had his memories for a while now."

"But, why does it say my father's name is Thomas?"

"Thomas…is your father. The man you know as your father is a very close friend of Thomas's. The two switched places after your mother disappeared. Thomas didn't want anything to happen to you, so he gave you to David when you were very, very young. Your mother disappeared a few days after you were born. He also changed your name to Gwendolyn. You remember your mother plainly because the magic inside of you feels her connection. You don't remember Thomas because he wasn't around you much as a child. He thought it was best to keep his distance for your safety. Thomas disappeared for a while after that. I don't know where he went or why."

"So not only is my life a lie, but so is my family?" I said scornfully.

Starletta looked at me with motherly eyes and then took me into her arms. "Oh child, they only wanted to keep you safe," She murmured into my ear.

"Hey, I have to ask. Why in the Grimm's book of fairytales is there a girl who looks a lot like me?"

"Oh that. That would probably be that merchant. She wasn't meant to look like you, again it was magic. She stole your mother's ring and used the DNA to make herself look beautiful like her. She's in one of the stories I believe. It was Beauty and the Beast. She was one of Beauty's sisters."

"How did Marybella's mother tell Marybella about the Prophecy?"

"I put the thought in her mind as she was about to die."

"Why?"

"Marybella and I hadn't met yet, and the woman needed help. She really did think her daughter had the Gift and she thought I could use it. I let her die with a happy heart. She needed some light in her life."

"Who was Aaron Star? I saw his name listed as my mom's father," I asked.

"Aaron Star," Starletta said. "He was a prince, a son of the Stardon family. He didn't always like his luxurious life and certainly did not enjoy some of the duties that were expected of him."

"He would act as common folk. He was very handsome, so the women in the town began calling him charming…"

"Wait," I interrupted. "you mean as in *Prince Charming*! Like from Snow White, Cinderella and Sleeping Beauty?"

"Technically, yes. Most of the time people lump together these princes, but they really are all different. The one I'm talking about is from Snow White, but she wasn't his first wife.

"Charming had a second wife?"

"No. Snow White was his second wife. His first wife, Felicity, is your biological grandmother."

"So, I'm related to Snow White?"

"Yes, in a way."

"I always wanted to have a famous relative."

"Aaron was a friend of Marybella's. When it came time to execute the spell, Aaron was to be left here with some of my sister fairies. I would die by using the spell. I would sacrifice the rest of my magic to make it work. Again, Marybella's magic wouldn't be enough. I didn't think logically about it and the spell came out…differently."

"Like, how differently?"

"The most important people, the ones from the Prophecy, are stuck in the Fairytale World with the Seven Sins."

"What happened to them?"

"Their stories never happened. They are each being held in a prison by the Seven Sins and have been there since the spell was cast."

"If they've been there and their stories never happened, how come people like the Brothers Grimm and Hans Christian Anderson have written the stories and put them in books?"

"This was meant to be the turning point in history. I saw that these stories would influence so many things. We couldn't let that go untold. So, I told all the writers the basics of the stories so that way they would be put out into the world. I knew it would get to you one day. I planted the stories in their brains even though the spell had been cast. They all weren't around at the same time, so at the correct points in history is when I put it in their thoughts. Pretty good for a dead lady, huh?"

"So, because you broke the law, did they banish you or something? Is that why you're a flower?"

"No, I wasn't banished. The Fairy Court allowed me to make that decision. I died from the spell as expected. I sacrificed my powers, even if the spell didn't work. When a fairy dies, we turn into a dream dust. The stuff the Sandman uses to make children go to sleep. That's why they have good dreams. Some of mine fell onto a flower."

"So, you're a ghost?"

"You could put it that way. I'm a living spirit basically. I came here because you needed answers. I would be the person to give the most honest ones. I also need your help."

"With what?"

"I need you to fulfil your fate - your destiny. I need you to use your magic as it was intended and give these people their lives back. Please Guinevere, they need their heroine."

I was faced with a perplexing feeling. I wanted to help these people. I wanted to change their lives for the better. But, how could I just take my life and change it, literally, like magic. I would be leaving behind a lot of people, not to mention going into an utterly dangerous place. The fate of these people, the people in the books I grew up cherishing, was in my hands.

"Can I ask you more questions before I make my decision?" I asked.

"Of course."

"Can you tell me who these people are in the Fairytale World? Blaire Whitman, Aiden Morns and Tori Fotter."

Starletta pondered. "Aiden Morns is the nephew to the girl I'm sure you know as Rapunzel. Her mother and father had another baby, a boy. He got married and they had Aiden. I believe his real name is Henry. Yes it was, I remember I talked to his mother the day that she wanted to know what she was having.

I'm a bit of a fortune teller, that's why I know all of these back stories.

"Tori Fotter - she is the niece to Alice. Alice's older sister is Tori's mother. I believe her real name was meant to be Elizabeth.

"Blaire, really Delilah, she is related to the fairy prince who married Thumbelina. Blaire's father, the prince's brother, was engaged to Blaire's mother. She got pregnant the first day in the Modern World and had Blaire there also."

I thought this over. Everyone I knew was connected to this world. Their families didn't know who they belonged to, but they should. Everyone should know where they belonged.

"Do these parents know they have siblings?"

"They do, but they don't know where they are. When they came to the Modern World, I didn't want them being confused and lost in such a new place. So, anyone that is in the Fairytale World will remember a little. But not where they are, or feeling the need to find out, until the spell completely wears off. And I don't know when that will be for everyone."

"Can I tell this to my friends? I think they should know where they really came from. They'll know at some point wouldn't they? So what's the harm in telling them now?"

"There really is no harm, dear. I'm just worried they won't believe you. Anyone from here would, but your minds have been taught differently in the Modern World. You believe different things, we're just stories to you."

"You're not stories! I know that what I'm saying is crazy, but forget crazy, I'm finally getting answers! I'm finally getting to know who my mother was! Who I am! I'm not letting my friends go through the same thing I went through when their memories start coming back. Feeling like no one will tell them the truth."

"I want this," I said. "I didn't realize until this moment, but I want to help this kingdom. I want to save it. I want everyone to have their happy ending."

"You'll do it then?" Starletta asked.

"Yes. Just tell me what I need to do."

"I'll come to that cave in your woods. It's like a portal to our world. I will be there waiting for you. Our time is different than yours, so use this clock to help you. There, I will show you how we're going to go to the actual Fairytale World." She handed me a silver pocket watch.

"Tell Thomas everything, he should know. And your friends should know, too. Oh, I almost forgot, this is a map of our kingdoms in the past." She handed me a folded piece of paper that came from the book.

"Why is Neverland and Wonderland on here?" I asked looking at the map.

"They're fairytales, too."

"Starletta?"

"Yes, Guinevere?"

"Thank you for everything. I finally have answers."

Starletta looked at me with a smile that made me feel more safe and secure than I had in a long time. The feeling I hoped my mother's smile would give me.

"Hey, just one more thing. So when I came here you were in that dream dust form. I know that you're like a spirit or something, but how are you talking to me?"

Starletta laughed. "I am a spirit now, so I can only talk to you at certain points. Most of them are when the magic is very strong and I can't tell you where or when that will be. You should be getting home, it's very late in your world." She turned back to her dream dust form and left.

I crawled my own way out. I walked out the castle doors and then I began to concentrate. I opened my eyes. I was still outside the castle.

Magic isn't thinking, it's believing. I heard Starletta's words as clearly as it would've been if I had been talking to her.

I began again. This time I believed. I knew I could get home. I wanted to get home. I would get home.

I opened my eyes to find myself right outside the small cave room. I plucked the ring from its slot in the rock and headed outside. It was still night. More stars had come out into the sky.

I raced through the woods and back to my house. The window I had used to get out was still slightly cracked open.

Using my upper body, I climbed the support for the awning on my porch up to the top. Then climbed to the window and pulled it open just enough for me to slip through. I shut and locked it.

By the time I could see numbers of my clock it was a little after 1:30 a.m. I unzipped my hoodie quietly and I slid into my covers.

A few minutes after I had settled in, I heard a *tat tat tat* on my door. I looked over and watched a small slip of light flood into my room. A figure stood in the doorway.

"Uncle Thomas? What are you doing up?" I asked wearily while sitting up.

"I just wanted to see how you were doing."

"Well, I think I'm doing fine for it being about two in the morning."

"Is the woods peaceful at night?" This stopped me.

"I suppose it might be," I said confidently. I could detect a smile on his face.

"Darling, I'm not mad. I know what's in those woods. I just think that you should tell me what parts of it *you* know," he said.

"Well, let's see. My mother was the princess of a kingdom in the Fairytale World. I am a princess and I am the magic that's supposed to stop these really messed up women named the Seven Sins. My best friend is half magic and my other friends are descendants of fairytale people. And, oh, this is my favorite one, I know that you're my biological father and the man I thought was my father is not even my relative. He's just a friend of yours. That's what I know," I said icily. I didn't see any reason to be delicate about this.

Uncle Thomas looked at me as he propped his shoulder against the frame of my doorway.

"How could you do this to me? My mom disappears and you think it is okay to just take yourself out of my life until now? You lost your wife, but I lost my MOTHER! I don't even know if she's alive, I have no clue where she is. The only person who has given me answers is Starletta. So, unless you can give me some as well, I'll just be getting my information from her from now on."

"Guinevere, I only wanted what was best for you. I still only want what's best for you, you're my little girl. What do you want to know?"

"Do you know where mom is?"

"I've been asking myself that question since she disappeared."

"Could she be in the Fairytale World? Hiding in one of the kingdoms?"

"It's a possibility honey, but a very slim one. As far as I know, no one has gone back there since the Seven Sins took over. Starletta put you in a dream state, so you only saw an illusion of our world."

"Well, I guess it is possible to go there, because tomorrow night I'm going back. As in going back to the real Fairytale World."

"Starletta found a portal?"

"I guess she did. She said she's going to show me how to get there."

"What did you mean that your friends are fairytale descendants?"

"Well, Aiden is a nephew of Rapunzel and his real name is Henry. Tori is the niece of Alice from Alice in Wonderland and her real name is Elizabeth. Blaire's uncle is the prince who married Thumbelina and her real name is Delilah. Macy is a descendant of Marybella. She had some of Marybella's magic in her and her name is Bella."

"Are you going to tell them all that?"

"I think that they should know."

"They may think you're crazy, honey."

"I'll figure out a way."

Uncle Thomas looked at me for a long time. "When your mother had you, it was the happiest day of my life. It was also the happiest days for the parents of Aiden, Blaire, Macy and Tori. They don't know where they came from. Neither do the parents. But, I think if anyone can convince them, it's you," he said smiling.

"Thanks Uncle...I mean Dad," I laughed a little. He did, too.

"Hey, I had one more question for you," I said.
"What?"
"Who is Dementia?"

CHAPTER 5
DEMENTIA

She was writing in her diary when pain shook her. She moaned as agony shot throughout her body. Gently, she rubbed her very large stomach. Thomas would get here soon she hoped.

She put her diary in its box then carefully moved her body back over to the bed. She heard a knock on her door. *Thomas?* She moved over to the door.

"Starletta, what are you doing here?" she asked, opening the door.

"Scarlett, dear, we have to go now. It's time."

"The spell is ready to start?"

"Yes, we must go," she tugged on her arm.

"I have to wait for Thomas," Scarlett stated, as she tried to stay in her room.

"He is already with the others. They have all gathered in the town square." Starletta looked to her pocket watch. "We must go now, dear." She nudged Scarlett down the castle stairs and into a carriage. They raced to the town square.

All of the kingdom's people were gathered in the square. Some looked tense and nervous. Most looked terrified.

Starletta guided Scarlett to Thomas, where she hugged him tightly.

"I have looked around the kingdoms Starletta, and you're right. They're coming," Thomas said hugging his wife.

"I was so worried you would be harmed, you weren't were you? I'll give her a bruise that'll never fade," Scarlett seethed.

"No, we never collided, but they're strong. Most of the kingdoms were in chaos."

"Where is my father?" Scarlett asked. Starletta looked off in the distance, but she didn't say anything.

"Where is he?" she repeated.

"He's not coming with us darling. He is a part of the Prophecy. He must protect the land, so we can return." A tear rolled down Scarlett's cheek.

"He'll be all right, won't he?" Scarlett asked.

"A few of my sister fairies are staying behind to help him. Come now, almost everyone is in the square." Starletta guided the couple up to the front of the crowd. They were all gathered around the statue of King James, the first king of Stardon Kingdom.

"Citizens!" Starletta's voice carried throughout the crowd.

"The Seven Sins have grown powerful, much more powerful than we predicted. The Fairy Court and I have made the decision not to fight, but to transport you all into a new land, thus trapping the Seven Sins here."

"I understand this is frightening. This is a change we hoped we would never have to make. You will not be able to take most of your belongings with you. That is why we have asked that each member of the family to pick only one or two items to take with them."

Scarlett rubbed the ring on her finger.

"This land we are taking you to, it is not bad. In some ways, it is better than our own. You will have larger homes and cleaner clothes. You will not be as poor as you once were and your children won't be either."

"How will the spell be enacted?" a woman near Scarlett asked. She was the blacksmith's wife.

"The spell will be enacted by me and this woman right here." Starletta gestured over to Marybella. Scarlett had seen the girl a few times. Marybella had been close with her father over the years.

"Marybella will be very helpful in this process for she, I now know, has the Gift."

The crowd murmured in awe. Everyone knew whoever had the Gift was somehow magic born. They would at some point meet the Fairy Court in person to learn what their magic was and how it would be used.

"Now, please, I would like to finish the rest of this announcement before we start the spell. This is terrifying, even for me. Especially for me. What none of you, except Marybella, knows, is that by performing this spell…I will die." A gasp escaped everyone's lips. Scarlett buried her face into Thomas's chest and cried. Starletta was like a mother to her. Now she would be hearing her last words.

"There is a small chance that I could come back, but it will be years from now. The last thing I want to say is specifically for the pregnant women of the kingdoms, since I will never be able to bless their wonderful children."

"This first praise goes to Mr. and Mrs. Thomason, whose oldest daughter, Penelope, will be giving birth to a little girl in the Modern World. I also bless the Thomason's youngest daughter, Alice, who always puts a smile on my face with that delightful imagination." Scarlett looked over at Penelope. She was holding Alice's hand.

"My second praise goes to the farmers, Richard and Elena, who I believe are about eight months pregnant with a boy, if my magic is accurate. I would like us to remember how hard it was for Richard's family when they lost his sister all those years ago."

"My third praise is to Marybella's younger sister, Ava, who should also be expecting soon. If that baby is anything like her aunt, she'll be a remarkable woman."

"My final praise goes out our very own Princess Scarlett, who is due quite soon. She would have been having the heir to our throne. By using my magic, I was able to make a fairly accurate guess to what she would look like so we gave her a painting of her own. What is the name you've picked out for this darling girl?"

"We wanted to name her Guinevere," Scarlett said to the people.

"I hope one day she and the rest of us may come back. Now we must start, our time is almost up." Marybella and Starletta faced each other. They took each other's hands and they began a chant.

> *"Om-ma lay-ya. De-sor-ta."*
> *"Om-ma lay-ya. De-sor-ta."*

"Ora, ary. Don-de-day."
"Ora, ary. Don-de-day."

A ball of brilliant light emerged in their clasped hands. It grew larger and larger. Then, at once, heavenly light became instantly black as pitch.

Confused whispers fluttered from ear to ear in the sea of people. Starletta stopped her chant. Everyone watched as a figure rose from the black, a stick curled in her long fingernails. A cruel grin formed on her lips.

"Am I interrupting anything?" the figure asked bitter sweetly.

"What are you doing here?" Starletta asked angrily.

"Do you not recognize me? I found black was a wonderful color on me. It reflects my personality." She was now facing Starletta, her attention focused fully on her. "You were my mentor. You wanted me to become a great fairy. You knew I had what it took. When I heard you were planning a great spell, I thought you would pick me. But, you picked a mere peasant. No matter, I still work on my craft. In fact, I even created something."

She spun her stick in a circle and a bird appeared on top. It was completely black from its head to its feet. Even its eyes were as dark as a shadow.

"This is a Bird of Black, its soul is darker than any night." She stroked its feathers. "I have created life, Starletta! I created a living, breathing object. Something fairies like you can't even fathom. You created a spell! That's all! To save who? Peasants? Sickly, elderly people who will die in your new world?"

"I know what I am doing, Dementia. Leave before you do anymore harm."

"You say you wish to come back. Well, I'm going to give the rest of the people some helpful information about that. She doesn't have the Gift. She doesn't have enough for your spell." Dementia pointed a long finger at Marybella. "She will let you down Starletta, I wouldn't have. You shouldn't have let me go." With that final word, she whipped her cape around and vanished leaving behind but one black feather.

The crowd was silent. They had no reason to trust Dementia. They knew that she was evil. She had taken away their daughters. She had no soul. Yet still, there was this lingering doubt. Did Starletta make an error?

"Do not let that fairy intimidate you," Starletta said to the people. She thought about her next words carefully.

"She is correct though. Marybella is not who we need."

Marybella looked over to Starletta, but she continued.

"I made an error. Marybella does have the Gift, she just doesn't have enough to make this spell perfect. I do not know how Dementia knows this information and I do not know how the spell will turn out. The magic we need will not be born in time." All of the pregnant women looked at each other. One of their children could be the savior of their homeland.

"The person we need is Guinevere Star, Scarlett's daughter. When Scarlett asked for the gender of her baby, I found it was a girl. I also found that this child was glowing. Magically glowing. The glowing that all the fairies and magic creatures have inside of them. I know that this isn't the time for doubting, but Marybella can still do the spell. It won't be perfect, but she can do what is needed. However, I won't force her to continue if she does not want to." Starletta turned her focus to Marybella. Marybella looked over the crowd of people. These were her friends and her family. Her people. It didn't matter if she wasn't perfect. She would get these people to the new world and get them there safely.

"I'll do this for my people," she said. Starletta smiled. They began the chant again. The ball of light began forming. Scarlett clutched Thomas's hand.

"Thomas, before we go into the Modern World, I just wanted to say this. Starletta said we would forget this place, but we would remember our loved ones. I…just wanted to say I love you so much. I love our child so much. I want us always to remember that."

"We always will." He kissed her head before the light spread around them like a tidal wave and soon all they could see was white.

CHAPTER 6
THE TRUTH

Bzzzzzzzzzz.

I pulled the cord from my phone. A text message was on it, but I didn't know the number.

> Hey Gwendolyn, this is Blaire. I know we aren't very close, but I have this problem and you're super sensible and I don't know... I just need to talk to someone. So can you meet me at Lonright Park in about a half an hour? You don't have to text back, I'll just be by the bridge that goes over the river.

What's the problem? I wondered. There was only one way to find out. I gave Dad, aka Uncle Thomas, the heads up on where I was going and set out.

Lonright Park wasn't that busy yet. I saw a few people by the gazebo setting up a birthday banner and two teenagers riding through on their skateboards.

I walked until I came to the bridge. There, sitting on one of the benches, was Blaire. Her hair was pulled into a limp bun that was bobbing above her shoulders. She was wearing an oversized turquoise sweatshirt and some yoga pants. I hadn't seen her look like that since last year.

She turned her head and saw me coming. I sat down next to her on the bench, I saw that her eyes were a bit puffy. She wiped her nose.

"Sorry, I look like a mess. I just threw some of my old clothes on."

"You look fine. So what's going on?" I asked.

She tried to stifle a sniffle. "Well, um, I've been keeping a secret. My parents are talking about divorce. My dad has moved out. I've been a wreck, but I've been trying to keep it together. That's why through the summer that was leading up to this year, I wanted to be in the popular group. I guess I thought that it would make me feel better to be on top."

"Do you know why your parents are getting the divorce?" As soon as I said, I wanted to take it back. "Actually, wait, you don't have to answer that."

"No, it's okay. My dad started having these weird dreams. And talking about this life he had led as a prince and how that he had to get in touch with this woman named Starletta. He apparently never told my mom. Then a few months ago, he just told her he had to leave. She didn't want him to, but he said he had to go. My mom is heartbroken. She and I don't know why my dad..." Blaire began to tear up again. "I got this letter from him a while ago. In it was this letter that's addressed to someone named Delilah. I don't know what to do. I just needed someone to talk to."

"I'm honored you confided in me, but I thought you would talk to someone like Macy or maybe Aiden."

"Well, Aiden and I had that movie date where he asked if I would go out again. I said yes and we're going to get pizza today. So, we're sort of a couple, but we're not that close. Then, well...Macy and I just got back to being friends, so I didn't want to drop this bomb on her. And you, well...you're just comforting and you've been very sweet to me. I just thought you would be a good person to talk to."

"Blaire, um, I think I know what your dad was talking about. Actually I was planning on talking with everyone about it. Do you live close to Tori?"

"Yeah, she lives just a few blocks from me."

"After you get pizza with Aiden I want you, her and him to all come to my house. I'm going to have Macy come over, too."

"What's going on, Gwendolyn?"

"It's hard to explain without me sounding crazy. Just make sure you're at my house at around 6:30 okay?"

"Okay."

"I have to get going. I'll see you then." I sprinted all the way home. I had no idea what I was going to say. How was I going to tell everyone about their lives? I knew that they would think I was insane, but I had to try. I thought about how Blaire felt. Her dad was remembering his old life. He wanted to find his brother. He probably didn't want to confuse Blaire and her mom. It would be hard to explain if their memories weren't coming back yet.

I thought about my own memories. At least I had some clues and people who could give me answers. Blaire, Aiden, Tori, Macy - they had no one. Neither did their parents. They didn't know how much their families missed them.

Weirdly, this made me feel strong. It made me feel like I could really help them learn about their pasts. And the pasts of their parents.

Back at the house, I was more nervous than ever. I was planning on how I was going to prove to them that I was telling the truth. I was going to take them to the cave and maybe show them some magic. If that didn't convince them, I didn't know what would.

Six thirty came much faster than expected. Pretty soon, I saw all of them coming up the driveway. Macy had a worried expression, Tori and Blaire's faces both appeared confused and Aiden looked surprisingly calm. It felt a little strange watching him hold Blaire's hand.

"Uncle Thomas," I called. It still felt a little weird to call him Dad. "They're here. I'm going to take them back to that cave."

"Okay," he said from where he was sitting at the dining table. "Guinevere?"

"Yes?"

"Good luck, princess." I nodded. I padded my pocket for my belongings and headed outside.

"So, what's up Gwendolyn? Why did you ask us to come here?" Tori asked.

"Guys, you're going to think I'm completely crazy if I tell you, so I'm going to show you. Follow me." I led them across the field into the back woods. I led them down the path and into the clearing.

"This place is gorgeous!" Blaire exclaimed.

"I agree, it's amazing. These flowers are so stunning," said Tori admiring the Starlettas.

We walked a little more as I led them to the cave. Macy came up and whispered in my ear.

"If you're going to show them the cave, they will think it's insane. They haven't had the dreams like you and I," she said.

"I know that Mace. But what I learned last night is even more insane. Even you will think I'm making it up."

We entered the cave. I carefully guided them to the stone door.

"It's a dead end," said Tori.

"Not for long," I pulled the ring from my pocket and put it into its slot. The entrance began to move and we all filed in. Like before, the crystal pedestal rose from the floor. I saw that Blaire wanted ask something, but she kept her mouth shut.

"You are all probably wondering where this is and what we're doing here. Well, I have your answers. This is a portal room to the Fairytale World."

"The Fairytale World?" Aiden, who had been quiet for most of the time, asked.

"Yes. The stories you've heard and read, they're not made up. They are actually your families. There was the first Fairy Godmother and her name was Starletta. She had seen a prophecy that these women – the Seven Sins – were going take over the Fairytale World and enslave its people. She knew about this fifty years before it happened and she also knew that certain fairytale people were the prime targets. She had told this Prophecy to Marybella, who is a fairy, and someone who she thought had the magic she would need to conduct the spell to save everyone. The spell would bring them to this world with no memory of their other life, but she made spell non-permanent, so they would get their memory back someday. Marybella ended up not having the exact amount of magic Starletta needed and the spell came out wrong. Which is saying that the characters from those fairytales are all trapped in the Fairytale World. Along with the Seven Sins, my grandfather Aaron and some other fairies. Therefore, their stories never happened. Starletta knew that Marybella didn't have the magic she needed, but she didn't have a choice but to enact the spell. The magic that she really needed wouldn't be born until after the fifty years were up.

"Look, I know this sounds totally insane. And you're going to say, 'Gwendolyn you're being ridiculous' and 'Gwendolyn you're making this up,' but I'm not. Aiden's real name is Henry and he's the nephew of Rapunzel, his father is Rapunzel's baby brother.

Tori," I said as I looked over to her. "your mother is Alice's sister. Alice from Alice in Wonderland. Your real name was meant to be Elizabeth. Blaire is related to the fairy prince that married Thumbelina. He's her uncle and her real name is Delilah. That's why your dad is acting so weird, he's regaining his memory. That letter is meant for you," I said looking to her.

"Macy and I have been having these weird dreams." I glanced over at Macy. "Well, you're having them because you're related to Marybella. Your mom's name is Eve right? She doesn't know it, but her real name is Ava and she's Marybella's younger sister. She gave birth to you and passed her magic into you. You're also technically related to Beauty from Beauty and the Beast because of your grandma. Your real name is Bella."

"What about you? Who are you related to?" Blaire asked.

"Well, not really anyone in particular, besides my step grandmother, Snow White. But remember that magic I was telling you about that was needed, but not born yet? It's me! We all started in the Fairytale World, but were born here. We all will regain our memories, but mine and Macy's came sooner because we have magic in us."

No one said anything for a while. Tori looked at the ground, Macy bit her lip and Aiden cupped his hand around the back of his neck. Then Blaire looked up. She walked over to me, looked at me for a second or two and then she put one hand on my shoulder.

"Okay everybody, I know this is super-wacko-crazy-bonkers, but I believe it. Gwendolyn has no reason to lie to us. I'm sure we've all gotten weird answers to questions about our family. So, whatever questions we have, I guess we better ask them now."

"Wait, how has it been fifty years and these people are like recent relatives?" Tori asked.

"Time works differently there and I'm guessing that the people in those prisons are frozen in time as well, but I'm not sure. I didn't get a whole lot of clarification."

"What have your dreams been about?" Blaire asked.

"Well," I started and looked over at Macy. "Mine have had me in a muddy field with fire and screaming. Another one with me seeing Marybella and hearing the Prophecy. One where I saw this lady Dementia in a town square. These were actually not dreams, they were memories Starletta had placed in my brain."

"How do we know about the fairytales if they never happened?" asked Macy.

"I asked Starletta the same thing. These stories were a big deal because these authors would inspire so many things. They couldn't let the stories go untold, so Starletta put the basic idea in each author's mind. She died from casting the spell because it used up all the magic she had left. She contacted me in this dream dust form."

"So, what do we do now?" asked Aiden.

"Well," I pulled the pocket watch from my pocket. "At some point, this watch should give me a time. Then Starletta will come and take me to the Fairytale World to reset everything and fulfill my destiny."

"Wait, you're going there? Where those crazy ladies are, all by yourself? Uh-uh, no way, we're coming with you," Blaire said confidently.

"But guys…"

"No 'but guys,' we're coming! Don't forget these are our families, too," she said.

"Yeah, Blaire's right," Tori said joining in. "These are our families and you're our friend. We're going to rescue them together." She placed her arm around my shoulders.

"Macy? Aiden? Are you with us?" I asked. They looked toward each other.

"I'm in," said Macy.

"I'm in, too," said Aiden. We crowded around each other in a huddle. It felt so nice to know that I wasn't going to be doing this alone.

I felt this tingling go through my hand. I looked down at the watch. It had blue waves of color vibrating off of it.

"I guess this means she's coming soon," I said.

"I'm already here, dear." We looked around the room for her and then all of our eyes landed onto a string of tiny white-blue dots floating over to us. "Hello Guinevere," Starletta said.

"Guinevere?" Tori said.

"It's my real name," I told her.

"Who are your friends?" Starletta asked.

"This is Tori, Macy, Aiden and Blaire. I asked you about their pasts earlier." I pointed to each of them as I spoke.

"They're coming with me. They want help save their families," I told her.

"Who am I to stand in the way of family?" she smiled.

"So, you were the first Fairy Godmother?" Blaire asked.

"Technically, I was meant to be, but I never got to. Most people called me Starletta. The godmother part came because I am actually Guinevere's godmother."

"What *exactly* are we going up against?" asked Tori.

"Well, you're basically going up against the beginning of evil, my dear. What you are going to do is get all these stories back on track by finding the story starters."

"What are story starters?" I asked.

"They are the beginners of the tales. I'm not talking about Snow White, but before that. When the mirror was created, when the queen became evil, that sort of thing. But, we do have to get them out of the prisons created by the Seven Sins."

"From what I take, we're just busting people out of jail. That doesn't sound like a big mission," Blaire said.

"Once we break them out of the cycle the Seven Sins put them in, the stories will start. Everything happens for a reason, even destiny. You must be there to make sure that the stories go accordingly and they get their happily ever afters."

"Why don't our families remember their sisters and brothers?" Macy asked.

"They remember the person, but they don't know where they are. I didn't want people remembering the Seven Sins, so I blocked memory from the Fairytale World almost completely.

They won't want to find their sibling until the spell completely wears off."

"Can you tell us more about the Seven Sins? They're going to be a pretty big threat and we should be prepared," I stated.

"The Seven Sins, as you may have guessed, are seven extremely dangerous fairies. They have power beyond imagination."

"How did they become so powerful?" Aiden asked.

"Some people are born with magic inside of them, like Guinevere. Others make themselves more powerful. The head of the Seven Sins, a fairy named Dementia, kidnapped six girls and somehow made them as evil as she was."

"Who are they?" Macy asked.

"There is Corona, Venema, Lexia, Sinica, Morna and Jellessa."

"What did you say Dementia did to those girls?" I asked timidly.

"Guinevere, is something wrong?" Starletta asked reading my expression.

"One of my dreams…was of Dementia. She separated all these girls from their families and looked them over. Then she came over and whispered into my ear 'such a pretty princess.' Did you leave that memory for me?" I asked.

Starletta looked at me with grave eyes. "I never left you that memory, dear. This is quite troubling."

"What did she do to Gwendolyn?" Macy asked moving closer to me.

"She sent her a dream. I made sure no one could communicate between worlds, except me. That way the Seven Sins couldn't send anything bad here. They must have weakened the magic somehow. Have you had any other dreams that were very destructive?"

"My very first one. I was on the ground and I heard screaming. And there was smoke and fire."

"That was when they were terrorizing the kingdoms. This means that their power has grown again. I thought I'd be able to give you more explanation, but you must leave now."

"Wait, we have to leave now? We need instructions, maps and rules. We need you," I said.

She looked back at me. "I know child. I'm sorry I have to leave in a rush like this, but I can't stay long. I will get you into our world. The book you saw in that small room, it will have some answers. Once in our kingdom, go into the castle. No one will be there, but still keep your guard up. Magic will be on your side, it will leave clues for you. You are the most powerful fairy. Trust me, you'll beat her. Now, all of you take care."

She turned her attention back to the crystal pedestal and pointed her wand at it.

"Lenis, coro, mava, metrone!"

A beam shot above the pedestal and a vortex opened. I shielded my eyes as best as I could, yet I still could barely see. Starletta motioned us toward the vortex. She yelled something, but it was hard to hear over the swirling noise of the portal.

"Beware the Birds of Black!" Then we were all pulled into the sea of light. In less than a second, I couldn't see Starletta's comforting smile anymore.

CHAPTER 7
THE QUEST BEGINS

When I opened my eyes, I was on the ground. It seemed to happen a lot whenever I came to this world. Dream version or not.

I looked around to make sure everyone was here. I hoped we hadn't fallen too far from each other.

"So, this is where we were meant to live?" Macy asked.

"Yeah." I looked around the landscape. It looked nothing like when I had come with Starletta. Everything looked burned or dirty, grey and black. The air smelled like fresh smoke.

"What did Starletta say before we went into that portal?" Aiden asked.

"Beware the Birds of Black," I said.

"What or who are the Birds of Black?" Tori asked.

"I believe those are." Our eyes followed to where Blaire was pointing. Two crows were sitting on a charred tree branch.

"Crows," Aiden said.

"I think those are the Birds of Black. What do you think they mean here? Danger?" Blaire asked.

"Maybe they're spies for the Seven Sins," Macy suggested.

"Possibly. Either way, Starletta told us to stay clear of them. I need to figure out where we are so we can get to Stardon Castle," I said. I looked around at our surroundings. It looked a little familiar. There was a broken statue in the middle of the cobblestones. Through the cracks, its face looked a lot like James Star.

We must already be in Stardon then, I told myself. *Now, where do we go?*

"Ouch!" Tori yelled. I turned and saw her grasping her shoe.

"What happened," I asked.

"I felt a singe on the bottom of my shoe."

She's not the only one who will feel pain. I turned. I must have just imagined hearing that voice, but it sounded so clear.

You all will feel pain. My pain. The pain they put me through. Humiliation. Shame. Rejection. You won't succeed. The prisoners are in a place even the crows do not go. The voice sounded more confident, like it knew it was playing me. A place where the crows do not go? Where would that be?

"Earth to Gwendolyn, come in Gwendolyn." I heard Macy's voice and it carried me away from my thoughts.

"Are you okay? You sort of zoned out," Blaire said.

"Yeah, I'm fine. I was just thinking about where we were. I'm pretty sure that we're in Stardon Kingdom. That is, or was, the statue of James Star, the first king. I think we're in the town square which means that the castle must not be too far. But when I was thinking about where we were, I heard this voice in my head. Not like my own voice, but like someone else. It sounded feminine and really calm. It said that we would all experience pain like it did. It said we won't succeed because the prisoners are kept in a place the crows don't even go. What does that mean?"

"Maybe it's somewhere dark. In any case, we first have to get to that room Starletta was talking about with the book. The more time we spend standing here the less time we have, so let's get moving." We walked for a good half an hour, based on the time on the pocket watch, before we stopped in a meadow beside the path.

"Are you sure we're going in the right direction?" Aiden asked.

"I think so," Blaire said.

"Is there anything to eat?" Tori asked.

"I don't think so. Did either of you bring your purses?" I said asking Macy and Blaire.

"I brought my small cross body, but I don't think much is in it," Blaire said rummaging through the bag. "All I have is this pack of breath mints."

"That works for me," Tori said taking the pack and popping a mint into her mouth.

"I'll take one too," Macy said.

"We should probably get going again," I said standing up from the grass we had all been sitting on. "Before it gets dark." Soon, after we had started walking, I could see the castle in the distance.

"How do we get in?" Aiden asked when we got there.

"I'm not sure. When I was here, the servants and guards were still here."

"Well, there has to be another way in. Hey Gwendolyn, you have magic. Maybe try focusing it or something. I've seen it done in movies, where you can just sense where things are. Of course, that was done by special effects," Tori said. I nodded, took a deep breath and focused my mind on finding a door.

I reopened my eyes. "We have to go around to the back of the left tower and find a brick. If we find it, it'll open a secret door." We headed around to the back of the tower and began knocking on the bricks to see if any were hollow.

"Found it," Macy said. We all went over and I focused my magic again. It didn't take as long for the magic to work. The bricks parted revealing an opening for us. We walked cautiously inside. I noticed we were on a staircase, so I began heading downward, assuming that it would lead us to the first floor. I knew that was where I had come in the first time.

Back at the entrance of the castle, I looked around to try and find the hallway with the portraits. Once I found it, I showed everyone down the corridor.

"Which is your mom?" Blaire asked. I pointed the portraits out for her. "Your mom is really beautiful Gwendolyn, she looks a lot like you," she commented.

"The passage way is behind my painting. All I had to do was press on it, so let's hope that it works." I stepped up to my painting and pressed it as I had done before. The painting opened and we all crawled into the tight fitting passageway.

When we were in the room, it was a lot more cramped then I remembered. Then again, there were five of us.

"So, where's that book Starletta was talking about?" asked Macy.

"It should be in a bookshelf, it's the one right behind you," I said. Macy ran her fingers over the books until I stopped her. She pulled it out and set it on the desk. The book had no title on the front, just a leather cover. There was a table of contents on the inside. I ran my fingers along until I saw the chapter title *PROPHECIES*. I turned to its page and started looking it over.

"This is the page."

"Read it, Gwendolyn," Aiden said.

"Ok. 'The Beginnings Prophecy: In fifty years, our world will change, everything will change. The Seven Sins will cloak this land in evil. Four women will go through tremendous things for true love, two girls will fill their craving for adventure, one boy and girl pair will risk anything to save one another.' I remember the mother adding something to the end, but I guess that was just for Marybella."

"Hey, Gwendolyn. If Marybella is my aunt then how come her little sister wasn't at the house with the mom?"

"I think she could've been. I didn't think about this earlier, but I did pass another room on the way to the mother's. I think I saw a bed in there. Maybe that was your mom's room."

"So, how do we figure out which people we need to help? It doesn't tell us their names in the Prophecy," Tori asked.

"We'll just break it down piece by piece. 'Four women will go through tremendous acts for true love.' Now we just have to figure out which fairytales have women who sacrificed or had been through a lot for love," I said.

"That will be a piece of cake," Blaire said sarcastically.

"Starletta knew that your families had been fairytale people and some of them sacrificed a lot. Like Rapunzel, her hair was cut for the prince," I stated.

"I thought the witch just hacked it off?" Tori said.

"Yes, but she knew it would happen. She knew she would be punished for seeing the prince, yet she still continued to bring him up into her tower," I clarified.

"That also means that Beauty is one of the girls. She raced back to the castle to save the Beast from dying because she loved him so much. She was sacrificing her heart to terrible heartbreak," Macy said.

"Okay, so we have two. Snow White is one. She didn't really sacrifice anything. But, she did go through a lot of things like being forced to be a maid, escaping death, being poisoned, but in the end was woken up by a handsome prince," I said.

"I think that means that Thumbelina would qualify, too. She was kidnapped, almost forced to be married twice and then a cute fairy prince told her she was great and married her," Blaire chimed in.

"That's four! Let's move on to the next part. Two girls will fill their cravings for adventure," I recited.

"If families are involved, then I think one of them is Alice. She wanted a world of her own, an adventure," Tori said.

"Who is the other, Little Red Riding Hood?" Aiden wondered out loud.

"No, she wasn't really looking for adventure. She was just going to her granny's house," Macy pointed out.

"What about Wendy?" I said looking up from the map Starletta had given me.

"Wendy?" Blaire asked.

"Yeah, Wendy from Peter Pan. She never really said she wanted adventure, but she always told stories about Peter's adventures. And she didn't want to grow up. I saw that Neverland is on the map of the kingdoms. Maybe that's a sign that it's part of the quest."

"Okay, so that's the two girls. What's the last verse?" asked Aiden.

"One boy and girl pair will protect each other at any cost to save one another," I read.

"The only boy girl pair I can think of are Hansel and Gretel," Blaire said.

"She did almost get pushed into an oven," Macy said.

"I know, but it just doesn't feel right," I said. "So many of these stories are different, except for the ones about the women. But, you don't hear about Thumbelina very often. I just get this feeling that these people are unique."

"What about the Snow Queen?" Tori inquired.

"What about it?" I asked.

"In the story it has two characters, Kai and Gerda. They loved each other and then the Snow Queen kidnaps Kai. Gerda does everything she can to get him back. They could be the boy and girl," said Tori.

"That would make sense. Good job Tori." I gave her a small pat on the back.

"All right, we have everyone. Now what do we do?" Macy asked. They all turned and looked at me. I knew that they felt like I had all the answers, but I was almost as clueless as they were. I didn't know things I wanted to know. It was like every time I got close, I would run out of time.

"We have to figure out that voices riddle. 'The prisoners are in a place even the crows do not go.' What in the world does that mean?"

"I've got nothing," Tori said.

"Neither do I," echoed Macy.

"Is this just strange to me? So, Starletta said that Dementia and the other women couldn't get through. How can the crows?" I asked.

"Starletta did say Dementia could've weakened the magic," Aiden put in.

"Yes, but to let hundreds of birds out. I don't think she could've made it that weak."

Do you want to know what happened to your people, Guinevere? My vision blurred and I just saw black in the back of my eyes. That voice again.

I made the crows. They are my minions, they obey my every whim. But, even a fairy can't make a living thing, I needed to use something else. Did you ever wonder where Marybella went? She looks very good in black, you know.

My stomach lurched. She had made Marybella a crow just to make me miserable.

Why are you doing this? I was surprised I could hear my voice even though it was in my own head.

I thought I made that quite clear. I want you to feel pain.

That doesn't mean you have to hurt my friends' families. If you're going to hurt anyone, hurt me. Leave them and their families out of it.

I am hurting you. You're letting your emotion get in the way of your mission. Why are you even paying me any attention? I'm the villain, remember?

You're in my head!

Even so, you have the power to block me out. I just didn't give Starletta enough time to help you learn it.

That's where you're wrong. I know you're wrong. Magic isn't about learning, it's about believing. And I believe that you're going down, Dementia!

I broke out of the mental state and found myself on the floor with eight pairs of eyes all looking down on me.

"Gwendolyn, are you okay?" Macy asked as her and Aiden hoisted me back up.

"I'm all right, really. I just heard that voice and I saw black. I guess I must've fallen to the floor."

"We were really worried. One minute we were talking about how the crows had gotten into the Modern World and the next minute you're on the floor," said Blaire.

I suddenly remembered what Dementia had told me. "I don't know how the crows have gotten into the Modern World, but I do know that Dementia created them and they serve her. She used humans and transformed them into crows. She's the voice I've been hearing in my head." I explained.

"How do you know it's her?" Tori asked.

"I just know."

"Anyway, how do we find the prisoners? Without them we don't have the stories," Macy pointed out.

"You said that Dementia controls the crows?" Aiden asked.

"Yeah."

"Well, that must mean that they fear her. Dementia seems like that kind of leader. If they fear her, that means that the crows wouldn't go anywhere near Dementia unless necessary. And Dementia wouldn't want the prisoners out of her sight since we're here now. So, I bet that Dementia has a dungeon somewhere and that's where they're held. Where the crows won't go!"

"That's brilliant, Aiden," Blaire said giving him a side hug.

"Where would be somewhere isolated enough that Dementia could keep them?" Tori asked. We all looked at my map.

"Maybe it's in here, where the Enchanted Forest is," Blaire stated as she pointed to the large area on the map. "That would have a lot of trees, wolves, witches, all sorts of dangers that would keep invaders out," Blaire said.

"Which creates a lot more obstacles for us," Tori mentioned.

"We have Gwendolyn, she basically has Dementia's power times ten. We'll get through it no problem." Blaire wrapped her arm around me and smiled.

"Okay, so we're going to the Enchanted Forest. First, I think we should get some supplies. We'll look around the whole castle and see what we come up with. How about Aiden, Tori and Blaire take the bottom and first floor and Macy and I will take the second and third floors? Sound good?" I got four nods in reply.

We all parted and began searching. Macy and I trudged up the wide stairs to the second floor. She was unusually quiet.

"Hey Mace, you all good?" I asked. She replied with a slight nod.

"Come on, you think I buy that? What's got you so silent?"

"Gwendolyn, I get that this is a big moment for you, but it is a little freaky. I am a descendant of a fairy. A fairy who is my aunt who is now some psycho's bird slave. And, I mean, this is our family. We have been living lies, our parents have been living lies, everything was orchestrated by some magic lady.

Don't get me wrong, Starletta is wonderful and I like her. But why did she have to do this? Why did everything have to change. We could've been living here, our lives could've been so different."

"They could've been different in a bad way, too. If Starletta hadn't done what she has, we would be slaves. Imprisoned by those awful women or we wouldn't have been born at all. I've met Dementia once, even if that was just in a dream, but I bet she wouldn't have thought twice about getting rid of me. And the rest of you."

"I just…I just don't like it. We have new responsibilities now, but what's going to happen once this is all over? Once we've gotten the stories back on track, then what? Are we just going to go back home, pretending like nothing has happened…"

"Macy." I put both my hands on her shoulders. "I know that we're not getting all the answers that we would want. But let's try to focus on the task at hand. Whatever happens after we finish the quest, we'll figure out after we're done, okay?"

"Okay." She wiped some snot from her nose. Sometimes it would run when she was worked up.

We worked out way up to the second floor and began searching through rooms. Everyone seemed to have left a lot behind, most of their belongings I guessed. Beds were made up neatly with all their blankets and pillows and the dressers were full of clothes.

"Have you found anything Macy?" I called across the hall.

"Some wool blankets that could be useful at night, but nothing else really. Mostly just clothes, a lot of people must have lived here."

"I haven't found anything yet. I'm going to check into the next room."

A vast, richly colored wood made up the floor that met stone walls. A grand bed was placed against a wall with a satin garnet comforter decorated in gold lace detailing. The bed had four beams that supported a sheer crimson canopy. A fireplace was opposite of the bed. Ashes were the only thing left in it.

As I walked farther in, I noticed that my mother and father were in a painting that hung above the fireplace. She looked so regal. I had only known my mother a little. Mostly because of the painting, old pictures from home and then me being inside of her once. It allowed me to partially sense her.

I stared at the picture. The gaze I got back was almost heart stopping, I didn't want to look away. If I did, it felt she would leave all over again.

"Gwendolyn?" I was startled by Macy's entrance. "Are you okay?"

"I'm fine Mace. I just saw the picture of my mom and I wanted to look…"

"Say no more. You deserve some time to connect. I was just wondering where you were, I'll check back in a bit." She gave me a smile and left.

I began looking through everything. I looked in trunks and closets, but I came up empty. Most of them were all locked. If they weren't, only useless things were in them.

As I searched through the closet, one of the trunks came down on top of me. I was able to move out of the way before it hit anything more than my foot. The trunk wasn't very big and it didn't look very difficult to open. It had rust spots scattered on it. I propped my feet up against the trunk and gripped my hands around the lock. On an inside count of three, I pulled. The lock popped off almost instantly, but the jerk still sent me flying backward onto the floor.

When I had pulled myself up, I looked down into the box. It had aged pieces of papers scattered around in it along with a leather bound diary on top. The papers were paintings, they looked as though they had been rushed. One was of a mirror. It was gold framed around the edges and on the glass it looked like someone was peering into it, but you couldn't really see the person. Another was of a rose. Its petals were done in a bright shade of red. There were seven paintings all together, all of different objects.

I looked at the diary next. The diary's pages had some faded coloring. I unclasped the buckle and peeked to the first page. My mother's name was printed on it.

Scarlett Rose Star

I had never known that my mother had exquisite handwriting. I assumed this must have been her diary. Due to our lack of time, I set it aside and began looking through more of the box.

A wand was wrapped in a scrap of cloth. It was made of wood as far as I could tell, with sapphires dotted in the twisted bark. This could be useful, maybe a wand would help me control my magic.

Also buried in the box was an even smaller box. It was a small oval shape, burgundy colored with gold and pearl trimmings. I looked on the bottom and found a small crank. I turned it three times, then opened the lid. A small girl was standing on a platform. She was about half the size of my pinkie, yet she was painted with extreme detail. She had dark brown hair, almost black, and her eyes were a greenish blue. She was dressed in a dark blue gown and looked like she was about to start dancing with the other figurine. This one was a man in suit with a crown on his head. The music began to play and the figures moved in a steady circle. The music was light and airy like twinkling chimes.

I looked through the rest of the box. It seemed like this had been my mother's memory box. Other things that were in the box were letters my mother and father had written to each other and a small bear with a bell around its neck. These were the things I had to connect with my mom, plus some of them could be clues. I put everything back into the box.

I met Macy back at the top of the stairs and we headed down to the bottom floor to meet everyone else.

"What did you find besides these pillows?" I asked her as we walked down.

"I found these blankets. I got four because one was pretty big. I found some candles in a box, so I got those and the three pillows that you're helping me carry." She nodded to the two pillows that were tucked under my arms.

"The blankets will be great at night and so will the candles. I bet we can find some flint to use to make a fire." We got to the bottom of the stairs and everyone else was trickling in from the other rooms.

Blaire wobbled in. She was carrying what looked like a towel or a blanket and some things in a box. Ropes were coiled around her wrists and sacks were slung over her shoulders.

"Here's what I got," she said setting her items down. "These towels are for us ladies. At least I think they're towels, because we're going to need to bathe at some point. I also got us some ropes because you don't know if we may need those. And I found some soap." She opened the box to show us the toiletries. "These we could use for bathing or for washing our clothes. Which reminds me, I got us all nightgowns so we can wash our clothes at night, I just guessed all our sizes."

"This is great, Blaire. This will keep us somewhat clean," Macy remarked. Next Tori came in. Her arms were as heavily packed as Blaire's.

"Hey guys, here's what I got. I found us some candles. It looks like Macy did, too." She gestured over to the candles Macy had laid out. "And I found food while I was searching the kitchen. A lot was left, but it's all pretty stale. I found a few apples that weren't too rotten and I found some rolls, but I don't know how spoiled they are."

"Maybe Gwendolyn can make food appear," Blaire said. At first I thought she was joking, but she didn't laugh. I began to wonder, *Could I do that?*

"Maybe I can. I mean, I could try," I said voluntarily. I was nervous, but maybe it could happen, I knew my power was strong. Still, I hadn't had any sort of training or anything.

I relaxed my muscles. I calmed my heartbeat down to a steady rhythm. I flexed my fingers as I shut my eyes. I took one deep, relaxed breath and let my mind do its work.

I opened my eyes and three peanut butter and jelly sandwiches were on the floor. Blaire, Macy and Tori were all looking at me deer-in-headlights style.

"It looks like we may not have to bring food with us. I'm a walking grocery store!" This made us all laugh.

Aiden finally came in and was carrying a bundle of things. From what I could see there was two boxes, a patched up, tarp like blanket and a wagon.

"Hey girls, look what I found. We can put everything into this cart and haul it, it shouldn't get too heavy. There are some loose boards, but it's better than carrying all of this by hand. The other thing I found was a tarp slash blanket. It could be good for making shelter or something."

"What's in the boxes?" Blaire asked.

"Food that wasn't spoiled is in one. In the other, is any medicine I found and some swords."

"Swords? Why did you get those? Gwendolyn can make food appear, so we don't need the box with food in it," Macy said.

"I got the swords for protection. Yes, Gwendolyn is a magical, powerful fairy, but we don't have that magic. At least Blaire, Tori and I don't, so we will need something if anything gets in our way."

"I think that it is okay to bring them," I piped up.

"Why?" Macy asked.

"It's a fact that danger is going to come our way. You and I both have some magic in us and we can protect them, but they should have some protection of their own. And, what if we weren't there right at that moment they needed us? What if you were washing clothes and I was exploring and these guys got attacked, what would they do? I just think it's good to play it safe." Macy nodded her head. Macy wasn't too keen on violence. She didn't like guns especially. I didn't know how she felt about swords or daggers, but I assumed that she wasn't thrilled that we would be bringing them along.

"Let's start packing everything into the cart. We should get going soon, the Enchanted Forest has the word 'enchanted' in it for a reason. And I don't want to find out that reason out in the dark," Blaire said.

"How much farther do you think we will have to go?" Tori asked. The Enchanted Forest was pretty far from Stardon Castle.

"I'm not sure. We should at least get to the edge of the forest and then we could set up camp for the night. Going into the forest in the dark is probably a bad idea. Dementia probably has spies everywhere," Aiden concluded.

"Hey, I just had a thought. Dementia, and this is just my opinion, and the rest of the Seven Sins seem like they would want people to control right? I mean they're clearly power hungry," I said.

"Yeah," they all said in unison.

"Well, no one is here. The only people that they have to control are their prisoners, but they want to enact fear. I think that if they can make people into animals, they can make animals into people."

"Are you saying you think they've turned animals into humans just to torment them?" Macy asked.

"Maybe, I just sense that there are people here. What else would they be doing? They're like dictators, they need someone to dictate."

"Why would your kingdom be empty then?" Tori asked.

"I'm not sure. I'm betting she hates my family, so she has forbid people from going there."

"That could be a possibility. She has probably made obstacles for us. She definitely doesn't want us to win," Blaire said.

"Guys…" Aiden said.

"I bet she would sacrifice all of her magic to beat us," Tori said.

"Guys…" repeated Aiden.

"She is a ruthless woman," Macy said agreeing.

"Guys…" Aiden repeated a third time.

"I just can't understand how she can just hold them…"

"Guys! Look!" Aiden shouted. We all stopped and followed Aiden's finger up to the sky. A thick cloud of black smoke was rising quickly over the trees. In the swirls of blackness, I could see purplish stripes looping through, dotted with flecks of gold, just like the sun.

"Dementia," I muttered. What was the cause of smoke? Had she blown something up? Had she hurt the prisoners?

Don't worry, they're still alive, she calmly said to me.

I'm surprised you've kept them alive, since you are a cold-blooded witch, I told her. I hoped I wasn't giving her any ideas.

I have my own reasons for keeping them alive. For now. And it gives me the pleasure of watching you figuring out the puzzle. The pleasure of me being able to taunt and torment you. You can't handle the magic you have.

"Guys, its Dementia."

"What is Dementia?" asked Macy. The cloud was getting closer now.

"That cloud of smoke. It's one of our challenges. She's trying to hurt me by hurting you. You guys need to get out of here before it gets to close. I can handle her."

"We're not leaving you, Gwendolyn," Blaire shouted over the rumble of the oncoming storm.

"That's right, we're staying," Tori chorused.

"I'm not leaving," Aiden said. They had all moved about a foot closer to me.

"I wouldn't think I would have to say this. But, girl, do you really think I would let you kick this tantrum throwing fairy's butt without me?" Macy asked.

"I don't know how strong she will be. I don't know if I can protect you all."

"You can. We know you can, just don't overthink it. It's in you." Macy padded my shoulder.

We watched as the clouds grew larger, dark purple strips mixed with the charcoal mist. Thundering noises were booming from within its walls. I hadn't wanted my friends to stay, but I was glad they were there. I wasn't sure how I would protect us all. I just knew I had to.

The storm had come very close to us, about a football field length away. I didn't want to think about what would happen if I couldn't protect us, but the thought kept coming to my mind. What would happen? Would we vanish? No, that wouldn't make sense. Dementia didn't want us gone, she wanted us to suffer. Would it take us to her? Maybe she wanted us to be her prisoners as well.

"Gwendolyn, it's close," I heard Aiden's voice.

"Okay. Everyone get around me in a circle. Keep together and then make sure that when the storm gets close enough that you don't look into it. I have no clue what's in there, but if Dementia is using powerful magic, then I don't want you guys to get hypnotized or something," I shouted to them all. They all huddled around me and I braced myself for what I was going to do. I had it planned.

The storm was a couple feet away now and moving fast.

"Everyone, close your eyes," I said. We all did. I raised my hands. My hair was almost being pulled out of my head from the dangerous wind. I concentrated. *Please, let this work.*

I reopened my eyes. We were still standing. I looked around, every one of us was here. We were all in the same condition as we were before the storm cloud. Then I noticed my hands. A blueish colored bubble surrounded us. I had done it, it had worked!

"Gwendolyn, that was amazing!" Tori exclaimed and hugged me tight.

"I can't believe I did that," I said.

"Gwendolyn, can you put the shield down now?" Aiden asked. I had almost forgotten that my hands still had it up.

"Yeah sure," I laughed. Once I lowered the shield, we looked around everything became grey. The forest was covered in ash which also coated the ground like fresh snow. My magic must have camouflaged it at first.

"What happened? It was nice just a minute ago?" Blaire said exasperated.

"I guess the shield concealed that the land had been destroyed. It looks like everything is just covered in some ash. Nothing too bad. We should keep going, we want to get the edge of the forest before dark." Macy picked up one side of the cart and the rest of us followed her lead.

At the end of the forest, we began setting up a camp. We took one of the blankets and used it as a roof by tying ends to low hanging tree limbs. Then we took the other ends and tied them to the cart making a lean-to. I figured out how to make fire and started a small one for us. Then I used magic to whip us up some protein bars and fruit as something to eat.

"I'm so happy we have you, Gwendolyn. We would starve if you weren't here," Tori joked as she bit into an apple. But I didn't really hear her. I kept feeling like I should've heard Dementia after that storm. She should've tried to taunt me. Saying I had gotten lucky and that the next one would be worse. But she hadn't.

"Gwendolyn?" Blaire asked, noticing I wasn't responding.

"Mmm?" I said.

"Are you all right?" she asked.

"I'm fine. I think I'm going to take a walk though, just relax a little."

"I'll go with you," Aiden volunteered.

"It's okay Aiden, I'd much rather go alone."

"I insist. We should get more wood for the fire anyway." He got up and began walking. I didn't really have the choice of going in another direction since there were woods everywhere. So, I followed Aiden.

"We had plenty of wood back at camp. You didn't need to come out here to get more," I said when I had caught up to him. He didn't answer me, but I saw there was a hint of a smile on his mouth.

"You caught me. I wanted to come to talk to you."

"Talk to me? About what?"

"You set me up with Blaire because you thought I still liked her right?"

"I *knew* you still liked her, but go on."

"Well, that was true, but… it feels strange. I like her, but now that we've gone on some dates it feels…different. And I'm not sure that we like each other in the way we thought we did."

"Have you told Blaire this?"

93

"No. This isn't the time. We're in such a strange place with so many things happening, I don't want to put more questions on her or confuse her." This was my chance, I could tell him how I felt, finally be honest with him.

"Here's what I think. I think you feel weird because I set you up with Blaire and you're still not sure what you want. You know you like her, you just don't know what you want to do about it. My advice is, just go with the flow. Let her do her thing and you do yours and it will all work out. If you're not meant to be together, there will be a clear sign."

"Thanks. This really helps out."

I handed him some branches I had picked up as we were walking. "Take these back to camp, so they won't wonder why you didn't bring any wood back. I'll be back soon, I just need some time to myself." He nodded and headed back while I continued on my walk.

The forest seemed very calm now, very still, very silent. I found a small lake not too far from where our camp was. It felt familiar to me and then I recognized it. This was the area where the huntsman tried to kill Snow White. It looked just like the picture in the book.

Snow White. Aaron's second wife. Aaron who was my mother's father.

Mom.

I remembered that I had slipped her diary and music box into my pocket before I'd left. I took them out and turned the box over in my hands. I wanted to hear that beautiful music again, it made me feel oddly safe. I turned the crank a few times and the song began to play. It felt like a distant memory, buried deeply within myself. I tried hard to place it and then it slowly came back. It was a lullaby my mom had sung to me. I was so surprised I remembered. I had known her for only a few days.

> *"Rose of red, locks of gold,*
> *Things, oh things, of a time ago,*
> *Small, little girl, lands far away,*
> *Things, oh things, of a time ago,*
> *True love's kiss and apple like blood,*

Things, oh things, of a time ago,
Palace of ice, queen of snow,
Things, oh things of a time ago."

The lyrics matched things from each story. I placed the music box down and opened up her dairy to the last couple of pages.

The dangers are growing, the time is coming. I remember when she took those girls. They were innocent and young and she turned them into the wicked creatures they are. I blame her.

The Seven Sins, their name fits perfectly with their personalities, have made threats to the kingdoms, even the Fairy Court. My husband has gone into the forest with a group of men to the neighboring kingdoms to see how much damage has been done. What the Seven Sins do not know is that we have a plan. Starletta has selected a woman who has the Gift and she will perform a spell to send us all into the Modern World. It is a world outside of ours, one where the Seven Sins will not be able to reach us. Starletta has used a lot of her magic to make this spell very specific, she wants to make sure that we will be safe in this new place.

No mother should ever know the feeling that her daughter will have to go into a dangerous situation, but some must. I am carrying the most magical fairy to ever be born, for Starletta has seen it. She will have to come back home to defeat these terrible women and restore peace to our land. I know she can do it. But she's my baby. I don't want her to be harmed.

I flipped to the last page of the book.

Guinevere, if you ever get the chance to read this, you must be back into our kingdom. I don't have a lot of time before I have to leave, but look at the paintings they are

The writing stopped there. What were the paintings? They were just of objects. Not everything is as it seems though, certainly not in this world. I packed everything back up, my friends would know what to do.

"We were about to go out looking for you," Macy said when I got back to camp.

"Was I gone that long?"

"You were gone for a while. You left your pocket watch, so we knew you had been gone almost an hour," Tori explained.

"I'm sorry, I didn't mean to be gone that long. I took this diary I found in my mom's room at the castle. I read just a few pages of it. I think my mom left us some clues."

"What kind of clues?" Blaire asked.

"The diary was in a box. In that box, was also some other stuff my mom left behind and some of those things were these paintings. They were of different objects - a rose, a mirror, something that looked sort of silver like and it was pointed. All of the paintings looked rushed and a little smudged, so some of the pictures are a little blurry. But, she wrote that the paintings are… and the writing stops. I have the paintings. I want you guys to help me figure out what they mean."

We clambered into a huddle and laid the paintings out. "Okay," began Blaire. "we have a red rose, a mirror with someone looking in, some shimmery, pointed things, an acorn and thimble, a hole, a man climbing up a tower and a white castle. How are these helpful clues? They don't make any sense."

"Maybe the meanings are hidden in plain sight. Like, they're right in front of us, but we don't know what they are because our brains are looking for a more complex answer," Tori said.

"Okay. Plain sight. We have to make sure that we don't overthink, just keep it simple," said Aiden.

"Let's start from the beginning. So, there's a red rose. The clues are most likely connected to fairytales. It has to be a fairytale with a red rose in it," Macy said.

"What if it's like the Prophecy? These items are from each story. That would mean this rose would be from Beauty and the Beast," Aiden stated.

"Do we know how these items will help us?" Tori asked.

"We'll probably know once we have it all figured out. The mirror looks like it has someone looking it in, but I can't think of any fairytales where someone looking in a mirror would be significant," I said.

"I don't think that it's someone looking in a mirror. I think it's someone looking out. The Magic Mirror from Snow White," Blaire said.

"The shimmering pointed things could be wings from Thumbelina, who got turned into a fairy," Tori excitedly shrieked.

"The tower the man is climbing is where Rapunzel is held," I said.

"The hole could be the rabbit hole from Alice in Wonderland," Aiden exclaimed.

"The last things are an acorn and thimble and the white castle," said Macy.

"The castle is from the Snow Queen, it's where she lives," Tori announced.

"The last story was Peter Pan. That must be where the acorn and thimble come in," Blaire stated.

"Well, what do we do with this information?" Aiden asked. I didn't really know what to say. Most of this all has to do with the stories, their beginnings. Their beginnings are the key. Starletta had said magic would be on our side and give us some clues. These were it. We had to get the stories back on track, but we couldn't just expect them to know what to do. Special events and spectacular things happened to make these characters who they were.

"I think I know what the pictures are for."

"What?" they yelled at the same time.

"I think they are our way to beat Dementia."

CHAPTER 8
MOM

Mom. It kept popping into my head as I tried to sleep. She had left me so many clues. Clues to help me fulfill who I was meant to become. Clues to help me save our people, but she hadn't left me clues about her. How did her and my dad meet? When did they get married? What had she done when she came to the Modern World? Who had taken her?

Where was she now?

I didn't want to think about her. I didn't want to think about where she was and if she was in danger. If the person took her only to traumatize me, then it was my entire fault. If I had been somebody else, anybody else, she would still be here.

No, I didn't want to say *if* she would still be here because I didn't know if she was dead. But, I didn't know if she was alive either.

What other explanation was there? She had been gone for years. It was like those fairytales, at least those girls knew their mothers were dead. Fate decided to make me wonder for the rest of my life and drive me crazy.

I turned over on my bed of grass and tried to make my mind shut down. I pictured black, pure darkness. I drowned out sound from ears and relaxed my limbs. I tried letting the slumber carry my mind deeper and deeper away from reality.

And then I smelled smoke.

My eyelids slid open a little at a time. I was so tired. There was something in them making them sting. I noticed that I was being carried, but I couldn't see my feet, my vision was too blurred.

I tried to see Macy or Blaire or Tori or Aiden. I saw small dark figures being carried, but I couldn't tell if it was them. I tried to lift my head to see who was carrying me, but all I could tell was that he had masculine features.

Before I fell back into sleep, I could see he looked down toward me. He said something, but it sounded like he was underwater. I read from his lips. All I was able to make out was 'Guinevere.'

When I woke up again, I knew we weren't at the camp. For one thing we were in a tent and I was on a cot, covered by a quilt. I looked around and all of my belongings were also there.

No one else was in the tent, so I got up and went outside. This looked nothing like where we had been. The grass was greener and flowers were actually blooming. It was still early morning and without my shoes, I could feel the fresh dew.

I saw men in armor walking around, including two that stood by the entrance to the tent. I went past them and out into the commotion.

"Where are all of my friends?" I asked turning back to the guards.

"They should be with King Aaron. Would ye like us to take ye to 'em, Princess Guinevere?" The taller of the two asked.

King Aaron has to be the Aaron that's my grandfather.

"Yes please," I replied. They guided me to a much larger tent, one that was covered with dark maroon velvet with gold fringe. They opened the curtains for me.

"King Aaron?" I asked a young man who was sitting at a desk. I curtsied, remembering he was royalty. But, I was also a little anxious because I was potentially meeting my grandfather for the first time.

"Please dear, the king piece really isn't necessary. I'm your grandfather." He gave a bear hug and directed me over to a chair in the dimly lit room.

"Why did you bring us here?" I asked as he poured me some tea.

"My men and I were patrolling around the borders and we spotted smoke. As we got closer, we noticed some of Dementia's birds were setting fire to your supplies. We fought them off and that's when I noticed it was you. You're the exact image of Scarlett. And I decided you'd be safer in our camp."

99

"I appreciate your concern, but we have to finish our quest. We can't stay in this camp."

"I know, dearest. Starletta explained that she hoped you would come back. And once you did you would be trying to put our world back together."

"Grandfather, do you know why these stories were chosen? I mean, some don't really connect. Some of the stories are very different from each other."

"To be honest, dearie, these stories, they have meanings that only you will understand. Come now, you must want to see your friends." He got up from his chair and led me outside.

My friends were all out sitting at one of the tables. They jumped up when they saw me coming.

"Gwendolyn, what's going on?" Macy probed.

"Everyone, this is my grandfather, King Aaron. He saved us last night."

"Your Highness," Blaire said curtsying. Tori and Macy both followed her lead and Aiden bowed.

"Please, there is no need. If anything I should be the one bowing to you. You're the ones trying to save my kingdom," grandfather said.

"Are we going to be staying at your camp for long?" Tori asked.

"That will be up to my granddaughter. I'll let you chat for a bit, I have some things I must take care of." He headed back to his tent. I sat down with my friends.

"Your granddad is nice, Gwendolyn," Macy said.

"He's not too shabby looking either," Blaire commented.

"Blaire, ew," I said.

"Sorry, I've always known him as Prince Charming, not your grandfather."

"He's a little young to be a grandfather. He's in like his mid 40's," Aiden said.

"We're in a different time period. You got married young because you didn't live long. And he's already been married, to my biological grandmother Felicity. She died somehow," I explained.

"I'm sorry," he said apologetically.

"Well, aside from Gwendolyn's young grandfather, are we staying here?" Macy asked.

"It would be a lot safer than camping out every night," Tori stated.

"I can't say that it would be bad to stay for at least the night. I want to talk to my grandfather and I want to talk to some of the fairies that are here."

"Also, I don't know about you, but I want to take a long bath," Blaire said.

"Same here, our soap got burned and they have some extra," Tori said happily.

"I wanted to see if I could check out some of the guards' weapons," Aiden said. They all seemed so happy to be here, I couldn't help but smile. I wanted to talk to those fairies for another reason, but if I told them they wouldn't understand.

Hard being the powerful one isn't it?

Can't you use somebody else's brain as a hangout?

No need to get sassy. You know they will never understand. About your magic, your potential or how you, deep down inside, feel connected to these people. I froze.

Gotcha didn't I? Yes, I know your little secret. I know everything about you, Guinevere. Your dreams, your doubts and my most favorite... your fears. That's why I'll win you know. Because you may be powerful, but you don't know how to use it. I do. I can get in your head and you can't get in mine. Don't fret though, at least once it's over, you'll get to see your mother.

I got up from the table and walked away. This was crazy. I couldn't let Dementia freak me out like that. Except the problem was...she did. She knew everything about me. Everything I wanted to be and everything that scared me. Everyone I cared about. *At least once it's over, you'll get to see your mother...* It was probably just a ploy to get to me. I couldn't let that get in my way. I needed to talk to those fairies about my magic.

After getting some directions from my grandfather, I found the fairies gathered around a slightly decayed tree in the forest.

"Excuse me?" The three of them turned their heads toward me.

"I'm Gwendolyn Star, you may know me as Guinevere." Their facial expressions didn't change, though I thought their eyes became wider. One of them was dressed in a purple dress. She had long white hair put in a half up, half down fashion with stars scattered in her strands.

"We know who you are young princess. I am Luna and that is Giselle and Ember. I can imagine you're here to talk about your unique gifts?" With her hand on my shoulder she brought me over to where the others were sitting. Ember had dark skin and her black hair had streaks of red and orange in it. Giselle had fair skin and her hair was a pinkish color. Her dress had vines and petals all over it.

"How much magic have you done here?" Giselle asked me.

"I can make food appear. I can make fire start and I made a shield that saved me and my friends from a storm that Dementia created."

"You're doing well for someone who hasn't had any practice," Ember commented.

"But, I want to know how to use it. Not when I have to concentrate and work for it to happen, but to be able to summon it whenever I need it."

"At the rate you're going it shouldn't take long. The thing of it is, we don't really have any training for you. Yes, we can teach you how to do spells and potions and all of that, but you're so gifted that you know it already. It's in your head. You're more advanced than any other magical creature conjured before," Luna explained to me. I felt lost again. These were some of the top notch fairies in all of the worlds and even they couldn't help me.

"Thank you anyway," I said I tried not to sound disappointed.

"A wand could help," Ember suggested. "It would be an easy way to summon your magic and use it."

As I walked back to the camp I thought about what Luna had said. I was more advanced, more unique, than any other magical creature ever created. Talk about being an odd ball.

No one could train me because everything would come naturally. Dementia was right, no one would understand me.

"Gwendolyn? Can I come in?" Macy asked.

"Sure," I replied. I was sitting on my cot in my nightgown. It wasn't the most comfortable thing, but it was wearable.

"How have you been?" she said, sitting beside me.

"Why?"

"Can't a best friend ask? You know, someone who knows you inside and out, left and right, up and down, black and white..."

"Okay Mace, I get the message."

"So, what's been going on with you?"

"You won't understand."

"Try me."

"No, you really won't. No one will get this but me, because there is no one like me." I hadn't meant to sound sarcastic, but the stress just came out.

"I'm guessing this has something to do with your magic?" she asked. I nodded.

"What did the fairies say? Have you talked with them?"

"Yeah and they told me just to work at it. They can't help me because I'm more powerful than any fairy or magical being. Dementia was right, nobody would understand me."

"Dementia talked to you again?"

"Yeah."

"Why don't you block her out or something?"

"I can't get myself to. I've tried. She did tell me something though."

"What?"

"She said once this is over, I'll get to see my mom."

"She's probably just trying to make you vulnerable."

"But, what if she has my mom? She's been gone for so long. She could've been with Dementia this whole time."

"So what are you going to do? Let Dementia win? Blow this off? You can't, you have to keep fighting..."

"It's my mom, Macy!"

"And your mom wants you to do this quest. She wants you to defeat Dementia and the rest of the Seven Sins. That's what your mom wants. Not for you to give it up." Macy was staring hard at me.

"Well, look at it this way. I'm the one you're all depending on for answers and direction and protection and I'm trying to figure this mess out myself. I don't have all the answers. And when my grandfather told me that our stuff was being burned and they were probably planning to kill us in our sleep and I realized there was nothing I could have done. It made me panic. You guys wanted to come. I get that you want answers about your families but..." I couldn't think of anything else to say. I couldn't say that I didn't want them here, because I did.

"But, if you guys got hurt, when I could've saved you, I would've never forgiven myself." Macy and I both stopped talking. We were the best of friends, but even so, sometimes we just didn't have anything to say to each other.

"Do you wish we hadn't come?" she asked.

"Do you want an honest answer?"

"Yeah."

"Sort of. I don't want you guys to get hurt, you don't have magic like I do. Yes, you have some from Marybella, but you haven't been able to summon it unless it's within those dreams. But, I know what it's like to not have real answers about your family. So, I understand that you want to know about them." She was quiet for a moment.

"I love that you care so much Gwendolyn, it's one of the reasons you're a wonderful friend. I know you'll make sure we're okay and we're going to make sure that you're okay. Tomorrow will be better, goodnight."

"Goodnight." She smiled and walked out. I rolled over on my cot and tried to sleep, at least a little.

I was woken up halfway through the night by a sound. I slipped on my shoes and walked out into the night. I couldn't believe what I saw.

"Starletta? What are you doing here?"

"Hello darling, I thought you might like to chat."

"Talk about perfect timing."

"What's troubling you? Come sit with me." She patted a boulder.

"My friends almost got hurt. I was there and I could've saved them, but I didn't know we were in danger. Thank goodness my grandfather was there, but that was just luck. If it happened again and they got hurt, I don't know what I would do with myself."

"Do you want your friends to go back home?"

"In some ways, but at the same time I don't want them to go. I don't know how they would get back. I don't know where a portal is around here."

"Well, you're in luck. You're right by one." She pointed toward the river.

"The river?"

"The most ordinary things make good portals. Come take a walk with me." We got up from the boulder.

"You know Guinevere, it is hard being a leader. These people care a lot for you though."

"And I care a lot for them."

"Why are you so worried about them getting hurt?"

"I'm not sure. We were all so different just a while ago. Blaire and Macy were just fixing their friendship and Tori and I were becoming friends. Aiden and I almost had a relationship. I dragged them into this mess, so I guess I feel like it's my responsibility to make sure they're safe."

"Guinevere, look at me." Starletta placed her hands on my shoulders. I noticed she looked a little different.

"I wonder who will keep them safe while you're taking a swim." Her white robe vanished, leaving long black cape. Her strong hands gripped my shoulders and she then shoved me backwards. The last thing I saw were those purple eyes before I plunged into the water.

CHAPTER 9
MORE HISTORY

My head broke through the water's surface, sucking in a gulp of air. I turned my head left and right. Water was glued to my lashes. The current was vicious and fighting against it was a huge struggle.

I saw a log drifting toward me. I reached for it. I felt my fingertips hook around its rough bark. I clung to it then pulled myself up onto it and looked at the water. It glowed faintly purple.

I calmed my heartbeat and spread my hands out. The water immediately slowed. I pushed myself over to the side of the river and got up onto the bank.

I had to get back to grandfather's camp. Hopefully, before Dementia did too much damage. The only problem was I had floated a good ways down the river. Also, my head felt strange, every direction felt the same. I didn't know which way I had to go. Dementia must have put some sort of spell on me when she touched me.

I couldn't let that distract me. I relaxed myself and thought about what Starletta had told me. *Magic is about believing.*

I started to run back to camp. I could feel I was going in the right direction. Then I heard a scream. It sounded just like Blaire's voice.

If Dementia hurt a hair on her head I was not going to be responsible for my actions. With that bolt of adrenaline, I shot to the skies.

I could see Dementia clearly once I was over camp.

"Dementia!" I yelled. I was hovering over the ground. She turned to me, holding Blaire with one of her hands. "Let her go. Now!" She smiled wickedly. She pointed upward without turning her eyes away from me. Macy, Tori and Aiden were suspended in the air.

"I hate to leave things just...hanging, but we must be going." With a snap of her fingers, they all vanished.

"Gwendolyn, dear, are you alright? We saw Dementia and tried to fight, but when she picked up your friends I didn't want to risk getting them harmed," grandfather said.

"I'm okay. I have to find out where they went. I can't let them get hurt."

"First and foremost, we need a plan, and a good one. Dementia is a very clever woman and she wants your friends for something. She won't give them up easily."

"Do you know where Dementia's dungeon is? The one where she holds the others?"

"No, I'm afraid not. We've looked and looked, but Dementia has hidden it so well that it's like it's invisible."

"Invisible...That's it! Grandfather, you're a genius! Starletta used this spell to conceal her house from Dementia when she was one of her students. Dementia probably learned the trick as well and is using it to keep her dungeon invisible."

"That's a start, but it doesn't narrow down the search."

"Yes it does. Get your men prepared, we have a long journey ahead of us."

"So, where exactly are we going?" grandfather asked. We were in a carriage that Starletta had supplied him with.

"Where was the kingdom that Marybella lived in?" I asked him.

"It was the Rosemoor Kingdom. Marybella's mother had two sisters that also lived there."

"That's where Starletta's house is and I believe that's also where Dementia has placed her dungeon. You'll have to show me where Marybella's house is though."

"How are you sure that you'll find it?"

"I've visited it once, in one of my dreams. Well, they are kind of dreams. Mom and Starletta planted them into my brain, so I could figure out how to get back here."

He chuckled. "There's so much of your mom in you it's astounding. She would be proud to know that you're fighting for our people."

"Well, it was either that or playing games on my computer."

"What is a computer?"

"Never mind. Look, we're getting close to a kingdom, it's just through that pass in the hills," I pointed. When we came to the pass, my grandfather halted the carriage and soldiers.

"Why are we stopping?" I asked.

"We must be careful as we go through here. We've noticed one of the Seven Sins, Corona, in the mountain pass. She can be very dangerous, so before we try to go through I want to make sure she's not going to try anything."

"Corona won't be a problem, trust me." He hesitated a moment, then motioned for the soldiers to keep moving.

As we got closer to the pass, I could tell grandfather was getting more anxious.

Thwump. "What was that?" grandfather wondered.

"I'm not sure."

Thwump. "There it is again. I'm telling the coachman to halt."

"Oh, no you're not, Aaron," A voice called. The carriage rocked as bright colors flamed across the window.

"Corona?" The carriage rocked some more, harder than before.

"We have to get out, before this thing tips." We opened the doors and jumped out.

"Are you all right, dear?" he asked me.

"I'm fine, but look out." He rolled out of the way just as Corona threw a massive fire ball at him. Her ruby hair blazed and her copper eyes danced with amusement.

"So, I see you've finally met your granddaughter. You know, Dementia would really like to speak with her."

"Dementia will never get the chance," he growled, eyes blazing.

"No need to be hostile Aaron. Or would you like me to give her a lesson in magic. This is how you burn something, Princess." She aimed a fireball at my head. I quickly ducked, hearing the sizzle zip past my head.

"Corona. I demand you let us pass, immediately," grandfather told her.

"You don't have any control over me Aaron. Maybe you should've thought about that beforehand."

"Hey, Corona," I yelled to her. "You need to take a chill pill."

"A chill what?"

"It's a saying from my world. Though here, I think you should take it a bit more literally." I took out my wand and blasted her feet with ice. She struggled against the cold restraints.

"Come on, we have to get into the carriage before the magic wears off." We rushed into the carriage and commanded the driver to go.

"You won't get away, Aaron. You ruined too many! Too many!" Corona cried as we fled the scene.

"What does she mean you ruined too many? Too many what?" I asked.

"She means I ruined too many hearts. You see, I am more of a romantic fellow. I don't really want to dabble with the ladies, I want to find my one true love. But, I was once married to a woman named Felicity. She was kind, beautiful, intelligent, everything I wanted for the girl of my dreams. She gave birth to your mother, but she died when your mother wasn't that old. Before I had met Felicity however, I had been matched with several ladies, two of whom were fairies. One of those fairies was Corona. She became more in love with me than I was with her. She thought I wanted marriage, but I didn't. When I told her this, she became very angry and hurt. She swore she would make me pay for it."

"Who was the other fairy?"

His shoulders tightened. "It was Dementia," he said a quietly.

"Did you ever... love her?" I asked slightly horrified.

"No, I never loved her. We were paired by her mother. She was beautiful yes, but she was very jealous. If she saw me talking with other ladies, girls who were my friends, she'd turn them into creatures that she called trolls. Finally, I got the courage to tell Starletta. My family had been long time friends

with hers and I knew her very well. I told Starletta what
Dementia had done and she expelled her from her teachings and
wouldn't let her perform the spell."

"Is that why she hates our family?"

"Yes. And I regret the decision deeply every day. I wish I
could reverse it and change the outcome. Maybe if I hadn't made
her mad then we wouldn't be in this situation."

"It's not your fault, she let her anger consume her. You
can't blame yourself for her actions."

"After that, I gave up finding love. It seemed like it
wasn't out there for me."

I felt terrible for him. His true love was out there, he just
didn't know it yet. And I couldn't tell him, he had to fall in love
on his own.

"Don't worry, I'm sure she's out there."

"I really don't know any more, dear."

I couldn't think of anything else to say. I began fumbling
with the treasures that were in my pocket. I looked over to him.
He twisted a gold ring that was around his finger.

"My mother gave that to you didn't she?" He looked up,
surprised by my knowing.

"I can sense it. I keep things of hers also, mainly these." I
pulled out the diary, music box and wand. "These were all hers.
I've read a few pages of the diary and I've played the music box.
Was the wand hers or was it meant for me?"

"She had a portion of the Gift inside her. It wasn't a lot.
Mostly she could do things with the elements of fire and water
and a few things with the mind. Starletta helped my wife and I
realize that."

"So, this was the wand she used?"

"Starletta gave it to her to help her focus her magic."

"Ember told me that wands can help beginners. The
fairies can't help me actually. They said they can't coach me
because I'm too magical. Everything that they could teach me I
already know somewhere in my brain, so it will come naturally. I
have no one to guide me. I could've saved my friends, but instead
I let them be taken away by that witch." I blinked my tears back.

"I'll guide you sweetheart. I love you very much and I'm going to make sure that you're alright."

"This is the first time you've met me."

"I knew you while you were in your mother's stomach and I loved you then, too." He smiled so lovingly. I hugged him. I hugged him and felt that family warmth that I missed so greatly.

"Grandfather, you'll find your true love. I know it. Someone is waiting out there for you."

"How can you be so sure?"

"I just am."

"Do you have your sights set on some young man?"

I laughed a little. "I guess I did at some point. It was the boy that was in my group. His name is Aiden. He's very nice and very sweet, but it was more of a little fling thing. He's with someone else."

"Why would he choose this girl over you? I can knock some sense into him if you'd like." I laughed again. "No, I told him to go with this other girl. I knew he liked her more than he let on. It was weird seeing them together at first, but he's a great friend. And he's happy and that's what matters to me."

"Well, I believe you're wonderful. You should get some rest. We still have a long journey ahead of us." I stretched out on the seat of the carriage and snuggled into the soft cushion.

I woke up and we were still riding in the carriage. At least I was. I couldn't see my grandfather anywhere. I looked out the window.

"Good morning, Guinevere. The coachman got tired, so I took over. I wanted to give the chap some rest."

"Mind if I come and sit?" I asked.

"Not at all." He stopped the carriage and I got up and slid next to him.

"How much longer do we have to go until we get to Rosemoor?"

"Not much longer. That is, as long as we don't run into anything."

"What could we run into?"

"Trolls, witches, those nasty birds. Pretty much anything Dementia has made her slave."

"She made witches?"

"One of the things she turned some of the peasant girls into. She has a quick temper."

"You don't say?" I said sarcastically. "How did Dementia create all these…people?"

"She has great power. No fairy can create an actual human just by using their magic. No matter how great it is. They must start with something else that is already alive. Then they may turn it into something else. But you have to firmly concentrate. Sometimes they won't fully change over. Like those horse people and fish women."

"You mean centaurs and mermaids?"

"Yes, they were some of Dementia's practice work."

"Wow. So that's how she turns people into birds and birds into people?"

"Yes. And Dementia being Dementia, she has given all the kingdoms new residents."

"She's so terrible! How did her mother think you'd like her?"

"Her mother was a sweet woman, she only wanted her daughter's happiness. Though finally, she saw Dementia's true colors. We all make mistakes in our life."

"True."

"We all have first impressions of people. Sometimes they're wrong,"

"And it can go the other way around. Sometimes people seem mean, but turn out to be nice. One of my friends was like that. She's the one dating Aiden now."

"She was not a pleasant girl?" he asked.

"She just made some choices she thought she had to make to be happy. She knows now that she didn't need to do those things."

"At least she knows. Rosemoor will just be over this hill." He pointed to show me. At the entrance of the town, I got glimpses of the people. Their faces were pale and hollow. Their eyes were lifeless.

"King Aaron, what has brought you to us?" A woman asked us. Her clothes were tattered, hanging together by threads.

"We've come to pay a visit to Marybella's house, Wilhelmina. This is my granddaughter, Guinevere," he whispered to her. She looked toward me. Her eyes looked bloodshot and her face was smudged with dirt, but you could see that she was pretty underneath.

"Oh," she said as she smiled kindly at me. "The house is quite a mess, no one has lived there in years. I can't take you there though. Lexia has put us under strict orders not let anyone near it."

"Is Lexia one of the Seven Sins?" I asked.

"Yes, she's terrible. She's taken so much from us and we were already so poor. All my livestock have perished. And Dementia, that wretched woman just put us here for her own selfish purposes. But you're here now, you're our blessing, thank you child." She held my hand and smiled.

"We must get going now, give our love to Regina and Malcom," grandfather said. She waved to us as we rode off.

"So, Dementia really just put people here to torture them?" I asked a little while after we got out of town.

"She's a very horrible woman, Guinevere."

"But that is being more than horrible. She's a...a...I can't even think of a word, she's so terrible. Wilhelmina has children, Dementia really has no soul."

"You seem very emotional about this."

"Well...I somewhat understood that she wanted revenge on people that hurt her, but these people have done nothing to her. She put them here to make them miserable, it doesn't make sense to me."

He placed a hand on my shoulder. "I want you to go into the house alone. I think you'll find more clues that way. I'll keep watch for Lexia."

"Okay."

The house was much different than I remembered. Wilhelmina wasn't kidding though, it was a mess. The roof was half caved in and rubble was everywhere.

"On second thought dear, maybe this isn't so safe," grandfather said.

"No, I'll be fine. I bet I can move most of this with my magic. Watch…" I lifted one of the wood planks that had fallen in onto the ground and tossed it aside. "See, I'll be fine."

"Alright, be careful." I set off to find a way to get inside. I found a hole in the door that was just big enough for me to squeeze through.

The inside was even worse. Some of the walls you could tell had water damage and some of the wooden furniture had been torn apart by termites.

I went up what was left of the staircase while practicing my art of levitating. I navigated through the bits of wreckage trying to examine them for anything useful. I came up empty.

Guinevere? Can you hear me? I knew it wasn't Dementia, but I couldn't tell who this new voice was.

I can hear you, but I don't know who you are.

I'm a friend.

Look, I've been tricked before by magic, so if you're trying to hide your true identity then it won't work. I want a name.

I can't tell you that.

Why not?

Because… I promised your mother I wouldn't.

CHAPTER 10
MOTHER'S FRIEND

You promised my mother that you wouldn't tell me your name?

Yes.

Why is it so terrible if I know your name?

If I tell you my name, then your mother will never be let free.

How do I know that you're not one of Dementia's spies. Or if you're my mother. Or if you're telling the truth at all?

If I didn't want to help your mother, I wouldn't be risking my life to save her and you.

Fine. Is there something you wanted to tell me?

Yes. Your mother is safe, for the moment.

Can you tell me where she is?

No, I'm sorry. I am restricted from doing that.

Who is restricting you?

I can't say that either. You have to trust me, my interest is in her safety.

If, and this is a big if, you really do want the best for her, is there anything I can do to help?

Make sure the Prophecy gets underway. Make sure those couples find their true loves. Make sure those girls have their adventures and make sure that that boy and girl save each other.

That's it? That's all I can do?

For now. Please be patient, I promise you will see your mother again.

The voice went away after that. I tried to reach it, but I couldn't. It was like a wall had gone up in my mind.

I continued on my way throughout the house. I looked everywhere and couldn't find anything of value. The new voice kept coming back to my mind. I couldn't place the voice anywhere from my memory. It was smooth and calm, like one of those operators when you call 911 and they ask what your emergency is.

I turned a corner into another room. It looked like Marybella's room possibly. I started searching through the remains of anything that was still put together. All I was able to find was a few books and shredded pieces of a quilt.

This wasn't working. I needed a strategy, something that would guide me to clues. I relaxed. When I reopened my eyes some of the objects were glowing. I picked up one of the books that had the glow and turned the page. It was some sort of log.

Two rose petals

Five sunflower seeds

Five pine needles

Place the two petals on the needles and then the seeds over that. Chant spell. Done properly, it should make a healer.

It was a spell book! Starletta must have had her write the spells down. I picked up another thing that was glowing. It was a piece of ripped, black cloth. It looked familiar. It felt sort of leathery, but smooth. Dementia's cape was black. And none of the other houses were trashed this bad. Dementia could've wrecked it looking for something. It certainly sounded like her.

I went back out and showed the items to my grandfather.

"Do you think that Dementia destroyed the house?"

"It seems like a reasonable guess."

"I would agree. We should start looking for Starletta's house. We'll have to be quick, Dementia has lots of ways to watch us."

"The house is nearby. We have to go through those woods until we get to a clearing. In some blackberry bushes are two stones that I can use to do the spell." I led the way until we came the clearing. I used the rocks to do the spell. Nothing happened.

"Nothing is happening, what do we do now?" grandfather asked. I didn't say anything. I just stared at the stones still in my hands.

"Guinevere, what do we do?" As he said this a second time, I saw that the stones were beginning to glow. I quickly set them down and pushed my grandfather back. Light erupted from the stones and a house appeared.

"How did you make that happen?" he exclaimed.

"Your guess is as good as mine." We went closer to the house. When I looked behind me, I noticed that grandfather wasn't with me. He was standing a few feet away.

"Come on, we have to hurry."

"I can't go any farther dear, I'm blocked." I went back to look and as I tried to touch him an invisible wall appeared.

"I bet I can break it." I started to get ready when he stopped me.

"You can do this on your own, Guinevere. I'll be alright. Go in there and get everyone." I sucked in breath. I could feel everything shaking. I braced myself for what might be in there. I prayed it wasn't what I was thinking.

CHAPTER 11
RESCUED

The house looked the same on the inside since the last time I had been there. On a hunch, I decided to go down to the room where I had first saw Marybella and Starletta. I peeked through the keyhole and what I saw amazed me.

Nothing was in there. None of the spell books, none of the potions. Nothing.

I walked in and my foot knocked against something. I looked down, noticed a handle and realized I was standing on a door. I hadn't remembered it being there last time. Of course, I hadn't gone in all that far.

I lifted the door up as much as I dared. I saw concrete steps and a green glow creeping up from the floor.

It seemed wrong. Like a scene in a horror movie when the girl isn't supposed to go down into the basement where the creepy clown is, but she does it anyway. I basically did the same thing. Except in my scenario I would be blasted into oblivion instead of getting ripped apart by a chainsaw.

As I walked down, I felt like something was watching me. My head seemed to spin slightly, but I ignored it. It was just nerves. My friends were down here somewhere, I had to find them.

I kept walking. I heard voices.

"When is this plan going into motion?"

"We need to enact it at some point."

"Patience." I knew that was Dementia speaking. "We must wait for her to get there, if we don't, it won't work." I wondered if they were talking about me.

"She's a smart girl. She's bound to figure out this house is our dungeon."

"So, we move the prisoners. The villagers won't do anything, they can't."

"It's not that simple, my dears. I don't want any rumors going around the villages and I especially don't want any difficulties. Until we know she's onto something, then we don't do anything. Is everyone clear?" No one said anything, so I assumed that they nodded.

"Good. Now, I want the four children put in a very secluded chamber. They should not be easily found. The west corner will do nicely. I want guards surrounding that door like their lives depend on it, because they do." I saw the shadow of Dementia's cape as she whipped it around.

I waited until their footsteps seemed far enough away and then I turned myself invisible.

I followed Dementia to the west corner of the house. She went down a hallway, her cape fluttering just above the floor. She came to a wooden door with no window and a heavy iron lock. She took a key from a ring by her belt and unlocked the door. Inside was Tori, Aiden, Blaire and Macy. All with an iron shackle around one ankle.

They all stood up when they saw her, but they didn't say anything. "You're being removed from this room," she said coolly.

"Where are we going?" Tori asked.

"Another chamber." She began unlocking their shackles.

"Where's Gwendolyn?" Macy asked. Dementia didn't respond.

"Where is she, you heartless monster!" Blaire screamed. Dementia looked at her and a purple beam of light gripped Blaire's throat and flattened her against the ceiling.

"Do not speak to me again unless you want your voice removed permanently," she said smugly. Then she dropped Blaire to the floor as she gasped for air.

"Let's get going." She had guards surround all of them as they moved up a flight of stairs.

She led them into a room that was in the wall at the top of the stairs. This room looked like the old one almost exactly. She dragged each of them in one by one. She took out her cane and spun it three times. Everyone's feet were chained once again, but this time the chains had an indigo color to them.

"If you try to break these chains, they will paralyze you. I suggest not to try." She smirked a little as she left. Just before she

119

shut the door, I slipped it. I looked through the keyhole. She put a spell on the lock and then said something to the three guards that stood in front of the door.

I made myself visible again. "Gwendolyn! You're here!" Blaire said moving over a little to give me a hug.

"We thought she had hurt you," Aiden said. I had to go over to give him a hug.

"Where were you?" Macy asked.

"I was with my grandfather. He told me all these things about Dementia and the Seven Sins, which I'll have to tell you later. Right now, we have to get out of here."

"But what about the other people, we need them, too," Blaire said.

"I know and we'll come back, but first I want to get you guys out, so hold on tight to me." They hung onto my arms and waist. I whispered a few words and the chains snapped off.

"Hold on." I jumped off the floor and we punched through the ceiling out into the sky.

"I'm so glad you're all safe," grandfather said as he wrapped his great arms around us, squeezing us all together.

"We didn't get the other prisoners, but we will. We're going to need a genius plan to get to them though," I said.

"What about this?" Aiden said. He told us the plan.

"That's good," said Tori.

"This is going to get her really mad, I can't wait," Blaire said excitedly. We planned to do it tomorrow. That night everything seemed perfect again. My friends were safe and we were all together.

"Hey, Gwendolyn?" Macy said coming into my tent.

"Yeah, what do you need?"

"You were saying that your grandfather had told you some things about Dementia. What were you talking about?" She came over and sat on my bed.

"Well, um, it's sort of hard to explain."

"If anyone is going to understand it's going to be me."

"Well, Dementia and him were…matched up. But he never loved her. When he started to keep a distance and talk to other girls, it resulted in her turning the village girls into trolls and witches. He told Starletta and she banned Dementia from her teachings. He caused the rage Dementia has for our family."

"Oh my God. Wow, that's heavy."

"It doesn't stop there. Dementia was really important to the fantasy world in a way. She created trolls and witches and mermaids and centaurs and all those things. Fairies can create a human using another living object and the other way around by turning a human into something else. I'm guessing that's where frog princes come in." We both laughed. "It's just a little crazy that I could make life if I tried."

"But, you don't have to use it like Dementia does. You can use it for good. Why do you let her get to you so much?"

"Well for starters, she has invaded the privacy of my thoughts."

"She can't make you do anything, you know."

"She did something that really got to me. She tried to harm my friends. If she wants to tussle with me, fine. She doesn't have to bring you guys into it."

"Gwendolyn, we're all right. Nothing happened to us. You were smart enough to figure out where we were and we never doubted that you would. You can take her on."

I thought about telling her about the new voice. It wouldn't be so terrible, if she was the only one who knew.

"There's another thing. I heard a new voice in my head. It sounded feminine, really calm, but it didn't tell me its name. It said my mother didn't want it to."

"What did it say?"

"I asked it why it couldn't tell me and it told me it couldn't tell me that either. It said someone was preventing it. I wanted proof it was telling the truth and it said it was risking its life to save me and my mom. I then asked it what I could do to help her. It said just make sure the Prophecy happens."

"That's all?"

"That's all."

"Could it be Dementia playing a trick on you?"

"I don't think so. When Dementia is in my mind, I'm completely unaware of everything else around me. She blocks everyone out, trapping me, making me feel vulnerable. When this voice spoke, I knew where I was and what I was doing. Dementia wouldn't let loose of her control. I'll still be cautious though."

"That's smart."

"Maybe she's here, Macy. You know I'd do anything to see her."

"I know. I just want to be smart about it." She closed my tent flap as she left.

Sleeping wasn't easy tonight. Nothing was troubling me, but I couldn't make my mind settle. I finally got up and wrapped one of my blankets around me.

Night was everywhere. I sat near the edge of the hill where we had made camp and looked out. I could see the whole village. I never imagined that a world so wonderful could be in so much pain.

"Hey." I jerked my head around.

"Blaire, what are you doing out here?"

"Couldn't sleep. Why are you out here?"

"The same reason."

"I wanted to talk to you actually."

"What did you want to talk about?"

"I know we haven't really been great friends for the last few years. I know I've been really horrible to you and Tori and Macy and everyone. I've lost some really great friends because of how I acted and I'm so sorry for everything I've done."

"I forgive you. You know now that it was wrong to do that."

"Tori and I were like sisters and I threw it all away to climb the social ladder. I used her."

"Blaire, you've made mistakes, but you're not the only one at fault. Macy and I did our fair share of name calling. Most of it was criticizing you. But still, you're not alone."

"I wish I could take so much of it back."

"You can. When we go back, apologize to Jennifer and Skylar. Tell Marco that you're not really interested. Ask Tori over for a sleepover. Maybe it won't change their opinions, but then you can't say that you didn't try."

"Thanks. But, you know it's only 'if' we go back."

"If?"

"We all know it and we're just not saying it. We don't know if we're going back. We don't know what our parents will say or remember. We don't know how the kids at school will react when we just show up again."

"Yeah, we don't know, but that doesn't mean we just stop. We're going to figure this out and you're going home."

"You're going home? Do you mean just Macy, Aiden, Tori and I?" My mouth locked. Her expression became questioning.

"Gwendolyn, do you want to stay here?" It surprised me. I expected her to be mad, hurt, possibly confused. But not relaxed and honestly asking for my opinion.

"I don't know. I do have a kingdom to run. Or at least my mom and dad do, if I can find my mom. This is a place where I wouldn't have to hide my magic."

"Well, make sure you think about it. Who knows, maybe we'll end up staying, too. We'll support whatever you decide. Try and get some sleep." She left and I was back with the night as my only company.

"Would you really want to stay?" This time Starletta didn't surprise me.

"Finally you come. Why'd it take so long?"

"I need the magic to be strong enough. I told you I wouldn't be around too much."

"I wish you could be."

"I do, too. So, you've been thinking about staying?"

"Maybe, it wouldn't be so terrible. I'm probably the youngest fairy to be able to travel between realms and I wouldn't have to hide my magic. I'd probably have to protect everyone, but I'd be fine with that."

She laughed. "Yes that's all true, but I know the real reason you want to stay."

"What is that?"

"You want to look for your mother. You're convinced that she's not in your world. And now you're positive she's here because a voice told you about her. I've been watching, too."

"Starletta, you don't understand. You know where your mother is, I don't. I haven't for almost all of my life. Now I'm hearing that someone knows where she is and is keeping her safe. All I have to do is complete this quest and I can see her again…I would stay here forever if it meant I could see her." She rubbed her thumb under my cheekbone.

"You have her determination. What did this voice say exactly?"

"Nothing too helpful. It said it couldn't tell me its name because it promised my mother. And it couldn't tell me where she was or who was keeping it from telling me all this. And it told me to make sure I was safe because I had to make sure the Prophecy was completed."

"This person is powerful. Anyone who can speak to you through your thoughts is."

"Why is it protecting my mom?"

"I'm not sure. The voice was restricted by someone?"

"Yes, but it couldn't tell me who."

"That's interesting. I'm not sure the Seven Sins would have anything to do with it. Although, they aren't your mother's biggest fans."

"Did she do something to them?"

"I don't really know. I do have to be getting back though."

"Back to where?"

"Back to the Dream World. It is a world in between this world and yours. It's more of a heaven for fairies and other magical creatures. I'll be watching - good luck." Her body evaporated into dust and for the second time I was back to being by myself.

I went back to my tent and grabbed my mom's diary. I leafed through a few more of the pages. I found a piece of text that was before the first page I had read.

I couldn't believe I had found what I found. It proved all the rumors. It showed the deceitful way she had tricked everyone. It showed we could rid the world of her. All I would have to do is get that bottle. That was my goal. If I didn't, I would be risking missing out on my greatest joy – victory.

I didn't know what my mom had found, but it was something powerful. I knew the Seven Sins were a part of it, they always seemed to be. *How* they were is what I didn't understand.

"How did you sleep last night?" Aiden asked me the next morning.

"I hope that's a rhetorical question, because I don't have an answer," I said sarcastically.

"Now I guess we know."

"I'm sorry. I actually didn't sleep well at all."

"Do you know why?" Tori asked. Blaire and I shared a subtle glance.

"No, maybe it was just one of those nights."

"Well, today is the day. Do we have everything set for the plan?" Macy asked.

"Everything is good to go," Blaire replied. "We all know what we have to do right?" We shared a thumbs up.

"Dementia is going down and we're taking all the rest of them with her."

CHAPTER 12
PLAN OF ATTACK

We all crouched by the side of the trap door talking over the plan. We were surprised to find that no guards had been posted there.

"You're still sure about this, right Gwendolyn?" Aiden asked.

"Heck yeah I am, I'm showing this nut job she can't mess with my friends."

"Okay, well, it's now or never. We ready?" We put our hands atop Macy's.

"One, two, three, go," we all chanted. Aiden and Blaire pulled the door open and we all walked down. We placed everyone where they needed to go and went over last minute details. We had to get this just right. I cracked my knuckles and pulled out my wand. I plunged it into a crack in the cobblestone flooring and twisted it. A blue glow spread throughout the cracks around the stones until everything glimmered.

Just as I planned Dementia, showed up along with the other Sins.

"Hello, I hope you don't mind. It's dark in this basement," I smirked. I was just getting warmed up. I had to make her blood boil.

"I don't know how you figured out we were down here, but clearly you're too cocky for your own good."

"Maybe I am, but I'm half your age and I know more spells than you could ever master."

"What are you doing here? You have your friends back and I didn't come after you might I remind you."

"That's not why I came. I came for the others. Now, we can do this easily if you'd just kindly show me their cells and there'll be no trouble."

"Over my dead body, apprentice," she spat.

"If you say so!" *Whaaawhoomp*. Tori did a summersault as she flew down from one of the ledges. She held up her index finger and two lightning bolts sparked on the tips. She blew them away and smiled.

Whoosh. Aiden and Blaire emerged from a sea of smoke. Both held a sword lit by flaming blue fire.

Ffffffttttt. Macy flipped over me. She landed with one leg extended and her arm over her head holding a staff with a fiery blue crystal.

"Let's do this, Dementia!" My wand flared and I smiled. She wasn't going to win this time.

"I thought your friends didn't have magic?" Her voice was calm, but her body was anxious.

"You thought wrong. Now, would you still like to do this the hard way or do you agree to my terms and we may be shown the way to the prisons."

"I will die before giving in to you," Dementia snarled.

"As you wish." I gave a look to the others. We all stood in a line and pointed our weapons toward her. Everything began to rumble. The light illuminated the room. I took one final shot to the floor and we disappeared from the room.

"That was so cool!" Tori said.

"We were so awesome," Blaire said in agreement.

"We totally were, but that knockout spell will only work for a while. We have to find these prisons," I said.

"We have to think like Dementia," Macy said. "She was very concerned you would find us, so she must be extra concerned you would find them. I bet they're also in the west corner, just more hidden."

"Maybe I can make a locator spell and then we can find them," I suggested.

"Wouldn't you need a something from that person to find them?" Tori asked.

"I don't know." I thought about who we needed to find, why we needed to find them and where they were at that exact moment.

"It worked. I know where they are, follow me." I began shuffling through the passageway, the rest following behind me.

We passed several guards that weren't a problem. You can't tell someone not to do something if you knock them out.

"This is it, I know it is," I said when we reached a door at the end of the passageway.

"We ran through a hallway being shot at by guards and chased by crows to find a door with no one guarding it?" Blaire asked in exhaustion.

"I know this is it."

"How do we get in?" Aiden asked.

"I'll show you. This will open it." I held my mother's ring out.

"What is that?" Tori asked.

"It's my mother's favorite ring. I guess Dementia didn't think I would have it. It's going to fit in this crevasse to open the door for us." I placed it carefully in the slot. It turned around three times and then the doors creaked open.

"What?" I said.

"Gwendolyn? What happened?" Macy asked. I had no words. Nothing. There was nothing.

"Nobody is in there," Blaire commented.

"How is this possible, maybe you got it wrong?" Aiden said

"No, I couldn't have. They have to be in here somewhere," I reassured him.

Gwendolyn, just keep going. Sometimes things aren't always as clear as you think they are.

The last thing I needed was that new voice. But she did give me a hint.

"Come on, they're in here. We just can't see them yet."

"Are they invisible?" Tori asked.

"Something like that. Just follow me."

"What do we do? Just look around for a trap door or something?" Macy asked.

"I guess. Truthfully, I'm not really sure. They just have to be here." I looked over and saw Blaire was knocking on the bricks. "What are you doing?"

"I saw it in this video game. You knock on the bricks and the sound will be different if one is hollow. The hollow one could be a door or something."

"I didn't know you were into video games," Macy said.

"Oh, um, I'm really not. I just heard about it when I was looking through an article in a magazine."

"I think it could work. Let's all give it a try over here," I suggested. We all lined up against a wall. "On the count of three - one...two...three!" We took our fists and pounded into the brick. It crumbled like a house of cards. On the other side was...light.

"Man, that's bright!" I said hiding my eyes with the back of my hand.

"Yeah, and it doesn't really help that my hands are in severe pain," Macy remarked.

"Well, let's see where it goes. We broke down a wall to find out," Blaire started to walk through it.

"Yeah, remind me how we did that?" Aiden asked.

"I may have used a spell," I grinned.

"Now that makes more sense than my theory of us having this hidden super kid strength that only happens when needed," he joked.

"Come on you guys, something is on the other side of the light," Blaire called to us. We walked into it. It was sort of like what you would picture an angel's bedroom would look like. Lots of ethereal light and cloud like fluff.

"Where is the end of all this?" I asked as we pushed our way through.

"Why don't we ask Blaire? Blaire...Blaire?" Tori called.

"Where is she?" Macy asked.

"Hey, I think I see the end, come on!" Aiden darted ahead. Once we reached the end, we looked all around. It looked sort of what I pictured the Fairytale World would look like. It did seem a little gloomy, but the plants were all green and I could see hints of sunlight.

"Where's Blaire?" I asked.

"I'm right here."

"Where?" Aiden questioned.

"Right...here!" She jumped out of a bush right onto Aiden's back. While he proceeded to scream like a school girl, the rest of us doubled over in laughter.

"Don't ever do that!" he shouted in a high pitched voice.

"Oh, Aiden it was a harmless joke. She was just having fun," I said.

"Why does fun have to scare the crap out of me?"

"Relax, you're fine. Now, back to what we were doing. How do we find these people?" Macy questioned.

"Well, Starletta said she put them in prisons, so where would they be? I'm sure Dementia had plenty of ideas."

"What about the castles? If all of the women are princesses, they would all be in a castle," Blaire suggested.

"That doesn't work. Thumbelina, Rapunzel and Beauty all married into royalty," Tori pointed out.

"I thought Thumbelina was a princess?" Blaire said.

"No, she married into it."

"How do you know so much about fairytales?" I asked Tori.

"It's sort of strange," she laughed. "My mother is a book collector and she bought some Hans Christian Anderson books and this other book by Charles Perrault. She let me read them, so I learned a thing or two."

"That's cool. I didn't know you liked them."

"I've done a few paintings with inspiration from them. Oh, I just got an idea. In a lot of stories, the heroines were trapped at the beginning and then a man comes and saves them. Which, though I love these stories, I think is pretty sexist. But, maybe that's where Dementia put them. After all, in the stories, it seemed like they were pretty miserable in the beginning."

"That's a wonderful idea, Tori," Blaire exclaimed. "Now, let's just think of where they could all be."

"The easier ones are Snow White's castle where she was a servant to her stepmother and Rapunzel who was trapped in her tower," said Macy.

"Where would Beauty's misery be?" Blaire asked.

"I think that would be at her house with her two snotty sisters, right?" Aiden asked.

"I think that's right. Her sisters treated her horribly."

"Sounds good to me. Let's get this show on the road," Aiden said.

"What about your grandfather. He'll worry about us," Macy pointed out.

"I'll send him some sort of telepathic message or something. We're so close, he will receive it. I can provide food, water, shelter and warmth, we'll be fine. I don't think we really have the option of going back out there unless we want to be caught." We started our journey. I hoped that the sleeping spell had worked, at least for a little while longer. I wasn't really sure how long the spell I had put on them would last.

As we walked away I looked back. I swore I saw something, I must have just been imagining it. I sure hoped so.

CHAPTER 13
THE FIRST ONE

"Gwendolyn?" Macy whispered to me as we walked.

"Yeah."

"How's that whole 'new voice' thing going?"

"It's been fine, why?"

"Well, I was just wondering you know. My best friend has voices in her head and most people would take that to mean you're insane. And I'm ok if that's happening also, you know."

I chuckled. "I'm fine Mace. I appreciate that you care, but I am completely okay."

"Okay, just making sure."

"Macy? Gwendolyn? Are you guys ok?" Blaire noticed we were lagging.

"We're great. Macy was just wondering about something," I said. "How far do you think we are from her castle?"

"Well, Aiden's figuring it out. But, last time I checked we were about a woods distance away."

"So, Snow White is going to become your step grandmother in a little while?" Macy said.

"Yeah."

"You get to watch their wedding, it's going to be so romantic! I mean he wakes her up with a kiss. A kiss! Then he carries her off into to his castle and they get married. Oh, it's just so wonderful," Blaire said dreamily.

"Blaire, I didn't know you had the hots for romance. I should set you two up," said Macy jokingly.

"Make fun if you must, but I think it's wonderful. He sweeps her off her feet and they barely even know each other. Then they end up spending the rest of their lives together. That's just so sweet." She did a little spin.

"How are you and your boy doing by the way?" I asked.

"He's a thirteen year old boy. He's sweet, but fairytale romance isn't always their forte."

"Hey, that thirteen year old boy is my stepbrother!" Macy said.

"Girls, come here, I think we're at the castle," Aiden called. The castle was just a few hundred yards ahead of us.

"So what's the plan? How are we going to get this girl out of here?" Blaire asked.

"Well, how about we find her and then we'll think of a plan," I suggested.

"Don't we need a plan before we go in, in case something happens," Tori said.

"Maybe you guys just want a plan so you have an excuse to use those powers again," I said with a smirk.

"We were pretty awesome with them, you have to admit," countered Macy.

"Yeah, you were awesome. Well, here's a mini plan. Since this is just illusion magic, I bet you'll be able to scare away any of the guards. If you can't, use these." I handed them blue, marble sized shining balls. "These are small, but they have a ton of blue dust in them. It's comes out like thick gas and it will temporarily blind them."

"Where did you get these?" Macy asked.

"I was thinking about it as we were walking. Basically, I used the method of a stink bomb and just made it stronger."

"That is so cool," Aiden said.

"I'm going to go and try to find Snow White. Can you guys cover me and make sure no surprises get through?"

"Sir, yes, sir," They all said with an army salute. I giggled before leaving.

In most stories, Snow White was cleaning somewhere in the beginning of the tale. I started a search around the castle and was finally able to spot her out in the courtyard sweeping.

She was older than I expected, in her late twenties, maybe thirty. Then I remembered that she had been here for years. She was frozen in this part of her story, but she probably aged a bit. Trapped here until she dies. Sounds like something the Seven Sins would come up with.

She was just as everyone described her. Her black hair was tucked under a grubby bonnet. She had skin pale as the moon, but with pleasant, rosy cheeks. Even as she worked, she hummed a little cheerful song.

"Who's standing by the entrance?" she asked noticing I was there.

"I'm Gwendolyn," I said coming out into the courtyard.

"Please to meet you Gwendolyn, what may I do for you?" she asked joyfully.

"I wanted to ask you something. Let's sit on the bench and talk." We went over and sat. I looked at her eyes, round and innocent. Fully oblivious to the fact that today her life would change.

"Do you like living here, with your stepmother?"

"Are you one of her maids? Is she making you ask this? If I say the wrong thing, I'll be punished…"

"No, no I'm not working for her. I just really want to know."

"Well. If I'm being sincere, I don't. I hate to say it, even think it, but I'm not happy. She doesn't love me." Snow's eyes fell to the cobblestones. That's when I saw it. She put up with this to try to win her affection. That's all she wanted. It was something she couldn't ever have.

"Would you like to leave?"

"I would. I want to go somewhere outside of these walls. I haven't left in such a long time. Since I was just a girl."

"I'm going to help you. I have some friends that will help us as well. Some of things that will happen may be strange or even scary. But, I promise it will all work out for the best, alright?"

"I understand. Why are you helping me, I don't even know you."

"Well…I'm…"

"Oh, it doesn't matter. You're helping me. I owe you dearly," she said clasping my hands with hers.

"You don't owe me anything, let's clean you up." I spun my fingers and dish of water and a rag appeared. Snow White stared at me in astonishment.

"You possess the Gift!"

"Yes. I was told you were in this situation and that you need some help. So here I am."

"You're so young, it's incredible."

"I suppose it is a little. Here, let's wipe that dirt off your face." I scrubbed off the dirt and dust from her cheeks making them extra rosy. I took off the bonnet and let her hair fall down her back. The wispy strands fell down to her waist. I snapped my fingers and a lip stain was in my hand, which I put on her lips.

"There you go. Now, just continue cleaning. And why don't you sing a little bit too, light and sweet. I'll take care of the rest. Oh, one more thing, where is the queen's room?"

"Well, her bedroom is on the first floor, but her beauty room is up on the second."

"Thank you." I went back into the castle and caught up with everyone. "Did you have any trouble?"

"No, we were fine. But, you will never believe who the Evil Queen is," Macy said.

"Who? Actually, tell me later. I met up with Snow White and now we have to make the Evil Queen really mad. I've come up with a plan, follow me."

We headed to where Snow White had told me - the Evil Queen's beauty room. I knew this was the room that would hold her mirror. I had to find that mirror.

The room itself looked very elegant. It had black marble flooring, a crystal chandelier hung from the ceiling and a huge vanity was up on a stage. Behind the vanity was a satin curtain. I motioned for the others to follow me in and we pulled back the curtain. Behind it was a huge mirror with gold frame and baroque embellishments.

"Nothing is in the mirror. I don't see the face," Tori said.

"Neither do I. That was our clue, what do we do now?" Macy asked me.

"I don't know. What if I make the face? I'll do a spell. I don't know how strong it'll be though or if it'll be permanent."

"She's coming, we have to go," Blaire told us from the door.

"Do it! It doesn't matter how long it works as long as it just lasts enough to convince her," Macy said. I thought about how you could put a person in a mirror. Magic was tricky. Someone created all the spells at one point and then others just copied them. In my case, I had to just search my brain.

"We need something to go into the mirror. I can't just make a person appear out of thin air, remember."

"Hurry, hurry," Blaire repeated.

"What if we use a mask? In some versions I've read, it's not been a face, but a mask. Like a masquerade one," Tori told us.

"I can make that. Here." I made a gold one appear in my hands.

"Now, put that into the mirror."

"Okay." I focused. I had become pretty good with my magic, but for stronger spells I still had to seriously focus.

"Sena, sora, gona, gana, shebeesh!"

The mask was in. "We need to see if it works."

"We don't have time, we have to leave now." We closed the curtain and then I gathered everyone near me. We hid in the bathroom, just as the Evil Queen walked it.

"The Evil Queen is…"

"Yes, it's her," Macy said finishing my thought. "I remembered Starletta mentioning her name. I heard one of her maids say it."

"I can't believe it." I watched as Corona walked over to the mirror. "Ah, my most prized possession. I can't wait to see my glorious complexion in you," she cooed to it. She opened the curtain.

"Ahhhhh!" She screamed. "There's a face in my mirror! I demand you leave my castle this instance," she ordered.

"I can't escape this prison, you clearly see,
But I have a special quality.
If you give me the command,
I'll tell you who's fairest in the land."

"If you can do what you say, then prove yourself!"

"My Queen you have beauty, a great deal so,
But there is another, who is more radiant though,
It doesn't matter if you make her dirty or give her no
   care,
Snow White, by far, is the most fair."

I saw Corona's temper spike. Her face was flushed, her eyes became slits and her knuckles were squeezed so tight they became white.

She yanked on a cord and a maid came rushing in. "What do you need Queen Corona?" The maid asked meekly.

"Where is Snow White?"

"I imagine she would be in the courtyard sweeping, why do you...?" Corona stormed from the room and down the hall. The rest of us followed behind.

Corona was staring down at Snow White in the courtyard. The plan was in motion. This had to get her blood boiling. She wasn't dirty, she wasn't in rags. She looked pretty on the outside and was on the inside. And Corona could see both.

I had just seen Corona mad. But now, now she was *really* mad. She was red all over. Her eyes were so tiny, it looked like they weren't even there. Her fist was so tight it looked like she might break the skin.

She plunged down the stairs into the throne room and slumped onto her throne. She yanked another rope and another maid came in. "Bring me my huntsman now!" she commanded. The huntsman was brought in and he bowed before her. It made me sick. She didn't deserve to be bowed to.

"I want you to take Snow White into the forest and kill her."

"My Queen, she is the princess," the huntsman argued.

"I don't care. I want her gone. And to prove that you killed her, I want her heart. Here is the blade that you shall use." She slid it over to him. It came to a stop under his boot.

"My Queen..."

"You will do this. If not, you *will* pay a price. Am I clear?" He nodded. "Good. Be gone." He bowed before leaving the room. She stayed in her throne, now grinning from ear to ear. I had been wrong. *That* made me sick.

"So what do we do?" Aiden asked when we had left the castle.

"Well, the plan is currently working. We've made the queen jealous. Now what we have to do is make sure that the huntsman feels guilty for Snow White, so he won't kill her," I said.

"Doesn't he already feel bad for her though?" Blaire asked.

"Maybe, but having to face death from a Seven Sin or kill someone and be rewarded. He may choose the latter," I said sadly.

"So how are you going to make him feel sorry?" Macy asked.

"I'm going to put an enchantment on the blade. As he goes to strike, the enchantment will take over and he won't be able to do it."

"Sounds good. We should get some sleep, it'll be a long day tomorrow," Aiden said, getting up from the fire we had made.

"I'm going to stay up for a little bit. I'll be back in a while, don't worry. The rest of you go to bed."

I headed back to the castle and flew around looking for Snow White's room. I found her looking out her window.

"Hi."

"Gwendolyn, you're back. My stepmother was in such a bad mood today. Is that part of your plan to get me out?"

"Yes, I'm sorry if she was horrible to you. But, I promise that it'll be alright."

"I trust you. Why did you come to see me?"

"I wanted to ask you another thing. Do you believe in love?"

She laughed and smiled. "Yes, I do. I want to get married, although I'm a little old by now. I'm happy to wait though. I want true love, my one and only. I'm not the kind of lady who just wants a man for riches. I want to love him for him and I want him to love me for me. Why do you ask?"

"I just wondered."

"Well, I think you'll find someone." I looked at her strange, but she just winked. "I know a good heart when I see one."

"I'll see you tomorrow." I flew out the window and back to our tents. I couldn't help but be happy. It had worked, the plan was working. I was doing it. I could do it.

CHAPTER 14
OFF TO THE DWARF'S COTTAGE

"Hey Blaire, you woke up. We were about to send Aiden in to kiss you," Macy said as Blaire came out yawning.

"Shut up! I needed beauty sleep. Lots of things are going on and I want to be refreshed."

"Regardless, we're all awake and we have to get moving. Is everyone clear on the plan as we discussed?" I asked.

"We're waiting for your say so boss," said Macy.

"Let's go." We headed up to the castle and I put an invisibility spell on everyone to make sure we would go undetected. We found the huntsman and we followed him out as he prepped his bag. Making sure he wasn't watching, I used levitation to lift the knife out of his satchel and bring it to me.

"Okay Macy, hold this while I enchant it," I instructed.

She held it out for me as I did the spell. "We're good." I floated it back over to his satchel and placed it in. "Okay, now we just have to make sure everything else goes well," I explained.

"And if it doesn't?" Tori asked.

"We'll figure it out." We watched as he went and asked Snow White to come with him hunting. She eagerly agreed and we followed them out to the woods. They went to that place where we had last camped.

"Huntsman, shouldn't we go somewhere where more animals are? I don't see any here."

"Trust me, they'll come." Snow White went over to a rock and began to sing. This was perfect. The more innocent she seemed, the better this would work.

He reached into his satchel and pulled out the blade. He got closer and closer to her. "Gwendolyn, he's getting really close," Blaire said nervously.

"Just be patient, it'll kick in."

"Gwendolyn, I think Blaire's right. He's two inches from her!"

"Trust me, it'll work." I never took my stare from the blade. I was putting her life at risk, but it would work. I knew it would. I saw his hand began to tremble and his walk became slower. He was losing his confidence. I let out a small breath when he dropped the dagger.

Snow White turned around and gasped at the dagger lying in the grass.

"My Princess, please find it in your heart to forgive me. The queen wishes you dead, but I cannot kill you."

"I owe you a debt of gratitude for sparing my life."

"Run into the forest, never come back. If you do, she will kill you. Run - run now." He waved off toward the forest.

"Will the queen punish you?" she asked him.

"Do not worry about me. Just go and hide." She nodded once before fleeing into the forest.

"Okay, you follow her into the woods and I'll take care of him. Make sure she goes towards the dwarfs' cottage." I handed Tori the map.

"Where did you get this?" she asked.

"Last night I was thinking over the plan and I summoned that book we found the first day we came here. I found maps for the different stories. Just follow this and I'll meet up with you as soon as I can." They set off into the woods. Using my wand, I transformed my grimy clothing into a sparkling purple dress with wide false wings and a flower crown.

"Excuse me, huntsman?" I called as I floated towards him. His jaw fell as he saw me. "How may I service you, fairy?" he asked bowing.

"I saw what a kind act you did for that girl. I would like to repay your services." I bit the inside of my cheek to stop from smiling.

"To make sure your queen does not lose her temper, I give you the heart of a humble deer in place of the girl's. It is enchanted and will fool the queen for a short time. Give it to her and then get out of this place. This orb will lead you to an exit. Go through it and it will get you safely out of a dungeon into another version of this world. I also give you this bag. Go to the town of Rosemoor. There, find Wilhelmina, and give it to her. You both will find happiness." I tossed him the objects.

"Bless you kind fairy, I will do as you ask." He took the items and ran off. I grinned. I had killed two birds with one stone. Now I had to go and find the others.

It didn't take long to find them. They were a just little ways behind Snow White.

"Has she found the cottage yet?" I asked.

"She's close. What's that outfit you're wearing?" Macy asked.

"I had to close a deal with the huntsman. It was part of my disguise."

"You look like the sugar plum fairy," Aiden snorted.

"Hey, he bought it."

"How do we get her to go in?" Blaire asked.

"We need something to give her a hint," Macy said. "Like have an animal guide her or something."

"Any volunteers?" I asked.

"I'll do it," Tori said. I tapped my wand on her head. Blue dust fell over her and changed her into a sparrow.

"Just get her to go inside and then come back here," I told her. She gave me a little tweet to say she understood. She flew over to Snow White and fluttered around her until she looked up.

"Yes, little birdie?" Tori motioned to the cottage with a tip of her wing. "You want me to follow you?" Tori flapped her wings. Snow White followed her over to the door of the cottage and pushed it open.

"Do you want me to go inside?" Snow White asked. Tori chirped.

"When do we execute the next part of the plan?" Tori asked when she was back in her human form.

"When the dwarfs return, I'll turn us invisible. Then we'll go inside and make sure they let her stay. That's how we'll enter and exit the house, they won't see us at all."

"So, we're going to camp in the woods again I'm guessing?" Blaire said.

"Unless you've found a hotel, the answer is yes," Macy said.

"I'm just saying, we should upgrade our living conditions. We know a girl who could do it."

"We're supposed to be as hidden as possible. I don't want the Seven Sins to see us, find us, anything. We have to be completely off the grid," I said.

"Actually, how are the Seven Sins in the other Fairytale World *and* here? The last time we saw them they were in the dungeon," Aiden said.

"Well, this is their greatest scheme ever. They've trapped these people in the worst parts of their stories until they wither away and die. They would want to watch them suffer," I explained my theory.

"Why haven't they attacked us then?" Macy wondered aloud.

"What?" I asked.

"They have to know we're here. They may be psychos, but they're not stupid. Why haven't they come after us?"

"Gwendolyn's with us, they won't attack us as long as we're with her," Blaire concluded.

"It didn't stop Dementia from sending that storm. And they had the chance to get us when we were in the woods while Gwendolyn was with the huntsman. It's just strange, I'm getting one of my feels and they're rarely wrong. This doesn't feel right."

"Let's not jinx our good luck. We have some of Gwendolyn's portable blinding orbs with us if we're alone. In a worst case scenario, we just run," Tori told us.

"Look, the dwarfs. They're coming," Blaire pointed. We saw the line of short, bearded men marching in a line toward the house, pickaxes in tow.

"Here we go." We closed into a circle and I turned us invisible. We followed the dwarf line right into the house.

"Someone has been in our house!" A dwarf with glasses cried.

"They've eaten some of our bread," another said.

"And some of our apples," said one more.

"I bet they're still in the house," the glasses wearing dwarf said. The seven of them began searching around the house. "Something is in this bed," one of them said. He was smaller than the rest and his shirt was too big. They all crowded around the bed and then pulled down the covers. Snow White was sleeping peacefully.

"It's a girl!" the dwarfs exclaimed.

This awoke her. She looked up, startled. "Who are you?"

"The question is who are *you?* You're the one in *our* house," one of the dwarfs said grumpily.

"I am Snow White. I'm terribly sorry for intruding. But my mother, the queen, is trying to kill me and I needed a place to stay. Please let me stay here, I have nowhere else to go. I'll make sure that I won't make any messes and I'll even cook if you'd like." The dwarfs went over into a huddle and began a series of whispers. "Welcome to the cottage Miss Snow White," they all said as one. Snow White went over and gave them a joyful hug. I nodded to the others and we left the cottage.

"Well, that worked out wonderfully. She gets to stay," I said.

"It's amazing what guys will do for girls," Blaire said with a laugh.

"Whatever do you mean," I said in a phony voice.

"Oh come on, she's gorgeous. Guys will do just about anything for pretty girls, in my opinion anyway," she stated.

"Do you think that's true Aiden?" I asked.

"Yeah, in some ways, I'll admit it. It depends on the girl though. But, we'll also do anything for girls we care about."

"Aww, that's sweet," Tori said.

"So, what do we do now. It's not very late," Macy said.

"I'm going to go for a walk," I said.

"Gwendolyn, can I come with you?" Tori asked getting up.

"Sure, if you want."

We walked in silence for a while. She had something on her mind, she kept twirling her hair.

"Is something bothering you Tori?" I finally asked.

"Well…it's this problem that I have been keeping secret for a long time."

"Do you want to talk with me about it?"

"Yes, that's why I asked to come. I've never told anyone this and for now let's keep it between you and me."

"Alright."

"I don't live with my mom or dad, I live with my grandma. My mom is a flight attendant and my dad is an archaeologist, so they travel a lot. I don't tell a lot of people because, one, it's not their business and, two, I like to keep it private. To cope with them not being around a lot, I found peace with art. What I'm trying to get at here is…I don't see my parents much and my grandma has been thinking it's time to get a new house. So…maybe we'd move here."

"You want to stay?"

"Well…possibly. My grandma has been saying that the condo we live in is just not the right fit anymore. She works as a small time photographer and would like somewhere more scenic, so she could work out of the house. I know it's crazy, but maybe it wouldn't be half bad."

"Tori, are you sure this is what you want? You wouldn't be able to go back and forth without a portal. And those can be very hard to find. Actually, almost impossible right now."

"Aren't you staying?" I bit the inside of my lip. "I overheard you talking to Starletta. I didn't eavesdrop. I thought I heard something, so I looked out and saw you two talking."

"Its fine, I know you didn't mean to and I don't know if I am. I don't know if I want to. It's very complex."

"I get it. You have a lot of pressure. I shouldn't burden you with my problems." She started to walk away. I stopped her.

"I didn't know how hard it was for you, but here's something I'll share with you. I don't know where my mom is. I haven't ever known. She disappeared a few days after I was born. It's one of the reasons I want to stay. No one has found her in the Modern World, maybe she could be here."

"Oh my gosh."

"Yeah, it's pretty heavy. I just thought you might like to know. We should be getting back, they'll wonder where we are."

"Gwendolyn?"

"Yeah?"

"You're going to find her you know. I've read enough fairytales to know everyone gets a happy ending." I smiled at her. I saw Tori differently now. She always seemed timid, smart, but a follower. To want to move to an entirely new place with very different people was very brave, very bold. Very heroic.

CHAPTER 15
COMPLICATED

The next day we were up early. We had to prepare for the long day ahead.

"So let's review. I checked and Corona has asked the mirror who is the fairest and it's still Snow White, of course. After the dwarfs leave, she will come in her first disguise to kill Snow White. We have to make sure that the dwarfs get back in time to save her, got it?"

"Got it."

"Affirmative."

"Understood."

"Gotcha."

"Let's do this." Back into our invisible forms, went inside. A few hours later, Corona showed up in her first cover. It was a long purple dress with a large bag on her shoulder. Her nose looked bigger and her hair was brown instead of red. She knocked on the door and Snow White came out.

"May I help you with something, miss?" Snow White asked.

"I be sellin' pretty things for pretty girls."

"What sort of things?"

"Oh, ribbons, bows, laces, everything for pretty dresses. Oh, you have such a wonderful waist. So tiny and petite, you must try this bodice." She pulled out a bodice from the bag. It was a very light yellow with gold ribbon to lace up the back.

"It is very nice," Snow White said admiring it.

"Turn around an' I will show you what it looks like on." Snow White turned around and Corona placed the bodice on her. We saw as she pulled tighter and tighter.

"That's a little tight," she wheezed.

"It will make you look so flattering though," Corona said.

"I…can't…" Snow White fell to the floor.

Corona smiled triumphantly. She laughed as she fled the scene. I turned Aiden into a deer and sent him off to find the dwarfs.

Soon, he came back with the dwarfs running behind him. I quickly turned him invisible and we turned our attention back to the dwarfs.

"Hurry, cut the ribbon," a dwarf said. One pulled out a pocket knife. He began cutting loose the ribbons that were fastened to her body.

"Snow White, what happened?" the dwarfs asked. She told them about how a woman had come to the door selling things. She tried on a bodice and it became too tight and she fainted.

"She could have just accidently tied it too tightly, but it also could have been the queen is disguise trying to kill you. Don't open the door to anyone but us from now on," the dwarfs warned.

"I won't," she promised. The dwarfs went back to work and Snow White began her cleaning. I checked again and Corona was outraged the dwarfs were able to revive her.

"She's going to come back again. Get ready," I told the others. And I was the right. A few hours later, there was another knock on the door. When Snow White opened the door, Corona was in another disguise. Her skin was several shades darker and her eyes looked smaller. She wore an orange sparkling veil and an oriental looking dress.

"May I help you?" Snow White asked. She only opened the door a crack.

"I have been on a long journey. May I please rest?"

"I cannot let you in, but you may rest outside." She sat down the cart she had been holding.

"You have such pretty hair. You must have a lovely brush to make your hair so fine," Corona said.

"No, I do not have a brush."

"I sell many things for beauty, such as brushes. I'd be happy to show you some." Snow White nodded excitedly. Corona pulled out a selection of brushes from the cart. Snow White's eyes locked on a copper one with encrusted emeralds.

"That is one of my best brushes," Corona said noticing her. "You must let me comb your hair with it."

"I can't open the door for anyone."

"I'll just stand by the doorway. Don't open it much and I'll brush it from there."

"That would be lovely."

"Turn around." Snow White turned around in the small space of the doorway. Corona placed the comb on her hair. As soon as the comb touched her scalp, she fainted to a lifeless form on the wood floor.

"Let's see if they can bring you back from this one," Corona taunted. She cackled with maniacal laughter as she left.

I turned Macy into a squirrel and sent her off to fetch the dwarfs. When they saw Snow White, they frantically tried to wake her. One noticed the comb in her hair and tugged it out. She told them about how an Asian woman selling hair brushes combed her hair, but she never opened the door more than a crack.

"It was that dastardly queen again, I reckon. If she comes again, and she will, don't open the door at all," the dwarfs instructed.

"I promise. The door won't open for anyone but you."

The dwarfs headed back to work for the second time and we stayed and waited. And waited. I was about to tell the others we should leave and come back in the morning, when I saw through the window something moving up toward the cottage.

"Hello, hello. Would you like to buy my apples? They're red and juicy?" a voice sang. Snow White looked around at the empty dinner plates.

She cautiously opened the window. Outside stood an old woman with a rosy round face and childlike eyes. "Hello miss, would you like to buy some of my apples?"

"They do look delicious, but I can't. I have no money to pay you with."

"Well, how about we split one, free of charge." She pulled out an apple from her basket and cut it in half.

Snow White looked at the apple in her hands. "You wouldn't want to hurt my feelings that you didn't like my apples would you?" the woman asked.

Snow White brought the slice to her lips and took a bite. She let out a hushed gasp and dropped the apple. The thud of her body was unheard over the sound of Corona's cry of joy. "*I am the fairest. And always will be!*" She echoed the chant as she vanished from the cottage.

This time I didn't send anyone. This time we sat there. The dwarfs came home whistling a jolly tune, until they saw their beloved Snow White. They looked around her for something, anything, to wake her up. When they couldn't find anything, fourteen pairs of eyes filled with tears as they came to accept that she was dead.

They placed her on a bed for the night and then all found other places to sleep.

We left the cottage, our work was done. And I couldn't watch any longer.

"Did you see how sad they were? It was so heartbreaking," Blaire sniffled as we sat around the fire.

"It was so depressing. Tomorrow, we have to watch the funeral," Aiden said.

"How will your grandfather get here?" Tori asked as she wiped her eyes with the back of her hand.

"I'm going to teleport him here, I guess. I'm sure he's been wondering how we've all been."

"You didn't tell him?" Macy asked.

"We've been kinda busy."

"I suppose. Is anyone going to stay up a little longer? If no one is, I'm putting the fire out," Macy announced.

"I'll stay up a little longer," Aiden said.

"I will, too," I said.

"Have fun," Macy said tiredly.

"Not too much though," Blaire warned playfully. The three girls went into their tents.

"So, how has it been with Blaire, since the last time we talked," I asked after some awkward silence.

"Umm…we actually broke up."

"What?"

"We broke up. It wasn't bad or anything. She said she doesn't want to be in a relationship now. At first I was a little upset about that, but then she said that she has been having some issues with some things, personal things. So I backed off. If it's family issues, then it's her business, not mine."

"That's very kind of you to respect her privacy."

"I've had my share of family problems. I got a great stepsister out of the deal though. And a great stepmom and a pretty good friend." He nudged me a little with his elbow.

"You're a pretty good friend, too."

"Look, there is something I wanted to tell you. I know you told me to go out with Blaire. I did have a good time, but I also had a good time with you and…"

"Aiden…"

"Please let me finish. I just wanted to say you're a wonderful girl and I know I'm not the guy. But, I know that you'll pick an amazing one, because that's the kind you deserve."

"Thank you."

"I do have something else to ask."

"What?"

"Did you like me before we went to the dance?"

"Yeah, I did. I had liked you for over a year before the dance happened."

"It's definitely the wrong time to say this, but I liked you, too. It's why at the movies, I just had to ask Macy about you. She convinced me to ask you to the dance."

"I never knew she did that for me."

"Yeah, she really cares about you."

There was a little silence after that. I had never known that Aiden liked me until now. After I had gotten over my crush. A perfect time to make things complicated.

"Nothing is going to happen with us now, huh?" he asked.

"I don't think so. I'm Blaire's friend now and…I've grown out of my crush. I'm sorry. Maybe in the future possibly, but right now…it won't work."

"That's what I was thinking. Hey, you were honest with me, I respect that. I'll put out the fire, you go to bed."

"Okay."

I went to bed with confused feelings. Aiden told me he had liked me. Words I had wanted to hear for a long time. I turned him down. He wasn't what I wanted. I didn't know *who* I wanted. I was thirteen. I didn't need Prince Charming. I had whole lifetime of liking, loving and kissing before I would. I was in a fairytale, but I didn't live one. And it made me the coolest princess ever.

CHAPTER 16
THE COOLEST 13 YEAR OLDS

The coffin was beautiful. I had heard the dwarfs working on it all night. It was a shining rose gold with a glass lid. Bright wildflowers were laid around its edges and a bouquet of forget-me-nots was placed in her hands.

She looked so stunning. Her hair was shining almost as bright as the gold, her lips and cheeks were a romantic shade of pink. I had changed her rags into a cream white dress with lace on the cuffs and collar. She was so peaceful. I couldn't help but cry both tears of joy and sadness.

"When is your grandfather going to show up?" Macy asked me.

"Oh, I have to get him here. Make sure nothing comes up." I went pretty far out into the forest. This spell would be harder to do. Moving an object was one thing, moving a person was another.

After I had focused myself for what seemed like a year, my grandfather was standing in front of me.

"Darling, I was so worried. When you didn't come back out, I assumed that you had found the prison. But then I thought maybe you had been captured. I couldn't get in contact with you," he said hugging me.

"Don't worry, everyone's alright. But you have to come with me. I've found your true love."

"What?"

"I've found her. But, you have to know you love her. If you don't, please walk away."

"How will I know?"

"I can't tell you. Go in that direction and you will find a coffin covered with flowers. Some little men should be standing by it weeping. Ask them who's in the coffin and if they'll lift the top for you. Take this horse." A white steed appeared in front of him, dressed in a saddle and reins. "Now go, hurry." Grandfather speed off on the horse to where Snow White was. I transported myself back to where everyone else was hiding. "Is he here?" Tori asked.

"He's coming, he should be here shortly." Soon, we heard the sound of hooves and I saw my grandfather coming toward us. He climbed down from the horse and walked over to the coffin. "She's so lovely, what happened to her?" he asked a dwarf with a large nose.

"She's dead. The queen poisoned her," he choked.

"Can you lift the lid, please. I must see her closer," he pleaded. The dwarfs wavered, but gave in. They went over and lifted the lid. The sunshine landed on her face making it glow. Grandfather looked down at her and stroked her cheek with his thumb.

"He's going to do it, he's going to kiss her," Blaire whispered giddily. We watched as he knelt down onto his knees and lifted her up, bracing her body and head with his forearm and hand. He gently pressed his lips onto hers. He pulled away from her and laid her back on the coffin. He stood back up. We held our breath.

"Wha…" we all silently screamed. She was awake!

"It's you!" Grandfather said breathlessly.

"It's you," Snow White said softly.

"You're the one, my true love. Please, let me have the honor of making you my wife."

"You don't even know my name."

"It doesn't matter, I know I love you. I've known enough love to know what pure love is. You're more pure and true and wonderful than I ever thought I could find. Share with me a lifetime." He intertwined their fingers together and was down on one knee. He pulled the ring my mother had given him from his finger and held it up to her. I had only known Snow White for a couple days now, but she never smiled as big and as bright as she did when she saw that ring.

"Yes, yes, I'll marry you…"

"Snow White Stardon. That sounds perfect," He kissed her again and lifted her onto the horse. "Thank you so much, kind dwarfs. I'll never forget you," Snow White said as they started to ride off.

"Did you tell Aaron and Snow White each other's names?" Macy asked.

"No. I guess they just knew. Love can make you believe in crazy things."

I met them out in the forest. "Guinevere, I found her! This is Snow White, my bride to be," grandfather said with a huge grin.

"Wait, Guinevere? You're the girl I met back at my stepmother's castle. You're Gwendolyn."

"Yes, I am that girl. I am a fairy and I helped you two get together. Also, I'm his granddaughter."

"Well, thank you. I will never be able to thank you enough for helping me find my true love." she hugged grandfather's torso.

"It's what I do. I need to get you back to safety. I want you two back at Stardon Castle. I'll transport you out of the dungeon with this dust I made. Wish for anything with it. It will be your wedding present since I can't be there."

"Wait, you're not coming back to see us get married?" Snow White asked.

"I can't, I have to help other people. People who are in a position like you were. I can't abandon them."

"Then we'll wait. We'll wait until all of this is settled and then we'll have the wedding. It will give us a chance to learn more about each other." He intertwined his fingers with Snow White.

"All right, as long as you're okay with that," I asked Snow White.

"I would like nothing more than for you to be there," Snow White said with a warm smile.

"I'll see you then. Goodbye." I spun my hands around and watched as they faded away back to the castle.

"How did it go?" Macy asked.

"I sent them to Stardon Castle. They have some magic for food and stuff, so they'll be fine."

"Aren't you going back for the wedding?" Blaire asked.

"No. They're going to wait and have the wedding after we've finished our work."

"I still can't believe it. They haven't even known each other a day, not even an hour, and they're engaged. This marriage seems shaky," Aiden complained.

"My parents got married early. They had only known each other eight months and they're still together," Tori noted.

"I don't know when my parents got married," I said looking at my feet.

"Haven't you asked your dad?" Macy questioned.

"I don't think he would know. David's not my dad."

"What! How?"

"I'm about to dump a big bombshell on you guys," I warned.

"Then do it."

"Uncle Thomas is my father. When my mom disappeared, he gave me to David who is one of his oldest and most trusted friends. He changed my name to Gwendolyn Star so if anyone came after me they would be looking for a Guinevere. Then he left. I don't know where he went, but he did it because he thought if he hung around something might happen to me. Once his memory started coming back is when he came back into my life."

No one said anything or really even moved. Their jaws hung open and their eyes were wide. I was surprised this shocked them more than the other stuff I had told them.

"Your uncle is your dad?" Aiden said breaking the ice.

"Yes."

"Your uncle is your dad!" he repeated.

"Yes, I stated that."

"How…how did you find out about this?" Blaire asked.

"Well, in the dream I had where I saw Starletta, I walked through a hall in Stardon Castle. The one we walked through. One side had all the pictures of the kings and the other had the all the queens. When I found my mom, I saw that the king she was married to was Thomas."

"I knew that picture of your dad looked off," Macy said.

"Yeah. So, I've just started learning about my real family history. And I haven't really learned much about my mom, but I know that for almost thirteen years she's been missing. And no one can seem to find her in that world, maybe she's in this one."

"Are you going to look for her?" Blaire asked looking concerned.

"Wait, Macy and Tori know my feelings about wanting to see her. Blaire knows my feelings about this place. Starletta does, too, but how 'bout I clue you all in now. I've been thinking about staying. Not because I want to be apart from you all, but because…I am a fairy. I'm not like every other thirteen year old kid. I have magic and lots of it. Here I wouldn't have to hide that or worry about someone seeing me. My parents might have to start ruling again. And my mom, she has to be here, she just has to be. I don't know what will happen, but I want you all to know that if I do decide to stay that I will visit. I'll see you for your birthdays and holidays and art shows and baseball games and I'll go shopping with you and have sleepovers. It may be less than what it used to be, but if any fairy can do it, it's gonna be me. I will see you, I promise."

Macy snorted. "Gwendolyn, Guinevere, whatever you want to call yourself. Yes, you're not a normal thirteen year old, but neither are we. I can have very real magical dreams. Blaire is also a fairy and related to Thumbelina. Tori is Alice's niece. And Aiden is a nephew to Rapunzel, which means that I am a step niece to Rapunzel. We're all pretty non normal, but we're non normal together and that means we stick together." She held my hand and thrust it into the air. "Now, let's go finish this quest!"

We all laughed. We laughed like how we would what seemed like ages ago when we didn't know any of this. Like when our lives were typical. When Aiden had his first concert for a paying crowd, Blaire and Macy were patching up their relationship and Tori and I were becoming friends. It all seemed so long ago, like years had passed since we had all came here.

That life seemed so boring. Now we were fighting fairies and restoring fairytales. We were being invisible and using magic.

We were the coolest thirteen year olds ever.

CHAPTER 17
A BEAST NAMED ANDREW

"So where is Beauty's house?" Tori questioned. We had travelled to Rosemoor the night before after saying our goodbyes to my grandfather and Snow White.

"It should be somewhere here in Rosemoor. Marybella's mother is Beauty's sister and they lived there," I told her.

"How far is Rosemoor from here?" Macy wondered.

"It should be a ways that way," Aiden said as he pointed. "According to the map."

"I never knew Beauty had two sisters," Blaire said.

"Yeah. In the original story by Jeanne Marie Leprince de Beaumont, Beauty's family is wealthy until the father loses his fortune and they have to move into a small cabin in the forest. The sisters treat Beauty like a slave and make her do the housework," Macy told her.

"Wait, I'm getting déjà vu," Aiden said scratching his head sarcastically.

"The father has to go on a trip and asks his daughters what they want. The sisters want fine clothes and jewelry, but all Beauty wants is a simple rose. As the merchant is coming back with no money, he sees a castle. He is invited in where he eats a wonderful meal and stays the night. As he is about to leave the next morning, he saw some rosebushes and picks one for Beauty. As he does, a menacing beast comes out and threatens to kill him unless he brings Beauty back to his castle to live with him. The father tells his daughters and Beauty tells him she'll agree to the demand. So, she goes and lives in the mysterious palace with the beast. He asks her to marry him, but she says no because she doesn't love him. Finally, she asks to go see her family, but she must return or the beast will die. She goes and her sisters trick her into staying longer hoping the beast will be angry with her. When Beauty goes back to the castle she finds beast among the roses dying. She sobs for him and tells him she loves him and will marry him. Her tears bring him back to life and he becomes a handsome prince. And, of course, then they live happily ever after," Macy explained.

"Wow, you know a lot about that story," said Tori.

"It's a favorite of mine," Macy says sheepishly. "My mother would read it to me when I was younger. She said she always felt connected to the characters. Boy, did she hit that one on the nose."

"Well, you're going to be a lot of help since you know the story best. And you'll get to meet your family," I tell her.

"I'm excited for it. I get to meet my grandma,"

"And your great aunt," Blaire pointed out.

"Yeah, I'm a little intimidated. She is going to be a queen," Macy said.

"Don't be nervous, my grandmother is going to be a queen, too. And Beauty is one of the nicest and smartest princesses," I said to her.

"Well, if we do want to see your great aunt, then we better get moving," Aiden said.

"Can't you teleport us, Gwendolyn?" Blaire asked.

"I don't know. I'm starting to get good at it, but that's with objects. With humans, it takes a while and I don't know how well it will work."

"It's going to get dark in a couple hours. If we want some spare time than we need a much better alternative to walking," Macy said.

"I can try," I channeled my magical energy and we were plopped down into the town.

"Just work on the landings," Blaire smirked.

"I'll second that," Aiden agreed.

"It's so depressing here," Macy said looking around.

"Everyone looks so sad," Tori observed.

"We need to know where Beauty's house is, who do we ask? The Seven Sins probably have it on lockdown," Blaire said.

"I guess we'll just have to ask anybody, someone must know," I said with a sigh. "Excuse me sir, do you know where a girl named Beauty lives?" I asked a weary man. He was old and his wobbling hands weakly held a walking stick.

"She lives with her father and sisters. Follow the path that leads out of town until you get to the creek. Turn right and the creek will lead you to the house," he said in a scratchy voice.

"Thank you so much." Just before we left, I turned the stick into a fine cane with carefully done carvings of mountains and animals. It shimmered slightly and would make his back feel better. He was about to say something, but I stopped him. "You just take care of yourself and give these to your wife." I handed him a bunch of daisies. He smiled at me and tipped his patchy hat before heading down the road.

"How did you know he had a wife?" Tori asked.

"I sensed it. It's one of the things I've noticed I can do. I also knew he had terrible back pain. That's why I made the cane charmed to help it feel better."

"That is so sweet," Blaire said.

"Well, these people have done nothing to the Seven Sins. They put them in this place to dictate and torment. It's stupid. And I couldn't stand to see that old man pay for it. Or anyone else for that matter."

"That's really noble. This isn't even your kingdom and you're sticking up for them." Macy laid her arm across my shoulders and squeezed.

"Thanks Mace. We should be trying to find Beauty's house before it gets too dark, so we can get some work done." We walked down the path until we found the creek and turned right following the man's instructions.

Beauty's house was quaint. It was a log cabin with a rickety wood fence making a lane to the door. It looked similar to the picture in the Grimm's' Fairy Tales. There was a well near the house. A girl came out of the house that looked similar to Macy's mom. It was Marybella's mother.

"Beauty, get out here!" she yelled.

"I'm coming Martha," Beauty said in a soft voice. Beauty was petite. She had wide, brown eyes with brown curly hair very similar to Macy's.

"Well, come faster. I want my water," Martha whined. Beauty was obedient and lowered the bucket into the well. Once it was filled, she hauled it out. She was a small thing and not very

tall. The bucket seemed far too heavy for her. I didn't expect
Martha to help. She didn't.

"Take it into the house," she barked. Again Beauty did as
she was told. She said nothing, but I saw her lower her head as
she passed Martha.

"My grandma is one rotten sister," Macy mumbled.

"Let's go," I whispered. I enchanted us to be invisible as
we walked inside.

"Beauty, get me some more bread," the other sister
snapped. She was chunkier than Martha and appeared shorter.

"We have no more, Natasha," Beauty said meekly.
Natasha smashed her fist into the table. "What do you mean we
have no more?" She growled.

"We ran out two days ago," Beauty said even quieter.

"Well, then get me something else to eat. Go!" Beauty
hurried into the kitchen.

"We never had this problem when were wealthy," Martha
said irritably.

"If we didn't have Beauty we would save a lot," Natasha
said in agreement.

"Maybe we could ship her off to a work house," Martha
said with a high pitched laugh. I saw Beauty standing near the
doorway. She brushed a tear from her eye. Macy saw it, too. If
looks could kill, Martha would be dead.

Beauty came out silently and set a plate in front of
Natasha. "Go start on the washing," she told her as she shoved
food into her mouth. Beauty headed outside as the girls continued
to make fun of her.

"I think Macy and I should be the only ones who go," I
told the others.

"I agree, you need to be there and this is Macy's family,"
Blaire said.

"We'll stay in here and pick up on any interesting
conversation," Tori told us. Macy and I followed Beauty to the
creek.

She sobbed as she washed the clothes. I changed us out of
our invisible state and gave us some wings. I nudged Macy.
"Excuse me?" she said.

Beauty whipped her eyes and turned around. "Yes?"

"We're here to help you. This is my friend Gwendolyn and my name is Macy."

"How are you going to help me?" she sniffled.

Macy looked over to me. "We know you're picked on by your sisters. I'm a fairy, as is Macy. We know you have a wonderful heart and you shouldn't be treated that way. We want to make sure you get the life that you really deserve."

"How?"

"We can't tell you, but just know some strange things might happen. But, I promise everything will work out for the best." I smiled sweetly at her and she smiled at me. It was the first time she looked anything other than sad.

"Will I see you again?" Beauty asked.

"Possibly, we'll be watching. Your suffering is about to end." I floated us into the air and whisked us away.

We flew around a little bit before I landed us a little ways from the house. We watched Blaire, Aiden and Tori sneak out.

"Hey, how did it go with Beauty?" Blaire asked us.

"Good, we told her that some weird things were going to happen, but that everything is going to work out," Macy said.

"Remind me why are we telling them this would happen?" Aiden asked. I thought about it. I didn't really have a good answer. It just seemed like they should know why this happened to them. It wasn't about recognition, but I had gone through a lifetime without answers. I didn't want to make these people wonder, too.

"I guess it's because if something wonderful happened to me, all of a sudden, when my life was terrible, I would want to know why."

"Good enough."

"Anyway, did you guys get any information from the sisters?" Macy asked.

"We heard them talking about the Prince of Rosemoor and how this lady was going to ask for his hand in marriage again," Tori recited.

"Did you get the lady's name?" I asked.

"It was Lexia," Aiden said. "And judging by your face she is not a good person."

"Lexia is one of the Seven Sins," I explained.

"We have to deal with another one," Blaire groaned.

"I didn't know Lexia was in love with the Beast," Tori said.

"I guess she is. We have to get to that castle and see them. And I have a new way of getting there." I raised everyone up into the air. "Levitation powers," I grinned.

"We need to travel this way more often," Aiden said grinning from ear to ear.

"Totally," Tori said doing a flip.

"Just follow me." We went high above the tops of houses. When I looked down, it looked like a dollhouse town with little figurines.

"There's the castle," Tori pointed. We veered and landed just outside. I saw a woman walking up to the doors. I couldn't deny she was pretty. Her light blonde hair was pulled in a long braid down her back. She was wearing a satin green cape.

"Why do you wish to pass?" One of the guards at the door asked.

"I'm here to see him. He knows why." The guard opened the door for her. I motioned for the others to follow. "What is your business..." I blew some dust in his face and we rushed in through the door.

The castle was very grand with stained glass windows and statues between them. Grey flooring lined the hallway.

We followed Lexia into a room which I guessed was maybe the Grand Hall. It had a gigantic chandelier hanging from the ceiling.

"Hello Andrew," Lexia said seductively. Andrew was sitting on his throne. He looked unimpressed that Lexia was there. She bowed before him and placed a rose at his feet.

"Andrew, once more, I bring you a single rose and ask for your hand in marriage. Share with me a love that will be unbreakable." She stood back up.

"Lexia, I have told you once before that I cannot marry you. I do not love you," Andrew said calmly. Lexia tensed.

"Is there another woman?" she asked.

"You ask me this every month. You are the only woman from outside the castle that I see personally. Any other visitors my advisors accompany me to see."

"Andrew, I am not stupid. You have rejected me for two years now. There must be something that is holding you back."

Andrew stared her down. And she stared back. "A fairy once told me that after a great crisis, I will find my one true love. She told me she would be the one who would see beyond my flaws. You are not her. You don't care about the people or me. You hurt them. Those are the reasons I won't marry you."

I saw Lexia become very still. Nothing moved. Even the birds became silent. Lexia picked up the rose, climbed the stairs up to Andrew and stood less than an inch from him. She placed her hand on his shoulder and pressed her mouth against his. She crushed the rose into his hand. "Something so beautiful will now become your biggest disappointment?" Green mist swirled around Andrew. The chandelier's lights went out. Andrew's appearance began to change. He grew three times his size and hair sprouted over his body. His small nose became a large snout. His fingernails became claws and we saw fangs as he roared in pain.

Lexia vanished as Andrew began his transformation. The only thing that showed she has been there was that rose. A petal broke off and fluttered down to one of the steps.

"Time to go," I said. We rushed out of the Grand Hall.

"That was pretty harsh of her, don't you think?" Aiden said.

"Yeah. I know he rejected her, but he doesn't love her. He can't help that," Blaire said.

"Shouldn't we be getting back to Beauty's house?" Tori asked.

"We're not staying there," I said casually.

"Where are we staying then?" Macy wondered.

"I thought we would stay here. Most of the events are going to happen here, so I figured that it would just be easier."

"I think it sounds wonderful," Blaire said.

"I would be a nice change of scenery," said Tori.

"Let's find some rooms then." We quietly ran up the stairs and picked out some small, unnoticeable rooms.

"Will Andrew find us?" Macy asked.

"I'm sure he won't, but just in case I'll make a spell so only we can see the doors," I told her.

"Let's get some rest and start fresh tomorrow morning," Tori said.

"Yeah, that sounds great."

"Gwendolyn?" Macy said a while after we had gone to bed. "Are you awake?"

"Yeah," I said.

"I can't sleep."

"I've been having trouble, too."

"Can we talk?"

"Sure, about what?"

"Have you heard from Dementia lately?"

"No. I wish I had though."

"Why?"

"I don't like not knowing what she's plotting."

"Can you contact her?"

"I haven't figured out how. I think my mom stumbled upon one of her secrets though."

"What did she find?"

"She had found out about a bottle. It would prove rumors about something really bad that someone did. I'm pretty sure it's Dementia, but I don't what that bottle holds."

"What do you think it could be?"

"Maybe it's how Dementia held everyone here and why. Like a piece of paper with the plans on it or something."

"It annoys me that she keeps us guessing. And that she keeps making us hide and irritating us constantly. If she had never lost her cool, then we wouldn't be doing this."

"We also would have completely different lives. Maybe we would have never become friends. We met each other because of school. Maybe your mom would've have married Aiden's dad."

"Maybe my parents would still be together," she grumbled. Macy's dad was a sensitive topic. A topic even we didn't bring up a lot.

"I'm sorry, I shouldn't have said that."

"It's fine, I really shouldn't be so bitter about it. I just hate that they had to get divorced."

"I know."

"Let's move onto another subject."

"Okay. Do you want to live here Macy?" She didn't say anything right away, but turned toward me.

"I don't know. It would scare me. This place is so different from the Modern World. It would just be hard. I know you want to, even if you said you're just thinking about it."

"Why do you have to assume that? It's a 50/50 chance."

"Gwendolyn, you were meant to be here. This is your home, you're needed here, we aren't. People need their happily ever afters. You're the one who's going to be able to give it to them."

"But…"

"Gwendolyn, it's okay. You just gave us that talk about how you would see us. How you would be there for our birthdays and art shows and go shopping and see concerts. You promised that you would see us, I have no doubt you will keep that promise." I could see her smile in the dark.

"Thanks Macy."

"No problem. It's my job to make you feel better."

"You do an excellent job." At some point we fell asleep between our giggling and talking.

I had sent Aiden out to see if the father had tried to recollect his fortune.

"Did you see him?" I asked when he came back.

"Yeah, he went out the shipyard to meet a ship. It'll be a four hour journey. He told his daughters and they asked for the fine clothes and jewelry and the rose. He'll pass the castle on the way back. Also, can I just say that flying while invisible is amazing?"

I smiled. "We could make it permanent."

"Really?" he said excitedly.

"Yeah, I can give you some wings. I'll make them big and pink and sparkly." We all laughed.

"Hey, did you notice this before?" Blaire asked looking out the window. We looked down and saw a massive cluster of rose bushes all around the castle.

"This is what Lexia meant. Something once so beautiful will now become your biggest disappointment. He has to look at those roses everyday so he will always be miserable," I said horrified.

"That's terrible," Blaire said.

"I'm going to do something," I said. I stormed from the room and ran down the steps. All the staff seemed to have left. I went into the Grand Hall. The curtains were drawn making the room very dark. Andrew's throne was on its side and one of the legs was broken. Vases were on the floor in pieces and the roses in them were torn to shreds.

"Andrew," I said calmly and softly. I changed my clothes into a more high class, Renaissance style dress. He didn't turn his face.

"Andrew, I know you can hear me. Look at me." He turned his head around to look at me. "You're not ugly. You're not a monster. What Lexia did to you was wrong, she has no just reason for it."

"How do you know about that? How do you know my name?" he asked in a gruff voice.

"That's not important. I can't stand to see you in this pain. I want to make it easier for you, so I'll give you some advice. Take very good care of those roses. They'll make her happy."

"Her who?"

"Your true love. Those roses will make her happy beyond belief."

"Why are you being kind to me?" I looked into his eyes. His eyes were still human eyes. A deep chocolate brown, scared and unhappy.

"That's also not important."

"Tell me your name."

"Gwendolyn."

"Thank you, Gwendolyn."

"Don't thank me yet." I started to walk out of the room when he grabbed my hand. My hands looked so small against his large paws. "Tell me more about her." I shook my head. "Please, I beg you."

I thought about my answer. "Once a rose is taken, a grand love will awaken. That's all I'll tell you." He let go of my hand and I gave him a reassuring smile. I walked out and back up the stairs.

"What did you say to him?" Tori asked me when I came back up.

"And what's up with the fancy clothes?" Aiden asked.

"The dress was just because I didn't like my clothes, they were getting grubby. I just told him about the roses and how they were important."

"Why did you tell him that?" Macy asked.

"I was mad that Lexia hurt him so bad. He was sitting the dark with broken vases and roses all around him. He hated himself. I told him that the roses would make his true love happy."

"Well, he needs to be mad at the father for picking the rose, so making him protective of them actually works out," Aiden said.

"Hey Gwendolyn, can you change my clothes, too?" Blaire asked.

"That wouldn't be a bad idea. It would make us blend in more and the less attention on us the better. Let's see, we can't make them very fancy like this one because the peasants don't have a lot of money."

"Just make them comfortable, that's all that matters to me," Tori said.

"Put a little color in them to," Macy said. I pictured how we should look and then I changed each of us. I put Macy in a chestnut brown dress with a dark brown bodice. Blaire got a pale, yellow dress with a tan bodice and Tori received a grey dress with a white bodice. I put Aiden in some brown pants with an off white shirt and gave him a hat. I put myself in a pale blue dress with a white bodice. All the dresses had long skirts and everyone had brown shoes.

"You have very good taste," Blaire said approvingly admiring her dress and bodice. "And the bodice isn't too tight."

"I made sure they weren't."

"This hat is awesome!" Aiden said adjusting it.

"How much longer do we have before the father is supposed to show up?" Tori asked.

"Maybe an hour still," Macy said.

"Yeah, that sounds about right."

"Check your pocket watch," Macy suggested. I had forgotten that I had it. I pulled it out and checked it. "I don't know what time Aiden saw him, but I'm guessing it was sometime in the afternoon. So yeah, it'll be a while before we see him."

"All these stories seem to go by so fast. When you read them it seems like the story took much longer," Tori said.

"The authors probably had to stretch the story out. If they didn't add some dramatic details, the stories wouldn't have been as good," Blaire said.

"How'd you figure that out?" Tori asked.

"I took this class and it taught you how to piece together things that didn't make sense. My friend recommended it to me," Blaire said. I looked over at her. I knew that class. I had taken it. It was for kids with separated parents.

"What did you get to do?" Aiden asked.

"You learned how to answer questions that didn't always seem right. Sometimes you would write your answer, sometimes you would tell it in front of the group. Stuff like that."

"Which friend recommended it to you, was it someone from our school?" Macy asked.

"No, she went to another school. She was a bit older," Blaire said swiftly.

"It sounds fun," Tori said. "Are they doing it again?"

"I'm not sure," she shrugged.

"We should get a plan ready for when the father shows up," I said changing the subject.

"What are we going to do?" Macy asked.

"We're going to have to open the door for the father and prepare a room and meal."

"I'm a pretty good chef," Macy volunteered.

"I can open doors," Aiden said.

"Blaire and I can set up a room," Tori offered.

"I'll make you guys invisible, we shouldn't let them see us," I told them.

"Let's get started then," Blaire said tugging Tori toward a room.

"I'll get started on thinking up a meal," Macy said.

"I'll help you," Aiden said and followed her as they looked for the kitchen.

I felt like I should've been happier. Nothing was in our way and these people's lives would soon be so wonderful. I just couldn't make my face smile. I kept thinking, these women knew one thing and one thing only - evil. They were told it was the only way they would finally find happiness. And the sad thing was, they truly believed it.

CHAPTER 18
FINDING HIS PRINCESS

"I see him," Tori said looking out the window. We had been waiting anxiously for his arrival.

"Finally," Aiden said pushing himself off the wall he had been leaning against.

"We'll meet back up in the middle room. Good luck." I zapped us with my wand. Aiden and I stood by the door. We saw the father coming up the walkway and then, just before he knocked, we opened the door. He walked in to a hot plate of food lit by candlelight in the dining room. He ate his meal slowly, only looking up once in a while.

After he ate, he walked into the room where we had left the door ajar. He shut the door and we flew up the stairs to meet up with everyone.

"That worked out really well," Macy said when we were all gathered.

"Yeah, it was really simple," said Tori.

"I have to say, I like the simple way," Blaire said sitting down on her blanket bed.

"It's been nice," I admitted.

"It's going to be a pain when they find us," Aiden said.

"We've stayed incognito this far," Macy noted. "What makes you think they'll find us now?"

"They're not stupid."

"Neither are we," I interjected.

"Yes, but they are cunning women who have been bent on making these people pay. I'm sure they're bound to figure out that they now have better lives."

"That's why Gwendolyn put them in the other Fairytale World," Macy stated.

"I'm just trying to be cautious."

"So, what do we do now?" Blaire asked.

"Wait until tomorrow morning. That's when we'll have to pay close attention," I said.

"It seems like our days are short and nights are long," Tori said as she straightened her bed.

"I would rather have that than long days and short nights," Macy said. She and I headed back to our room.

As I slept pictures entered and left my mind like flashes. I saw Dementia, an ancient room, something covered with a sheet, the other Sins and a bottle that had something in it.

My eyes flew open. I tried to recall all the images I had seen. This wasn't something Starletta had sent me. This was something I had remembered on my own.

I pulled my mom's journal out of the sack I had been carrying it in. I flipped to the page where she was talking about the bottle. I went back a few pages to try to recall anything that might explain the sudden flashes.

Rumors have been going around the village, rumors about her power. She wasn't that strong when she was young, so I understand why they are skeptical. Everyone disliked her, but after she kidnapped those girls it was different. It was a new kind of disliking that became fear. A fear that she could be far more ruthless then we ever thought.

The girls she chose were not random, I saw that clearly. She inspected them. I watched. I was a little older, but the same terror in their hearts was in mine. Six girls were chosen. I learned why. One girl was prideful, one obsessive. Another selfish. One greedy, one saw herself as a failure and the last was extremely jealous. I became intrigued with them. Why would Dementia want these types of girls? I took it upon myself to find out.

I stopped reading after that. Each of those girls was a sin from the Bible. I quietly snapped my fingers and I had a pencil and paper. I wrote down each sin and matched them up. The girl who was prideful was pride. The girl who was obsessive was lust. The one who was selfish was gluttony. The one who was greedy was greed and the one with the jealousy issues was envy. That meant the girl who thought she was a failure was sloth. That was six. Rage was the last sin. The thing in the bottle my mother found had something to do with the Seven Deadly Sins. I just wish she had told me what.

Everyone was up around the same time the next morning. Macy had woken up first and saw that the father was leaving, so we all got up and rushed downstairs to watch.

I saw Andrew standing by a window in hiding. The father plucked a rose from the bush and Andrew charged toward him. I saw him screaming. The man's face became pale. Soon, the conversation calmed down and the father nodded in understanding. He was still shaking. He got back on his horse and rode home. The rest of us ducked back inside.

"I couldn't hear anything, could anyone else?" Aiden asked. We all shook our heads.

"It seems like everything went accordingly. Andrew wouldn't have let him leave if he didn't promise him Beauty," Tori said.

"That's true. We'll have to wait and see if she comes," I said. We did wait. We waited until sunset and then noticed something was coming toward the castle.

Beauty rode up and climbed off her horse. She tied it to one of the iron rods of the gate. Then she walked up to the castle.

I didn't have time to give everyone a warning before I made them invisible. I pulled the door open for Beauty and she cautiously walked in. She walked down the hall into the ballroom. Andrew was fixing his throne.

"Are you, Beast?" Beauty asked him. He stopped what he was doing and turned around to face her. "Yes."

"Do you prefer me to call you something else?"

"No, Beast is fine," he said flatly.

"Where do I sleep?"

"Wherever you would like. Everything in this castle belongs to you, do with it what you will." He turned his attention back to his throne. Beauty climbed the steps and began helping him. They didn't look or say anything to each other.

"That is so romantic, he gives her everything he owns," Blaire said happily.

"It still seems rash to me," Aiden said.

"He loves her," I said softly.

"What'd you say, Gwendolyn?" Macy asked.

"He loves her. He already knows that he loves her."

"What? No. He can't love her already," Aiden said.

"He does. I gave him that clue and I know he knows for sure that she is the one."

"Why do men in this world do this? They see a woman one time, fall in love and want to marry them. That's crazy. Knowing someone for six weeks and getting married doesn't even compare to this," Aiden said.

"How do you know that this won't work out?" Tori asked him. "How do you know that they aren't soulmates and he already has figured that out?"

"I don't know. I just don't believe that a healthy marriage will come out of knowing a girl for not even a day and then deciding you love her," Aiden stated. "Remember I have a divorced father, I know how bad a marriage can get."

"But this isn't like our world. Love isn't just love, its true love," I said. I hadn't taken my eyes off Beauty and Andrew through the whole conversation.

"Gwendolyn, are you crying?" Aiden asked gently. I didn't brush them out of my eyes, I allowed the tears to roll down my face.

"Gwendolyn, what's wrong?" Macy asked kneeling by me.

"Nothing's wrong. It's just so perfect." We all watched them fix up the rest of the Grand Hall together, not saying a word.

We watched as they ate dinner. We watched as he asked her if she loved him. We watched her say no. She said it comfortingly and sweetly. We watched as she went into her room and Andrew went to his.

The next day was a rollercoaster. We took turns watching Beauty and Andrew. They walked around the castle together, admiring the statues and the roses out in yard. I hadn't seen Andrew look as happy as he did when he was with Beauty. Especially around the roses, he hadn't smiled at them once.

"They're doing wonderful, they're laughing and talking. They're in the backyard looking at the fountain," Tori said after she finished her shift. I turned back to visible and made Blaire invisible.

"Good," I told her.

I heard a knock. "Who's at the door?" I asked. They shrugged their shoulders. I went over and opened the door.

A man was standing outside. He didn't look too old, but sort of scruffy.

"What can I do for you, sir?" I asked.

"I have a message for Beauty. I was told she resides here now."

"That is correct. Beauty is unable to come to the door at this moment, can I take the message?" I said it like how I would answer the phone at my grandma's.

"Her father wishes her to come home. He says only for a day and that would satisfy him."

"Thank you. I will get this to her right away." I closed the door and headed out to the backyard to tell Beauty the message. "Miss Beauty, I have a message for you," I said. I knew that she remembered me, but she didn't say anything. "Your father wants you to come home. Just for a day and he would be happy." I did a small curtsy and then I left.

I saw that Beauty and Andrew start talking before I went back up.

"What was the message about?" Aiden wondered.

"Her father wants her to come home. She's talking to Andrew about going."

"He's going to let her right?" Tori asked.

"Yes, she's going to go home and then all the sad things happen," said Macy.

175

"Are we going to follow her back to the house?" Tori inquired.

"I wasn't planning on it. Andrew will begin to get sick. Someone should be here to make sure he doesn't die before she comes back," I said.

"What if Tori, Macy and I go and make sure everything goes fine at the house. You and Blaire stay here and tell us when we need to send her back," Aiden proposed.

"I'm cool with that."

"So are we," said Macy and Tori.

"Here's some luggage." I clapped my hands together and two sacks appeared. "Just some food and water. When Andrew falls ill, I'll send a message and Macy can put it in Beauty's dream."

"Wait, what do I have to do?" Macy asked nervously.

"You'll be just fine. Relax your mind and then concentrate. Magic is about believing," I told her. She nodded weakly.

"I guess Beauty will be leaving by tonight, so just follow her as she leaves," I said to them. Beauty left at sunset and Blaire and I said goodbye as a part of our troop departed with her.

"So, I guess it's just you and me. You can stay in our room if you want," Blaire said with a smile.

"That would be nice." I took a small portion of my clothes and put them in her room.

"Aiden told me you and he broke up," I blurted out. I don't know why I did. The silence was getting a little too uncomfortable.

"Yeah, I just didn't want to be in a relationship anymore." I decided not to bring up the whole thing about him liking me. It would just cause more confusion.

"At least it wasn't a messy breakup."

"Yeah, it was an easy conversation. Aiden comes off as a little sarcastic at times and a little skeptical about things. But he's really very mature for a boy his age."

"He always has been."

"I did feel bad though."

"Why?"

"Well, I basically threw myself at him after I stood him up. Even though he was your date. I don't even know why I stood him up. He's really a nice guy. For some reason I feel like I always pick jerks to go on dates with, ones that aren't that sweet. Then, I find this one guy that likes me and what do I do? I dump him. I felt so awful, he was your date. I tried to win him back and he said no. I don't know why he said yes later, but I feel like he shouldn't have."

I didn't want to say anything. If I told her that I had told Aiden to go out with her then she might feel worse. It didn't matter anyway, I had wanted him to. I wanted to give them a fair shot and that's what they got.

"It was his decision Blaire, you don't have to feel guilty for it. He chose to give you two a chance and it went well. We're thirteen, there's no rush to find Mr. Right right now. As the old saying goes, you have to kiss a lot of frogs before you find your prince."

She giggled. "I'm not kissing any frogs, but I get the point. Also, I want you to know, you and Aiden would've been great together."

"Thanks, he would make a great first boyfriend."

"First?"

"Oh yeah, I've never had a boyfriend," I said sheepishly.

"I never knew that. You're such a wonderful person I assumed you had."

"Thank you. I've never really found a guy that I wanted to give that title to. The only thing that came close was a valentine from Marco. And it was meant for another girl."

"Marco is an idiot to not see that you're wonderful."

"Marco is a player."

"No kidding. I don't know why I ever thought he was good looking."

"Well, I won't say he doesn't have charm. Once you know him though, he becomes very un-charming."

Blaire and I both laughed. "If you want, I may know a guy," she offered.

"That's okay. I'm going to wait a while. Maybe I'll meet a boy here."

"Does that mean you've decided to say?" she said it calmly, but her lip quivered a little.

"Well…"

"Gwendolyn, it's your choice. Don't feel bad about your decision."

"It's not that I feel bad, I just can't make the choice. It's more difficult than I thought. On one hand, I could stay here and my magic wouldn't have to be a secret. On the other hand, I go home with you guys and I would continue living a normal teenage life with this secret. And I have to think about if my dad wants to live here again? Would I continue living with David or live with him? It's just a lot to take into account and I'm not really sure which the best one is. Either way I would lose something."

"You know we could end up living here again, too."

"Why do you think that?"

"Well, my dad seemed very eager to find his long lost brother, maybe he'll want to live with him. That could mean that I could end up here with him. And Aiden's dad could want to see his sister and Tori's mom could want to see her sister. Maybe Macy's mom will want to move back, too. We all could end up living here again."

"Yes, but it would be difficult. To travel back and forth, you have to go through the portals and those can be hard to locate. Plus, it would be a big change from our world. No cell phones, computers, tablets. No technology at all. We were raised with that stuff, going cold turkey would be a bit hard…"

"But, if it meant we got to learn about our real heritage, it would be worth it. Did you not see how excited Macy was to meet Beauty? Aiden and Tori will be so happy to meet their aunts and I would be thrilled to know my uncle. Look how happy you were to meet Snow White, we're all going to go through that."

"I guess I just wouldn't want any of us living here and then having regrets."

"Well, first we have to make it the magical place we always dreamed it was. Then we can worry about moving. If any of us choose to."

"Oh, when the rest of them get back, I'll have to tell you all this theory I've developed. I think each sin is connected to the Seven Deadly Sins from the Bible."

"What are the Seven Deadly Sins?"

"Pride, Lust, Gluttony, Greed, Sloth, Envy and Rage."

"So you think each of the Seven Sins is one of the Seven Deadly Sins?"

"I think so."

"Well, if so, they picked a really good name."

"And I think Dementia planned it. In my mom's diary, she was talks about a bottle of some sorts. I think it belonged to Dementia. She also mentioned when Dementia kidnapped those girls, the girls were described like each of the sins."

"And Dementia picked them because of it?"

"Precisely!"

"Dementia just keeps throwing more curve balls at us."

"Yeah, it's getting a little tiresome."

"I think that's the goal," she said with a snort.

"Do you ever think that there's more to her?" I asked seriously.

"What do you mean?"

"Do you think that Dementia has something more evil planned out? That this is just the beginning?" Blaire sealed her lips together. "Dementia to me is someone that wants go down in history. I don't know what she plans to do to get there, but I know it'll be something big."

"I guess I'm wondering about it because…everything she says, everything she does is part of something else. The way she would talk to me, it was arrogance. She talked like she knew everything before she said it. Then, she pushed me into a river, but the enchantment wasn't strong enough. She knew I could get out. I don't understand why she took you guys and never tried getting any information out of you. It doesn't make sense knowing her other behaviors."

"She's the kind of person who likes to keep people confused. She wants to hurt you, play with your mind."

"She actually hasn't spoken to me in a while."

"Don't let it psyche you out. It might be good that she's not talking."

"How so?"

"It could mean she's panicking. She doesn't want to sound weak and lose her edge."

"That is a good point."

"As of right now, we're ahead of the game. As long as we just keep doing what we're doing, we'll be fine."

"I still do want to talk with everyone about that Seven Deadly Sins theory. They may have some input on it."

"Yeah, I agree." I laid out my blankets onto my makeshift bed and drifted off.

The next morning I woke up early. I crept downstairs to see how Andrew was doing. He wasn't in the dining room. He wasn't in the Grand Hall. I finally found him in the courtyard. I didn't go up to him, but he called out. "Gwendolyn." I kept walking.

"Gwendolyn, wait." He was bigger now and caught up to me with ease. "I've found her." Those eyes lit up.

"Oh, you have?"

"Yes, she's wonderful. When she comes back, I'm going to ask for her hand in marriage."

"So, you must love her?"

"Yes, I love her more than the stars and moon and sun. She is my whole world." His gruff voice became very kind, almost dreamy.

"I have a friend and he is very doubtful about things like that."

"How so?"

"He doesn't believe that you can look at a person, instantly fall in love, get married and the relationship will last."

"Do you believe that can happen?"

"Well...I think both can work. I believe that falling in love with someone over time is wonderful and I believe that sometimes people can just know that they're meant for each other."

"The advice I would give your friend is…he can have faith in whatever he chooses. The reason I say this is because I was once just like him."

"You were?"

"Oh yes. I didn't think that people could know each other for a short time and be together forever. I just didn't believe that it would work out."

"What changed your mind?"

"When I look at her eyes and when I hear her laugh. When I saw that she could be so kind to everyone and everything no matter what they looked like. When I saw what her name truly meant."

"That's poetic, Andrew."

"You look about the age to be thinking about the lads."

"I haven't really been thinking about it all that much. Beauty is quite a few years older than me and she is just starting to be interested."

"I guess some folk would assume twenty five is a bit old."

"Possibly. I have to be going now." He walked back to the courtyard and I went to wake Blaire.

"Andrew is doing fine right now," I told her.

"That's good," she said rubbing her eyes.

"After today, we have to start keeping a close eye on him," I said. She nodded and stretched her arms out. "You're up really early," she said.

"Yeah, I do that sometimes."

"I don't. I'm not a morning person at all."

"School starts at 7:30. How do you look all fresh if you don't like to get up?"

"I wake up at 6:10 and then watch reality TV for twenty minutes. Then it's not so hard."

"Good trick."

"So, is Andrew going to die tomorrow?" Her words were soft and low.

"No, he's just going to get very sick."

"I don't know how good I'm going to be with that."

"You were fine when Snow White was sleeping."

"I knew she was just sleeping. This time he's actually dying."

"You know Beauty is going to come and save him."

"That's only if we get her here in time. I'm very emotional about death."

"Don't worry, she will get here and save him. The stories always end in happily ever after."

"Yeah, but this time that pressure is on us. All the authors had to do was write a couple words. We have to actually make it happen."

"True, but we're going to do fine. We should do something fun. We should go into town."

"That sounds good!" Blaire got dressed and we headed into Rosemoor.

"I hate that this town is in so much poverty," Blaire said as we walked around. The town did look very dreary. All the people seemed miserable. We wandered into the market.

"Look at those shawls," Blaire said pointed at a booth. She made a bee-line to it and began perusing the merchandise. I stood on a street corner where a little girl was sitting. Her hair looked more brown than blonde, but her eyes sparkled like the fields of Ireland.

I started humming the lullaby my mother had sung to me.

"What is that song?" she asked me.

"It's a lullaby that my mother taught me."

"Can you sing it?" I stared at her round eyes and melted.

"Of course," I said.

"Rose of red, locks of gold,
Things, oh things, of a time ago,
Small little girl, lands far away,
Things, oh things of a time ago,
True love's kiss, apple like blood,
Things, oh things, of a time ago,
Palace of ice, queen of snow,
Things, oh things, of a time ago."

"That's beautiful." She smiled and that made the dimples on her cheeks pop out.

"Thank you."

"I'm Cecile," she said in a giddy voice.

"Nice to meet you, Cecile. Where's your mother?" I asked.

"She's in the market selling the last of our wool. We had to sell our sheep for money." She stared sadly at the ground. She had obviously loved the animal.

"What if I told you I could give you another sheep?" I said grinning. She looked up at me with curious eyes. I clapped my hands and a lamb trotted up to her. Her jaw hung open in a grin. "Give this to your mother." I handed her three silver coins.

She stood on her tippy toes to give me a hug. I reached my arms down and hugged her, too. She took hold of the rope around the lamb's neck and guided it to her mother's booth. I walked back over to Blaire who was still trying on scarves.

"What do you think about the purple one?" She modeled it around her shoulders.

"It looks good."

"I thought so, too. Let's be getting back." She took the scarf off her neck and put it back on the stack. "You're not buying it?"

"I buy shawls for parties at the country club and I already have a few. You're right though, we should be getting back." We left town and headed back to Andrew's castle. It was late when we got back, so we just headed upstairs.

"Do you feel like going to sleep? We might be up for a while tonight," I asked Blaire.

"Yeah, I'm kinda tired. You can stay up if you want."

"I was just going to look through my mom's diary a little more. See if there was anything I missed."

"Go right ahead, it won't bother me. I'll be asleep in about five minutes." She was indeed asleep in five minutes. I searched through my mom's diary. Everything was very vague, she didn't call a lot of people by name. I closed it and set it beside my bed. Dementia wasn't the only one who had secrets.

"Gwendolyn, Gwendolyn, get up!" Blaire pleaded. I blinked my eyes open. Blaire was standing over me looking very pale. "What time is it?" I asked.

"I don't know, it's sometime in the evening, While you were taking your nap, I went to check on Andrew and he's lying in the courtyard. I'm pretty sure he's breathing, but he looked so still. We have to get Beauty here," Blaire said while taking short, fast breaths.

"Blaire, it's alright, I'll get Macy." I closed my eyes. It was hard to relax with Blaire's panicking, but I sent a message to her. *Andrew's lying in the courtyard. Get Beauty here now.*

"I told her, we just have to wait until Beauty arrives," I said rubbing Blaire's back. The sun sank lower into the pink sky. We checked periodically on Andrew, his position didn't change.

Just as the stars were coming out, we heard the oncoming patter of feet. I saw Beauty sprinting toward the castle with Macy, Aiden and Tori a short ways behind her. Beauty's speed never slowed as she pushed open the gate doors and rushed to Andrew's aid. We all gathered in the courtyard. Tori and Blaire were both crying, Macy's nose was running and she kept wiping it with her sleeve. My eyes got wet, but the tears didn't come. The one who was crying the most was Beauty. A waterfall of tears fell onto Andrew's suit. She laid her head against his chest and murmured. "I'm sorry, I'm so sorry. I love you, I love you and now you're gone." After she said that, we saw a part of him move. Beauty raised her head and we watched as green light wrapped around Andrew's body. His snout shrank back to a nose and his claws went back to fingernails. The matted fur on his body disappeared. He became the handsome man we had seen that first day in the castle.

Beauty looked at him in astonishment. Before she could say anything, Andrew spoke. "My name is Andrew. A fairy changed me into the beast you have known. She changed something I loved into something that gave me sadness. You undid that curse. I am the king of this kingdom and I would like nothing more than if you would rule beside me as queen." Beauty's hands covered her mouth, but her eyes smiled. She nodded her head and Andrew took the ring he had been wearing and slid it onto her ring finger.

"I only wish I could thank that fairy, Gwendolyn," Andrew said.

"I know a fairy named Gwendolyn and another named Macy. When I was crying back at my old home, they were telling me that my life would get better. I wonder where they are." Aiden nudged Macy and I. I took her hand and we were visible.

"Gwendolyn, Macy," Beauty said surprised. "How did you get here?"

"It would be a very long and complicated story if we told you," I said to her barely containing my laughter.

"Well, we would just like to thank you both. You helped me have faith that my life would turn around and now I'm engaged to a wonderful man." She wrapped her fingers around Andrew's.

"I haven't met you Macy, but thank you for helping my fiancé. Gwendolyn, I really want to thank you for making me believe I wasn't an ugly man and for letting me know this amazing woman was coming to me." The former beast and Beauty shared a loving glance.

"You know Macy, you look so much like Martha when she was younger," Beauty commented. Macy bit her lip. I knew that she was battling the decision of telling her.

She'll know soon enough. It won't kill her. Starletta told me.

"Actually, Macy has some surprising news for you," I nodded to her.

"Um, Beauty, this could seem a little farfetched, but hear me out. Your sister, Martha, will have two daughters in the future. The youngest one will get married and have a daughter of her own. I'm that daughter. You're my great aunt." Beauty instantly rushed over and hugged Macy. They didn't cry, but laughed. Short little laughs and they clung hard to each other.

"You're my great niece? Oh, you're going to have to be the flower girl at our wedding," Beauty said.

"I don't know if I'll be able to come, we have this quest we have to finish. You can have the wedding without me."

185

"We'll have it tomorrow then," Andrew announced.

"Oh yes, I'm not an extravagant girl anyway. A simple wedding would be perfect," Beauty said happily.

"Do we have a minister that could perform the ceremony?" Macy asked.

"Someone of the Fairy Court normally would," Andrew said.

"Gwendolyn could do it, she's a very advanced fairy for her age. You'll find out why later," Macy said.

"I would be honored to do it," I said breathlessly.

"We could get some flowers and I'll need a dress. Who will we invite?"

"Leave it all to me, we'll call it your wedding present," I said. "But, we do have a few people we would need to add to the guest list. Come on out guys." It looked like they were walking out of a mirror when they became visible. "This is Aiden, Blaire and Tori. They're some friends of ours." Beauty and Andrew gave everyone a hug. "They're more than welcome to come," Andrew said.

"We'll have it tomorrow morning at dawn, it'll be beautiful," Beauty said. I looked over to Blaire and giggled. The morning was going to be very interesting.

CHAPTER 19
SURPRISES AND SECRETS

"Queen Beauty, you're beautiful," Tori gushed when she came out in her dress.

"Oh, you can call me Beauty, sweetheart."

"Do you like the dress?" I asked her nervously. I knew Beauty was simple, so I went with an A-line cut, cream white dress with a semi sweetheart neckline and lace sleeves.

"It's beyond stunning! Thank you so much! And on short notice," she said giving me a hug.

"Aunt Beauty, we need to do your hair," Macy said pushing over a chair. She pulled Beauty's hair into a Gibson bun leaving out a few curls to frame her face. The last thing was adding a crown of rosebuds onto her head.

Blaire handed her a bouquet of roses. "I never dreamed that if I got married I would be having thirteen year olds as bridesmaids," Beauty said with a laugh. "Yet, you are the most wonderful ones I could've asked for." Aiden knocked on the door. "It's time ladies. Gwendolyn, we need you at the altar," he called.

"I'll see you up there," I said. I rushed into the brisk morning air. The grass was concealed in a thin layer of dew and the sun was just peeking over its imaginary edge. It looked so ethereal.

Beauty's sisters had come. I couldn't figure out why based on how they viewed her. Beauty's father came, but he was sick and coughed terribly. Besides them, there was the harpist that Macy insisted on and us.

The harp began to play and I watched as Macy, Blaire and Tori walk down in their pale pink dresses. Then we saw Beauty. She had never looked more gorgeous. Aiden was her substitute father for the moment.

"Dearly beloved, we are gathered here on this morning to join two people in holy matrimony. Beauty and Andrew are destined for each other. She could see past any flaw he had and he could open up his heart to her and find love. Their love is a special kind because it isn't traditional. They have known each other for a short while, but I have no doubt they will love one another until the end of their days. Do you Beauty, take Andrew to be your lawfully wedded husband? To have and to hold, in sickness and in health, for richer or for poorer, for better or worse, til death do you part?"

"I do."

"Do you Andrew take Beauty to be your lawfully wedded wife, to have and to hold, in sickness and in health, for richer or for poorer, for better or worse, til death do you part?"

"I do."

"Then, by the power vested in me, I pronounce you..."

"You can't marry her!" Lexia screamed. She plunged down from the sky onto the rose covered aisle.

"Lexia! What are you doing here? Leave my castle and kingdom immediately!" Andrew yelled defiantly.

"You have known me for two years and denied my proposals. You've known her not even a week and you're marrying her? It's preposterous and it's not going to happen to a fairy such as I." She pulled roots up from the ground and they coiled around Beauty lifting her to the air.

"Release her!" Andrew shouted. He dove toward Lexia, but she pinned him to the ground with a wave of thorns. "She'll be released when you wed me. Wed us," she said to me. I didn't move. "Wed us you incompetent little girl!" she bellowed.

"I'm sorry, he's taken." I took my wand and a bolt of white magic slapped Lexia backward. Beauty plummeted from the skies. Released, Andrew skidded on the dewy ground to catch her in his arms.

"You!" Lexia said when she got a good look at me. "You're, you're..."

"I'm telling you to leave. Now." Lexia looked at me dumbfounded. "Now, Lexia!" She picked herself up and without another word vanished.

I turned back to Beauty and Andrew. "I'm sorry we had that small interruption. By the power vested in me by the Fairy Court, I now pronounce you husband and wife. You may kiss the bride." They looked at me wide eyed. Then they looked at each other and remembered they needed to seal the deal.

"Are you sure that is the best idea, Macy," Beauty asked at the reception.

"It'll be safer there than here," Macy said.

"She's right, I can transport you two there," I agreed.

"It does sound better than risking it. I wish you could stay with me though," Beauty said.

"I do, too, but the sooner we help these people the sooner they get happy endings like you two," Macy said.

"Take one of my carriages for traveling," Andrew offered. "They are the fastest horses in the kingdom. It's the least we can do."

"It would take stress off of me to use less magic, I barely had enough to fight off Lexia," I noted.

"We could use it to sleep in also," Aiden said.

"Then it's settled, I'll get the carriage," Andrew said heading for the doors. We went out to the stables and Andrew had his servants bring out a carriage.

The carriage wasn't very fancy. It was a box shape with four large wheels and a step to reach the doors. It was painted white with red curtains in the windows.

"These horses are not only fast, but they're also magical. Just say any destination and they'll take you there," Andrew said.

"This is so generous. Thank you, Uncle Andrew," Macy said hugging him.

"One more thing. Do you know of a tower hidden somewhere in the forest that holds a girl with hair of gold?" I asked.

"I've heard little about it, but I know it's near the kingdom of Northton," Andrew said. "Go out through the mountain pass and continue in that direction."

"Thank you, Andrew. You'll be at Stardon Castle, look for King Aaron," I said. Macy gave them both a quick hug then jumped in the carriage beside us. After the cloud of dust had faded, they were gone.

"How long do you think it will take us to get to Northton?" Aiden asked in the carriage.

"I bet it's a good hour. We have a lot of time though, it's like 7:30 in the morning," Macy said yawning.

"It was worth it to get up though. That wedding was darling with the sunrise and the roses and her dress. Gwendolyn, besides being the all magical fairy, you should think about a career in fashion. Beauty's dress was amazing," Blaire complimented.

I blushed a little. "Thanks."

"Maybe you could officiate Rapunzel's wedding, too. Wouldn't that be nice, Aiden," Macy asked with a smile. "I mean, she is our aunt." Aiden didn't say anything. He kept looking out the window.

"Aiden, aren't you excited about seeing her?" Macy asked.

"I guess."

"What's wrong?" Tori asked puzzled.

"I don't really want to talk about it." I saw Blaire was about to ask him something, but I spoke first. "Aiden, you don't have to tell us. We won't make you, but if you're going to talk about it with anyone, talk about it with the people who would understand the best."

He turned away from us again and shut his eyes. "I'm not upset at seeing her, I'm mad at my dad," he said slowly.

"Why are you mad at Luke?" Macy asked.

"He's been acting sort of funny lately, going through family albums, going to grandma's. I went in his office and he was drawing a family tree. I think that he's remembering things. I'm ticked that he didn't tell me. If he thought I had an aunt somewhere, why couldn't he tell me?" Aiden said frustrated.

"Maybe he didn't want to get your hopes up until he actually knew," Tori said.

"Or he could've thought you wouldn't believe him," Macy suggested.

"But I would've believed him. Macy's mom at least told her that she had a sister, but she lost touch. Which is true and so what if it was a cover. She didn't know where she was. She was honest with her kid," Aiden said raising his voice a little.

Blaire and I didn't say anything. She looked over at me biting her lower lip. I shrugged as if to say, *it could make him feel better.*

"Actually guys, Aiden has a right to be mad," Blaire said in a soft tone. Aiden looked at her a little staggered. "My parents…are talking about getting a divorce and the reason why is because my father has been talking about needing to see a woman named Starletta. He's been having strange dreams about a life he led as a prince and magic and all that. He didn't talk about it with my mom until recently when he left. He said he didn't want to drag her into this mess. He sent me this letter addressed to Delilah. He didn't tell me he thought he had a brother until later and I was mad and frustrated, too. I understand why Aiden is."

"What did the letter say?" Tori asked.

"I didn't read it. I wish I had though."

I envisioned the letter and it was transported in my hand. "Here. If you want." I handed it to her. Her hand shook as she unsealed the flap. She held it in her trembling fingertips.

"I can't read it, can you?" she said as she handed the letter to Macy.

Dear Sweetheart,

I can never tell you how sorry I am that I have to leave. I will never stop loving you or your mother, but this is something that has to be done. I need to find your uncle. What I am going to tell you will sound ludicrous and you don't have to believe me. But please listen. I am a prince and so is your uncle. We come from a place that is full of fairies, castles and magic. We were brought to your land by a powerful spell that a woman named Starletta cast. The spell dictated we wouldn't remember the land that we left. Lately though, I have been remembering. I remember my brother, the flowers, the magic. I have to find answers and I didn't want to pull you and your mother into it. I didn't think you would believe me. I promise I'll come back. This time I'll keep it.

P.S. - Your mother and I got married in the Modern World, but we hadn't told anyone that we got pregnant the day before the spell was cast. That's why this is addressed to Delilah. It was the girl name we had picked, but I didn't remember it until recently.

She handed the letter back to Blaire. Blaire took it and folded it into the envelope.

We all stayed quiet. Blaire didn't look at any of us, just at the note on her lap.

"Blaire..." She looked up at Tori. "At least he tried to explain it to you. He feels terrible I bet. Actually, from this note I *know* he feels terrible. You know he didn't tell you because it sounded senseless. You would've thought he was going crazy."

"I know he feels awful," Blaire said in a tired voice. "I'm not mad."

"What did he mean when he said he would keep it *this* time?" Aiden asked.

"My father isn't the best at keeping promises," she stated flatly.

"He's going to keep this one," I said assuredly.

"I think so, too."

"I care about you greatly Blaire, but let's move past the family drama for a minute. What's our plan for finding Rapunzel and the tower?" Macy questioned.

"We just get there and get directions. Like Andrew said," Tori answered.

"I know that, but how are we going to get the prince to find her? Does anyone know single royalty?" she asked.

"The prince in Northton," I replied

"Is he married?" Aiden asked.

"I'm not sure, but what other prince could it be?" I asked.

"What kingdoms surround the area?" Tori asked. I handed her the map. "It looks like the two kingdoms that are close are the Lakeshore Kingdom and the Redthorn Kingdom. The Lakeshore Kingdom looks farther away though." She pointed to where it was located. "The Redthorn Kingdom looks much closer."

"I wonder if the Redthorn Kingdom's prince is married," Macy said.

"It would be a pretty big detour on our ride. If we don't stop there, we could reach Northton and maybe find the tower before it gets dark. If we do stop we won't be able to," Aiden said gazing at the map.

"I'll fly there and see what I can find out about him. You guys know how to work the horses, right?"

"I went to an equestrian camp for three summers, I can handle it," Tori said.

"Okay, I'll meet you in Northton." I climbed out the window to the top of the carriage and jumped off into the wind.

Redthorn was much more cheery than Rosemoor. It was smaller, but more people were on the streets. Children were playing and it looked like even a few were smiling.

Probably because there's not an evil fairy living here making their lives miserable, I thought to myself.

I walked around for a little while before I saw a woman who looked friendly enough to ask.

"Excuse me, miss?"

"Yes, what can I do for you," she asked.

"I was wondering about the ruler of this kingdom. I'm a fairy and I've been seeing these strange pictures in my dreams. It's something about who runs this kingdom. Can you tell me anything about him or her?" I asked politely.

"Our ruler is King Drake. He's a magnificent king. He cares for his people and his family has kept this kingdom safe for generations."

"Does this king have a queen?"

"Sadly, no. His father passed sooner than anticipated and he was thrust into power immediately. He hasn't had the time to try to find a bride."

193

"That's tragic," I said solemnly.

"Yes. Does that help at all with what you're looking for?"

"It does, thank you. One more thing though. Have you heard of a maiden locked in a tower?" She looked up at me intrigued. "No I haven't. Why is she in a tower?"

"Well, a witch is keeping her there. I don't really know why, but I suspect it is because of her great qualities. The tower is somewhere in the woods between Northon and Redthorn. You know, she may be a wonderful fit for your king."

"She sounds promising," she said not trying to sound interested.

"Thank you for the information." I dropped a silver coin onto her cart. "Keep it as a gift." I walked away with a satisfied smile on my face.

"Hey, did you find out anything?" Macy asked when I met up with them.

"Yeah, and he isn't a prince, he's a king. King Drake and he isn't married. So, I told this woman in town about Rapunzel, hopefully word will get around. Did you guys find out where Rapunzel is?"

"No one in town knew for sure, but we did get some vague information. Tori and Aiden went out to look for it," Blaire explained.

"How long ago was that?" I asked.

"Five minutes maybe, they should be back in a while. We told them we'd find a place to sleep," Macy said.

"I thought we would just sleep in the carriage," said Blaire.

"I don't think that can house five people," Macy said doubtfully.

"I don't mind sleeping outside," I offered.

"The most that can probably fit in here is three, so someone else will have to camp out with you," Macy said looking inside the carriage.

"Hey, Gwendolyn, you're back," Tori shouted as she and Aiden emerged from the woods. "Is the guy married?" Aiden called.

"No, but I told a lady in town about Rapunzel, so maybe the word will get around," I called back.

"Did you find the tower?" Blaire asked when they were at the carriage.

"We didn't go all the way to it, but we did see the top of it. It's not a great distance from here once you enter the woods," Tori said.

"We thought it would be a good idea if we parked the carriage by the edge, so that way it wouldn't be a long walk to get there," Aiden proclaimed.

"Speaking of the carriage, we thought that would be a good place to stay. But we think that the max would be three people to stay in it. Gwendolyn already said that she would sleep outside, so someone else needs to also," Blaire asked looking around.

"I will," Aiden volunteered.

"Okay, all set then. Is there anything else we have to do?" Macy asked.

"I don't think so. How about we move the carriage." Tori and I guided the horses over to the side of the woods and then her and the other girls climbed in and started unpacking. I heard them giggling.

"Something up?" Aiden asked.

"No, I'm fine," I said nonchalantly.

"You sure? You don't seem fine."

"I'm just being quiet."

"But, you're thinking. I can tell when you're thinking about stuff. It's in your expression."

"If you're so good at reading me, then tell me if I'm thinking about good or bad."

"You're thinking of neither. You're thinking about something complex. And it's standing in front of you." He grinned, but it was a sad smile. "I never meant to confuse you…"

"You didn't confuse me," I lied.

"Yes I did. I made you rethink your feelings which I shouldn't have done. Making you question your emotions isn't fair."

"You don't have to apologize. Yes, what you told me surprised me, but it doesn't change how I feel. I don't have those feelings for you anymore," I said gently.

"And neither do I."

"Good, we're on the same page."

"Yes."

"Good." I went back to unfurling my blankets.

"But…"

"But what?"

"Nothing."

"Aiden come on, we have to be honest about these things."

"When you told me you liked me, I knew if I didn't tell you how I felt I would regret it. So I did. I guess a part of me hoped you would say yes."

"But I'm not going to. I'm really sorry, but if I pretended that I did I would feel terrible. We have to make peace with the fact that nothing is going to happen. At least not right now."

"Then when?"

"Why would you think I know that? I don't know when, I don't know if ever. I'm sorry Aiden, but we aren't meant to end up together. We're thirteen! What is the big rush? All we would do is go the movies and eat pizza. I'm sorry, but we want different things. That's not an opinion, that's a fact." I started to head for the woods.

"Where are you going?"

"On a walk."

"Gwendolyn."

"What?"

"I'm sorry. You're right. I don't want to fight."

"Thank you. I'll be back in a while." I ran into the woods and sat at the base of a tree. I hugged my knees close to me and cried. I didn't want to be dealing with this. I didn't want to be thinking about it.

Love hurts, doesn't it?

Dementia?

You didn't answer the question. Love is disappointing, isn't it?

And why would I talk to you about it?

I'm in your head. I know what you're going through better than you do. Trust me, it is overrated.

It's not overrated. It's just not the right time and place.

I was just a year older than you when I had my first love. He was handsome... kind... Charming.

My grandfather was never in love with you!

Ah, indeed he was not. He wasn't in love with Corona either.

And she became an enraged maniac who tried to keep his true love locked in a castle cleaning until she died. Although, you aren't that much different.

We all have our own ways with getting revenge.

Why did you pick them?

Pardon?

The girls you kidnapped. They are the Seven Deadly Sins. Versions of them anyway.

Your point?

Why would you want girls that are driven by these emotions? One who was too prideful, another selfish, another greedy. One who saw herself as a failure, another that was obsessive and the last who was envious.

The qualities they possess assist me.

How?

It's another piece of the puzzle you'll have to figure out.

Well, I did figure out an important piece. Tell me Dementia, did you ever keep things in bottles?

I don't know what you're talking about. Her voice had suddenly become shaky.

Oh, I think you do. And whatever you're hiding in that bottle, I'm going to find out what it is. Then, I'm going to destroy it.

I jumped up and rushed back to the carriage. "Guys, come out here, I need to tell you something," I called into the carriage.

"What do you need to tell us?" Tori asked when we were all outside.

"When I was reading my mom's diary, I came across something. She was talking about the girls Dementia kidnapped. She described them with traits that were each like that of the Seven Deadly Sins."

"So the Seven Sins are like each of the Seven Deadly Sins?" Aiden asked.

"Yes, the Seven Deadly Sins are Pride, Gluttony, Lust, Sloth, Greed, Envy and Rage. She described the six girls Dementia took as six of those sins."

"Why is that important?" Macy asked.

"I think it also has something to do with another thing she wrote about. She said that she had found this bottle and whatever it held would prove the way she tricked people. I'm guessing the 'she' is Dementia."

"What's in that bottle?" Blaire asked.

"I don't know, but it's important. Dementia just spoke to me. And when I brought it up, her voice lost its confidence."

"Did she say anything about the Seven Deadly Sins?" Tori asked.

"Sort of. When I asked her about them, she said those qualities would help her,"

"Well, if this is part of Dementia's sick puzzle, then we need the upper hand. We need to know what's in that bottle. Can you look through her diary again? You could've missed something," Blaire said seriously.

"Yeah, I can look through it again," I said unsurely.

"Gwendolyn, are you okay with doing this?" Macy asked putting a hand on my shoulder.

"Yeah, I think so. It's just that my mom's involved with them now. I thought it was bad that my grandfather was on Dementia's death list. But, I hate the idea of my mom being on it, too."

"Wait, back up. How is your grandfather connected to Dementia?" Aiden questioned.

"Dementia's mother set Dementia and my grandfather up. He said she was controlling and turned any girl that was so much as glancing at him into a troll or witch. Grandfather told Starletta and she expelled Dementia from her tutoring and wouldn't let her do the spell. It's why Dementia hates my family," I explained.

"I hope your dad hasn't done anything to upset her," Blaire said concerned.

"You and me both," I said. "I better get reading, I don't want to be up too late."

"Tell us if you find anything, we'll talk about it before we set off in the morning," Macy said before going in the carriage with Tori and Blaire. Aiden went out pretty fast, so I went to my reading. I flipped through scanning for anything.

Dementia is good at covering her tracks, but I haven't given up. I know that those girls represent something connected to the Seven Deadly Sins. I've been piecing together who is who. I know Corona is Pride and Lexia is either Lust or Envy. I haven't gotten the chance to get a close look at any of the others. I wish I knew where that bottle was and if what I think it is, is really in it. Dementia loves to bluff the cards she holds, but she can only lie so long before someone calls her.

So, she had a theory about what was in that bottle and which sins were which. I wished she could be more specific. I flipped to the next page.

So much of Dementia is lies. She has built layer upon layer of secrets. I hate the way I found out that she and my father had a relationship. I hate that I had to hear it from her instead of him. I felt so betrayed. She told me so much that day, I still don't understand why. I wish it was because she was my friend and she wanted me to know the truth. She's not my friend. She doesn't care about me. You can get rid of friends, but you can't get rid of family.

CHAPTER 20
MEETING IN THE TOWER

"Are you sure that's what it said? Maybe you read it wrong."

"Macy, I know what it said. Somehow Dementia and my mother are related," I said. My head was still running a million miles a minute, thinking of Dementia's DNA coursing through me. She was part of me. My insides felt like trillions of knots had been tied in them and they were tightening by the second.

"On the plus side, she did say she knew which sin Corona was and she had a guess on Lexia. That brings us closer to figuring that out," Blaire said positively.

"I guess."

"Gwendolyn, don't stress about it. We'll figure it out." Macy put her arm around my shoulders and pulled me into her.

"It didn't give any hints on male or female?" Aiden inquired.

"No. She wrote 'you can get rid of friends, but you can't get rid of family.' It didn't mention if the relation was boy or girl."

"We have to learn about Dementia's family history," Tori said.

"How could we?" I asked unconvinced.

"Could you ask Starletta?" she said.

"I can try."

"Before we try to resolve any of this, we need to get this quest rolling," Aiden said standing up. "Where do we start?"

"We should go to Redthorn and see if Drake knows about Rapunzel and if he is leaving today. If he isn't, we need to speed the process along."

"Will we be traveling by air or land?" Blaire asked.

"I was thinking air," I shot her a grin. "It's more efficient. I'll put a force field around the horses to keep them safe."

In less than five minutes, we were up in the clouds looking down at the greenery. I couldn't believe the rush it gave me. It felt natural, like I had known how to do it all along.

"Is that Redthorn?" Blaire called.

"Yes, we need to dive." I tilted my legs upward, ducked my head down and glued my arms to my sides.

"It looks nicer than Rosemoor," Blaire remarked when we arrived in town.

"It does. People are actually smiling," I said.

"How are we going to find out where Drake is?" Aiden wondered.

"We could split up and ask people if they know. With us everywhere, we'll cover more ground. We can meet back here," Blaire pointed to the entrance. "Five minutes." We rushed off.

Who should I ask... I lost my thought as I crashed onto the dirt.

"I'm so sorry, miss. Here, let me help you up."

"Thank you." I looked behind me and noticed there was a boy. He was tall. His face was smudged with dirt, but it made his green eyes shine bright.

"Can I ask you something?" I asked once he pulled me up.

"Sure, I won't guarantee an answer though."

"Do you know where King Drake is today?"

"He left this morning, rode right out of town. It was strange, he didn't bring any knights with him."

"Thank you, for that. And for helping me up."

"It was nothing. I have to go, I can't be late to the watermill again."

"I have to get going, too."

"Before I go, what's your name?"

"Gwendolyn."

"I'm Jamie."

"Goodbye, Jamie," I called as I headed to the gate.

"The king headed out of town earlier," Tori said when we were back at the entrance.

"I heard the same thing," I said.

"Gwendolyn, you're skirt's ripped," Blaire noticed. I looked down and a small piece of fabric was missing from my hem.

"It must've torn when I fell. I'm fine though."

"Shouldn't we be following the king?" Aiden asked.

"Yes, let's get going." We ran out of town and followed the trail of faded hoof prints.

"I can't see the tracks anymore," Macy said.

"Now, we take to the skies." I shot us above the treetops. I spotted his horse and we tailed after them.

"Is he heading to the tower?" I asked Tori.

"Yes, he's a little off course, but he'll run into it." We flew behind them until I saw the top of the tower. I lowered us to the ground a few feet away. We all watched as a lady called for Rapunzel to let down her hair. Rapunzel did and the lady climbed up.

It was almost dark before the woman came back down and left. Drake came out of hiding and asked for Rapunzel to let down her hair. She let her long braid fall again and he was pulled to the top.

"He's been in there for like twenty minutes," Blaire complained after a while. "Let's go see what they're talking about."

"You mean spy on them?" Tori asked.

"We've been doing it to everyone else."

"Good point."

"I'll get us up there." We went to the base of the tower, but tried to keep our distance from the thorn bushes. "I'll turn us invisible and then fly us up," I said.

The inside of the tower was actually very cute. There was a wooden table with a little vase of marigolds on it. Her bed was by a wall with the book shelf beside it. Rapunzel and Drake were sitting on the bed talking.

"I was told by a villager woman that there was a beautiful maiden held in a tower by a witch. I didn't truly believe it until I saw that woman climbing up your hair."

"She doesn't want anyone coming up here," Rapunzel said softly.

"Why not?"

"She never tells me exactly why. She always says I should respect her wishes. There isn't a reason why I should question them because she raised me and has been the only one who's taken care of me. I can't believe I actually let you come up here. I've never disobeyed her," she said on the verge of tears. "You need to leave." She stood up from the bed and gathered her hair.

"Please let me come back. I'll come when she isn't here," Drake pleaded.

"I...I...alright, come tomorrow at least one hour after sunset." Drake smiled at her and she turned her face away so he wouldn't see her blush.

When he was back on the ground, she had a dreamy look on her face. She was doing twirls around her bedroom.

"Let's head back," I said.

"You're not going to talk to her?" Macy asked.

"I guess I didn't think about it. Aiden, do you want to come?"

"No, I'm alright. She's got a lot going on right now, I'll tell her later," he said.

"Okay, I'll meet you guys back at the carriage." I watched them leave and then I looked up to the window. It seemed so far away now that I was at the bottom.

I didn't know if I actually wanted to go up there. What would I say? It was easier to talk to Beauty and Snow White for some reason. I told them who I was because I wanted them to know that someone was watching out for them. That someone cared.

Rapunzel should know that, too.

I rocketed myself to the window and climbed in. Rapunzel looked over and screamed. "What are you doing up here! How did you get here? It doesn't matter! Get out, get out!" she hollered.

"I flew up here. I can fly," I said over her shrieks. She stopped screaming and looked at me. "I'm a fairy and I flew up here because I had to tell you something."

"What did you have to tell me?" she asked cautiously.

"I know your life is a pain. You've been in a room the size of a closet for your whole life and have never met anyone other than that lady. I know that you've never seen another face. It frightened you and that's why you wanted him to leave. I also know that you thought he was nice and handsome. You're so happy that he wanted to come back and see you again."

"How…how do you know all that?" she stammered.

"Like I said, I'm a fairy."

"I don't know a lot of things, but I do know about magic. My mother – the lady – is magic. You seem young to know you have power."

"You don't know how much power I actually have."

"I did know my life is a struggle by the way," she said smiling weakly. "And for the first face I've seen besides hers, I'm really glad it was his."

"I saw what he looked like, he certainly is good looking."

"He is. I want to see him again so much. I can hardly wait until tomorrow's sunset."

"I thought you didn't want to disobey your mother?"

"She's kept me inside these walls for years, she can't keep me forever. She can't control me forever." Her blue eyes got very serious. She didn't seem so afraid then. She seemed determined.

"Well, I just wanted to come and tell you that. Things will get better." I started to head to the door. "Can you tell me your name?" Rapunzel asked.

"It's Gwendolyn."

"I'm Rapunzel."

"Goodbye, Rapunzel." I jumped off the ledge, dropping toward the earth then bolting up into the night sky. Instead of flying to the carriage, I went past it. I kept flying. I had no idea where I wanted to go.

I stopped at the edge of a forest and I instantly recognized it.

It was the Enchanted Forest.

I didn't come there to think, but it just didn't feel like I shouldn't go back yet. But, even though I didn't come there to do think, my mind took over anyway. I tried answering the unanswered questions. What was funny was that I now knew the answers to some of life's important questions. I knew how mermaids and centaurs had been created. I knew that there were other worlds. I knew magic existed.

I thought about *our* unanswered questions. Why Dementia did all of this? Why my mother had been taken from me? What did those painted pictures mean?

I had forgotten about the pictures. They hadn't really seemed that important. I knew they were big parts of the stories, but nothing was just important for the sake of it. No, they were important to us somehow.

I had made the Magic Mirror. The rose was a symbol of Andrew's sadness and happiness. Drake climbed into the tower to see Rapunzel. They didn't connect.

"They actually do," a familiar voice said. I turned and Starletta's shimmering figure was behind me. I wanted to cry.

"Oh dearie, don't be sad." She came over and handed me a handkerchief. "What's got you troubled?"

"It's just difficult trying to figure out each part of the puzzle."

"You knew it wouldn't be easy."

"Yeah, but I didn't expect so many layers and secrets and surprises. It's just a little overwhelming. Especially being a teenager."

"But, that's the wonderful part. You don't think like an adult and you don't think like a regular child. You're a mix of magic and modern, it will serve you well."

"Can you please help me answer some questions?"

"I can try."

"I found these pictures in my mom's room. They each have a symbol from a story from the Prophecy. I know they're important to the story, but there's always another meaning. How are they important to us?"

"What are the pictures of?"

"The red roses from Beauty and the Beast, the Magic Mirror from Snow White, the prince and tower from Rapunzel, the rabbit hole from Alice in Wonderland, the wings from

Thumbelina, the acorn and thimble from Peter Pan and the Snow Queen's palace."

"You're right, everything has a deeper meaning. These items are major parts of the story because they change the way it could've gone. Take the roses for example. They already made Andrew unhappy, but because he finally told Lexia the real reason he couldn't marry her, she made it even worse. If the roses hadn't been everywhere to make Andrew miserable, Beauty's father wouldn't have picked one to take to his daughter. And she wouldn't have come to the castle, they wouldn't have fallen in love, broken the curse and gotten married."

"I think I get it. It's the same thing with the mirror. If we hadn't taken the mask to use as the face then it wouldn't have told Corona the cruel truth. She wouldn't have tried to have Snow White murdered and Snow White wouldn't have ran into the woods to the dwarf's cottage, gotten poisoned and awakened by my grandfather."

"Precisely my darling. Now you have to figure out why Rapunzel's tower changes things."

"Can I ask you one more thing?"

"What?"

"I was reading my mom's diary and she wrote that she was somehow related to...Dementia. Do you know anything about that?"

Starletta didn't move. She stared at the trees. "Guinevere, there are going to be many things that I can't explain to you now."

"Why not? You've always been honest with me."

"I know. I promise once this is all taken care of I will explain everything. The answers will be nothing but honesty, but its...it's not the right time."

"Starletta, please, I have to know."

"I can't. I'm so sorry." She got up and started to walk away. "Starletta, please, you can't leave. You can't hide things from me. You're the only one who doesn't! Please!" I cried to her, the tears were dripping down my face like raindrops from a storm. She turned around and looked at me with a look of great sorrow. She was hurting just as much as me, even more. "I'm sorry," she mouthed. I watched as her body dissolved into dust and was carried high up into the sky until it mingled with the stars.

I kicked the dirt in frustration. I choked between my sobs, I was so angry and frustrated. The clouds had come together and it was raining. I heard the thunder clash as my foot hit the ground.

I stopped mid kick.

Dementia was full of anger and rage and she let it control her. It didn't matter if we shared blood, I wouldn't let that overpower me. I took a deep breath and fell back onto the grass. The clouds moved back apart and I could see the sky again. I hunched into a ball. Not knowing things scared me. But becoming like Dementia scared me so much more.

CHAPTER 21
RUNAWAY GIRLS AND
RUNAWAY BRIDES

We watched as Drake and Rapunzel did their routine for two nights. On the third night, we were going to make sure that the Rapunzel's mother found out. As she departed, I moved a spool of thread from her basket and placed it a few feet away from the tower. She walked over to get it and saw Drake being pulled into the tower window.

She stomped over to the tower and yelled for Rapunzel to pull her up. We heard a lot of screaming and then we saw Drake being pushed from the window and landing in the batch of thorn bushes. He cried out in agony. Rapunzel and her mother both climbed down her braid. We heard a loud snip and saw the braid crumple onto the ground. I heard Rapunzel's pain filled cries as her mother dragged her away.

After they had gone, we rushed over to help Drake. His eyes and face were covered with scratch marks. He wouldn't open his eyes.

"Is he blind?" Tori asked.

"Yes. You see this glowing," I said as I pointed out the glow around his eyes. "I bet that is a sign of magic. Her mother probably cursed the thorns."

"I bet she's one of the Seven Sins," Macy guessed.

"Which one?" Blaire asked.

"We can find out when we find Rapunzel," I said.

"Who is speaking? If you are speaking about Rapunzel then, I must find her," Drake said beginning to sit up.

"We're some friends of hers. I'm Gwendolyn, and this is Aiden, Macy, Tori and Blaire. I met with Rapunzel and she knows me. We saw where she went."

"Then we must hurry, we must catch up to her and Venema."

"Venema is her mother?" I asked.

"Yes."

"Okay, we'll guide you." Drake stretched his arms over the shoulders of Aiden and I and we held onto his forearms to help support him. "We'll tell you when to walk and stop," Aiden told him. "Start walking when we do," he instructed.

"Venema and Rapunzel went this way," Macy stated as she pointed. "Can you fly up and try to find them overhead, Gwendolyn?"

"Here, switch me places." I slid out of Drake's hold and Macy took my spot.

"This is Macy. She's Aiden's step sister," I told Drake. "I'm going to fly up and see if I can see them." I went a couple feet above the trees and scanned the ground. I saw Rapunzel and Venema heading into the thicker regions of the forest.

"They're going that way." I pointed. "The forest is going to get denser, we have to catch up fast," I yelled down to them.

"You need to transport us, Gwendolyn," Blaire called. I flew back down and envisioned Venema and Rapunzel running, deeper and deeper into the trees. When I looked up, we were just a little ways away from them.

"Venema!" She turned around startled. I could tell she recognized me. Her expression was angry, but also terrified.

"You!" she said. Her voice was low.

"Yeah, it's me. Let Rapunzel go."

"You have no control over me."

"Well, you must not be that powerful if you have to use her hair to get inside the tower instead of flying," I said matter of factly. She narrowed her eyes.

"You don't want to see how much power I really have."

"I mean really, why did you take a farmer's baby to raise as your own in such a small place? I get it when people ask for money or jewels or a palace, but you asked for a child. That's a lot of work for a young woman."

"That's not the point," she seethed

"Oh, but it is. Because it makes no sense. Why did you want a child just to keep in a room for the rest of her life? She wouldn't accomplish anything in there, she couldn't help you be evil. It doesn't add up."

Venema gritted her teeth. "I don't have to explain my life choices to a teenager."

"Fine, you don't have to. But, let her go. I'm not going to treat you as a child, but you realize that she's not one anymore either. She found someone she as a connection with. Someone she could be happy with. You're her mother. Do you really want her to blame you for not letting her have happiness?"

Venema looked from Rapunzel to me. "I don't care if she's happy." She pushed Rapunzel to the side and raised her arms up. Lightning bolts rained down from the sky sizzling the trees and grass to ash.

"Still think I'm weak!" she bellowed over the crashing lightning. "Well?" The lightning became fiercer.

"How about we settle this without magic?" I proposed. The lightning diminished.

"Keep talking," Venema said.

"We do this without any magical assistance. That would truly show who the best is."

"What's in it for me?"

She pondered. "If you win, I turn myself over to Dementia willingly and you and Rapunzel leave together."

"Alright, I'll do it. To make sure we both don't cheat, we'll get rid of our wands."

"How will that make sure we don't cheat? I just saw you shoot lightning with your hands."

"Wands are the center for any fairy's power. You keep them in your sleeve so no one can tell where your magic is located. It prevents them from stealing your wands." She said it like I should've known this.

"Okay then." We both dropped our wands.

"Now we must turn our backs and walk ten paces away from each other," I said. She looked at me oddly, but it was clear she didn't want to lose, so she turned her back.

"1...2...3..." Venema counted.

Macy, get the girls and hide in the trees. When I say 'now' jump out yelling for Venema to look in your direction. Make sure she doesn't see you. Have Drake near me.

"4...5...6..." They quietly raced around to their new positions.

"7...8...9...10. Hey..."

"Now!" I yelled

"Venema. Over here," Tori shouted.

"Over here," Blaire called.

"Venema, look at me," Macy sang. Her head was spinning like a top.

"Hey, Venema," I said. Her dizzy eyes tried to focus. "I just wanted to say...bye."

Aiden had gotten Rapunzel and they were holding up Drake. Macy, Tori and Blaire followed behind us as we ran for the trees.

"How did you know that it would make her so dizzy?" Aiden asked.

"What I know that Venema didn't was that I have used magic without a wand, which means it's not my center. I was able to make her dizzy and she didn't even know I was doing it."

"How much farther are we running?" Macy asked.

"Just a little longer. We have to get as far away as possible," I said.

"If we go any farther, my feet will fall off," Tori said. Her face was almost as red as her hair.

"Actually, I think we'll be fine here," I said slowing down. We all fell onto the dirt.

"I don't even care that I'm getting dirty," Blaire said fatigued.

"Where are Rapunzel and Drake?" I asked. Aiden lifted his arm and pointed off in the distance. "They went to talk."

"Then I guess we'll just stay here and catch our breath."

"If I can find mine," Tori said.

"I wonder what they're talking about," Macy said.

"We know the story. She's going to cry and give him his sight back," Blaire said sitting up. "Then they're going to live happily ever after."

"Aiden, when are you going to tell her?" I asked him.

"Tell her that I'm her nephew? I'm not sure. I know I have to, but how do you say that? She just got her freedom and now she has to deal with having a new family?"

"Aiden, her whole life she's never known anyone but Venema. Now she has someone she really cares about. She'll be overjoyed to know she can have more people to love," Macy said.

"She has you, too," he said smiling.

"Yeah, but you two share blood."

"Can I ask you guys something?" I asked everyone.

"Sure," Tori said.

"I got a chance to talk with Starletta last night. I asked her about the pictures that I found in my mom's room. At first I couldn't see how they connected, but they are the things that change the story. The roses are an example. They were there and Beauty's father picked one. As a result, Beauty had to come to the castle, she and Andrew fell in love and he turned back into a human. And the mirror. If the face hadn't told Corona she wasn't the prettiest, then she wouldn't have wanted Snow White killed. And Snow White wouldn't have gone to the dwarf's house, been poisoned and then awakened by grandfather's kiss. I haven't been able to figure out what Rapunzel's picture means."

"It was of Drake and the tower right?" Tori asked.

"Yeah."

"Well, Drake changed things because he was the first man Rapunzel had ever seen," Tori said.

"Couldn't it be the tower though?" Aiden asked. "Wouldn't that change everything? Once she met Drake then she saw that they were possibilities out in the world. And she had to stare at the one thing she knew was safe. Maybe it made her think, 'I can play it safe and stay here or I can take a risk and see what happens.' What do you think?"

"So, Drake does change things. But the tower is what made her decision," Blaire concluded.

"Exactly," he said.

"I think they're coming back," Macy said looking at the trees. Rapunzel was being carried by Drake and they were both smiling.

"Drake, you can see again," I exclaimed.

"Yes. I can see my darling's beautiful face once again."

"You both look so happy," Macy beamed.

"We are! Gwendolyn, I wanted to thank you and your friends for helping me escape Venema, who I now know is not my mother." She said the last part a little sadly.

"We're sorry she lied to you Rapunzel," Blaire apologized.

"I am, too."

"But we do have some news that we think is wonderful," Tori said.

"Oh, what is it?" she asked. Aiden stepped closer to her. "Rapunzel, your birth mother and father had another child and it was a boy. I'll have to explain the full story to you at some point, but he is my father. I'm your nephew." Rapunzel wiggled out of Drake's arms and hugged Aiden. "Oh my gosh, I have a brother and a nephew. I can't believe it!" They both laughed and cried.

"I'm so happy I have you as an aunt," Aiden said.

"I'm so happy I *am* your aunt."

"And I'm going to have an uncle, too." She pulled away from him a little. "Oh, I forgot to tell you. We don't know if we're going to get married."

"What?"

"Well, he's the first man I've ever met. I want to make sure that he is the one I want to spend the rest of my life with. I haven't had a lot of the experiences that a lot of other girls have had. And if there's something out there that I want to do before marriage, I want to make sure I have the chance do it."

"Oh."

"Come on dear. You don't think people can know each other for a short time and get married right?" We all burst out laughing, even Aiden.

"I guess you're right, take all the time you need," Aiden said. "I wish I could stay, but we have to be leaving."

"Where are you going?"

"We have to finish a quest. We're going to help people like how we helped you," he told her.

"Well, I'm going to start my own quest. So, all I'm going to say is be safe." She rubbed his head.

"There is one thing I want to say. With the Seven Sins out there, who Venema is working with, it's not safe. Gwendolyn can put you in an exact replica of this world where they won't find you until they're all destroyed," Aiden said.

"I think that's a good idea," Drake said. "If Venema is one of them, then I don't want her anywhere near you." Rapunzel nodded.

"Goodbye," they said to Aiden and then I whisked them away in a cloud of white. Before that, Drake had told us of a woman with a small child in a house outside of Lakeshore. It was our first clue to finding Thumbelina.

"Take us to Lakeshore Kingdom," I told the horses.

"This is the kingdom my dad was prince of," I said when we got there.

"It's nice that it's right on that lake," Blaire said looking through the window.

"That's pretty huge for a lake, maybe it's the ocean," Tori suggested.

"Then they should've named it Oceanshore," Blaire joked.

"How far out in the country do you think the lady's house is?" Macy asked.

"I don't know. All Drake said was that she lived in the country outside of Lakeshore," I replied.

"I wonder what she's like," Blaire said.

"The mom?"

"No, Thumbelina."

"Oh, I'm sure she's great. From her description she is pretty, has a beautiful voice and, of course, she's the size of a thumb." We giggled uncontrollably.

"I know that, but what's her personality like?"

"I'm not sure, but I bet she's everything that you think she's going to be. What made you think about that?"

"I don't know, just wondering I guess."

"Guys, I see a house," Aiden showed us this dainty little cottage with marigolds in baskets nailed up by the windowsill and a white picket fence around a stretch of land. Some birds were washing in the birdbath by the walkway.

"It's such a cute little house," Tori smiled.

"How are we going to get in?" Macy asked.

"She's not just going to let a bunch of strange kids in," Blaire pointed out.

"We need to become the size of Thumbelina, so we can watch the story from her point of view," I said.

"Are we taking the horses with us?" Aiden asked slowing them to a halt.

"No, they will be harder to hide. As we were driving up, I saw a shed. We'll hide them in there." Macy and Tori pulled them inside and I shrunk us down.

"Wow! Now I know what an ant feels like," Aiden said looking up.

"We need to crawl under the door," I instructed. The inside of the house was very cozy. We walked into the parlor. There were floral chairs and a vase of lilies on the table.

"I think I see Thumbelina," I said. We pulled each other onto the couch and then up onto the table.

"Where is she?" Blaire asked looking.

"Over there," Tori said. Thumbelina was on her knees with her arms folded on the bottom window pane. She was singing.

"Her voice is really pretty," Macy said.

"It's so sweet and soft," Tori said in agreement.

"It sounds sad though," Blaire said.

"It's an odd time to ask this, but where is her mom?" Aiden asked.

"I don't know, I didn't hear or see her when we came in," I said.

"Could her mom not be here at all?" Macy asked. "Then she really would be all alone."

"It sounds like something Dementia would come up with," Tori said.

"Should we go talk to her?" Blaire asked.

"I think you should," I told her.

"I don't know…"

"I'll go with you." I took her hand and we walked over to where Thumbelina sat.

"Thumbelina?" Blaire asked timidly.

"Oh my! You're like me, you're small. Um, who are you?" Thumbelina looked like an older version of Blaire. They had the same blonde hair, but different eyes. Thumbelina's were more ice blue than grey blue.

"I'm Blaire, this is Gwendolyn."

"I'm so happy to meet the both of you. I've been so lonely in this house, I never imagined that there were people actually like me," she said.

"Trust us, there are people like you. We just wanted to come and introduce ourselves. We had to stop here for a moment," I told her.

"Oh, couldn't you stay. At least for the night. It'll be close to dark soon anyway."

"I suppose we can. We'll stay on the couch."

"How did you know my name?" Thumbelina asked.

"You'll find out soon enough," I called back.

"It was nice meeting you," Blaire said happily. We hopped back down onto the couch.

"What's she like?" Tori asked.

"Oh, she's so sweet. She looks a lot like Blaire. She was so happy to meet someone her own size," I told her.

"Here's what I don't get. How can the fairy prince that Thumbelina marries be a fairy who is like an inch tall, but Gwendolyn can be a fairy that is a normal height?" Aiden asked.

"Why don't we look in that book with the Prophecy in it?" Macy suggested. I opened it to a page marked *FAIRIES AND PIXIES*.

"Fairies," I began. "are the oldest magical being. They were the first magic to ever be known. They avoided the humans to protect their magic, which they thought the humans would take and destroy. Every once in a while, a human would spot a fairy and tell tales about them. They became known as creatures with sparkling wings, pointed ears and were quite small. These in fact are pixies. Pixies and fairies are not the same, but in some ways similar. They both have magical properties and both can master the art of flight. Pixies, however, gain their flight because of their wings. Fairies can fly based of the amount of magic inside them. Pixie magic is mostly nature related, such as flowers, trees and occasionally animals."

"When people thought they were seeing a fairy, they actually were seeing a pixie, who did not keep their magic hidden as well as fairies did. Pixies are described exactly how they are. They're around an inch high with shimmering wings, pointed ears and you can identify them by a laugh that sounds like tiny bells chiming."

"Fairies can look like normal humans and will rarely ever grow wings unless they have pixie blood in them. Fairies are much more powerful than pixies because of how long they've been around and because they have learned how magic can be used properly. Since fairies are larger and look human, they have mated with the human species. This has resulted in humans being half fairy and half human. And because fairy blood mixes with the human blood, it will be passed down through generations. This means that there are humans that have fairy in them which provides them with magic. So, a fairy can be anyone with magic in them."

"Since there were a growing number of humans with magic in them, the fairy community elected a court to help decide who was 'gifted' and who was not. They were named the Fairy Court and the highest person in the Court was Starletta, a very powerful fairy. She could easily tell if someone had the Gift and how much they possessed. She would bring them into the Fairy Court and they would determine where your magic came from, to determine if it was nature focused, emotion focused or another of many sources."

"So, how am I both pixie and human if my dad was so much smaller than my mom?" Blaire asked.

"It says in here that a pixie can sacrifice their pixie heritage to become human. They must take their case to the Fairy Court and they decide whether or not they will change them," I read.

"That means that your dad probably gave up being a pixie to be with your mom," Tori said.

"Does that mean that I am or am not magical?" Blaire asked.

"We'd have to ask Starletta and probably talk to the Fairy Court," I said. "In the meantime, I was planning on going to bed."

"You're the one who normally stays up all night," Macy joked.

"I know, but I'm tired. Last night I was up for a long time. You guys feel free to stay up," I said. I headed over to a blanket thrown on the couch and snuggled into its soft fabric. For once, my head wasn't spinning with questions or dying for answers. For once, I was relaxed and peaceful.

"Thumbelina's gone!" Blaire scream jolted me from my sleep.

"What?"

"She's gone, left, not here," she said in a high pitched voice.

"Blaire, it's okay, it's part of the story," Tori said putting her arm around her. She took a few deep breaths.

"If the toad took her, then we need to get going," I said pulling together some things we would need.

"How are we going to catch up to them?" Aiden asked.

"There's a pond outside, it connects to a stream. I bet they are headed that way. We can find a stick or something and float down the stream," I told him. We crawled under the door and ran down to the pond. We found a piece of log and used that a boat.

"We need the current to pick up a little if we want to move any faster," Aiden said.

"We could get in the water and kick," I proposed.

"It's worth a shot," Aiden said as he nodded. "Mace, you were on a swim team right?"

"Yeah."

"Hop in." I grabbed a tree root sticking out from the bank as they climbed into the water. "Ready?"

"Ready," they said and I released my hold on the root.

"Now, we're moving," Tori said.

"Can you see the toad's house?" Macy asked.

"I can. We just have to go a little farther," Blaire said. They pushed even harder and we were right by the toad's house. Thumbelina was talking with a toad that had on a purple bonnet. They sounded like they were arguing. Then Thumbelina hopped into a little boat and crossed her arms. The toad with the purple hat headed inside.

"I guess they had a disagreement on the marriage," Aiden said pulling himself onto the boat.

"I don't blame her, I wouldn't want to marry a toad," Blaire said.

"What do we do now?" Macy asked wringing out her hair.

"We wait I guess," Tori said.

As night came, it became very cold and rain was pouring down in buckets. Thumbelina crawled under a leaf and rubbed her hands up and down her arms. We were getting soaked. We tied the boat to a rock with a piece of cattail and watched from under a plant by the riverbank. A mouse walked by and saw Thumbelina sitting under the leaf.

"Goodness child, what are you doing sitting out here in the cold? Come inside with me and we'll get you warmed up." She took Thumbelina under her arm and led her to a small mouse hole. We tiptoed behind them and became invisible as we walked through the door.

"You really didn't have to do this," Thumbelina said.

"Nonsense. I wasn't going to leave you out in the rain," the mouse said.

"What's your name?" Thumbelina asked.

"Mary Ann."

"I'm Thumbelina."

"Please to meet you, Thumbelina. Now, how long would you like to stay. I'd be happy to have you."

"I suppose I could stay for a little while."

"Wonderful! Tomorrow we have to go and visit one of my friends. He's a mole, so he won't be able to see you, but he's just a delight."

Thumbelina nodded at the idea. Mary Ann went and fixed them some tea and they chatted. Mary Ann did most of the talking. She got up after a while and went to her bedroom, while Thumbelina stayed out in the sitting room. She gazed through the small window and hummed that sad song again.

"Should we head outside?" I asked.

"Couldn't we just stay in here? She's going to be my family, I'm sure she won't mind," Blaire said.

"That's true, we can at least stay tonight." We walked over to the couch which had a lot of pillows on it. We each took a pillow and then sat over by the door. Aiden and Macy went to sleep very quickly, but I expected that. They had just pushed three people on a piece of wood. Blaire was lying next to me and she was snoring softly.

"Hey, Gwendolyn," Tori whispered.

"I thought you were asleep."

"I can't get my mind to shut down. Can I talk to you?"

"Sure."

"So, after we help Thumbelina, where are we going next?"

"We're going to go and find Alice."

"How are we going to get there?"

"We'll just look on our map."

"What do you think Alice's prison is?"

"I don't know. Nothing truly devastating happened to her. Except being on trial with the Queen of Hearts."

"I thought maybe it was at the beginning of the story. All of the other prisons have been at the beginnings of the stories. And it would make sense because Alice was bored at the beginning of her story. Which is why she wanted the adventure."

"Yeah, that would make sense."

"Thanks."

"Hey, so it was while ago, but are you still thinking the same things you were thinking before?"

"Maybe. I would be scared, I can be really shy. I was viewed as being this very popular girl, but I really never tried to be. I was only called the Queen Vicki because of my name. Which actually isn't even Victoria, it's just Tori. Skylar and

Jennifer are friends, and they're sweet, but I think they became friends with me just to get back at Blaire. They would ask about her a lot. Like, wondering who her friends were and what she was doing. I guess they thought I would know because we had been good friends. When they told Blaire how they felt that day after school, I knew why they did it. I had told them that Blaire had been upset in homeroom. I think they saw it as a chance to bring her down even more. After that, I was repulsed by them. It's the reason I was gentle about what I said to her, I was so mad at them. She was upset and all they could think about was knocking her down even lower. I should've probably been mad at myself. I didn't tell them that it made me feel crappy, I didn't say anything period. I haven't said a word to them since that day."

"You're not a bad person, Tori. You're a wonderful one because you realized what they did was wrong."

"I can't stop thinking that I should've said something."

"When we go home, you can. I'll even go with you if you want."

"Thank you."

"You know for a shy girl, you're pretty brave."

"You think?"

"Yeah. You came to another world to help fulfill a prophecy and meet your long lost aunt. You used illusion magic, became invisible multiple times and have flown. You don't give yourself enough credit."

"Well, thanks for that. I never considered that this quest would make me brave."

"It does in my book."

"Gwendolyn, you know, we're kind of in a book. The plot of it anyway." We muffled our laughter with our pillows.

"Goodnight."

"Goodnight."

CHAPTER 22
THE EMPIRE OF PIXIES

I heard the sound of rustling and blinked my eyes open. Thumbelina and Mary Ann were heading out the door. I shook Blaire and Tori awake. I asked Tori to grab us something to keep warm as I noticed Thumbelina had been wearing a cape. Macy and Aiden awoke as we were gathering our things.

"What's going on?" Macy said stretching.

"They left to visit the mole," Blaire explained. "We have to go after them."

We followed their footprints in the damp ground and we came to door much like Mary Ann's. It was still slightly open. We peaked through and saw that Thumbelina, Mary Ann and the mole were all talking. The mole got up and walked into another room.

"Mary Ann, I don't want to marry him," Thumbelina snapped.

"You would be lucky to be his wife. He's a respected animal in the community."

"But, I don't love him."

"I'm not going to argue. You're going to marry him in two days." She got up from the chair she was sitting in and went the same direction that the mole had.

"Thumbelina, come here and let me see if this is enough fabric," Mary Ann called. Thumbelina reluctantly got up and walked over to where Mary Ann was holding a pile of white material.

"Poor Thumbelina," I said.

"I don't see why that rodent has to be so rude," Blaire said.

"She's probably thinks she doing something nice for her," Tori said.

"By making her marry a mole? I wouldn't call that nice, I'd call it an arranged marriage. And a crappy one at that," Blaire said.

"Let's head back to Mary Ann's house. We won't have to worry about anything for two days," Aiden said.

"I'm bored," Macy said lying upside down on the couch.

"Me, too," Aiden agreed.

"Then let's do something productive. Does anyone have an idea how we get to Wonderland?" Tori asked.

"Where is it on the map?" Blaire asked.

"It looks like it's an island in the ocean on the map. But, I don't see how it could be so strange if it's just an island," I said.

"What if it's like the Bermuda Triangle? It's cursed. Or in our case, it's magical," Macy proposed.

"That's a possibility. It would help explain Neverland, too," I said.

"So, how are we going to get to it?" Aiden asked.

"Is there a harbor close?" Blaire asked. "If so, we could sail."

"That would make sense. Tori pointed out that what we thought was a lake could be the ocean. "Where there's an ocean, there are ships," I said.

"We can buy a boat," Aiden suggested. "My dad is a great sailor and I have my boating license."

"Wouldn't people think it's weird that five kids are buying a boat?" Macy said.

"Not if Gwendolyn gives them some gold," Aiden smirked.

"It sounds like the best idea to me," I said.

"Same here," Tori said.

"I agree," said Blaire.

"Well, I have no other ideas, so I'm in," Macy said.

The day of the wedding came quick. We snuck over and saw Thumbelina. She was in an ivory ball gown dress with puffed sleeves and white gloves that stretched up to her elbows. Her long hair was pulled into a bun in the back of her head with a white fishnet wrapped around it. She was leaning up against the doorframe. "I guess this is the last time I'll see outside," she said glumly.

"What do you mean this is your last time seeing the sun?" a bird asked. It was perched on a branch of a wild rose bush.

"I'm wedding Mr. Mole, so I'll have to stay underground with him," Thumbelina explained.

"Do you want to marry the mole?" the bird inquired.

"No."

"Then come with me. I'll fly you far away from here and you'll never see that mole again."

"I hate to leave Mary Ann without saying goodbye, but I just can't marry him. I'll leave her the dress, she worked so hard to make it." She came back out in her simple yellow dress and pulled the fishnet out of her hair.

"Take me somewhere with lots of flowers," she told the bird. He flew high into the sky.

"Here we go!" I lifted everyone up and we flew alongside them.

"Hello again, Thumbelina," I said to her.

"Gwendolyn, Blaire. I'm so happy to see you. Who are your friends?"

"This is Tori, Macy and Aiden," I said.

"Please to meet you," Thumbelina said politely. "You wouldn't believe the things I've been through."

"I bet we can make a good guess," Blaire said with a little laugh.

"Well, first I was taken by a toad who wanted me for her son's bride. But, I said I wouldn't, so when she went inside I snuck away. Then it rained! I've never been in a rainstorm before because I always stayed in the house. This mouse named Mary Ann let me stay at her house and she took me to her friend, Mr. Mole. He wanted to marry me, but of course I couldn't because I didn't love him. Mary Ann really wanted me to, but I just couldn't. So, here I am on the back of a bird."

"That's quite the adventure," Macy said.

"It really was. You know I always wanted an adventure, but I wanted it to lead me to people like me. All I got were animals that wanted me as a housewife."

"Every cloud has a silver lining," Tori said.

"I suppose. The flowers will be wonderful though. I haven't seen any other flowers besides the marigolds my mother had planted."

"Where is your mother," Blaire questioned.

"She raised me until about a year ago. She told me she was leaving for the market and then never came back." She snuggled closely into the bird's feathers.

"I'm really sorry," Blaire said sympathetically.

"It's terrible I know, but I manage well. I've taken care of myself for a long time. Now I'm ready to experience life outside of that house. I wrote a note a few months back and it's still lying on the kitchen table. In case she ever comes back and wonders where I am."

"We're almost there. I'm taking you to the Empire of Pixies. It's a meadow full of flowers of every color, shape and size. And, of course, full of the pixies and the pixie royalty," the bird said.

"Have you ever met the pixie prince?" I asked.

"Yes, we're great friends. His name is Edmund."

"Edmund? That's not too common," Aiden commented.

"I guess, but my name is Gilbert. That's fairly unusual, too. We're here." Gilbert glided down into a patch of violets. Flowers stretched for miles with colors as vibrant as a crayon box.

The flowers slowly opened and people climbed out of them. They wore outfits made of leaves with flower petal crowns and wings that were taller than they were. The sunlight glinted off them, like beams of light off a prism.

"This is the Empire of Pixies." Gilbert walked between the stems up to what looked like a stage. Three thrones were made of bark and had dandelion cushions. A man and woman sat on two of them, in addition to a young man on the other. He looked similar to Blaire's father.

"Your Majesty's, Edmund," Gilbert bowed. "It's a pleasure."

"It's a pleasure to see you also, Gilbert. So, old friend, what have you been up to?" Edmund asked. He looked over to Thumbelina and smiled a little. I knew that Thumbelina saw it.

"I would like to introduce my friends. This is Gwendolyn, Blaire, Tori, Aiden and Macy. And this is Thumbelina." He pushed Thumbelina a little way forward. "Everyone, this is Empress Esmerelda, Emperor Hugo and Prince Edmund."

"Oh please, Gilbert, the formalities aren't necessary. You're practically a member of the family. Esmerelda and Hugo are perfectly fine," Esmerelda said.

"It's a pleasure to meet you all. Thumbelina, I haven't seen you around the Empire of Pixies before," Hugo said.

"I've never been. Gilbert just brought me here today. I've had a pretty rough few days and he thought this would be a nice place for me to live."

"Well, we're happy to welcome you," Esmerelda said. Thumbelina and Edmund kept glancing at each other.

"Thumbelina," Gilbert said. "Can I speak with you and Edmund for a moment?" Edmund got off the stage and went with Thumbelina and Gilbert into a growth of lily-of-the-valley.

They talked for a while. A long while.

"Excuse me everyone, we have an announcement," Edmund said. "Thumbelina and I are engaged." He laced his fingers into hers. "We know it's rushed and the wedding won't happen for a while. But, we both feel this tremendous feeling when we look at each other. We both have never felt this way about someone before, and now that we do, we don't want to let it go."

The king and queen were both smiling huge smiles and Blaire looked like she wanted to cry.

"I have an announcement, too," Blaire said. "This is going to be a shock, but you had another son, correct?" she asked Hugo and Esmerelda. They nodded.

"Well, he got married to a girl. Her name is Diana and they had a baby. I'm that baby and Edmund...you're my uncle." She was crying now, but her smile was joyous. Thumbelina and Edmund both pulled her into a bear hug.

"This is so wonderful," Edmund said.

"I'm going to have a niece!" Thumbelina cried.

"When is the wedding going to be?" Blaire asked.

"We were thinking maybe in a year. That way I could get acquainted with the people and get used to the fact that I don't have wings like my fiancé." Thumbelina looked toward Edmund disappointed.

"Maybe I can help." I walked over to Thumbelina and looked her over. I placed my hands on her shoulders and shut my eyes. I felt the magic flow through my fingertips.

When I opened my eyes, the glittering outline of the wings had formed. They were the color of sunlight on water. White, with a gold lining, that sparkled like diamonds.

"Oh, thank you, thank you," she enclosed her arms around my neck and squeezed.

"You really don't have to thank me," I said modestly.

"None the less, thank you! I can't express how happy I am. Blaire, please promise me you'll make it to the wedding," Thumbelina said.

"I wouldn't miss it for anything."

"Excellent. Are you all going to stay the night?" she asked us.

"We can't, we have to get to a harbor," Aiden said.

"I can show you the way if you'd like, there's one that's not a great distance from here," Gilbert offered.

"That would be great," I said.

"Oh, Aunt Thumbelina and Uncle Edmund, there is one more small thing I have to tell you. I'm not you're height, Gwendolyn shrunk us down. So, I'm going to get much bigger in a second. I swear I'll watch my step," Blaire said.

"I sort of guessed this wasn't your natural height. My brother traded being a pixie to become a human. He and Diana have a long history together. When he knew he was in love with her, he asked the Fairy Court if he could become human," Edmund said.

"What do you mean they had a long history?" Blaire asked.

"Pixies are a little more vocal that we exist. Diana lived in a house beside the meadow. One night she saw Cameron. He saw her and they instantly became friends. When he was sixteen, he realized he loved her and told us he was going to become human to be with her. We were all supportive. Diana had protected us and she did love Cameron. We all knew that they would be together for a long time."

Blaire looked at me with a look that said, *can you tell them?*

"Blaire's parents are considering divorce. They've been getting closer to ending the marriage, but no papers have been finalized yet," I said seriously.

"What. No. They can't be splitting up, they just can't," Edmund said in disbelief.

"It's true," Blaire confirmed. "He told my mom he needed a divorce. He didn't want to bring her into this mess. He started talking about the life he led here. He wants a way back to see you."

"He wanted the divorce?" Edmund asked.

"Yes."

"I can't believe this."

"Uncle Edmund, it's going to be okay. He does still love her and he loves me. He wrote me a letter and explained everything."

"I promise you we'll get them back together." He held Blaire's hand tightly.

"I hate to cut in here, but there are these women called the Seven Sins. They are extremely dangerous and they're after you and a couple of others. I've put them in another version of this world. I think it would be a good idea if you were there, too," I advised.

"It would make me feel better, too. They're ruthless women and they have powerful magic," Blaire said.

"If you think its best, then I would agree," Thumbelina said.

"As do I," Edmund agreed.

"Alright, just relax." I moved my hands a little and light started to spread around them. As it cleared, the forms of their bodies vanished.

We walked out of the flowers into the grassy part of the meadow and I changed us back to our original heights.

"We need to get back to Thumbelina's house to get the horses," Tori said.

"How are we going to keep track of them on Wonderland?" Blaire asked.

"We could just leave them in that shed for now," Aiden said.

"They'll starve," Tori said.

"Let's go back, give them some food and then go to the harbor," Macy suggested.

"That's a good idea," I said. We were able to get to Thumbelina's house fast – this time we weren't the size of a pinkie – and I gave the horses three bales of hay and some water.

"That should be good enough. Lead the way, Gilbert." We flew along with him to the harbor.

"You know what I just realized?" Aiden said as we flew.

"What?" Macy asked.

"If everyone was transported to the Modern World, then how are the pixies and Mary Ann and the toad and the mole and everyone all still here?"

"Could Dementia have brought them here?" Blaire questioned.

"That could be the reason she wanted all the birds out. To find these people and bring them back here," Tori said piecing it together.

"But, that's…strange. Why would she bring them back? They're key characters in her enemies' happiness?" I said.

"Dementia has a reason for everything, we'll probably never know all of them," Macy said. "Don't stew over it."

"Yeah, you're right. Dementia is just a person who has a lot of skeletons in her closet. We'll never find them all. Let's just think about how we're going to get to Wonderland," I said.

"I can drive the boat. All I need is directions," Aiden said.

"I'll see if there is a map in the book that we can use," Tori said.

"The harbor is just ahead," Gilbert said. I could see the edge of the ocean just ahead of us and the tops of the ships.

"Thank you so much for getting us here," I told Gilbert.

"It was an honor to help you." He graciously bowed his head before he took to the skies again.

"What about that one?" Tori pointed. It was a small boat made of wood, but it looked very sturdy. On the side was a name, but it was hard to decipher.

"Excuse me sir, is that boat for sale?" Macy asked a man. He was tall and muscular. His beard was cut close, but his hair wasn't. It was ruffled and matted.

"How much you want to pay?"

"Name your price," I said, stepping up.

He snorted a little and smirked. "All right, I want $200."

"Bring it down to $150."

"So, you know how to bargain," he said chuckling.

"Does that mean we have a deal?"

"We do if you tell me what four young girls and a boy need a boat for."

"We need to use the boat to get to my aunt's. It's the only way to reach her," I said.

"You're a good negotiator. Bad liar."

I looked at my friends. *Should I tell him?* They nodded.

"Look, we have to get to an island because we're on a quest. There's a girl on that island and she needs help. She's probably only a few years older than me. Please sell us the boat."

He grinned and looked down. "What are you smiling for?" I asked.

He looked up. Right into my eyes.

"I know the girl."

"How?"

"She's my sister."

CHAPTER 23
MARK

"You're Alice's brother?" Aiden asked in disbelief.

"In the flesh."

"But how?" Blaire asked.

"Before Penelope and Alice were born, I was. They don't really remember me. I wasn't around much."

"You left home?" Macy asked.

"Well, yes. I left when I could. I was five years older than Penelope, but ten years older than Alice. So I knew Penelope better."

"Why did you leave?" Tori asked.

"I didn't fit in with my family. I was different." I walked up to him and looked him over.

"You're magic," I said.

"How did you know that?"

"I'm a lot more magic than I seem. Did your parents not like it?"

"My mother didn't like it. My father had never told my mother about his past. He had fairy blood in him and got the Fairy Court to remove it. But, not before my mother announced she was pregnant, just a few hours before the removal. He knew it was too late, but he never told her. He prayed that it wouldn't be transferred, but it was. I found out when I was seventeen. I was with my girlfriend and I was going in to give her a kiss. As I moved in, we floated up into the air. She freaked out. She refused to talk to me, saying that I should've told her even though I didn't know until that moment. My mother also was very angry at my father. She was mad that he never told her where he came from and that he knew the magic would be transferred into me. They fought and argued and finally I just went to the Fairy Court on my own. They told me that my power was driven from air elements and wind, which is why the floating happened. After that I left. I never used my magic. Penelope has tried to reach out to me, but I just didn't know what to say to her."

Tori went over and hugged him. She was on the verge of tears. "What's your name?"

"Mark."

"Mark, I have to say this. I'm your niece. Penelope is my mother. You are my uncle and Alice is my aunt. My name's Tori." Mark put his arms around Tori. "You're my niece…"

"That's why we need the boat. To find Alice."

"Then I'm coming with you. I'm not letting anything happen to you."

"How are you here? There was the spell and it put everyone…"

"Into the Modern World, I know. It was the craziest thing, but one day I woke up here at the harbor where I had worked before the spell was cast. I have no idea how though. I thought the entrance was sealed off."

"We did, too. We have to get going if we want to get to Wonderland," I said.

"Do you know how Alice ended up there?" Macy asked.

"I haven't spoken to her in years. I was sailing one day and I saw this girl standing on the beach of the island. As I got closer to shore, I thought it was Penelope, but she looked too young. Then I knew. I know she wouldn't remember me, so I didn't say anything. Your friend is right though, we should be going." We climbed into the boat and set sail for the island.

"You've been pretty quiet for a while," Mark said to me. I was standing at the side of the boat. Watching the waves softly slap over one another.

"Just thinking," I said.

"You said back there that you were more magical than you seemed. What did you mean by that?"

"Just that I'm magic, like you."

"I did some research on fairies. From what I know, most of the fairies that can sense magic are much older than a teenager."

"You caught me," I smirked. "I'm meant to save the Fairytale World and I'm the most powerful magical being that has ever been created."

"That's a lot of pressure for a kid."

"You have no idea."

"I do sort of. I was still a teenager when I found out I was magic. And I'm the only one in my family."

"That must've been hard."

"It was. But the people who truly care will be there for you."

"Like Penelope was?"

"Yeah. She wrote me letters after I left. I've kept them all."

"Were you sad when you had to leave her?"

"Yes. She was the hardest to leave behind. And then she gets taken away to another place and I end up back here again without her."

"I know what it's like to lose someone. My mother went missing when I was a few days old. I haven't seen her for thirteen years. It's one of the reasons that I want to finish this. I feel like one of them knows where she is. The Seven Sins, I mean."

"I'm really sorry that happened to you."

"When I was a baby, I got told all sorts of lies. Told 'she'll just be gone a while.' Now that I'm older, I want to know the one very real reason."

"You seem like a girl who wouldn't give up. You'll find her."

"Thank you. And thanks for listening to my problems."

"Thanks for hearing mine." He patted me on the back and walked across the deck into the wheelhouse.

I climbed up to the crow's nest. "Hey, what's up?" I asked Tori.

"Nothing really, just looking at the water."

"You seemed really happy to find out about Mark."

"I am. I can't even describe the feeling," she smiled and turned her face back to the ocean. "What's the game plan once we get to Wonderland?"

"First we have to figure out what the rabbit hole and Thumbelina's wings represent."

"I think Thumbelina's wings were important because she was finally who she was meant to be. She's clearly a pixie. No one else is that small that isn't one. She finally found her place in the world."

"Yeah, she was always thought of as this pretty girl, an object. Now she got to see herself as who she really was."

"And the rabbit hole, it's the way to Wonderland. It's the beginning of Alice's adventure."

"Well, it seems we didn't have to spend a lot of time on that. Okay, here's what I think. We'll dock on the island and find Alice and the rabbit hole. We make sure she falls down the hole and then we follow. Simple."

"Sounds good, we should tell the others." We climbed back down onto the deck.

"Guys, here's the plan for Wonderland. We find Alice and the rabbit hole. We make sure she falls down the hole and then we go down as well to make sure everything falls into place," I said.

"We're sure Alice will be on our side of the rabbit hole? Not on the bonkers side," Aiden asked.

"She could be with the Queen of Hearts," Macy suggested.

"I guess we'll find out when we get there," Tori said.

"Guys, look." We were nearing the island. I could feel the weirdness vibrating out like sonic waves.

"What's that in the water?" Blaire asked. Something was bobbing just above the waves. Tori fished it out.

"It's a bottle. And there's a note. It says - You thought I was confusing, you're in for wild ride. Try to keep your sanity. D." We all looked back and forth at each other.

"How did she send us this?" Aiden asked.

"She's everywhere," I said as I looked at the island. "And she knows this is the perfect place to make us go mad."

CHAPTER 24
WONDERLAND

"So, this is Wonderland?" Aiden said as we stepped onto beach. "It seems less creepy in the children's books." He wasn't kidding. The place had an eeriness to it, something you couldn't describe. Wonderland wasn't supposed to make sense anyway.

"We can't let it get to us. We have to find Alice," Tori said confidently. She walked farther up the beach.

"Look over there," she pointed to a girl sitting by a tree. She looked vaguely like Tori, maybe a few years older and with brown hair. She was reading.

"We should approach her carefully, we don't know how she'll react," Tori said. We strolled over to her.

"Pardon us miss, but could you please tell us where we are?" Blaire asked sweetly.

"I can't even answer that question myself. I've been here for forever reading the same boring book over and over again," she snipped. "We're on an island, that's all I know." She focused her eyes back onto the pages. I motioned for us to step back.

"She hasn't found the rabbit hole. Where can it be?" Macy asked.

"I don't know, she always followed the White Rabbit to it," Tori said.

"Does the rabbit have to be real?" I asked.

"If he wants to move, he has to be," Aiden said.

"No. I mean couldn't he be a hallucination?"

"What are you getting at Gwendolyn?" Mark asked.

"Well, I was thinking about how Alice woke up at the end of the book and people thought it was just a dream. Alice controlled where she went because this was her world. I can create the White Rabbit, but let it be controlled by Alice's imagination. She'll guide us to where the rabbit hole is."

"Sounds good to me," Macy said.

"Let's do it," said Tori.

"She's starting to doze off," Blaire called in a whisper.

"Okay Gwendolyn, time to do your thing," Mark said. I pictured what I wanted him to look like. Snow white fur, small black eyes, a tweed jacket and bowtie.

"Gwendolyn, look. There he is," Aiden whispered. Alice looked up and saw him hopping. She got up after him. He hopped over to a patch of dirt.

"Where's the rabbit hole?" Blaire asked.

"I don't know." The surroundings looked familiar, this was where it was meant to be. I inched closer.

"Gwendolyn, what are you doing?" Macy hissed. I shrugged her hand off my shoulder and locked my eyes onto the ground. It began shifting, falling deeper into its self. A faint light gleamed from the circle.

"Did you just…"

"Yep," I said cutting Tori off.

"He's going in it," Aiden said. Alice looked down. Her face was painted with the light. Then…she jumped.

"Here we go," Mark jumped first, followed by Aiden, Blaire, Macy and Tori. I was last. I was praying with my whole heart that we were going to the right place.

"Where did Alice go?" Mark asked when we had landed. We were in a hallway lined with doors.

"We have to think like people from Wonderland," Tori stated. "Anything that is supposed to make sense won't make sense and anything that isn't supposed to make sense will make sense. All the things they will say will sound like gibberish and a lot of it will be in riddles. We have to use our wit, but backwards. We'll say things that will make sense to them, but won't be logical. But, we still have to make it make sense to ourselves."

"Tori, that all went like this," Aiden whistled as his hand swiped over his head.

"She's saying everything will be opposite than what it normally is. We have twist reason around," I said.

"So, to find where Alice went, we can't pick the most logical door, we have to choose the most illogical door," Macy said.

"Exactly." We walked around the hallway until we came to a door no taller than a soda can.

"This is where she went," Tori pointed. "It's still wet."

"We need to shrink down again," I said. In an instant, we were small. And up to our waists in tears.

"We have to swim under the door," Macy said taking the lead. She dove into the water and we swam along with her to the other side of the door.

"She's not here either," Blaire said bobbing up.

"She probably found land and started walking." We swam over to shore and followed a fading trail of footprints.

"Are arms and legs supposed to stick out of a house?" Mark asked, pointing.

"In Wonderland they are," I said. "That's Alice, she's in the White Rabbit's house." We hid off in the distance. A lizard came and climbed into the chimney. A minute later, he came out and Alice's limbs disappeared inside the house. She came out running and we rushed to keep up.

The terrain of Wonderland was so different. Plants were taller than houses and animals were colored like rainbows. Yet, the more you saw, the more you thought it was normal. When we caught up with her, she was standing on the tips of her toes talking with a caterpillar who was sitting on a mushroom.

After they talked, the caterpillar disappeared and Alice studied both sides of the mushroom. She bit into one side and grew tremendously. We scrambled as she walked around. She took bite of the other side and shrunk back down to normal size.

"Hey, Gwendolyn, what are we going to do to get Alice out of here when the trial comes?" Tori asked.

"We'll have to watch and see if we can slip her out. First, we have to get her there." We walked with her as she strolled along and then came upon a cat. The cat had a toothy grin spread across its face.

"Little girl, you look lost," the cat purred.

"I am lost. But the strange thing is I don't have a preference for where I would like to go."

"Then, you're not lost."

"I suppose not."

"If you are fond of tea, I suggest going to the Mad Hatter's tea party with the March Hare."

"That does sound intriguing. Thank you, Mr. Cat." Alice walked off until she came to a garden. Inside the garden gate was a table with a man and rabbit.

"Those are the March Hare and Mad Hatter," Tori said in shock. Alice walked over to the table and sat down. They both began talking with her. Alice looked as puzzled as ever. They talked for a long time. Alice's expression was a mix of frustration, anger and confusion. She stood up from the table and marched off.

She walked for a while and then sat on a stump. She was saying something to herself.

"How is she going to find the queen?" Macy asked. "Where does she go?"

"I think I have to help her on this one," I said. I looked over at an open space behind Alice.

"Monoa, letrouse, seforma, letona."

A door with a heart shaped doorknob stood behind Alice.

"How did you know to say those words?" Mark asked me.

"They just come to me when I try to do a spell." We pursued after her as she walked through the door.

We stepped into the queen's garden. We saw some of her card soldiers painting the white roses. Alice walked over and asked. "Why are you painting the roses?"

"The queen wanted red roses, but we planted white. We will get beheaded if she finds out," one of the cards explained.

"Why would the queen behead someone for making a simple mistake? That doesn't seem fair," Alice said.

"She's the Queen of Hearts, she doesn't have to be fair."

"Still, it's not right to harm someone if they did something they can fix. But if you'd like, I'll help you." Alice was about to reach for a paintbrush when a trumpet was sounded.

"She's coming!" The cards bowed their heads and kneeled. Alice watched as the royal parties walked in. They were dressed in furs and jewels and had hearts on each garment. The guards did, too. Their swords had hearts on the handles and white hearts were displayed on their red armor.

The king and queen walked in. She was in a ball gown with a train that was at least three feet long. Hearts were on her corset, overskirt and sleeves. Lace was on the cuffs with a layered lace collar around her neck. A fur shawl was cradled in her arms. A golden crown was on her head, decorated in heart shaped rubies.

The queen walked right up to Alice and stared her down. "Who are you?" she asked, sounding pompous.

"I am Alice, Your Majesty." Alice did a curtsy.

"Who are *they?*"

"I do not know their names, but they are cards, Your Majesty,"

"Do you think I have a sight problem?" The queen asked.

"No, Your Majesty."

"Then why would you assume that I don't know what they are."

"I do not know, Your Majesty. You're the one who asked me what they were."

The queen turned to the cards, but then noticed the dripping rosebush behind them. Her face was as red as her dress. "Off with their heads!"

"Pardon me, Your Majesty, but that is preposterous!" Alice said defiantly. The queen looked over at her. "My dear, she's just a child, pay her no attention," the king said.

The queen looked back to the cards. "On your feet!" The soldiers stood up and looked at the queen terrified. "Have you been painting my roses?"

"Yes we have, My Queen," a card said.

"As I said before, off with their heads!" Some of the queen's guards snatched up the prisoners for execution.

"Alice, my dear, do you know how to play croquet?" she asked sweetly.

"Yes I do."

"Then you shall join me for a game." she lead Alice to another part of the yard. "Everyone, get to your spots!" she shouted. Everyone scrambled to get to a location.

The queen clapped her hands and a curled up animal was placed in front of her. She clapped again and a long bird was placed in her hands. The soldiers became the hoops.

The queen took the position for her shot. With ease she hit the little creature with her bird mallet through the card hoops. She smiled at Alice.

Alice stepped up, but her turn was difficult. The bird didn't want to cooperate and would go limp every time she tried to position it. The little creature finally got bored and walked off. Everyone was snickering.

"The queen has won the match!" a little man said. He had a mustache that curled at the tips and was holding a heart shaped flag.

"How has the queen won when I haven't even finished my turn?" Alice protested.

"The queen always wins," he replied.

"And who are you to decide that?"

"I am the Royal Scorekeeper. I say when the game is won."

"Excuse me!" the White Rabbit squeaked. "I must announce an injustice. Someone has stolen the queen's tarts." The people gasped. "We have found the culprit, it is the Knave of Hearts." Another gasp.

"Off with his head!" The queen thundered with rage.

"Wait, he needs a trial!" Alice said. "Before you can say someone is guilty of something, you must have evidence that proves the accusation."

"She makes a very good point, my dear," the king said.

"Very well," the queen huffed. "The knave shall have a trial. To the courthouse!"

We followed Alice and everyone else into the courtroom. With so many people, we didn't have to be invisible. But to be safe, I gave everyone a disguise so we wouldn't draw any attention. We sat down behind Alice.

The knave was brought in to the king and queen. "Bring forth the first witness, White Rabbit," the king commanded.

"The first witness is the Mad Hatter," the White Rabbit said. The Mad Hatter approached the stand.

"What evidence do you have for this case?" The queen asked.

"I don't know what this case is about. I was drinking my tea." He pulled out his cup and took a sip.

"Are you an accomplice in the case?" the queen questioned. The Mad Hatter took another sip.

"He doesn't deny it! Off with his head!" She cried.

"Now that's just plain stupid," Alice mumbled a little too loudly.

"What was that?" the king asked.

"Nothing, Your Honor," Alice said innocently.

The king looked slowly back to the Mad Hatter. "Hatter, if you have no evidence for this case, you are dismissed." He slammed his gavel down. The Hatter tipped his hat and slipped his tea as he skipped back to his seat.

"Next witness!" The king cried.

"The next witness is Alice," said the White Rabbit. Alice looked to him in surprise. She walked up to the stand.

"What evidence do you have for this case?" the king asked.

"I haven't any evidence, Your Honor," Alice replied.

"Off with your head then," The queen said.

"Now wait a minute, just because I have no evidence, does not make me guilty of a crime. And it certainly does not require my head to be removed," Alice said.

I noticed the jurors were writing furiously.

"And furthermore, I don't think that you are a very good queen. You behead people for no apparent reason and you clearly have horrid patience and a bad temper. That does not make for a very good monarch."

The queen looked down at her.

"Alice, do you know who I am?"

"You are the queen."

"Yes. I am the Queen of Hearts, the Queen of Wonderland. And *I* think that you are a little girl who doesn't know when to hold her tongue."

"Well, for the Queen of Hearts, I think your job must be very difficult considering you do not have one."

"OFF WITH HER HEAD!" The queen screamed so loud the courtroom shook. Everyone went silent. I could feel what people were thinking. No one talked back to the queen.

"There you go again. Just because someone said something you didn't like, doesn't mean that you get to be so cruel." As Alice's anger grew, so did she. Her height was growing at a rapid pace.

"I mean, why in the world must you be so bratty and arrogant and treat your subjects so poorly. You're putting a man on trial for taking a tart! It's rubbish, nonsense. It's so silly I can't even think of a word for it!" Her head was centimeters from touching the ceiling.

"You must leave the courtroom now, young lady," the king said. He summoned his guards.

"I'm not scared of these. You're just playing cards, I can crumple you up." She picked up one of the cards. He tried poking her with his spear, which she plucked from his hands stomped to the ground.

"You morons! She's a little girl!" the queen yelled. Alice picked her up and sat her in her palm.

"Look, Your Majesty. I understand that you are the ruler, but this place is madder than I could ever imagine. Foods and drinks make you shrink and grow, rabbit holes and magical doors lead to strange places, caterpillars and cats are asking odd questions, when a cat and caterpillar shouldn't even be able to speak. And the only reason I know that is because it's the last shred of sanity that I have left. You are no exception though, you are as mad as the rest of them." Alice's eyes were bulging from their sockets. Her cheeks were purple from her shouts.

But the queen was laughing. She was laughing hysterically.

"What is so humorous?" Alice asked in a high shriek.

"I finally won. I'm finally not a mistake. You're the crazy one, finally," the queen said and fell back on to Alice's hand laughing with delight.

"We need to get Alice out of here," I said. I got up and walked over to Alice's leg and touched my wand to it. She began shrinking and fainted to the floor. The queen fell onto the floor, still howling.

We carried Alice out of the noisy courtroom and back into the garden.

"We have to get her out of here. Before she really loses her mind," Tori said adjusting her on her arm. I swirled my wand around and another rabbit hole appeared for us to drop through.

"Alice?" Tori asked. Alice dazedly sat up, pressing her hand to her forehead.

"Where, where am I?"

"You're back on the island. You're safe," Macy said.

"Did, did I really go there? Or was it just a dream?"

"No, it was real. We got you out," I explained.

"You're the people who asked me what this place is," she remembered. "I'm sorry I didn't tell you before. This is my family vacation home and I've been staying here. My mother and father died a few weeks ago and my sister is gone. I was told I had a brother. I knew we kept a lot of our family documents out here, so I've been trying to find him."

"You don't have to look anymore," Mark said. He pulled Alice into a hug.

"Mark, it's really you? Penelope told me so much about you."

"All good things I hope," he smiled toothless grin.

"Yes, all wonderful things. Now, that place I went to, how did I get there?"

"You fell through a rabbit hole," Aiden said.

"Well, it certainly was an adventure. I had always wanted one."

"You still seem a little shook up," Tori noticed.

"I'm sorry I just…It's crazy, never mind."

"Try us. We've seen it all," Blaire encouraged.

"Well, maybe it was me thinking it was her or maybe she looked just looked like her. But, I could've sworn I knew the Queen of Hearts," Alice stated.

"Why do you think that?" I asked.

"Well, I used to be best friends with her."

CHAPTER 25
THE BOY WHO DID GROW UP

"You were best friends with the Queen of Hearts?" I asked in shock.

"It was before she became crazy," Alice said softly. "She wasn't always that way."

"I find that very hard to believe. You aren't just normal one day and off your rocker the next," Blaire said.

"I'm being sincere. She was a good person. It's long story of how she got the way she's become."

"We've got time," Tori said sitting down.

"All right. Sinica, her real name, and I were great friends at one point. She lived a little ways down from my house. I had always been different, I looked at things in a different way. I saw a painting as a story that someone was trying to tell and music that was foreign intrigued me. Because of that, it was hard for me to make close friends, but I didn't change. They were who I was and I was proud of it. Sinica and I shared that, we both saw things that way.

"As we got older though, Sinica started acting strange. She became very competitive about things, everything. To see who could sing the prettiest, ride a horse the fastest, play a piece on the piano more smoothly. I always told her she was wonderful. I honestly thought she was better at a lot of things than I was. But, Sinica always saw herself as not good enough, no matter what I said. I finally just couldn't take it any longer. I told her until she got over this we couldn't be friends because I couldn't keep competing with her all the time. I couldn't keep watching her demean herself. She never spoke to me after that, so I never knew if she ever changed."

"Would Sinica ever want revenge on you?" Macy asked.

"I don't know. She hasn't talked to me in years. She didn't seem upset at me when I told her we couldn't be friends, so I don't know if she wants revenge. She never seemed like she could hurt anyone."

"Just to be safe, I don't think it would be a good idea for you to continue staying on the island," Mark advised.

"Why not?"

"We believe that Sinica belongs to a group. They're called the Seven Sins and they're incredibly devious. Sinica's leader is the worst of them all and she'll destroy you to keep Sinica on her side. I can transport you into the real version of this world, I'm magic," I told her.

"And you're sure Sinica really hates me."

"I'm so sorry, but...yes."

"Will you come with me, Mark?"

"Of course," Mark said taking her hand. "But, there is something that I would like this young lady to tell you." He nudged Tori forward.

"Um, Alice. Do you remember your sister, Penelope?" Tori asked.

"I think about her all the time, why?"

"She's my mother and I'm your niece, Tori."

"Oh, oh my, come here." She hugged Tori. "Mark, did you know she was your niece?"

"Yes, she told me a while ago."

"I am so happy, this is so wonderful," Alice said smiling.

"I was over the moon when I found out," Tori said.

"I'm over Venus," Alice said with a laugh. "I'm sorry we won't get more time together, but I promise that soon we will be able to. Once this is all done," she said clutching Tori's shoulders.

"I can't wait!" Tori said.

"Well, I suppose we should get on with this." Alice and Mark held each other's hands as my wand made then vanish.

Tori was sniffling a little after they had gone. "Oh Tori, don't be sad, you'll get to see them soon," Macy said.

"I know," she sighed. "I guess I was just being emotional. But, did you guys hear how she talked about Sinica? She described her as one of the Seven Deadly Sins."

"Which one?" Blaire asked.

"I think its Sloth. Sloth in biblical terms is when someone fails to do something they should've done. This would make them a failure to God. In this case though, I think that Sinica just believes she a failure altogether."

"So, Dementia manipulated her just like she did the others. She takes their worst quality, brings it out in the open and it consumes them," Aiden said.

"Yes."

"That's what she meant when she said their qualities help her. She was talking about how they became evil," I said.

"Well, we have two more Sins, I wonder what roles they'll play," Macy said.

"We'll find out soon. Let's find Neverland."

"I thought the only way was to fly?" Blaire questioned.

"You're right Blaire, up we go." We flew over Wonderland and searched through the choppy seas below.

"There's something off in the distance, it could be Neverland," Tori squinted. I looked in her direction.

"It's the only clue we have, it'd be good to check it out." We flew toward the foggy shape.

"It's definitely an island," I said as we came closer.

"Owww," Aiden said as we were about to land on the island.

"What?" Macy asked.

"I don't know. It feels like I hit something." He reached his hand out and it revealed an invisible shield that surrounded the island.

"Is this how Neverland keeps in its magic?" Tori asked.

"I guess so. Neverland is like Wonderland, things don't always make sense. No one ages here, yet Captain Hook is a full grown man," I said.

"And that raises this question. All of the Seven Sins have had something to do with each story. We haven't figured out how they're involved with Thumbelina yet. Captain Hook is a guy, does that mean the real villain is another person?" Macy pointed out.

"So, if a Seven Sin is involved in this story, she has to play another role," said Blaire.

"Or she has to play one that is connected to Hook," Aiden said.

"Before we figure out anything, we need to get through this wall," I said poking it with my wand.

"Can't you just make it disappear?" Blaire asked.

"If I did, I could let all the magic out of Neverland or something worse. I'm not going to risk that. We have to float through." It felt like a wave washing over you. Time slowed down for just an instant, but then it sped up. When I opened my eyes, I was laying on the beach.

"What part of the island are we on?" Macy asked.

"The sandy part," Aiden said, dusting sand out of his hair.

"Hey, there's something out there," Blaire said.

"She's right, it looks like someone is coming to shore," Tori said. We walked out into the shallows.

"Hello," a voice called. It was female. The bottom of her dress was soaked from the knees down and her hair was stringy and damply glued to her forehead.

"What happened?" Macy asked.

"Our ship's bow cracked. It's going to take a few days' worth of repairs. My brothers and I need a place to stay, is there somewhere on the island we could stay?"

"Of course, I'm sure we can find somewhere. What's your name?" I asked.

"Oh, pardon me, my name is Wendy. Wendy Darling."

"Would you excuse us for a moment, Wendy? Guys…" I jerked my head farther up the beach.

"What are we doing?" Tori asked in our huddle.

"We just met Wendy. And we have no clue what her prison was or is," I said.

"Well, Wendy didn't want to grow up, but she never got her adventure. That could be it," Blaire suggested.

"Now, she pops up here and gets that adventure, that's too easy for the Seven Sins," Macy said.

"What if she did want to grow up?" I said. "We know that the authors just got the basics of the story. Maybe they changed details. Maybe Wendy has already had to grow up. Maybe she never got to experience the adventure she could've had with Peter."

"Now that is something the Seven Sins would enjoy taking away. She would never be able to reverse time," Macy said.

"We better get back to her," Tori said.

"Wendy, we'll find a place for you and your brothers," I said.

"Oh, thank you so much, I'll go get them."

"I can fly you over," I offered.

"Pardon?"

"Hold on." I took her hand and flew her over to the wreck.

"There are my brothers," Wendy said. "Michael, John, take my hand." They linked arms and then took her hand. I flew them back to her beach.

"You can fly!" the littlest boy said, gawking at me.

"Michael, it's not polite to stare," Wendy scolded.

"Oh, it's all right, it is a little strange. But I'll tell you a secret," I bent down close to his ear. "I'm magic."

"You're magic!" he squealed.

"Extraordinary," John said.

"I suppose," I said giggling. "Well, we'd better get going if we want to find a place to stay." We set off into the jungle.

"I'm going to go and try to find Peter's hideout," I told Macy. I slipped away from the group and flew up to get a bird's eye view of the island. I saw something that resembled a house. I flew down to it.

"Can I help you?" I turned around and saw a boy behind me. He had shaggy hair that was gathered in tuffs around his head. He had no shoes and his pants were ripped at the hems. His eyes were pine colored and sparkled like gold. He was just how he appeared. Wild. Free.

"Um, I'm looking for someplace," I said casually.

"Well, maybe I can help. My name's Peter."

"I'm Gwendolyn." My hand was shaking as I shook his.

"So, what are you looking for?"

"Oh, I have some friends that need a place to stay and I'm just looking for one."

"Why don't you and your friends stay with me? My brothers won't mind."

"You have brothers?"

"Yes, I call them the Lost Boys because I can never seem to find them all," he said chuckling. "I've raised them here for a couple years now."

"That must have been a little difficult."

"A little, but my pixie helps out a bit. The boys adore her. And everyone has to grow up at some point right?"

"You grew up?"

"Everyone does."

"Did you want to?"

"In a way, I think I had to. We got stranded here. I had to take on the role of being a guardian and with that comes responsibility."

"That doesn't answer the question."

"I don't really have an answer. I missed a lot of things in my life because I had to take on that role. But, they're my family and I'll do anything for them."

"So you didn't get your first love or do anything ridiculous? You didn't get to live the life of a teenager?"

"No. And we never seem to age here, so I guess I'll be their guardian forever. I'll have to be a grown up forever." His voice sounded sad, longing to experience those things.

"You are going to have those things. A first love, doing one crazy thing, being young again. You shouldn't be acting like a dad. Not yet."

"How am I going to have that"

"Hold onto my hand. And no matter what happens, don't let go."

CHAPTER 26
EXPERIENCES

"We're actually flying!" Peter cried as we flew over the ocean.

"Isn't it great?"

"Are you kidding? It's amazing! I wish I could feel like this every day!"

"You can. Here." I passed him a drawstring bag. "In this bag is dust that can make you fly."

"Thank you."

"This is just the beginning. I really think you should try and have those memories. They're worth it."

"Can't you give me a hint on any of them?" he smirked.

"Nope, they'll all be a surprise. Just don't be afraid to do something crazy once in a while. That's the whole point of this."

"All right, I won't be so stingy. I promise."

"Good. I have to get back to my friends. Can you fly on your own?"

"I think I can manage."

"Okay." I let go and I flew over the trees until I found them.

"Hey, I got us a place," I said when I reached the group.

"Where?" Macy asked.

"I met a boy named Peter and he offered to let us stay with him and his brothers." My friends gave me questioning looks. *I'll explain later*, I mind spoke to them.

"That's wonderful!" Wendy clapped her hands. "I don't know how I'll begin to thank you all."

"You don't have to Wendy," Tori said modestly.

"Well still, thank you so much. Where do they live?"

"It's just a little ways from here," I flew everyone to the hideout. The Lost Boys were outside wrestling with each other.

"Those are Peter's brothers," I explained.

"Gwendolyn, hello," Peter said coming out of the hideout.

"Hi Peter. This is Aiden, Macy, Blaire, Tori, Wendy, John and Michael."

"Well, there is plenty of room. Follow me." He led us into the hideout. We walked through a door in a hill and down some stairs into what resembled a living room. There were beds set up for the boys. Bows, arrows and slingshots were mounted along the walls.

"I hope it's not a problem to sleep on the floor," Peter said.

"Not a problem at all," I said.

"Good. As a warning, the boys are very rambunctious." Just as he said it, the boys came running into the hideout like a stamped of cattle.

"Boys, we have guests!" Peter yelled over the noise. They instantly halted.

"Please, say hello."

"Hello," they chorused.

"These people will be staying with us for a while and I want you to be very courteous to them. You can be hyper outside. Is that clear?"

"Yes," the boys said.

"Good, now get ready for bed." The boys walked quietly over to their beds and climbed in.

"Aren't you going to read us a bedtime story, Peter?" asked one of the younger Lost Boys.

"Oh, I'm really worn out boys."

"I can tell them a story," Wendy interjected. "It's no trouble."

"Oh, thank you. Please listen to Miss Wendy, boys. I'll be back in a moment."

I pulled everyone into corner.

"Okay, did anyone else think it's crazy that the boy who isn't supposed to grow up just acted like a father?" Macy asked.

"The Lost Boys are Peter's brothers," I said.

"So, Peter grew up and raised them?" Aiden asked.

"Yeah."

"So both Peter *and* Wendy grew up?" Tori questioned.

"Yes. And because of that, Peter isn't Peter. He can't fly, he hasn't battled pirates and he never experienced emotions like he should have."

"This means that the Seven Sins had two bones to pick - Wendy and Peter," Blaire said.

"I showed Peter how to fly and I got him thinking about all the adventures he could have. We have to make sure that Wendy is in them. I'll take care of Peter as long as you guys can make sure that Wendy is around."

"We got your back, girl," Macy said.

"Thank you, I'm going to go see where he went and possibly figure out who the seventh Sin is." I silently walked outside.

Peter was talking with a pixie. I stood frozen. How were they not seeing me? I realized that I was invisible. The shock of seeing him must have done it automatically.

"You're being ridiculous."

"I'm telling you Peter, you can't do this. You can't go back in time."

"Well, Gwendolyn is a better friend than you because she actually wants to help me try."

"I've helped you with those boys for years. I've been a friend to you through all the tough times. I helped you survive here and find happiness."

"I've never been happy here. I want those years back, even if it's just for a short time. Then I will have the memories that every other teen has."

"Peter…"

"Save it! Why should I even trust you? You're always slipping away secretly. You want me to always be honest with you, but then you aren't honest with me. You know what, I'm done. I don't want you around anymore. I'll let the boys know you're gone. Goodbye, Tinkerbell." Peter sulked back into the hideout. He was sad that it had come to this, but he knew that it was right.

Tinkerbell floated there for a minute. Her wings disappeared and she grew until she looked like a human. She pulled her hair out of the bun and let the curly, messy tresses fall down her back. She was now dressed in pirate attire - an off-shoulder top with a brown skirt and a laced corset.

She fled off into the jungle. I followed her down to the beach. A dingy came and took her to a ship a little ways out in the water. Once on the ship, she was escorted into the captain's cabin.

"Hello darling," she said wrapping her arms around his shoulders. My blood ran cold when I saw his face. And his hand.

"Hook," I said breathlessly.

"Hello, dearest." He spun around and kissed her hand. "How is the plan going?"

"There has been a slight...interruption."

"What kind of interruption?"

"There's a girl. She got him thinking about his youth. He's falling for another girl, this is ruining everything!"

"Did you try to talk him out of it?"

"He wouldn't listen to me. He's sent me away, permanently."

"I can eliminate this girl for you if you'd like," Hook said, kissing her.

"Don't worry, I can handle her. I should be going, I just thought I should drop by."

"Goodbye, Jellessa."

"Goodbye." She got back into the dingy and was taken back to the beach.

"Guys, are you still up?" I whispered.

"Of course we are and we have news," Blaire said.

"So do I."

"You go first."

"I followed Tinkerbell, only she isn't Tinkerbell, she's Jellessa. Starletta mentioned her name. She's a Seven Sin and she and Hook are dating. She has a plot against Peter and apparently I'm an 'interruption' to her plan."

"You know I'll crush her if she hurts you, right," Macy cracked her knuckles.

"I know, thank you." I patted her on the back. "What's your news?"

"Peter has a crush on Wendy. After she put the boys to bed, she and Peter started talking. They are still talking outside right now. Come here." Tori brought us over to the window at the top of the stairs. We saw Peter and Wendy flying around the trees. They were laughing and looking into each other's eyes. I felt the warmth they were feeling. They each finally felt like someone understood.

"They totally like each other," Blaire gushed.

"First love. Check," I said.

"So, when is he going to battle pirates?" Aiden asked with a devilish smile.

"I don't know, but you seem very eager to join him."

"Uh, yeah!"

"You are such a dude," Macy said shaking her head.

"It does sound pretty cool to actually witness one of Peter and Hook's swordfights," I said.

"I'd be down for it," Blaire said. "And you can always fly us out of there if it gets too dangerous."

"Mace, would you be okay with it?" I asked.

"I'm not really down with guns and violence, but I suppose I can throw that rule out the window for a day. All the rules have pretty much disappeared anyway. But, just observing, please."

"Of course, we know how you view stuff like that," said Tori.

"Thank you," Macy said.

"Well, I'm going to hit the sack," Aiden said.

"We all should." I stared into the glow of the candle before I finally felt my eyes drooping and my mind shutting off. Then I blew it out.

"Who is ready to battle some pirates?" Peter asked the next morning. "Because I sure am. Those cowards have been stealing from us for far too long, now it's time for some revenge. I saw a ship a ways out from the beach, let's go." I flew us to Hook's ship. It was in the same place as last night. My stomach knotted thinking about it.

"Peter, I have a friend and she really is against violence, so we're not going to go with you," I said.

"Not a problem, I can handle it on my own." He shot into the ship's crow's nest. He yelled something, but I couldn't make it out. Hook came out of his cabin and everything seemed to come to a standstill.

Peter bounced from the sail, down to the deck and drew his sword. Hook drew his. Neither of them moved. They seemed to be waiting for each other to start, but not wanting to back down either.

"How did it go?" I asked when he came back to the beach. He kept walking into the jungle without answering. We walked silently with him back to the hideout.

"What's wrong with Peter?" Wendy asked.

"I'm not sure, maybe you could talk to him? You two seemed to get along pretty well," I said.

"I think we do. He gave me something last night," she said, blushing a little.

"What?"

"This." She held up an acorn. "And I gave him this thimble I had. It was sweet." She looked at the acorn and I saw that spark. That spark that you see in movies.

"Can you go talk to him, please. I just want to know if he's okay." She headed over to Peter as he was restringing his bow. She tapped him on the shoulder and sat with him beside the bed.

She came back over to me a little while later. "Gwendolyn, I wanted to tell you he's okay. Being around pirates just reminded him of his dad. It was just hard for him."

"Thank you for making sure he was okay."

"You're welcome."

"Wendy, do you like Peter?"

"As a friend?"

"No, the *other* kind of liking."

She bit her bottom lip and the tips of her mouth curved up. "I do. He's different from the boys I normally meet, he's free spirited. I grew up pretty fast being an older sibling, but these past few days have been wonderful. I've gotten to be a kid."

"You both deserve it. Do you know if he feels the same way?"

"Wendy, can you come here for moment?" Peter asked.

"Sure, I'll be right back Gwendolyn."

"Guys, come here," I said after they headed outside. We went to the window.

"What are we watching them for?" Tori asked.

"Wait for it," I said. They began to talk. The light of the moon shined on them. I saw as she moved closer to him. He looked confused for a moment. She lightly sealed their lips. He was stunned at first, but then he seemed to relax.

"Aww, that's sweet," Macy said.

"How did you know?" Blaire asked.

"I'm not sure, just felt it. I saw the spark."

"What spark?" Aiden asked.

"You don't know the spark? It's the look you see in the movies, the one girls dream about," I explained.

"Oh, that's what Macy was talking about when we watched that romance movie."

Macy rolled her eyes at him.

"I'll be right back." I headed outside and flew over to Wendy's boat. I found the captain nailing some of the finishing boards into place. "Excuse me, Captain? Is the boat finished?"

"Yes, I was going to go and find Wendy to tell her."

"I can tell her for you. I'll send her here in the morning,"

"Thank you."

I flew back to the hideout. Wendy had come inside. "Hey, Wendy, I was just talking to your captain. Your boat is fixed."

"Oh, okay." She continued setting up one of the boy's beds.

"Are you alright?" I asked.

"Yeah, it's just... I'm going to miss this place. Time finally stopped and I got the chance to have some fun and now it's over. But, I guess I finally got the experience. We should get our things packed." She went over to Michael and John who were playing with the Lost Boys, pretending to be pirates. Their eyes were filled with tears when she told them that they were leaving. Hers were, too.

We all went down the beach in the morning to wish them well on their voyage.

"We're going to miss you, Miss Wendy," the Lost Boys said with heavy hearts.

"I'm going to miss you, too." She gave them each a kiss on the forehead.

"Wendy." Peter grabbed her arm before she stepped onto the gangplank. "These few days have been the best I've had in years. Gwendolyn told me that I needed these experiences, but you helped me realize how wonderful they truly can be. I've never felt this way about anyone before. I don't want it to end. When you come back I'll be the same, I won't have aged at all, even though you will have. When you're here, I want us to have more experiences like we just had."

"Peter, just like how you must take care of your brothers, I must take care of mine. I wish with all my heart that we could stay and I could be with you."

"There may be a way," I interrupted.

"What?" Peter asked.

"Well, Peter, this may be hard to hear. Tinkerbell is planning something against you. She's not a pixie, her name is Jellessa. She's dating Hook. She's also part of this group of women who want to hurt Wendy. They're the Seven Sins. For your safety, I can put you in a place where they can't get to you."

"Do it! I won't let anything happen to her," Peter said firmly.

"What about John, Michael and the boys?" Wendy said.

"I think they'll be able to go, too."

"Then we should to it. No one is hurting my brothers. I'm so sorry, Captain," Wendy said.

"It's alright Wendy. Do you lads and lasses need a ride?" he asked us.

"We will after this. Is everyone ready?" I asked. They huddled together. "Ready!" With so many people, I had to work a lot harder. I swirled my wand and my hands making clouds of white. The beach looked like a bag of flour had exploded. My knees were shaking. My head was achy.

"Gwendolyn, you look a little queasy," Macy said. She put her hand on my shoulder.

"I'm alright, it just took a lot out of me. I can rest on the boat." We walked the gangplank aboard.

"Where would you like to be taken to?" the captain asked.

"Well, we're not sure of the kingdom's name, but there is a girl named Gerda and a boy named Kai who live there."

"Oh, I know which kingdom you're talking about. You're talking about the Southan Kingdom. I'm friends with Gerda's grandmother and her and Gerda both live there. The kingdom is ruled by the Snow Queen. She kidnapped Kai and poor Gerda was heartbroken. The girl has never been the same."

"Can you take us there? We need to see Gerda," Tori said.

"I can take you to the harbor, but you'll have to find her on your own. The kingdom isn't too far, just a few hours to get there."

"That's good enough. And we'll pay you whatever Wendy was going to pay you," I said.

"It was just a favor to her, but you don't have to pay me," he said modestly. "We'd better get a move on." We set sail for Southan. As we sailed, a thought troubled me. Each Sin was a villain in a story. Dementia was the last one.

CHAPTER 27
THE SNOW QUEEN'S PALACE

"Thank you for the ride, sir," Aiden said as we disembarked after our short voyage. The trip short since the sea had been calm.

"You're very welcome," the captain said tipping his hat. We walked through the docks and into the quaint town.

"Where do you think Gerda is?" I asked.

"Normally, we're the ones asking that," Aiden said.

"She's probably at her house," Tori said.

"How do we find it?" Blaire asked.

"We do what we normally do, ask someone in town," Macy said. She walked over to a lady. "Excuse me, ma'am. Do you know where a girl named Gerda lives?"

"What business do you have with my granddaughter?"

"It's about Kai," I said. "It's urgent."

Her eyes got very wide. "Come with me." She rushed us through the streets to her house. "Gerda, come downstairs please," the grandmother called.

Gerda walked sluggishly down the stairs. She didn't look anything like the girl portrayed in the fairytale. Her face was drained of color. Her eyes had deep, dark circles under them. They looked dull. There was no life in them, no life in her.

"Gerda, they have some news about Kai," the grandmother said gently.

"You didn't see him. Whoever you thought was him isn't. Kai's with the Snow Queen. She's probably froze him to death. Please, don't make me hurt any more than I already do." Her voice was tired and weak. She began walking back up the stairs.

"Do you trust the word of a fairy?" I called to her. She turned around to me.

"We don't want to cause you any pain. Gerda, I know he's alive, please hear us out. If you don't believe us after, we'll leave."

She sighed. "Come upstairs and we can talk." We walked up the stairs to her bedroom. It was just as bleak as her. There were no pictures on the walls. Nothing was in the room besides a bed and a dresser.

"So what do you know about Kai?" Gerda asked us as we sat on her bed.

"I know Kai was taken by the Snow Queen. I know that he meant the world to you and you loved him very much. I know that you searched endlessly and you couldn't find him. Now, that sadness has finally taken over and you've given up on finding him."

"That's all correct, but do you have a point?" Gerda asked sadly.

"Kai is still alive and waiting for you to come and save him. I know it doesn't sound possible, but it is. You can't give up."

"But what if you're wrong?"

"What if I'm not? Wouldn't Kai want you to keep trying? He wouldn't want to see you holed up in a bedroom wasting your life away."

She stood up. "All right, I'll go. But, you're coming with me."

"We're what?" Macy said.

"The Snow Queen is one of the most powerful women in the world. I can't face her alone."

"We'll come," Tori said. "We know what it's like to face something terrifying."

"Thank you. There's so much to get ready, I'll be right back." It was the first sign of emotion she had shown, besides sadness, since we got there.

"Did you just volunteer us for a meet and greet with a psycho snow lady?" Blaire asked.

"Yes. She doesn't want to exist in the world because it scares her. All she needs is a nudge and some good friends by her side to encourage her."

"Tori's right. It would've been scary for me to come here without you guys. But because you were with me, I felt so much stronger," I said.

"That's true and we wouldn't change our minds if we had to make the same choice again. I'm just going to warn you now, I get cold easy," Blaire said.

"My grandmother is putting some food together for us right now," Gerda said coming back in. "I'm guessing you don't have winter coats, so let me see if I have some extras," she said as she opened up her dresser.

"If a couple of you don't mind wearing capes, then we're set."

"We don't mind," Tori said.

"Great." She passed around coats, capes and wool mittens. "You're going to want these when we get near the Snow Queen's palace."

"Children," the grandmother called through the door. "I've put together some biscuits, apples and a canteen of water."

"Thank you, Grandmother," Gerda called back. "Are we all set?"

"The sooner we go, the better," Tori said.

"Oh, I don't even know you're names."

"I'm Tori and this is Gwendolyn, Macy, Aiden and Blaire."

"Pleased to meet you all. I have a map here that will show us the way to the Snow Queen's palace." After grabbing the satchel of food from her grandmother, Gerda and rest of us began our journey to find the Snow Queen.

"How did you and Kai meet?" Blaire asked Gerda as we walked.

"We met by this tree when we were young. I had been going there for years. It was a willow tree that was right on the edge of a river. I was reading one day and Kai was playing this wooden flute he had made. He stopped by the tree and noticed my book of poetry. He recited a poem from it from memory. Ever since that day, that was our spot. We played and laughed and told each other secrets. He became my best friend.

"One winter, we were skating on the ice of the river and the Snow Queen rode up in her sleigh. Kai was hypnotized. He walked over to her, got in her sleigh and she drove away. Not before smiling at me though. A smug smile, like she was proving something."

"She sounds pretty horrible," Macy said.

"She is. She doesn't care about anything beautiful or wonderful or happy, she just wants cold. And that's all she'll ever be. We have to cross the river here," Gerda said as she pointed. "The problem is the crossing part."

"I'll float us over."

"You can float us over?" Gerda asked.

"It's a thing you can do when you have enough magic."

"That's amazing. Please, float away." I carried us over the water. Flying is cool, but standing an inch above the water just by pure levitation is so much more fun.

"That was spectacular," Gerda marveled. "We need to keep walking this way." She pointed down a dirt path by the river.

"Hello children," a voice cooed. A lady was standing on the other side of a fence. I hadn't noticed that a fence was there until now.

"Hello ma'am," Gerda said politely.

"Are you lost?"

"No, we're actually on our way to meet someone," Macy said.

"That's a shame. I have this beautiful garden that I just finished weeding. I wish someone could see it."

"I'm sure we could stop for a moment," Gerda said.

"Did we learn nothing from the 'don't talk to strangers' video in kindergarten?" Aiden whispered.

"We have to follow her," Tori said walking in. I will admit the garden was beautiful. It looked like a scaled down version of the Empire of Pixies.

"Let me show you around," the lady offered. She toured us around the garden. She seemed to be paying special attention to Gerda.

"I just remembered who this lady is," Tori whispered.

"Who is she?" Macy asked.

"She's a witch. Not a bad one, but she wants to keep Gerda because she never had a child of her own. We have to leave now."

"Gerda, you know, your mother is going to get worried if we don't meet her soon," I said, giving her a look.

She caught my hint. "Oh, I'm so sorry ma'am, we have to leave. Maybe we can come another time." Before the lady could protest, I flew us out of the garden.

"Just watching the sunset?" I asked sitting down next to Gerda. We had set up camp for the night. The location was scenic. Right from a postcard.

"Yeah, I always do."

"You know we're going to find him, right?"

"How did you know I was thinking about him?"

"I can send, read and sense emotions and thoughts. Another magical perk."

"To answer your question, I don't really know that we're going to find him. But you're right, he wouldn't want me wasting my life in a bedroom. And it feels so good to have hope again."

"I know what you're going through, I lost my mom. And until a few weeks ago, I hadn't had any hope that I'd ever find her. But now that I have that hope, I never want to let it go."

"Never do. The second you do, you'll end up like the girl you met when walked into my house."

"What made you give up on him in the first place?"

"I woke up one morning. It was snowing softly outside. As I watched the snowflakes fall, I realized that I couldn't see him anymore. When he first left, that moment felt so real every time I saw it. I could hear his voice and see his face. That morning, all of it felt like a picture or memory or something from the past. I had seen it, but couldn't really grasp it. I panicked, I didn't want to forget him. And then I just broke down. I realized I was forgetting him because he was gone and he wasn't coming back. I hadn't fought to keep him safe, I had been a coward."

"You're not a coward, Gerda. A coward wouldn't be trying to find him."

"But, I was one. I let him go. I shut him out just to make the horrible pain stop."

"And now you're fighting for him again. That shows courage, perseverance, faithfulness, love, hope - all of it."

"A few hours ago, I didn't dream I'd ever be doing this."

"But you are and it's because you realized that you can't let that pain control you forever."

"It's something like that. Let me ask you a question. Why did you so badly want me to try and find him?"

"Let's just say I have this thing for helping girls find what they need."

"Alright, that can be your excuse for now. But I'll get the real answer at some point."

"At some point, you definitely will."

"Well, I'm off to bed. We have a long way to go before we get to the Snow Queen's palace."

"Yeah, you're right. Goodnight."

"Goodnight. And Gwendolyn, I won't lose hope as long as you won't."

"Deal."

"We'll have to be careful around here, there are rumors of bandits. So, be watchful." Gerda warned the next day. We stayed close to the trees and made our steps light.

"Did you hear something?" Aiden asked.

"I don't think so, what did it sound like?" Macy asked.

"Rustling of branches or leaves. I'm probably just imagining it."

"Where did Gerda go?" Tori asked nervously.

"Help!" Gerda screamed from a little ways ahead of us.

"Put her down!" another voice said. It sounded young and girlish. We crept behind a rock and saw Gerda slung over a male bandit's shoulder with a young girl bandit standing next to him.

"I said put her down, you ninny!" the young girl demanded. The man set Gerda down, but held firmly onto her arm. "If you'd kept holdin' her that way, she'd screamed her head off. We'd better get goin', bring her with you," the girl snapped.

"We have to go after them," Tori said, getting ready to jump on top of them.

"We will, but we need a plan. There are probably more of them and if we charge now we'll get outnumbered," Aiden said, sitting a hand on her arm.

"Aiden's right, we need to do this smart. We'll follow them to wherever they're going. Then we'll figure out a way to get Gerda back."

We trailed the bandits to a decayed barn. We peeked through one of the holes on the barn's side. It was like an outlaw hangout. The girl and man walked in with Gerda. The girl said something to the man. He went and joined a card game, while the girl and Gerda headed somewhere that was out of my line of vision.

We walked around to the back of the barn where there was another door. I opened it a little and saw a stack of hay bales that led up to a loft. Some faded purple curtains made a cloth lean-to. Gerda and the girl's shadow were inside that triangle. We slowly climbed the hay ladder up to the loft.

"I'm really sorry that you have to live here, Piper," I heard Gerda said.

"It's not so bad. I steal because I'm saving up my money. When I get enough, I'm going to leave this all behind me and move to one of the kingdoms. One that's far away from here, like Stardon or Redthorn."

"Here, please take this. It's just a few copper coins, but you need them more than me."

"Thank you. I promise I'll get you out of here."

She smiled. "Oh, don't worry. I have some friends that are going to get me out."

"Gerda," Tori whispered. "We're outside the curtain." Gerda opened the curtain a little.

"I knew you'd come. This is my new friend, Piper. She got me away from that other guy. She's going to help us get out of here."

"Follow me everyone." We followed Piper outside. "If they ask where you went, I'll tell them I lost you."

"Will you get in trouble?" Gerda asked.

"I can handle them."

"Thank you so much Piper. Promise me you'll try to find me when you leave."

"You'll be the first person I come to. But you have to hurry, they could come out here any minute," she said keeping one eye on the door.

"Bye," Gerda whispered as we hurried away.

"How did you know to trust her?" I asked Gerda.

"Well, when she took me up to that loft, I noticed this little nest of patched up blankets, pillows and a few tea candles. I realized that that was her bedroom. She's my age and that was her life. And I just wasn't afraid."

"Do you think she's going to get out of there?" Tori asked.

"I do. She's a tough girl and she'll find her place. Because it's absolutely not there," Gerda said. "But onto the more pressing matter of where we need to go. We need to keep walking this way until we come to the mountains. It's the snowiest place in all the kingdoms. That's where her castle is," Gerda explained.

The hills became steeper to climb and the air became cold and thin as we climbed higher.

"Pull out your winter gear," Gerda said. We layered into our capes, coats and mittens. "It's just a little farther," she said. Once geared up, we hiked some more and soon we were close to her domain. The snow was up to our knees and it whirled around us like a mad tornado.

The palace was grand, but menacing. Tall towers of ice stretched to the heavens with spires pointed like animal fangs.

"Do we just walk in?" Macy asked.

"I really hope it's warmer in there, th...than it i...is out here," Blaire chattered.

Aiden, Gerda and I walked over to the door and pushed. It was surprisingly light and we walked into the palace. We walked down a hallway until we came to a wide room. The queen's throne was directly across from the doorway.

"Oh my God, look," Tori pointed at a figure lying on the icy floor. We ran over and flipped him onto his back. His face was a sickly color of blue and frost was evident in patches across his body.

"Kai, wake up. Please wake up," Gerda pleaded, sniffling through tears. She hugged his body close to hers.

"You were too late," a voice said. We looked around, but there was no one there but us.

"She's just taunting you Gerda, don't give up," I said.

"Please Kai. This can't be the end. Remember all those summer days playing in the cornfields and in the spring when we would read poems under the willow tree. Don't you remember that? Tell me you remember that," she sobbed into his frigid chest.

I looked around the room. Everyone was in tears, everyone was cold and unhappy. Just what the Snow Queen wanted.

I took a deep breath and braced myself. This was going to take a lot of magic.

"Gerda, keep saying those memories," I said.

"Okay. Swimming in the river, lying in the sunshine, having picnics, looking at the clouds." I took each memory into my brain. I felt the grass between my toes, the warm sun on my back. I could smell the flowers and see the flowy white clouds swirling in the sky.

"Gwendolyn, how did you do that?" Gerda asked. I wearily opened my eyes. All through the palace, flowers and grass were sprouting up and sunlight was pouring through the icy ceiling. A river was flowing through the center of the room with chunks of ice bobbing up and down in the current.

"Gerda," Kai said. The color came back into his face and the frost dissolved off his body into a puddle.

"I've never been so happy to see you!" She wrapped her arms around his neck and he twirled her around.

"You didn't give up," Kai said.

"No, but it did take some wonderful friends to get me here." She nodded toward us.

"Thank you for bringing us back together," Kai said. "I don't know how I'll ever be able to thank you."

"Seeing you two happy is thanks enough," I said.

"Where will you go after this?" Gerda asked.

"Well, we were thinking about going home. But we're not really sure how to get back," I said.

"Come back to my house. You can stay there until you figure it out," Gerda offered.

"That sounds good, thanks."

"We can take some of the horses out back," Kai said. Out of the corner of my eye, I saw something glint in the Snow Queen's throne. I walked over. Something was definitely shining in the back of the chair. One of the jewels was cracked on the side. I pried it open and inside was a round, purple bottle.

My hands were nervously shaking as I held it. This was the bottle my mother was trying to find. I knew it. I took off the top and peered inside.

CHAPTER 28
SHE'S HERE

"Gwendolyn, you've been quiet the whole trip back to Gerda's. Are you okay?" Macy asked me. But I didn't catch all of what she said. I couldn't stop thinking about the bottle and what I had seen.

"Gwendolyn," Macy repeated.

"What?"

"Are you okay?"

"Yeah, can I just talk to you about it later?"

"Sure, I guess. Why can't you talk about it now?"

"I just want to process it for a little longer."

"Okay, let me now when you're ready." I hated keeping this from her, but it was just so crazy that I found it. My mom had been looking for years. Somehow I knew it was going to determine how we would defeat the Seven Sins.

"Here we are," Gerda said. We trotted into town and off to her house.

"Grandmother, we're back," Gerda sang into the house.

"Oh, dear, how did it go?"

"Hello, Loretta," Kai said.

"Kai, bless my stars. I never thought I'd see your face again," Loretta said giving him a hug. "I'm so happy you're back. So, when will the wedding be?"

"Grandma," Gerda said blushing.

"You're twenty eight, you're not getting any younger," Loretta stated.

"Kai and I aren't even thinking about marriage," Gerda said.

"Actually," Kai bent down onto one knee. "I'd be really happy if you said yes."

Gerda gasped. "Of course I'll say yes!" He took her hand and placed an antique band on her finger. "I didn't have the money for a glitzy one, but I believe this will be fine for now."

"This one will be perfect forever," Gerda said, kissing him.

"Oh, this is wonderful. We have to pick a dress and the flowers and the setting," Loretta began listing.

"I think I have the perfect spot," Gerda said. "Oh, we need a fairy to officiate."

"I can provide that," I said.

"Well, what are we waiting for? Let's get married," Kai said. The eight of us traveled out to Gerda and Kai's favorite place.

"Your dress looks beautiful, Gerda," I said.

"Thank you. Blue is not the normal wedding dress color, but this isn't your normal wedding. My minister is a teenager."

"Gerda dear, come along," Loretta beckoned. Kai moved up to the front of the aisle. He didn't have a suit, so he just wore his nicest pants and a clean white shirt. Gerda was walked down the aisle by Loretta. She looked beautiful carrying a bouquet of snowdrops.

"We are gathered here today, to join two people in holy matrimony. Two people whose love for each other lasted through the bitterest times and the coldest separation. Gerda and Kai share a love most others only dream of. They share a love that can never be broken, tainted or ruined. I wish them a long and happy life. Do you Kai, take Gerda to be your wife?"

"I do."

"And do you, Gerda take Kai to be your husband?"

"I do."

"I now pronounce you husband and wife. You may kiss the bride." Gerda dipped Kai down and kissed him.

"Now that's adorable," Macy beamed.

"I just wanted you to know that you're welcome to stay as long as you need," Loretta said to us. "What kingdom are you from?"

"Stardon," I said.

"That's rather far from here. How did you end up in Southan?"

"It's a very long story," Blaire said.

"You can tell me the short version," she pressed.

"Well, we were given this quest that we needed to complete. One part of that was telling your granddaughter that her true love was still waiting for her," I said.

"It's strange for people so young to get a quest like that. What were some of the other things you had to do?"

"It was like a help-them-find-what-they-need sort of thing," Macy said. "There were some people who hadn't found what they needed to find in life, so we helped them."

"Do you have any idea why this quest was given to you? You see, I was once quite involved with the Fairy Court. My husband was on it and I have a little magic myself, which is why I can sense the magic coming from you. And you, my dear, have a lot," she said as she pointed at me. "And I also know that the Fairy Court is normally the group that dish out the quests."

"We were given it by a retired member of the Court," Tori said.

"Which member?"

"Starletta," I said. "Did you know her?"

Loretta sighed a small sigh. "Starletta. You're bound to hear that name once or twice in your life. I heard it on many occasions."

"What does that mean?" Aiden asked.

"Starletta was kind to everyone. She was a glorious fairy and wonderful person. But, even good people can create bad things."

"What kind of bad things?" I asked.

"She never forgave herself for it. She tried so hard to make it better, but it just got worse."

"What got worse?" I asked urgently.

"All I will say is that even the purest flower can have a dark seed."

"Everyone. Kai wants us to come to his father's house for dinner," Gerda said.

"I think we're just going to go to your house. It's been a long few days," I said.

"Oh, alright, that's fine. Do you know how to get back?"

"Yes. We are really glad you found each other again."

"We are, too. Thank you performing the ceremony."

"It was my pleasure."

"Please say goodbye before you head home."

"We will," I told her.

"Why did you decline her offer?" Tori asked.

"I have some stuff I have to tell you guys," I said.

"Can you tell us now?" Aiden asked.

"We're here for you Gwendolyn," Macy said.

"I found the bottle."

"You mean *the* bottle? The one your mom wrote about?" Blaire questioned.

"Yes."

"Where was it?" Macy asked.

"It was in a compartment in the Snow Queen's throne."

"What's in it?" Tori asked.

"I can't really describe it. I'm going to look at it again later. But we have it, we have leverage. We completed the tasks, but we still have the Seven Sins to deal with. We have to get rid of them once and for all."

"She's right," Aiden said. "We can't let them do something like this again."

"How are we going to find them?" Blaire asked.

"That's one of the things I still haven't figured out. Dementia obviously didn't want this found, but she would've tried to take it back by now."

"Could Dementia have wanted you to find it?" Macy proposed. "Maybe it's a trap. If you use this against her, it'll backfire on you."

"But this is all we have, it can't be another dead end," Tori said.

"Dementia wouldn't mind tricking us," I said. "We just have to hope my mom was right and this will help us."

"We need to figure out how to get to them. That should be the first thing we do," Macy said.

"What about the Snow Queen's castle? If Dementia's bottle was there, maybe that's where their lair is," Blaire suggested.

"I can fly us there now," I said. We sailed through the sky to the icy castle. The air chilled automatically. Everything was still. The snow wasn't spinning like before.

"Something feels off," I said.

"Yeah, I feel it, too," Tori said.

"We'll just slip in and look around," Aiden said. "But, to be on the safe side, we should be quiet." We pushed the doors open and walked back to the throne room. It still looked the same as when we left.

"This is where I found the bottle." I pointed to the jewel in the back of the chair.

"Maybe there is something left in there," Blaire said. She looked around inside. "There's nothing. Could she have left something lying around?"

"I don't normally leave things lying around dearie." We slowly turned to see the villain we dreaded. She was smiling cruelly, yet seemed very pleased that she had caught us off guard.

"Tell me. What were you doing snooping around my castle?" We stood our ground. We couldn't risk letting any information slip.

"Never mind, you won't be around long enough for it to matter."

"No!" I jumped in front of Dementia's blast. A pain coursed through me. It was like daggers were jabbing from inside me trying to puncture their way out.

"Not a smart idea, Guinevere. Injuring yourself won't help you save them." I looked up at Dementia who had encased the others in wraps of black mist.

"Ta da." She flicked her wrist and they were gone. Twice I had let her take them from me. That fury gave me enough strength to attempt to get up.

"And now that they are out of the way, I'll deal with you." She roughly grabbed my chin, making me face her. My brain was clouded and every inch of me screamed with pain, but I stared her down.

"I'm going to give you answers," she said calmly.

"The answers to what?" I snarled.

"Everything."

CHAPTER 29
DEMENTIA'S STORIES

She took me under her cape and we were projected somewhere. It was dark, but beautiful. Dreamlike. The sky was several shades of purple with misty grey clouds painted in between. We were in front of a platform of stone. Pieces of ruin were thrown about with vines coiling around them like snakes. Cracked pedestals flamed ablaze as Dementia walked past them.

I wanted to charge at her. I wanted to scream and cry. I wanted her to feel every sliver of fury that was in my body.

"I know you want to hurt me," Dementia said. "And I know why. But, for the moment all I want to do is give you answers. We're not friends, but I'm not going to play tricks."

"I'm still keeping my guard up," I said curtly.

"I don't blame you."

"What is this place?"

"This is where I've been for years, before I met the others. Have a seat." She pointed over to a chunk of stone.

"You still didn't answer the question. What is this place?" I pushed.

"It's a riddle - 'Where fairies divide, darkness will lie.' I found it a long time ago. It's this bubble in the Fairy Realm. Only fairies who have lost their goodness can find it and enter."

"Why didn't you destroy me like the others?"

"How do you know I destroyed them?"

"It seems like a valid guess."

"I didn't destroy them."

"Then where are they?"

"They're not in harm's way. Are these really the questions you want to be asking? I bet you have so many others. Go ahead, ask."

My head began to swirl. What should I ask her? More importantly what should I ask her *first*?

"Tell me about the Birds of Black, why did you turn Marybella into one of them?"

"For fun, I suppose."

"Why did you need them? You had the other girls."

"I needed eyes and ears that wouldn't talk back and wouldn't ask questions."

"Why did you release them into my world?"

"Again, I needed eyes and ears. Starletta made the spell so *I* couldn't get to the other side. She didn't make it so a bird couldn't."

"Were you the one who sent me those dreams? The ones that were violent?"

"Yes. There weren't real memories, just pieces of memories. The one with fire was when the kingdoms were being destroyed. The one with the all the girls was similar to when I was picking the Sins. I made the girls your age to make you feel more trapped. I wanted you to see me. To be afraid of me."

"Tell me about the girls you took. What do they have against these people?"

"I have this very keen sense. I can tell when a person is hurting and why they are in pain. When I saw these girls, their emotions were so crazed and passionate it was like nothing I had ever dealt with."

"Why were they so angry?"

"I'll start with Corona," Dementia said as she stood up and began pacing. "She thought she was better than a lot of the girls, because she was dating a prince. When he didn't marry her, she was distraught. I found her that way and I told her that she could make sure Aaron suffered like she did. I made her a queen and gave her Aaron's true love to be her maid. But pride can get to you and she let that arrogance overpower her. When Corona first met Snow White, she was furious. She kept saying Snow was prettier than her. That's where her pride came in, she thought she was better than everyone. When someone threatened that, she wanted them to die."

"Sounds like she has some issues," I said.

"Not nearly as bad as Lexia. She was like Corona in many ways, but much more naïve. She thought that any man that kissed her would marry her." Dementia said with a snarky tone. "Andrew was an interesting man and he wanted something real. I really didn't have to do much to make Andrew say what he said to her. He just knew that he needed to. But, their relationship went back much farther than that. They had puppy love when they were about your age, but they lost it. Lexia became obsessed with him. He was her first love, her first kiss. When she got old enough, she searched for Andrew. I showed her where he was. I told her that if she gave him a rose and asked him to marry him for two years, then he would finally marry her. However, when you came into the picture, your magic interfered with mine and caused him not to fall under the spell."

"Did you ever find out why she was so obsessed?"

"I never got a straight answer, but I know it was because the love she had for him turned into a fixation. Then, I think it just flamed into pure obsession."

"Continue your story."

"Then you had a bit of confrontation with Venema and she's not one to back off. Venema was very selfish," Dementia explained matter of factly. "She grew up taking what she wanted and that continued throughout her life. She wanted a child, but she couldn't conceive. I told her of a couple that owned me a favor and the lady was pregnant. She lured the man to her and told him that if he didn't give her the baby, I would make sure the baby would die and they would never be able to have another."

"Don't you have adoption?"

"Anyway, she was greedy and wanted Rapunzel's love to only be only for her, so kept her in a tower. She was confident no one would come because the story of a girl with exceedingly long hair locked in a tower with no doors sounded like such a stretch."

"What about Thumbelina? We never saw a villain in that story. Other than maybe the men that wanted to instantly wed her."

"Morna. Thumbelina's mother, Delia, was another woman, who couldn't have a child. So, she went to a witch who was known for odd jobs and asked for a baby. The witch was Morna. Delia didn't know it, but Morna was her stepsister. Morna had always been jealous of her and she let her envy get the best of her. She decided to give Delia a plant that would bloom and send a plague into the house causing her to die. But, because Delia took such good care of the plant, when it bloomed, instead of a plague there was a pixie. I showed Morna how to take away Thumbelina's wings, which would make Delia incredibly unhappy because Thumbelina would be miserable."

"Where was Delia when we went to the house?"

"Delia had left by that point. She saw that Thumbelina was so depressed because she always felt that she was missing something. Delia felt so terrible for her that she went on a search to find that missing thing. She ended up in a shipwreck a few months after she left. You really realize how far a mother will go to make her child happy," Dementia said sadly.

I think I already know.

"The next is Sinica. As you already know, she and Alice were close friends for a very long time. However, as they got older, Sinica started noticing things. She noticed Alice was the one who got a date to the party, while she just tagged along. She noticed Alice was the one who played croquet and won the match even though she was basically as good. Little things like that. Sinica thought that if she beat Alice just one time, then Alice would become the second wheel. All she really needed to do was work harder. She didn't try to reach out to people like Alice did and she didn't practice croquet as much as she should have. Sinica saw herself as second best and that started to drive her crazy. Really insane. She would be up all night trying to think of ways to beat Alice or be better than Alice. She wouldn't stop until she figured it out. After she and Alice split, I found her. I told her I could make her better than everyone and drive Alice nuts. I showed her Wonderland and made her queen. She was the Queen of Hearts, so every man around wooed her and she always won at croquet. I told her one day Alice would be the crazy one and she would finally win."

"But Alice was just confused, she didn't go crazy,"

"You're partially correct. All of those characters that Alice saw were make believe. There was no one really there. When you go down the rabbit hole, it's enchanted to make you think you see them, but they're really just a hoax. Sinica was the only one who could tell that they weren't real. That's why she was laughing so hard, because she knew Alice was imagining everything. There was no Mad Hatter, no White Rabbit, no card soldiers, they were all make believe. However, Sinica still took their compliments."

"They were all fake?"

"Yes."

"All that just to get back at Alice?"

"Emotions can do strange things to people," Dementia explained with a look that showed relief that she was getting this all off her chest. "Now, Jellessa was a woman that you didn't reckon with. She played on the dark side and wasn't afraid of trouble. I'm sure you guessed that by her partner, Mr. Hook. Jellessa and Peter were friends and they got along until they were about twelve. Once they were twelve, Jellessa realized that she didn't want to be proper or nice or play by the rules. She became a female pirate on Hook's ship and they fell into their version of love. Jellessa was mad at Peter though. She was mad because Peter didn't try to stop her. She thought Peter would beg her to stay or plead with her to come with him. She wanted to stay young and rebellious and didn't see how many responsibilities Peter had as an older brother. She decided that because he didn't try to have his youth, then she would trap him in that state forever. I helped her cause a storm that would shipwreck Peter and his brothers onto the island that was cursed to keep him young forever. She disguised herself as a pixie to make sure Peter would never try to reverse the magic. When you showed up, you broke that cycle and Peter got to live experiences Jellessa didn't want him to have. She was selfish and immature and wanted to have those adventures to herself because she thought Peter didn't deserve them. In a way she was greedy, but she basically got a rush from breaking the rules. From hurting people. She became addicted to it, she thrived on it. A strange form of gluttony, but still."

"What about the last one?" I asked seriously. "That's only six."

Dementia looked at the fading purple sky and let out a big sigh. "The last one is my story. Gerda and Kai were the best of friends and I was very close to Kai. I thought that Gerda would take him from me and I would never see him again. I didn't kidnap him, he went with me back to my castle of ice by choice. A lot of my power has to do with weather - big storms, fire and ice. When we got to my palace and I touched him, he became so cold. I pulled back, horrified at myself. I was hurting him, which was the last thing I wanted to do. I tried everything, but his eyes were frozen shut. When you came, I hid. I hid because I knew Gerda could wake him up. I knew that if he was alive, even if he wasn't with me, that I'd be happy."

"Why were you so connected to Kai?"

"He's my son." Tears welled on the edges of her lower lashes. She wiped them away. "After Aaron, I found another man that I loved and he loved me back. One thing led to another and Kai was born. His father left shortly after, taking Kai because he thought I was a danger to him." She got up off her stone.

I didn't have any sympathy for Dementia. She had hurt so many people that I loved. It was hard to imagine her having pain within her and sadness toward herself. I didn't want to feel sad for her, but I didn't want to be like her. I wasn't going to shut people out.

"Dementia, I lost someone I care about very much. I have no clue where she is. At least you know where your son is. And daughter-in-law. I don't think that you're cruel enough to hurt my mother. Because you know what's it's like for a mother to not be with her child. My mother told me that you and she are related, which makes me related to you. How are we related Dementia?"

She turned her back to me and said. "How much do you know about your grandmother, Felicity?"

"Not much, except that she died when my mom was young."

"Do you know her parents?"

"No."

"Her mother was Starletta. Felicity was magical, very magical. She passed it on to your mother, but most of it went into you."

"But how does that make you and I related?"

"I'm Felicity's sister. When a fairy - a powerful one especially - is conceived, they have this magical glow that other fairies can detect. When we were born, Felicity shined like a star.

It was bright and warm, everything Starletta wanted. My glow was black and cold. Right away, my mother was a bit frightened, but she still tried to help me. It was no use, I was destined for darkness and I gave into it. I didn't want to hide it any longer, I didn't want to pretend. I found out about the Prophecy and discovered that I was going to be the villain. I decided then and there that there was no use trying to hide or stall it. Starletta expelled me from her magical teachings just like I wanted. And I found the girls I was going to use to ruin these lives. I saw that these girls were angry. They had emotions that were stronger than everyone else had. I didn't want them to deny their potential like I had."

"So, my grandfather didn't force you to become like this?"

"No, Aaron added to my anger, but I found about the Prophecy on my own. I needed to get away from my mother so I could start the search for the other Sins. I was just as powerful as Felicity, so I got these very graphic dreams that showed me who I needed to find."

"Why do all of this? Why go through all this trouble to make sure these girls can get their revenges when you knew that other magic was going to come and fix it? It wasn't to take over the world or something, it was just to make these people feel bad."

"You're clever girl, Guinevere. You know that each of these girls is one of the Seven Deadly Sins. Do you know who is who?"

"Corona is Pride. Lexia is Lust. Venema is Greed. Morna is Envy. Sinica is Sloth and Jellessa is Gluttony. And you're..."

"Rage."

"Why do you have all this anger?" She stared through me like a sheet of glass.

"Enough questions."

"You said you would give me all the answers..."

"Enough! It's time."

"Time for what?" I asked with half suspicion. She didn't say anything. I walked over to her. She swirled her hand circularly and a vortex opened. She began to walk in and tilted her head for me to follow.

With little deliberation, I stepped in after her.

CHAPTER 30
THE ENDING OF THE
BEGINNINGS

I was taken into an ancient castle. Thick strands of greenery dripped down from the ceiling. Along the sides were large walls of stone.

"Are you ready?" Dementia asked. She was wearing different clothes. It was a sleek black dress with slits coming up the sides and a band wrapped around her head with a black onyx in the center.

"I'm ready," I said. I realized my fists were tightly clenched.

"What if I were to tell you that if you fought me, you would lose the people you really care about?" She blew out one of the walls.

I felt all my breath sucked away from me. Aiden, Macy, Blaire and Tori were pinned to another wall. The other one must have been a decoy.

"Gwendolyn!" Macy yelled.

"Oh, and that's not even the best part," Dementia said with a laugh. A draped object dropped down from the ceiling.

"One more thing," she blew out the opposite wall. All the fairytale characters were still restrained to one of the two remaining walls.

"You know what I've never figured out about you, Guinevere? You wanted to help these people who had done nothing for you. You had never met them, they weren't your friends. Why did you do it?"

"Because I do know them. I read about them and loved them. They taught me so much, so many things that people need to know in life. They showed me to be optimistic about things. They explained that you're going to be in some pretty tough situations in life and you just have to remember that everything will eventually work out. Love and family and caring about people are the most important things and you can't give up on the dream that you want. That's why I helped them. And you know what else? I finally know why these stories were chosen. It wasn't because of you, it was because I needed to meet these people and learn these lessons. Everything is connected to something else and I was put in the position to be the center of it all. Even though you're my great aunt, if beating you is what it takes to save my friends, then bring it on."

"I'd be happy to." She raised her hands up. Lightning obliterated the floor and a hole quickly grew larger. It created a forceful wind swirling everything with its pull. My hair whipped across my face.

I pulled out my wand and aimed it at Dementia's chest. It smashed her against one of the walls. She pushed herself back up and blew out part of the ceiling. Rubble rained down on us.

Dementia propelled me against the last wall with a blast. As the throbbing in my head grew, she hit me again. My arms were burning and my eyes were watery. My will to fight was diminishing.

"Gwendolyn, don't give up!" Aiden shouted.

"Show her what you're made off!" Blaire called. I tried to push myself up.

"Guinevere, let's be honest. Do you really want to continue fighting? You're tired and frustrated. You're homesick. We can end this right now. All you have to do is give me your wand, that's it," Dementia cooed. She offered her hand.

"No, Gwendolyn, don't. It's a trap!" Macy screamed.

"Come on, Guinevere, this can all be over. Just hand over your wand and this will all be done," Dementia whispered. She almost looked loving.

I looked at everyone. They wanted me to win, they wanted me to fight. But I didn't have it in me. My mom wasn't here, my strength wasn't with me. I had no tricks, no strategy to beat her.

I grabbed her hand.

"No!" My friends shrieked.

"That's right, Guinevere. Now, give me the wand," Dementia coaxed.

"Before I do, I have one more thing to ask you," I muttered. "Do you have any more surprises?"

"The fight is over. There are no more surprises."

"Well, you're not totally right." I twisted my hand free from hers and pulled out the bottle.

"Remember this? This proves that you can't hurt anyone. You've been living a lie, what you told me was a lie. You weren't born evil, you chose to be evil. You didn't want to be compared to your sister for the rest of your life, so you turned yourself the way you are. You don't have anyone to blame, but yourself. This is what you used to be." I pulled out a very small piece of light.

"This is your glow. You removed it so you would become completely dark. So you wouldn't feel anything. This proves you're not heartless. You can still feel, Dementia. You don't have to live in anger anymore, you can be happy. Please, take it."

I had never before seen Dementia sad, but right now she looked like a scared little child. Lost and confused, trying to be one thing when they were never truly happy with the choice they made.

"I can't." She fell backward into the churning hole.

"No!" I caught her hand and gripped it tightly. My nails dug into her skin.

"Let me go, I have nothing to live for. My sister's dead, my mother's dead, I'm dead," she cried.

"No Dementia, you're not. You've thought you were worthless for so long, but you're not. You can change, I know you can."

"Guinevere, there's something you have to know. Your mother's alive, she's under the drape. There is more, there's always more. Even if I didn't show it, even if I don't deserve it back, I do love you and I'm so sorry." I felt it. I knew she meant it. I knew she loved me and she cared. She always had, but the anger had been too strong.

"I love you, too." And we let go.

"Gwendolyn, what happened? Are you all right?" Macy said hysterically. I was staring down into the empty pit. Everything had disappeared once we'd let go.

"I'm fine," I whispered.

"Where's Dementia?" Aiden asked.

"She's...gone." The words tumbled out of my mouth, choked and squeaky.

"Oh, Gwendolyn," Blaire said kneeling beside me.

"She was my great aunt. All she wanted was to be different. She told me she loved me and she meant it. I loved her, too. I didn't know until then, but I do now. And then we just...let go."

"It'll be okay, Gwendolyn," Tori said.

"Did she say anything else?" Macy asked.

"My mom is still alive, she's here. And there's more, I don't know what more is though. She didn't say."

"Your mom is alive? We have to find her!" Blaire said.

"She's under the drape." We pulled the draped object down from its chain and set it on the ground.

We pulled the cloth off. Under it was a black, bird like cage with a crystal ball locked inside.

"She's inside the ball," I said knowingly.

"Go for it, Gwendolyn," Aiden encouraged.

I looked sternly into the crystal. I began seeing it all. I heard my mother's voice. I saw myself as a baby. I saw crows and her firing magic at them.

The vision was so very real.

"How are you here?" Mom asked as she blasted the crows.

"It really doesn't matter Scarlett, all I need is for you to come with me," I heard Dementia's voice and saw her appear.

"Why would I go with you?" Mom asked bitterly.

"I don't want to hurt her Scarlett, but I will."

"You will not go anywhere near my baby."

"Who's stopping me? She is my great niece. Scarlett, come with me. I know something about this Prophecy you don't know."

"And what is that?"

"She'll only be driven to do it if you're not here. You can't be around. I know you tried to look for my bottle, but you failed. She has to be the one to fix this. She'll only want to complete this quest if it means finding you again."

Mom looked from me to Dementia.

"You have to swear she won't be harmed. When she's here or when she's there."

"I promise. Scarlett, I do love her. Even if I don't show it. Now, close your eyes and visualize that you're back home."

"Just a moment." She picked me up and held me close to her.

"I love you, Guinevere. I'll see you again soon." She kissed me and set me in my cradle.

"I'm ready."

"What did you see, Gwendolyn?" Macy asked.

"She went with Dementia to make sure I did this. She made her promise not to hurt me. She loved me that much."

"I still do." I turned around and there she was. With her curly, dark hair and shining blueish eyes. Just like the pictures of her.

"Mom!" I ran over and squeezed her.

"Guinevere!" We were both crying hard and smiling so much that my cheeks hurt.

"You did it baby, I knew you could," she said.

"I couldn't have done it without your diary."

"I knew you'd find it."

"Oh, Mom, these are my friends, they helped me. Their family members were parts of the Prophecy. This is Blaire, Aiden, Tori and Macy."

"It's wonderful to meet you all, I can't express the gratitude I have for you that you helped my daughter."

"We care about her and she cares about us. We weren't going to let her do it alone," Macy said.

"Thank you so much."

"How are we going to get home, Mrs. Star?" Tori asked.

"Well, my daughter is the only one who can answer that."

"I am?"

"Yes sweetie, you know how."

I closed my eyes and clasped my wand between my hands. I felt the magic flowing through my body. It was the best sensation. It was like flying at the speed of light, yet time was standing still.

"We're home!" Aiden cheered. We were standing in the abandoned golf course.

"Why are we here?" I asked.

"This is where everyone landed when we first came here. It's like a magic hotspot. Whenever you come back here, this is where you'll come," Mom said.

"Guys, don't we need to talk to your parents?" I asked.

"Yeah, we probably should," Macy said.

"I'll get them here," I transported each of the parents to the course. They looked around, all dazed and confused.

"Blaire, what are we doing here?" Mrs. Whitman asked.

"Aiden, Macy, where have you two been?" Mrs. Poen inquired.

"Please, parents, let us explain," Mom interrupted. "My name is Scarlett Star, I'm Guinevere's mother. You come from the Fairytale World just as I do. Your children just saved it from the Seven Sins and their leader, Dementia. Your memories were erased when you were brought to this world. They were erased by Starletta, so you wouldn't search for your family members that we trapped there. Please tell me you remember."

They looked at us dumbfounded.

"I remember." An older woman stepped forward. I assumed that it was Tori's grandma.

"So do I," both Luke and Mrs. Poen said.

"Connor, you were telling the truth!" Mrs. Whitman cried running into his arms.

"I was Diana," Mr. Whitman said. Blaire rushed over to them both. Aiden and Macy were locked in an embrace with Luke and Mrs. Poen. Tori was being hugged and kissed by her mother, father and grandma.

"We did it, Mom," I said wrapping my arm around her waist.

"No, sweetheart, you did it. You're the hero."

"Wait, look. There's Dad!" I pointed. He was running over to us.

"Scarlett, Gwendolyn." He scooped us both into his arms. "Oh, my girls. I'm so happy to see you both."

"I'm happy to see you too, Daddy."

"Thomas, I'm so glad that I'm back."

"I was so worried about you both. After Gwendolyn left, I was so frantic. But I knew you could do it and you did. Now you're both here, safe and sound."

"What did you say her name was?" Mom asked.

"After you disappeared, I thought changing her name might help. Dementia would be looking for a Guinevere Star under my care. So, I put her with David and changed it to Gwendolyn, hoping that it would throw Dementia off."

"Why didn't you change my last name then?" I asked.

"I was in hysterics. The night your mother was taken, I handed you to David and had the forms signed to change your first name. I didn't really think of much else besides getting you to safety."

"Aww, Dad. You know, I kinda like the name Guinevere. I wouldn't mind changing it back."

"It's your choice, honey"

"Whatever you decide, we'll be happy."

"Hey, Mom I have something to ask you. Do you know who the voice was who told me it couldn't tell me its name? It said you'd be in danger if it told me."

"I don't know who would've told you that. I was in that crystal ball the whole time."

"Then who was that voice?"

"I'm not sure."

Guinevere.

"Did you hear that?"

"Hear what?" Dad asked.

Guinevere, come here.

"I'll be right back." I walked away from everyone onto the island, to where I saw the Starletta flowers.

I did what you told me to do. I fulfilled the Prophecy. But, my mother doesn't know who you are. Who are you really?

I'll be honest with you Guinevere, I lied. Your mother didn't make me promise not to tell you my name, I chose not to. No one is controlling me. But I did need you to complete the Prophecy.

Why?

Once it was completed, we would truly know if your capabilities were as strong as perceived. You have gained more knowledge of magic than most fairies learn in their whole lives. You've completed tasks in single days that take years to master.

Why did you need to know if I was good enough? And what is your name?

My name is Twyla. I am the first fairy. I'll be in touch.